The Esoteric Design
Disbanding Hope

Written & Illustrated by

A. R. Crebs

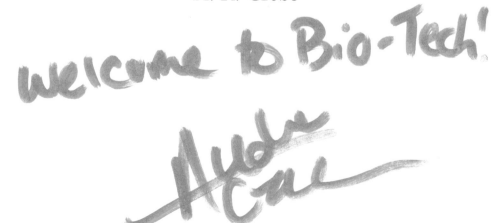

Welcome to Bio-Tech!

The Esoteric Design

Copyright © 2014 A. R. Crebs

The Esoteric Design: Disbanding Hope

Copyright © 2015 A. R. Crebs

ISBN-13: 978-1508512981
ISBN-10: 1508512981

DEDICATION

I'd like to dedicate this book to all of my fans. You continue to inspire me every day. Thank you for your support, and thank you for reading. I hope you enjoy this work and the many others to come in the future. Enjoy!

CONTENTS

"Scarlet Warrior"

ACKNOWLEDGMENTS

A special thanks to Michelle for being my guinea pig and reading a proof of the book. Your feedback is extremely helpful. Thank you to those who pushed, motivated, and cheered me on. Thank you to my friends and fans on the internet; you continue to inspire me to follow my dreams. Thanks to Richard. I'm pretty sure you're my biggest fan. And thanks to Marcus for once again listening to me as I read, pointing out all the flaws in my art and forcing me to fix them, and for helping me with some of the weapon designs. And a shout-out to my buddies at Nerd Barrage. Why? Cuz I can!

Thank you to Jade Macalla for allowing me the use of your amazing stock for reference. You're an extreme help to those in the art community. www.jademacalla.deviantart.com

The following are links to sites that I used for stock reference for some of the artwork within this book.

www.fotolia.com

www.dreamstime.com

www.freerangestock.com

www.texturez.com

Visit my websites for updates, more artwork, and to participate in some contests!

www.ARCrebs.com

www.ARCrebs.deviantart.com

www.facebook.com/ARCrebs

i

PROLOGUE

4 months earlier....

CRACK!

"Stop the drill! Stop the drill!" A man covered in grey dust and mud waved his arms in the air as he shouted. The orange of his mining uniform was barely seen by the drill operator. Crystalline particles covered his middle-aged face, blending in with his chin stubble.

"I said to stop the drill!" he yelled into his DNAIS.

Abruptly, the machine droned in a low tone from its previous high-pitched whine. The massive ridges that each stood two meters high spiraled from an unrecognizable blur to a steady spin, clanking against the thick barrier of the rocky mantle the miners had been drilling against the past few months. They were now at the lowest point of the mines, had cleared an entirely new level, created four tunnel offshoots, and were now beginning their fifth. The miner wasn't exactly sure what they were looking for, but the eerie glow that emanated from the front of the drill was a good indication that he had met his goal. Wiping his hands over his uniform, smudging the dirt across his Walten Mining name patch, the worker walked toward the colossal wheels of the ten meter wide drill. The ridges slowly crunched against the rock beside him.

"Did we finally find it?" the operator asked, pushing his helmeted head through the small window of the cab.

Looking up with a hand shielding his eyes to see his fellow miner, the older man shouted, "I think so. Back up the drill and come down here! There's some strange light coming through."

The driver followed orders, backing away from the newly created hole. A harsh light beamed from the opening that gave an odd hum. Stopping the drill, the driver excitedly opened the door and leaned out, his mouth hanging open. The peculiar gap gave him an uneasy feeling.

"Shouldn't we call Walten?" he questioned, climbing down the ladder of the vast machine. He dropped from the bottom rung, landing roughly on the ground, a hand pressing against his helmet.

"Gotta make sure it's the right thing first," the other man said. He strolled to the front of the borer, leaning over the edge of the hole, eyes narrowing against the harsh orange glow far beneath.

"Think we hit a molten patch?" the driver asked.

Giving a sharp intake of breath, the older man replied, "I want you to get Walten and his team on the line ASAP."

"What is it?" The young man watched as the glow flickered increasingly brighter, the low hum resonating within the enormous hollow cavern of the underground mining facility. The blaring rose in volume, eventually vibrating and echoing against the walls, threatening to shatter the very pillars above that held up the City of Fountains.

"Git! Call the team!" the worker shouted at the driver, his voice cutting short as his body began to tremor and all his limbs were pulled in separate directions.

"Shit! Shit!" the driver screamed, watching in horror as his coworker slowly pulled apart. With a sickening pop, his uniform was smothered in red. Swiftly, the driver turned and ran up the incline back to the main base of operations. "Driver 25 to base! Driver 25 to base! We've cracked it! We've cracked it!" he shouted through his DNAIS radio. His boots stomped wildly on wobbly ankles through shimmering dust over misshapen rocks.

"Roger, we hear you. Walten and team are already headed your way," the receptionist called back.

"No! Not safe! Not safe! Worker 263 is dead!" Driver 25 barked. "I repeat, Worker 263 is dead!"

"Acknowledged. Walten and team are on their way."

"No! No, you don't understand...." Driver 25 gasped as a couple of speeding trucks neared his position. He waved his arms, shouting and jumping frantically, his coworker's blood sprinkling from his uniform. A small whimper slipped through his quaking lips as the vehicles passed him by, heading straight for the hole in the Earth's mantle.

Dust clouded the tunnel as the trucks slammed into an emergency stop, the thick tires grinding against the hard floor. The headlights rested upon the glowing opening at the base of the drill's point. One by one the doors of the trucks opened. Walten's crew—his secret service, those with no name, not even identification numbers—was dressed in high-class military uniforms. They stepped from the vehicles, their boots crunching softly against the pebbled ground, the sound loud within the chamber. A second later, Walten's door was opened. The young, clean-shaven man, dressed in his fashion of charcoal-grey and amber, stepped out with his shined leather shoes. Slowly, with a trembling hand, he ran his fingers through his chestnut hair. He looked at the glowing pathway with anxious eyes.

"Sir?" one man asked, looking over the expanse of the drilled hole.

"This is it, right?" Walten asked with a shuddering breath, his eyes dropping to the splattered stain of whatever was left of Worker 263.

"It appears so," another answered, looking over a display map on his DNAIS. The familiar blue glow radiated against his stony features.

Clearing his throat and adjusting his ornate tie around his neck, Walten neared the flickering anomaly. He stopped a meter ahead, matching eyes with General Jeron Feyette, who insisted on coming with the young CEO.

"Would you like for me to do it, sir?" Feyette questioned.

"No, no. I, uh…I will do it," Walten stated apprehensively.

Reaching into his coat pocket, Walten pulled out a small device, one with notches that fit in his palm—an ancient frequency tuner. He eyed the gleaming hole, another rumbling hum beginning to drum noisily from its unknown origins. Walten clicked the mechanism, turning it up to maximum strength. It vibrated in his hand. Giving one last look at Feyette, he chucked the item directly into the cavity. The pulsating resonance abruptly stopped. Silence consumed the cavern. Cringing, Walten waited and waited…and waited. Nothing happened.

"Sir?" Feyette's deep voice alerted the CEO.

Slowly opening one eye and then another, Walten gaped at the fluctuating, sparkling opening. It crackled and sizzled, a strange disturbance taking place. Something faint and dark darted back and forth, growing in size. A towering silhouette neared him and his men. The shadow jostled from side to side, disappearing and reappearing before clouding over the whole expanse of the glowing gap. Terrible shrieks and screams sounded, rising in volume until it was at an ear-splitting level that caused tremors to vibrate within the men's bodies.

"WHO ARE YOU?" a deep voice, dual-toned and quaking with malice, barked through the entry.

"I, I am just a man," Walten stammered.

"FOR WHAT REASON DO I HAVE TO DEAL WITH A HUMAN?" the voice returned. The sound was unnatural, almost mechanical as it warbled in warm, piping tones.

Trying to make eye contact with the nearly nonexistent eyes of the oscillating shadow on the other side, Walten rolled his shoulders. Gripping the front of his dress coat in a snobbish manner, he daringly called out, "I believe I could be of good use to you. You see, I have a plan."

The figure remained unmoving, silent.

"I believe it is something you'd be interested in," Walten called out again. "I think it would benefit the both of us."

A thunderous crash erupted, light exploding from all sides of the cavern. The shrieking screams quickly re-tuned to a different sound, one that was eerily out of place–the giggling of a thousand children, flowing into one single pitch. With the light quickly fading back to normalcy, the giggle sounded in one voice–that of a little girl. Walten pressed his mouth shut in a firm line as he uneasily gaped at the small child. Pale skin, pale hair, grey-blue eyes. She smiled at him.

"So, you have a deal you'd like to make with me?" she curiously asked.

"The Deal"

CHAPTER 1

A harsh rumble shook the cave system, alerting the semi-unconscious Aria. The woman groaned as her senses slowly came to. Turning her head and trying her best to ignore the stiffness and dull pain coursing through her body, she looked through glassy eyes toward her partner, Troy. He was sprawled similarly on the rock floor, unmoving.

"Troy," she whispered, her shaking hand grasping his shoulder.

The man awoke with a start, tightly gripping her hand. A moan then erupted from him at the sudden movement he had made.

"Aria," he groaned, "are we dead?"

"I don't think so. At least, not yet," she grumbled, slowly pushing herself into a sitting position. She felt heavier than usual. Probably due to the amount of body armor she had on.

"What the hell just happened?" Troy whined.

"We got our asses kicked; that's what happened." Aria noisily exhaled.

She still felt groggy and lightheaded from the morphine shot she kicked into her system only moments before she and Troy were carelessly shoved out of the chamber by a transforming Ivory. Never in her life would she have guessed Ivory to be a biomechanical android. From Bio-Tech Military Corporation no less. There was no doubt about it. Camery was directly involved. But how had he become caught up in the first place and why?

"Dovian…where's Dovian?" Troy asked, his helmeted head hitting the rock wall behind him. He gave a short grunt upon impact.

"He's still inside. Probably crystallized in Ivory's Amasser Particle Beam."

"Hope she got that little bitch, too," Troy hissed, trying to stand. The thought of the little girl called Sapphire sent shivers down his spine. "What in the hell is she, anyway?"

"I'm not sure. Whatever she is, Dovian was scared of her. That means we should be scared, too."

Aria slowly rose to her feet, her knees buckling beneath her weight. Luckily, the meds were still doing the job; she barely felt a thing, but judging by the creaking in her ankle, something may have been broken. She didn't want to imagine how her body would look if she hadn't worn her armor.

'Most likely in pieces....' She cringed at the idea.

"Um, Aria," Troy's voice interrupted the woman's thoughts. "Ivory is an android, right?"

"Yeah."

"Camery's cloning and biomechanics operation was closed down a few months ago, right?"

"Yeah."

"Well…I don't think the bodies were actually disposed of."

Pointing a finger ahead of him, the man looked over his shoulder at the woman. She stumbled to his side, looking into a crevice in the wall. Inside the cavern on the opposite side was a frightening sight. Suspended by cables inside thick tubes were full-grown humans. The bodies floated weightlessly within placental containers, appearing lifeless. There had to be dozens of them just from what the soldiers could see. Marked on the sides of all the tanks were the metallic insignia for Bio-Tech.

"That damn bastard gave up his clones. Why would he do this?" Aria asked through gritted teeth.

"I think they are preparing an army." Troy gaped through the crack.

A low growl sounded from inside the room. The two continued watching as a tall, thin creature with abnormally long arms–the one Aria affectionately dubbed Stilt-Man–neared the tubes. It watched, staring upward at the hovering bodies. The creature howled quietly, running a long, clawed hand over the surface of one glass container. It tilted its head, looking at the clone's messy hair, his sharp nose, his closed eyes, his toned chest, and proportionate floating arms with normal-looking hands. Giving another growl, this time angry, the monster smacked the surface of the glass noisily as it threw a small fit.

Another rumble shook the cave, threatening to tear down the corridor Aria and Troy were occupying. The crevice before them splintered more, cracking wide enough to cause part of the wall to fall. Troy and Aria stumbled back. Both reached for their weapons and, to their horror, found that they were missing. The Stilt-Man turned, its dark eyes locking onto the two intruders. Opening its large, toothy mouth, it howled with a tremendous ferocity. The sound echoed within the chamber, bouncing down the tunnels in repeating waves. Drool funneling past the creature's lips, it screamed again, throwing down its arms as it broke out into a sprint toward the two, its fiery-red mane flowing behind it.

"Run!" Aria shouted, pulling Troy with her.

They spun together, heading the only way they could down the tunnel. From behind, they could hear the howling monster. In seconds, the channels were full of similar sounds as the creature alerted all the others of their location. Troy and Aria kept running in a straight line, passing a couple small passageways where the noises grew louder in volume. Eventually, they came to a fork of equally-sized tunnels. They skidded to a halt; both tugged each other to go one way and then the other.

"Which way?" Aria shouted.

"Straight! Just go straight!" Troy pushed her along.

The cave was full of howls and shrieks and the clicking of talon on rock. One beast lunged out from another fissure, chomping at Troy. The man dodged to the side, narrowly escaping the rabid creature. It slammed into the wall behind him and continued without pause after the humans.

"I see light!" Aria shouted.

Troy glanced over his shoulder and gave a cry of surprise. "Good! Cuz all I see are monsters on our asses!"

The boisterous howling continued, causing the loose rubble of the walls to crash down. It didn't help that Ivory had blasted the inner chamber with her particle beam, weakening the cave system. Perhaps she was still fighting. Perhaps she annihilated the entire center, and now the whole place was caving in on itself. If that was the case, Aria hoped Dovian was able to save Ivory from destroying herself.

"Dovian where are you?" Aria asked through her mental chip, hoping the Sorcēarian would pick up on it. The woman frowned when she heard no response. Maybe she was too far away.

The vibration of destruction neared her and Troy's position. The angry cries from the monsters were beginning to sound frantic, panicked, and a bit frightened. Next, a horrendous crackle and crash erupted. The floor beneath the soldiers' feet quaked as the roof over their heads dropped in large chunks in single file from the back of the tunnel up toward their position. With each thunderous boom, there came a high-pitched shriek from the demons that were smashed into oblivion, the screams only worsening as the thunder neared.

Aria cried out as she was shoved harshly forward by Troy, her body shooting out the exit of the tunnel into the bright sunlight of the outside world. Clattering and rolling rather ungracefully on the rocky ground, the woman spun onto her belly, lifting her head to look back at the cave's entrance. A large cloud of dust covered her view, making it impossible to see where her partner was.

"Troy!" she shouted, trying to scramble to her feet. After a couple of tries, she gave up and dropped to her knees. Catching her breath, her eyes never left the dusty passageway. "Troy!" she called out again in a hoarse voice.

"What?!" the man finally replied.

Aria let out a shuddering sigh as her pounding heart finally slowed within her chest.

'Thank God,' she thought.

"Where are you?" she asked. Finally gaining enough strength to stand, she moved into the dispersing cloud, her helmet's viewer flickering to find Troy's heat signature.

"Right beside you," he said.

Aria gave a slight jump and turned, smacking him in the chest. "Don't sneak up on me like that!"

"You're the one who sneaked up on me! And you passed right by me!" he protested, running his hand over his chest.

Aria quickly strode away from the cave's blocked entrance. Clicking on her DNAIS, she picked up her location and flagged it for Aren so he could catch their coordinates.

"Aren, we need a ride," she called through her mental chip.

"Is everyone alright?! I've been picking up some bizarre seismic activity in your area. What the hell was that flash? It shot out of the cave and all the way across the island!" Aren replied.

"That would be an Amasser Particle Beam." Aria stumbled over a rock.

"Should I even bother asking how?" Aren asked.

"We'll explain later…." The woman froze as she heard a familiar buzz. Turning slowly, she glanced back at the cave. A deafening boom sounded, and a new cloud of dust blew through the cracks of the barricaded entry.

"Brutes, Troy." Aria tapped on his shoulder.

"Well," Troy mumbled, watching another puff of powder erupt from the cracks, "that's dandy."

Without another moment's thought, the two began running once again toward the valley they had originally come.

"Problem with the coordinates you sent me!" Aren called out. *"Electrical storm seems to be heading this way! I can't get a read on your exact location!"*

"Just get your ass over here! We need an evac immediately!" Aria mentally called out as an explosion of noise came from behind her as the Brutes finally crashed through the wall of the cave.

With heavy footsteps, the two soldiers moved at a pace that was less than satisfactory. Wave after wave of destruction fled past them as the Brutes ran in pursuit, their arms swinging crazily to send their bursting attacks. Aria and Troy zigzagged in their run, trying to avoid each blast the best they could. The pounding of the monsters' footsteps grew louder as they neared the humans.

"We're going to die!" Troy gasped for air as he floppily hopped over a boulder.

"Just keep running!" Aria grunted.

A tumultuous jolt shook the earth. Aria and Troy both stumbled, crashing to their hands and knees. The woman looked over her shoulder. Even the Brutes had stopped their chase, staring at the ground. Another quake shook and cracked the land, splintering from the cave toward the two militants. They both rolled to the side, the fracture stretching in a broad dark line past them toward the horizon. A low wail sounded, echoing with a metallic tone that bounced off every rock and pebble and valley. It was a menacing sound, one that screamed death was approaching.

"What the hell was that?!" Troy shouted, quickly climbing to his feet. He helped Aria to hers.

The Brutes spun, moving in all directions as the ground burst open beneath their feet, an explosion of rock and Brute bodies spiraling outwards. One massive, fleshy hand rose from the hole in the ground, its fingertips digging into the rock surface like it was mud. The low moan sounded again, and another hand shot out.

"We should be running," a trembling whisper slipped past Aria's lips.

The two stumbled backward, their heels skidding against the loose dirt as the cracked ground directly behind them broke away and sank far into the earth. Aria and Troy grabbed onto one another, dropping forward so not to fall into the bottomless fissure behind them.

"Can today get any worse?!" Aria growled, her hands digging into the soil.

Troy gaped at the monstrous being that pulled itself out of the ground near the cave. Its head was large; two massive black eyes sat at the top of its skull between two thick nostrils. Its toothy grin wasn't a happy one but was menacing and angry as it growled. Two bulky, though squat, legs pushed out of the hole. It was like a Spewer, only bigger, much bigger, and there were no magma sacs on its back.

A soft hiss came from across one of the gaping cracks on the right. Aria quickly turned her attention to the source of the noise, expecting to find more fiends on the opposite side. Her eyes widened as she saw a slightly familiar sight instead.

"Hector!" She quickly scrambled to her feet.

The lizard scuttled from the left to the right, hissing as he shook his neck flaps.

"That looks like Dovian's lizard," Troy murmured. He tore his eyes away from the reptile to look back at the giant that was trudging slowly toward them. Its dark eyes were pointed in their direction; its head cocked to the side as it snarled. Each stride the monster took, he was meters closer.

A little bark erupted from Hector as he scampered back and forth, darting to the side of the cave system where there was a high wall of boulders. Aria and Troy both looked at the gaping hole behind them, then to the crack on the right. One simple jump, and they'd be on the other side with the lizard. However, they would also be nearing the cave system again. Their options were limited. If they stayed, it was either death by freefall or death by a giant monster. Aria was willing to take her chances on following the lizard.

"Come on!" she shouted, running toward the smaller crack to the right. She leaped over, crashing onto the other side as her ankle gave out. Giving a short yelp of pain, she brushed it off and pushed to her feet.

As Troy landed beside her, they followed after the trotting lizard. In a few seconds, they were by Hector's side, walking briskly to keep up.

"Come on; where are you taking us?" Aria asked.

Troy glanced at the woman skeptically. She was talking to a lizard. As far as they knew, this lizard was only out for an afternoon jog, and they were bothering it.

Hector rounded the corner and stopped, his tiny head looking up high. Aria and Troy rounded as well and came to an abrupt halt as a loud roar greeted them. The source of the sound came from a massive, beastly reptile. It was a dinosaur of sorts. And it didn't look at all pleased with its golden eyes glaring hungrily upon Aria and Troy. The two soldiers twirled about-face and ran back around the corner, halting again as they noticed the colossal enemy was now near the crevice they had been only moments before.

"Shit! Where in the hell is Aren?!" Troy cursed.

Another small bark came from Hector. Aria looked over her shoulder and then up at the giant lizard that awaited them around the corner. It remained still, wasn't trying to attack, but continued to stare at them with fiery eyes. The woman swallowed thickly, noticing the creature's neck flaps and the tattoos lining the side of his body. There was a name scrawled across the lizard's neck just as Hector's name was—something along the lines of 'Pete' or maybe 'Petey.' Despite being written in Legacy, Aria could make out most of the letters. It also appeared to be someone's pet at one time. Hector hopped and hissed, running toward the lizard named Petey.

"Troy, I think he wants us to ride him," Aria muttered.

"What?" Lifting the visor of his helmet, the man looked back at the woman as if she was nuts.

"That lizard….His name is Petey. He looks just like Hector…" she glanced back at the impatient lizards, "…only bigger."

"You're crazy, you know that?" Troy asked.

Aria lifted her visor as well. Her eyes were glassy; her face was pale. She didn't look well. Her pallid features, drenched in sweat, were slightly alarming to the man.

"Fine! You can deal with that giant; I'm hitching a ride with the dinosaur!" Aria quickly turned to the massive lizard. Holding out her hand, Petey watched her with vicious eyes. "Please don't eat us," she whimpered.

The creature bucked, his flaps expanding outward, nearly knocking the woman over. He called out, the vibrating snarl shivering throughout the valley.

"Aria, be careful!" Troy huffed, watching the nearing colossus.

Stamping his talons into the dirt, the lizard straightened in posture as he looked sideways at the woman. Hector yapped as well, glancing from Aria to Petey and back again. Aria noticed a small nod from Hector, and she smiled.

"Who's a good boy?" Aria asked, running her fingers upon the creature's scales behind his large flaps.

Petey honked, stamping his feet again. Troy watched the woman in disbelief as she climbed onto the lizard's back, gripping the fringe at the base of his neck.

"Get up here!" she ordered Troy.

The man quickly walked around Petey, eyeing the lizard's intimidating glare. He didn't think Petey liked him very much. Aria scratched Petey's neck once again and grabbed Troy's hand, helping him up onto the beast's back.

"You ready to," Aria gasped as Petey took off at a full frenzied sprint, "GO?!" She quickly pulled down the visor of her helmet.

Petey lunged directly in front of the colossus and turned, running away just as the monster's enormous fingers snatched for them.

Aria looked over her shoulder back at little Hector, who got left behind. "RUN HECTOR! Get to safety!" she shouted. Relief washed over her as she saw the small scuttling creature dart into a hole beneath a rock, his tail dragging in the dirt behind him. He would be okay.

Giving a loud honk, Petey continued his sprint, each heavy trudge bouncing Aria and Troy's bodies up and down on his back. It wasn't the smoothest of rides, but it was better than nothing. Petey ran for a few hundred meters. The colossal demon fervently growled and roared as it followed after them, its slow, heavy pace chunking away at the rock until it reached full speed like a freight train. Petey was quick, but if he remained in a straight line, the enemy would reach them soon.

"He's catching up with us!" Troy shouted as he looked back.

"Petey! We need to get away! He's going to catch us soon!" Aria scratched the lizard's neck.

Petey kept up his current pace, his golden eyes looking to the side where the crack in the valley split the earth. Digging a little deeper, he turned to the left, pulling away from the crack and back out into the open. He ran a great distance, the colossus having to slow down to make its turn to follow, and then Petey turned around again, running straight for the nearing beast.

"What are you doing?!" Aria shouted, her grip tightening on his fringe.

The ground shook with each of Petey's and the giant's footsteps. Dirt spilled between each of the lizard's toes, rocks clattering against the floor. Troy's arms wound tightly around Aria's waist. He clenched his teeth, preparing for a violent impact. The giant neared so close, Aria could see her own reflection in its dark eyes. Petey turned abruptly to the side, twirling in a quick circle as the giant's open arms tried to close around them and continued driving forward. The massive beast howled, stumbling to the side. Digging its thick fingers into the rocky ground, the demon turned and pulled backward in the opposite direction, continuing its pursuit.

"Don't do that again!" Aria groaned.

"Agreed," Troy sighed.

Petey kept up his pace, but a rumbling pant was beginning to sound in his chest. He was going to tire out soon. Running in a straight line, he neared the bottomless fracture of the valley.

"He's not doing what I think he's doing…" Troy whimpered.

"Just hold on tight!" Aria moaned, closing her eyes.

Four more steps and Petey was leaping up high into the air, his stubby lizard legs reaching out for the other side. The gap itself was at least ten meters wide. Petey landed, giving a grunt as he did so, and lunged forward again, continuing his sprint.

"Are we alive?" Troy whispered.

"For now," Aria replied.

A moment after they passed, a loud thump sounded from behind as the enemy cleared the jump without effort. Aria admitted she wasn't shocked, but it didn't keep her from feeling disappointed.

A sudden droning rumbled over the pounding of the lizard's galloping.

"Finally! I've been looking all over for you!" Aren's voice crackled into Aria's ear.

"Damn it, Aren, where have you been?!" she cried out.

"I'm sorry! The storm's nearing and getting worse!"

Aria lifted her head, noticing that the previously clear blue sky was now being eaten away by bubbling black clouds. An eerie orange glow was cast on the horizon as lightning flashed in violent intervals.

"How could you miss the giant monster and dinosaur with people riding on its back?!" Troy returned.

"How about you lecture me after I figure out a way to get you out of here?" Aren replied, sounding a bit irritated as well. He was silent a moment before adding, *"Shit! Where's that lizard taking you?"*

"Not sure, why?" Aria replied.

"Are you all suicidal? He's taking you straight to the edge of the valley! That's hundreds of meters deep, and if he jumps…you're not going to make it!"

"Petey! What are you doing?!" Aria shouted out loud.

The lizard barked back at the woman.

"He's nuts!" Troy cursed.

"Hold on; I'm lowering the Hawk. I want you to fast-rope in!" Aren said.

Petey gave another cry. The sound warbled deep in his chest, rising in volume and pitch as he repeated the howls over and over again. The soldiers grimaced in pain at the shrill calls.

As Aren lowered the Hawk, dust spiraled up, clouding over Petey and his riders.

"Providing a bit of cover for you guys," Aren said. He turned his attention to the colossal monster. It didn't slow down as it entered the dust cloud. Shifting gears to auto-pilot, Aren unbuckled himself and rushed into the cabin. Snatching up the rope, he looked over the open side of the Hawk. In the eye of the dirt storm, he could see Aria and Troy looking up at him from Petey's back. "Here it comes!" he shouted, dropping the line down for the two.

Troy snagged the cable and quickly fastened himself and Aria to it. Giving a whirl with his finger overhead, Troy signaled for the pilot to bring them up. Aren hoisted them without hesitation. Aria gasped as she instinctively reached out for Petey. The lizard continued running, despite losing his riders. Aren assisted the two as they climbed into the cabin. Once unclipped, he returned to his seat without a word, lifting the Hawk to a safe distance above ground.

"Wait! What about Petey?" Aria shouted, looking over the side of the Hawk. "That dust cloud may have shielded us from that monster, but it also blocked Petey's view of the valley!"

Far below, Petey kept up his eager pace. He was only a few hundred meters away from the valley once he cleared the cloud. The enemy was right on his tail, growling and snarling all the way. Petey must've sensed him so near and flicked his tail, smacking the beast's hands away. Over the sound of the copter, another warbling call erupted from the lizard, vibrating over the hills and cliffs. Not even a second later, the landscape was covered with flurrying specs as hundreds of frilled monitors darted from their hiding places beneath rocks and inside cracks of the dried land. Together, they all traveled to the giant demon, leaping, biting, clawing, and swiping at the fiend. The attack worked on slowing the beast down, but Petey was still heading directly for the massive valley and was showing no signs of slowing down.

With each pull of his talons, Petey sprang forward with more and more might. As the valley neared, he prepared with his quickest speed. From behind, he could hear the demon's cries and the shrieks of his lizard kind. From above, he heard the faraway shout from the pretty woman that had been on his back. She had a scent so like his mother's—the scent of candy and orchids, a sweet and comforting smell. Petey smiled, and then he leaped, pushing with his hind legs as hard as he could. He was flying, the wind in his flaps as he crossed over the deep, dark crevice. His golden eyes watched the nearing ledge; only a few more meters and he'd make it.

Petey honked as he felt a hard tug on his tail. The wretched monster had jumped after him and had somehow managed to snag him. The lizard's talons jabbed into the rocky ledge on the opposite side. He frantically clawed, honking loudly as the rock pulled away from the surface. And then he was falling, falling far below into the deep, dark abyss with the demon and all of his tiny lizard friends who helped to take it down.

Golden eyes watched the orange sky as it was eaten away by darkness, the silhouette of the flying man-machine swooping over the gap. Petey thought he heard his name, smelled the sweet smell of orchids. He thought of his home once again—a home full of lavender blankets and bowls full of fruit. It was so comfortable and nice, unlike the feeling of the sharp, pointed rocks tearing up his sides as he crashed down into darkness–an unknown depth, an unavoidable death.

"Petey!" Aria shouted as she lifted her visor. She hung over the side of the aircraft and watched the massive lizard get violently tugged down by the demon into the darkness.

Troy grabbed her shoulders and pulled her back inside the Hawk 90. The woman covered her face, giving a quiet sob. Her nerves were wrought; she was exhausted beyond reason, her body was broken, and she was in pain. Above all, she was surrounded by death and monstrosity. Petey was a giant lizard; he belonged to someone at one time. He was as old as Dovian. And now he was gone, killed by a disgusting, violent creation. Everything on Ives was slowly being brought to ruin. And all Aria wanted to do was return home.

A jolt shook the two soldiers causing them to moan. The morphine in their systems was finally wearing off. Aren returned to the cabin, his face holding a look of concern.

"Should I circle back? Where is Dovian?" he asked.

Aria and Troy were silent a moment.

"We need to regroup later. If we go back now, we'll surely be killed. Dovian can take care of himself," Aria murmured. "We need reinforcements to take care of this job. Things are much worse than we thought."

"Is he going to be alright?" Aren asked.

Aria's eyes dropped to the metal floor. She stared at her hands, feeling numb. "I don't know," she whispered.

"And what about the other woman? Ivory?"

"She…she's with Dovian. She's safer with him than she is with us," Aria mumbled, watching the dark clouds pass the Hawk.

"We'll get them back. There's nothing we can do right now, though," Troy added.

"R-Roger." Aren nodded.

Aria deeply inhaled, her lungs suddenly itching. She gave a raspy cough and felt the warmth rising in her throat. Choking, she coughed again, her hands gripping at the metal of the cabin floor. Her coughing fit worsened, and the red hot blood gushed, slapping against her hands and the floor. She dropped to her side, giving a rasping breath as she tried to calm the fit. Her ears were ringing, the blades of the Hawk thumping into her mind. She thought she could hear her name being called. Was it Troy? Or was it Aren? She couldn't tell.

"Dovian..." Aria tiredly called out in her mind. The Sorcēarian wasn't there to heal her wounds this time.

With glassy eyes, she continued to watch the gloomy clouds. She felt her body shake as a bright flash of lightning pushed from one cloud to another, causing an eruption of thunder to rumble as it splintered into the earth. Large droplets of water fell from the sky, some of the specks splashing against her pale, sickly face. She smiled, trying to record the look and smell of natural rain, lock the memory in her mind. It always rains on Ives. It always rains when Dovian has a bad day.

"We have to get her to a hospital!" Troy shouted. He tried speaking to the woman, but she seemed too far away. The torrential rain flooded into the cabin, mixing with her blood. "Get us home ASAP!"

Troy removed the woman's helmet, running a hand through her wet hair. He had only seen her like this one other time, and if they didn't get her to the hospital soon, he feared she wouldn't make it.

"Aria!" he shouted.

Looking at his partner, Troy groaned, feeling the effects of his morphine wearing off. Grabbing his side, he dropped next to the woman, grimacing in pain. He didn't realize he was in just as bad shape as she was.

"Troy?!" Aren called out.

The soldier didn't respond. Instead, he stared at his partner, not noticing the sides of the copter closing in as the Hawk 90 took the form of a jet and took off at full speed back to the City of Fountains.

"Trusty Steed"

18

CHAPTER 2

Walking through the dark tunnels, stoic as ever and lost in his thoughts, Dovian made his way into a large, cavernous opening. He needed to get away, think a little about what had just happened to him. Did he actually agree to join Sapphire's side? Did he actually throw away the last fifteen thousand years of his life? Everything he had fought for, everything he had lived for, should have died for, was now all for nothing. He simply threw it all away. The thought stirred in his brain, making him realize that if he had simply done that to begin with, all he had ever known would still exist. Heaving a heavy sigh, Dovian slumped his shoulders as he lifted his head and finally noticed his surroundings.

Covering the floor of the great cave were dozens of lizard bodies. Dovian's sight moved from one body to another, taking in their closed eyes, their drooping neck flaps, their unmoving clawed hands. He frowned. They were all dead. His little, scaly friends were all dead.

A trail of corpses carried his gaze to another monstrous beast—a rather large demon, one of Sapphire's creations. Dovian noticed the hundreds of claw and bite marks marring the giant's skin, revealing the reason for the lizards' demise. They had tried to take the creature down.

Dovian looked up toward the light source flooding in from the top of the cavern. It was quite an extreme fall. It pained him to know that the poor, little reptiles were probably frightened in the last moments of their life. But why would they try taking down one of Sapphire's creations? Frilled monitors weren't necessarily known to be brave creatures when it came to

19

teaming up against foes much larger than themselves.

A low howl echoed from the opposite side of the hollow room, alerting Dovian. He slowly walked around the giant, careful not to step on any lizards. Cautiously, he tilted his head to look at the source of the sorrowful wail. A low, shuddering breath huffed, and the clattering of small rocks sounded as the air gushed out of another giant beast's nostrils. Dovian's frown deepened as he looked upon the king-sized frilled monitor that lay broken and bloodied on the cave floor. Pitiful golden eyes stared at Dovian. The large creature puffed out another breath, a wheeze rumbling as it tried to bark at the nearing Sorcēarian.

"Look at the mess you've gotten yourself into," Dovian mumbled, placing a hand on the lizard's snout. The creature clawed at the ground, trying to move. Another garbled moan escaped it as it attempted to breathe through a collapsed lung.

"Now, now…." Dovian ran his hand along the creature's neck, eyeing the faded tattoo. He gave a crooked smile. "King Petey. You are always getting yourself into trouble. First you steal the onions from the gardens, then you eat everything in the kitchen including the tables and chairs, and then you get yourself into all sorts of peril even when thrown into the caves…looks like you haven't changed a bit."

Blue light trailed from Dovian's fingers as he began healing the creature, his staff glimmering with a similar hue.

"Only bigger," he sadly whispered. "You get bigger every time I see you."

Memories from long ago flickered in the Sorcēarian's mind as he watched the suffering creature that was once considered a pet. Dovian's eyebrows raised; his lashes fluttered at the sudden onslaught of remembrance. Taking a sharp breath, Dovian trailed his fingers over the tattoo. "She…she would be so proud." He shivered.

After so many years, he tried so hard not to be taken down by the memory of her. So hard, in fact, that he had somehow managed to force her from his mind. How could he forget? How could he even forget for one second, let alone so many years, her?

"My God! What have I done?" Dovian moaned as he lowered his head. Who was he? How terrible was he to have even forgotten her? "My sweet Lita. My dear, little Lita." One of his hands gripped the robes covering his chest. Tears lined his eyes as faint memories of an adorable, spunky young woman with green eyes and wild hair of silver spun with gold flew through his mind. "I'm so sorry. I'm so sorry!" Dovian whispered, gripping his chest with a shaking hand. "I couldn't save you, either…."

Lita's death was as painful as I'Lanthe's, possibly even more so. Perhaps the constant memory of her would have broken him further. Dovian had to filter something in order to spare his sanity, for what little he had left. But he didn't understand why he would choose to forget her. No, there was no excuse for it. The possibility that he had even forgotten one memory of her, along with so many others he had known, left Dovian feeling ill. What did he have left to hold onto if he didn't allow himself the joy of their memory?

A small groan sounded from Petey once again, bringing the Sorcēarian back to reality. Dovian sniffed, abruptly composing himself. He looked worn and tired; the constant reminder of his past was beginning to wear him thin. Patting the lizard on the side, he smiled again.

"You're not as good at healing yourself as you used to be, are you?" Giving another call of light, Dovian finished treating Petey's wounds. "Still spoiled as ever. Always getting what you want. I think she taught you that as well." He hummed a small laugh.

Petey slowly stood, his golden eyes flickering with radiance within the dark cave. Rearing, he gave a loud and proud call, the sound rippling against the walls. Dovian folded his arms, unimpressed at the spectacle, eyeing the creature.

"And I see you've been eating a few too many albatross eggs. You're rather plump."

Petey eyed the tall man. Dovian stared in return.

"And what, precisely, put you in this predicament? You didn't try to eat this demon, did you?"

Petey honked in response, hissing with his tongue flickering as he hunkered low, eyeing the dead monster behind Dovian.

"Let me see." He placed his palm between the lizard's eyes. At the touch, the reptile's pupils turned milky-white as Dovian searched the beast's memories.

Like the flickering of photographs, the last couple hours of Petey's life played in a jostled order. There was the recollection of eggs, dark caves, demons, lizards, bright sunlight and rocks in the deep valley. There was a helicopter, Aria and Troy looking up in fear, a very familiar frilled monitor that had a very familiar waddle, and more eggs. Next was a vision of Aria calming Petey and climbing on his back. Then finally the long chase that involved the greatest leap of faith which led to Petey sacrificing himself and his little friends in order to save the two soldiers.

"How very noble of you, Pete," Dovian murmured.

Aria and Troy were able to make it safely off the island. Dovian's heart fluttered with hope and fear at the revelation. They were still alive, which pleased him. However, that meant they would end up crossing paths with him and Sapphire once again. It also meant they'd be getting in the way of the child's plans and be in the path of danger and destruction. And when their paths did cross, Dovian would be expected to kill them. Was he ready for that? He swallowed thickly.

Petey gave a loud snort. Dovian shook his head, looking at the lively creature.

"I was correct in my assumption that you've been eating too many eggs. It's all you think about," Dovian lectured.

Petey squawked, not minding that Dovian pointed out his plumpness as much as he cared about hearing the word 'eggs.' He stamped his squishy pads against the rock, his talons clicking. Dovian arched an eyebrow.

"Come, I will feed you some eggs. You deserve them. But I expect you to share with my Hector. He has done a good deed, too, and I noticed from your eyes that he now looks a bit frail."

Scratching behind Petey's fringe, Dovian led the way back into the tunnels from whence he came. Petey obediently followed. As the lizard waddled from side to side, he barely managed to fit through the opening.

Cold sensations smothered her. From faraway, she could sense her body moving but not of her accord. Slowly her awareness brightened, pulling from the darkest reaches of her mind up toward the front, an expression of light flickering before her eyes. She couldn't breathe. Something weighed her down, and the cold sensation–water–was too much for her fragile senses. Sputtering, she tried to take a breath but only found herself choking. The struggle caused her to awaken, her green eyes bursting open as another dousing of water gushed over her.

Coughing, Aria tried to catch her breath as wave after wave barraged her. It was warm for a second and then cold as the air hit her. The sight before her left a searing white in her retinas.

"She's awake!" a foreign female voice called out.

"Stop the rinse cycle! You're going to drown her!" another shouted.

"Sally, stop the rinse cycle, please," the first voice commanded.

Aria continued choking, her hands gripping the sides of her bare arms. She was shivering, her teeth clattering noisily in the white spinning room. Looking up, she caught the strange eyes of the robot above her. Its blue lit orbs flickered at the registering of its master's command.

"Rinse cycle aborted," a low drone sounded.

The water halted its frenzy, and Aria continued shivering inside the tub. Quickly, a burning sensation began to boil her insides. Groaning, she covered her bare stomach and began to curl on herself, falling back.

"Catch her!"

"Damn it, sedate her! The drugs are wearing off far too soon; we need to double the dosage until everything's set back into place."

"Administering sedation," the robotic tone alerted.

A sharp sting poked the woman's spine. Her vision blurred, colors of white and metallic-grey mixing with the glowing blue eyes looking down at her.

"D...Dovian..." she whispered.

As Aria's body became weightless, lifting high above the tub, she trembled in the cold. Her dilated eyes tried to catch her surroundings and the source of the voices around her.

"What's she saying?"

"No clue, she's not here with us right now."

"Do..." the word sputtered between her lips, "Do-Dov...Do."

Aria's vision faded fast. With fuzzy awareness, she felt her body being wrapped tightly in something soft and warm, her shivering quickly halting, and then she was placed onto a surface just the same. Her hair was tugged as something brushed through her locks with robotic fingers.

Looking to the side, Aria noticed a blur of other colors. Her mind was numb to the frantic shouts and calls as a series of doctors and nurses ran toward the bed beside hers. Her ears were ringing with an atrocious high-pitched whine.

"Not again!" one male voice yelled.

"Get the epinephrine and the defibrillator; he's going into cardiac arrest again."

A horrible shock sounded. Aria's eyes widened as she recognized the man on the bed beside hers, his blurry body focusing momentarily as he jolted at the violent current. His messy brown hair matted against his unshaven face—Troy. Another blast caused his chest to rise, and Aria's eyes were burning, her heart rate monitor beeping noisily in the room. The stress sent her mind into a whirlwind; her eyes rolling back as she felt her body grow heavy. Her sight went first, turning black as her heart pounded in her chest. The thumps were loud in her ears; her shaking hands gripped the blankets as the noise of the drumming beeps and bursting shocks faded far into the distance, vanishing with her consciousness.

Blackness consumed the woman for an unknown amount of time. It could have been minutes, hours, or days. In the darkest recesses of the mind, time did not exist. Dreams did not exist. As soon as Aria's eyes had closed, she found them fluttering open once again. This time, her vision focused after only a few seconds. Her body was no longer burning on the inside. She wasn't cold and shivering. She could breathe just fine, and there was no ringing in her ears.

Taking a slow deep breath, Aria let the air pass through her nose. The room smelled like antiseptic. She stared blankly at the ceiling above her. Long straight lights were implanted into the flat surface above her, shining with a dimmed fluorescence. Turning her head, she looked upon the bed beside her. It was empty. Frantic, Aria sat up.

"Troy!" she gasped.

Trying to stand, the woman groaned as she bent her knees to twist in the bed. The long thin IVs tugged at her arms, tangling with her as she fussed with the blanket. She was already breathing heavily, feeling drained and light-headed. The sight of the fresh scars running down the length of her legs from her knees to her ankles was alarming.

"You had best stop moving so much, missy!" a nurse shouted from the doorway at the front of the room. She was middle-aged, small, round, and had her dark hair pulled tight behind her head.

"Troy! Where? Where is he?" Aria asked, sitting half-turned on her hospital bed.

The nurse looked over her shoulder, nodding at someone in the hallway. She quickly waved her hand toward herself before holding it out, gesturing to allow someone else to enter the room before her.

"Troy? I'm not sure who you are talking about. You mean Sean? He's fine. You shouldn't worry so much," the woman said.

"S-Sean?" Aria asked with confusion.

From the hall came Troy. Aria sighed with relief, unsure as to why the nurse was referring to Troy by his middle name. He was wearing colorless hospital attire—a long-sleeved shirt and baggy pants with matching slippers. A mechanical brace was secured about his hip and knee joint to help support him as he hobbled toward his bed. His eyes were dull and lined with dark circles, but as he looked at the alert Aria, they flickered back to life, and he gave a large lopsided grin.

"Hey, look who's finally awake," he said, his voice raspy. "Certainly got your beauty sleep."

"I woke up, and you were gone," Aria spat without much thought.

He looked at her, his smile fading momentarily. "Well, that's because I was out for a nice little walk."

"I thought you were dead."

Troy slowly lowered himself to sit on the edge of his bed; the nurse helped by holding onto his elbow.

"What would make you think that?" he chuckled. "I'm indestructible; you know that."

Aria finally sat back onto her pillow, watching Troy from the corner of her eye. "I woke up once. I was being washed and carried back into my bed. Alarms were going off. I heard someone say you were going into cardiac arrest."

Troy dropped his head, not making eye contact with the woman. His hand reached for the sagging collar of his large shirt, and he tugged downward to reveal the top of his chest. It was bruised, the skin dark in the center, gradating into a bright red on the outside. A bandage hid the rest.

"Burned me a bit, but I guess they were able to get me back," he mumbled.

"Sean is lucky. He had coded for about a minute before they got his heart back beating," the nurse interjected.

"You were dead?!" Aria shrieked, sitting up in bed again. Troy jolted at the volume.

"It's not that big of a deal." He shrugged.

"Not a big deal?! Damn it, you almost died on me! Forever!" she shouted.

The nurse looked at the two soldiers, her eyes bugging slightly.

"Yeah, well, so did you!" Troy snapped.

"I didn't...did I?" She stared at the nurse for answers.

"You were in pretty bad shape when they brought you in. You were coughing and spewing up blood like I'd never seen. Most of your internal organs had been smashed in some way. Both of you had multiple broken bones. Sean's chest had collapsed, and he was retaining fluid in his lungs and around his heart. Your lower legs were shattered. If it wasn't for those armored suits and whatever kind of drugs you injected yourself with, you two woulda been in pieces." She pointed at Aria's scars on her legs. "We were able to place the bones back together, but you'll need to rest a few more days to let the alloy set in."

"A few more days?" Aria gaped at the woman. "Oh my God, how long have we been here?" Her head twisted to the left and then the right.

"You've been here for about three days."

"Three days?!" Aria screamed again.

"Please, Ms. Clarke, lower your voice. You'll wake the other patients, and you need to relax."

'Clarke?' Aria thought. Now it was starting to make sense.

"Relax? How can I relax? We've been in the hospital for three days." Her eyes narrowed at Troy. "We are in Fountains, aren't we?"

"Of course you are," the nurse replied. "Your pilot dropped you off. Luckily, he knew about your medical history. If not, we wouldn't have been able to tell what your blood type was since your dog tag was missing, and both of your DNAISs were burnt to a crisp."

Aria glanced at her wrist, noticing the bandages. Her eyes then fell to Troy's which was similarly dressed. Bringing her attention back to the man's chest, she noticed he was wearing his necklace that only contained one tag instead of his usual two. She gave a wry smile.

"Courtney never wears hers. She's gotten herself into trouble before because of it," Troy said, glancing at Aria with piercing eyes.

"Well, I don't like being treated like some spoiled brat's pet," she replied, folding her arms.

"Still, it could save your life if you wore it like protocol instructed," the nurse stated. "And I couldn't find any active files on you."

"It's because she doesn't wear it. Every time she's been in the hospital, she's been listed as anonymous," Troy explained.

"Well, I guess that would make sense. Still, they could've checked your DNAIS the previous times…" the nurse muttered, glancing at her watch. She quickly stood up. "Anyway, it's dinner time. I've got to check with the kitchen to make sure your food order has been updated to solids. I'll return shortly."

Troy and Aria both remained silent, watching the older woman slip out of the room. After a few more seconds—to be sure no one was within earshot—Aria sat up in bed and faced the man.

"What in the hell is going on?" she hissed quietly. "How long have you been awake?"

"Chillout; everything's fine. I woke up this morning. Luckily, Aren came to check up on us not long after. He knew Walten would be keeping a close eye on any records that revealed our names. He's a smart kid. Before he brought us in, he tore off my dog tag, leaving only Dad's. Don't know how the idiot doctors didn't realize he's been dead for nearly forty-six years….I'm sure Aren came up with some good excuse."

"And how'd he know about the Courtney bit?" Aria asked.

"Not sure; I figure he did some digging. Funny, a kid can look up anything he wants on us, and Walten can't seem to ever find us."

"Nobody said Walten was smart."

Troy snorted a laugh. "Or his cronies."

"So…I guess Aren also went the extra mile and burned out our DNAISs," Aria said, running a hand over her bandaged wrist.

"Yeah. He says 'sorry' by the way. It was the only way he could keep our identities private. Good thing you had given him a backup of all your files. He said he had a plan, been working on a project the past few days with the information you gave him." Troy stretched out his leg, the joint popping loudly. He winced. Even Aria cringed. "Not sure if that was a good sound." He rubbed his knee.

"Should I be concerned about his little project?" Aria asked.

"He said that if you asked that, to tell you not to worry; he's got it all under control," Troy mumbled, still running his palm over his leg.

"I hate being out of the loop," she groaned.

"You hate not being in charge."

She glared at him, frowning the more he smirked.

"Okay, dinner is served," the nurse called out as she entered the room. Aria and Troy quickly turned their attention to the woman. "You know, I've worked here for over twenty-five years, and I still cannot tell you what, exactly, is in the meatloaf," she laughed.

As she set the trays down, Troy gave a cockeyed grin at the sloppy tan-colored mess on his plate.

"Just like how mom used to make," he cheered.

Aria wrinkled her nose. "This looks like my cooking."

"And I expect you both to eat it all. You need your strength and health." The nurse's expression turned into a hard look. "Especially if they are in such a hurry to get as many soldiers out on the field as possible."

"What's the hurry?" Aria asked. She rolled her eyes as the woman tucked a napkin into her shirt.

"Oh, I suppose you wouldn't know with everything you've been through. The war…against Cherno, Saray, and Roma. They need as many soldiers as they can get."

"Saray and Roma, too?!" Troy shouted.

The nurse quickly pushed him back onto the angled bed and placed a napkin in his collar.

"Yes. War's been declared. Apparently Cherno was so angry with Mr. Walten for buying out Elixis during the Stock Talks that they nuked Athenia just to keep him from having it! And then, Cherno teamed up with Saray, who is also allies with Roma. Ever since they attacked the Underbelly, both President Clarke and Mr. Walten have turned up missing. General Jeron Feyette has been in charge of all the military ever since. I suspect that it's Cherno who has kidnapped the President and CEO. And now being teamed up with two of the largest militaries in the world, Cherno is very dangerous."

"Cherno had nothing to do with the attack on the Underbelly!" Troy argued. "Nor did they nuke Athenia!"

The nurse was taken aback by the man's angry outburst.

"When did Feyette mobilize?" he asked, not bothering to explain the truth to the nurse. Walten's propaganda clearly was already in full effect with the general populace.

"Well…three days ago they sent out drones and mechs," the woman stammered. "Troops were sent out about two days ago."

"Shit! We need to get out of here! We've got to find James." Aria tried standing from her bed, her arms tangling with the IVs again. As her bare feet hit the floor, she began to topple over, her knees buckling.

"You need to sit down! You're not healed yet! You've got a few more days before you'll be walking out of here." The woman guided Aria back into her bed.

"No…you don't understand," Aria said, her breathing heavy from the small amount of movement. "We are all going to die if we can't get out of here."

"Honey, there are plenty of soldiers out there right now. Those Cherno bastards will get what they deserve for killing all those innocent people down in the Underbelly. As messed up as a lot of those folks were down there, they didn't deserve that," the woman said, tucking in Aria. She then proceeded to remove the IVs. "And neither did Athenia. I'm sure Saray and Roma will get their just deserts, too, for allying themselves with that terrible Lebedev."

"Lady, there's something out there you can't comprehend, and it's going to destroy us all," Troy snapped.

The nurse placed her hands on her hips, frowning at the male soldier. "Are you one of those conspiracy theorists that think monsters are doing all of this?"

"Pull your head out of your ass! What reason did Cherno have to destroy the Underbelly? If they were going to attack, why not attack the side that counts–Bio-Tech? When are you people going to open your eyes and realize the truth to what's really going on here?" Aria said, her eyes flaring with hostility.

The nurse gaped at Aria in shock. Irritably, she folded her arms across her chest. "You two just be quiet and eat your dinner. I don't need you working up all the other patients in this hospital. Any more complaints and I'll have you both sent to psychiatric care. Then you won't be getting out of here for a while." She quickly spun and marched to the exit, dimming the lights to the vibrant white room, and shut the door.

"Well…that didn't go so well," Troy said. Picking up his fork, he poked the questionable meat on his plate. "You know, it's probably better that she dimmed the lights. Doesn't look so nasty that way."

Aria scoffed. "I'd rather eat field rations."

Troy followed with a scoff of his own. "I'd rather eat your cooking."

"I wouldn't go that far." She scrutinized her meal.

With a huff, the woman plopped back onto her pillow, staring at the pale ceiling. She was hungry but didn't feel like eating, especially the mush sitting in front of her. She angrily tugged on the napkin tucked into her shirt, crumpled it, and dropped it to the floor. Why couldn't she have a cheeseburger? That sounded good. Or pizza. Even then, could she stomach the food? The smell itself was making her feel nauseous. Closing her eyes tightly, she took a deep breath, trying to ignore the clatter of Troy's fork as he ate the cafeteria mess.

"You better eat that," he mumbled with a full mouth.

"Don't think so," she muttered.

"Do it, or I'll spoon feed you."

"You eat it."

"I would, but I know you need it more."

"It'll just make me barf," she groaned.

The room was silent after that. Aria sighed; her eyes remained closed.

"You need to eat. Why are you always so stubborn?" a familiar voice grumbled. It seemed quite aloof and rumbled with a bass tone. Aria wasn't sure where the voice had come from, but she had nearly fallen asleep when it sounded.

"I'm not being stubborn; I *will* barf," she replied.

"I didn't say anything," Troy spoke up.

Aria opened her eyes, looking at the man in the bed next to hers. He had nearly eaten all of his food already and was gaping at Aria like she had grown a second head.

"You said I was being stubborn," she stated.

"No, I didn't. I've been eating while you've been sitting over there snoring."

Aria's face twisted. Maybe she had fallen asleep. Dismissing the argument, she lowered her head. As the woman lay in her bed, she thought of the times she was sick as a child. Her mother would venture to the nearest store and bring her back some sweet treat. When she did that, it always made Aria feel a little bit better.

"Oh, I see why you aren't eating," Troy said with an accusatory tone.

"Why?" Aria asked, irritated.

"You've gotten full off of chocolates."

The woman's green eyes popped open. "What chocolates?"

Troy pointed. "Didn't notice 'em before. Someone must've visited while I was out."

Aria looked to the opposite side of her bed where a small table was. Beside her lamp was a petite pink box that had a matching bow.

"Those look like the ones from Saray," Aria whispered.

With a shaking hand, she gripped the decorative box. Carefully, she opened the small note tied to the top. With beautiful handwriting, there was a message scrawled inside.

'For the tummy ache....'

Aria's breath hitched, her heart pounding in her chest. Who would give her this gift? No one knew of their trip to Saray except for Clarke and Lebedev. It sure as hell wasn't from Lebedev, and Clarke's handwriting wasn't that nice. Aria rubbed her eyes, thinking of the voice she had heard only moments ago. It wasn't Troy who had called her stubborn. Was her mind playing tricks on her, or did she actually hear Dovian's voice? And were these from him? If so, why wouldn't he show himself to her? Where was he? Was he safe?

"Who's it from?" Troy asked, tearing the woman from her thoughts.

"Uh, it…it doesn't say," she grumbled, quickly opening the package. "I'm sure it's from Kovacevic or something."

'Yeah, like he can write in cursive,' she thought.

"Why would he send you chocolates? Would he even know we're here?" Troy asked.

"Maybe there's another one of those bakeries here in the city. I mean, it's just a pink box. Anyone could have bought this from anywhere. I bet it was Aren."

Troy shrugged, not thinking much of the whole ordeal. Aria, however, couldn't shake the feeling that there was more to it than that. Maybe she had just hoped there was.

Looking inside the box, she heaved a tired sigh. There were four truffles, each individually wrapped. Sure enough, her suspicions were correct. Inside was another message: *'a little piece of heaven'* and a tiny smiley face drawn in the corner.

"Troy, we need to get out of here," she whispered.

"Are Those Chocolates?"

CHAPTER 3

The chill of the cave froze Ivory to her core. Though she didn't feel it as much as read it in her senses that she should be cold. After all this time, the young woman never once thought about how she wasn't feeling things correctly like an ordinary human being. Sure, she knew it was cold. And as she sat on the slick crystalline floor of the chamber, her knees drawn to her chest with her arms wrapped around, she didn't feel uncomfortable. Pastel-blue eyes stared back at hers through her reflection in the ground. Who was this woman with fair skin and matching pale hair? As hard as she tried, no memory would surface from her previous life. Perhaps she had no memories because of the damage to her brain caused by the gunshot wound that stole her life away nearly a year ago. But was she even that same person? Perhaps she had no memories because she was nothing more than a simple clone, a clone of a dead body. She was a mere representation of a deceased woman named Ivory that once had a family–a mother, a father, and an adorable little sister who loved her dearly.

'Fiona.' The name bubbled in her mind.

She had no recollection of the girl outside of the miniscule memory from nearly a week ago. Though she had no idea who Fiona truly was, Ivory felt a deep connection to her. And for a few minutes, she almost had hope, hope that she could figure out who she was and where she belonged. But all that bright hope was brutally crushed thanks to General Feyette and his team of murdering soldiers.

That's what you get for always trying to think positively. Your optimism only makes the cruel reality more painful.' She glared at her reflection in the shining floor. Her angry expression made her seem harsh and distant, a complete contrast to her typical joyful appearance.

Ivory blinked away her tears. Her hands gripped her forearms tightly, nails digging into her flesh painlessly. She was living in an unknown world surrounded by unfamiliar humans, monsters, and a Sorcēarian. The Sorcēarian, a man whom she knew nothing about but felt everything in the world for, the feelings of another, filled her with both hope and fright. Dovian was once calm and kind, but his presence the past few days left even her skin crawling. But what was she afraid of? Why was she feeling anything at all? She was a biomechanical android. She, herself, was a monstrosity, built only to destroy humanity. Last thing she knew, robots didn't have feelings. They weren't supposed to understand or feel anything.

"Maybe I am just a robot, and this is what robots go through. Maybe they sit on the inside always contemplating their existence and reason for feeling anything at all," she whispered.

"You feel things because you are alive, Ivory," a male voice rumbled inside the dark chamber.

Ivory shivered a little at the sound. It was Dovian's voice, but something behind it made her heed warning. He was in another one of his moods. She twisted her head, looking upward at the tall, lean man. He had his hood drawn; his piercing blue eyes stared coldly upon her. In his right hand was his staff. The orb cast light around him.

"Why are you sitting in the dark?" he asked. "You haven't even bothered leaving the cave."

"It's not like it will grant me any freedom," she grumbled harshly.

Dovian never tore his eyes from hers. He frowned at her spiteful glare. She was obviously angry with him.

"You are as free as I am," he returned.

"You are a slave as I am," she mumbled.

"And how is that?"

Ivory slowly stood, her once beautiful masquerade gown was now tattered and torn, covered in stains of dust and burns from her heated thrusters and particle beam. Only one hand was gloved, the other article had been demolished in the amassing of her weapon. Her filigree mask was also long gone, probably lost during her travels with Euclid to this terrible cave. It was in that instant while looking at the beautiful glaring blonde that Dovian had realized he never once asked her if the other Sorcēarian had ever harmed her.

"You are only here because you are too scared to stand up for yourself and do what is right," Ivory stated. "You are afraid of *her*."

Dovian finally tore his brilliant eyes away. "And what is the right thing, Ivory?"

"Why are you even questioning it?" she hissed. "You know very well that you are wrong."

"You should be careful what you say," Dovian warned.

"Why? Because the horrible child will overhear? The monster that wants to destroy everyone and everything will only kill us both once she gets what she wants!"

"Lower your voice! You have no idea what she is," Dovian growled.

"I don't care! I want to go home!"

Dovian snatched her by the arm then. "And where is that, Ivory?" he said through gritted teeth. "You have no home. You and all you've ever known in the past life have all been destroyed by the humans."

"And you let Aria and Troy die!" she shrieked.

Dovian tugged her close. His voice lowering, he said to her, "They are not dead."

Ivory's glare finally dissipated as her eyes widened, and her breath halted. "They are alive?" Her voice raised in pitch.

Dovian nodded in affirmation.

"You know this for fact?" she asked, her tone lowering again.

"I've seen them myself. They survived the attack and are currently in a hospital in Fountains. Things were looking bleak at first, but now they seem stable. They will be alright."

Ivory's glare returned. "No thanks to you!" She pushed away from him.

Dovian lowered his head. "And what in the hell would you have me do, Ivory?"

The woman spun around, her finger pressing against his chest as she lectured him. "Protect them! Like you said you would! They aren't just allies, Dovian, they are our friends! Even in the short amount of time we've known them, we've been through so much!"

"How can I protect them when I have you to protect?" he asked.

"I can take care of myself, Dovian." She folded her arms.

The words reeled in the Sorcēarian's mind. Was this I'Lanthe speaking to him right now? Ivory indeed was growing stronger in her demeanor.

"But, before I found out that you are..." he hesitated, watching Ivory's face fall into sadness, "...an android, I had to find you. None of us knew what we were up against. None of us knew what Euclid wanted with you. He could've killed you for all I had known."

"So you came here for me…and once you found out that I was an android, capable of all kinds of monstrosities, you still made a deal with her and agreed to her plan. You didn't help Aria and Troy escape. You didn't ensure their safety. You left them out there to die with Sapphire's demons! If it weren't for me shoving them out, they would have died!" Ivory's eyes were nearly aflame like a Sorcēarian's; the crystalline torches that decorated the chamber pillars glimmered against her irises.

"I didn't kill them, though!" Dovian shouted back. His white teeth clenched tightly together in anger.

In a way, Ivory was right. He was a coward. He did nothing to help Aria and Troy, and because of his fear and selfishness, he allowed the two to be in further danger. It was a miracle they made it off the island, let alone survived their wounds. But, he also couldn't risk leaving Ivory. What would have happened then?

He turned away from the woman, staring at the floor. "They are still alive," he whispered. "I may not have done much to help them, but they are still alive, and that's all that matters."

Ivory watched him, her folded arms lowering to her sides. Slowly, her face softened. She knew it wasn't his fault. All of this was Sapphire's fault. There was nothing she nor he could do to stop the child. At least, not yet. For now, Ivory would have to focus on her friends. The thought of Aria and Troy alive made her feel a little better about the situation, but the two militants remained in grave danger on all sides—human and demon both.

A flicker of distortion fluttered and spiraled from in front of the stone throne beside them. Ivory quickly stumbled away, leaning against the wall. Dovian sidestepped toward her, watching the black vortex bend the visual plane, revealing the small white body of Sapphire. The girl stood firmly in her place with her eyes locked onto Dovian.

"And if I hadn't found my creation dead at the bottom of one of the tunnels, I wouldn't have known whether the two humans had survived or not," Sapphire spoke with her sweet, innocent voice. She ran her thin fingers through her blonde hair. "But it's not a concern of mine. They will be dead soon along with all the others. It won't take much longer before all my plans are set into motion. I also expect that if we ever do cross paths again, which we all know we will, you will kill them without hesitation." Her blue-grey eyes narrowed as she smiled sweetly at Dovian.

Ivory looked at the Sorcēarian. His fingers wiggled open and closed around his staff as he remained silent an extra second.

"That…is called hesitation, Dovian." Sapphire's tone lowered.

"We'll worry about it when it happens," he replied coolly.

Sapphire looked upwards at the ceiling, taking a slow deep breath. It wasn't the answer she wanted to hear. As her lids closed, her long dark lashes brushed the tops of her cheeks while she smiled. Releasing her held in breath, the little girl opened her eyes again, the dark pupils widening to fill even the whites of her eyes.

Dovian flinched but couldn't prepare for the invisible blast that knocked him sideways onto the floor. His scepter clattered and rolled away. His head smashed against the crystal surface, blood bursting past his lips.

"Dovian!" Ivory shrieked. She quickly pressed herself against the wall, holding herself back from interfering.

"I don't want any hesitation from you, Dovian," Sapphire said. "If you hesitate, I will punish you. And I will punish you without hesitation, remember that."

Dovian groaned, his hand gripping his jaw. Dazed by the forceful blow to his face, the colors of the cave swirled in his vision.

"I will not hesitate to prove a point, either. I expect things to be done right the first time, just as I expect people to learn their lesson the first time," Sapphire said, her cheerful, childish voice lowering yet another octave.

Dovian's body spiraled so that he lay on his belly. The feeling of a dozen hands gripped at his robes, tugging them from his arms and back, lowering them around his waist. Dovian struggled, but the invisible force was much stronger than he was. Fingers trailed over his shoulders and back, scratching at his spine and shoulder blades. He began to panic, his back apparatus blinking in assorted colors as it filtered his energies.

"Wait! No!" Dovian called out, trying to pull free from the force.

"Begging won't help you, Dovian. It's too late," Sapphire said without emotion.

"Leave him alone…" Ivory whispered, watching Dovian struggle as the back apparatus began to tug upwards away from his body, pulling his skin.

"Quiet, or I'll tear off one of your limbs," Sapphire sputtered in response. "I won't warn you again."

Slowly, the metallic wings of Dovian's back apparatus separated from his body, his flesh bleeding and tearing like cloth. He was screaming; the noise no longer muffled as the notches of the centerpiece that lined his entire spine was torn nerve after nerve from his body. The machine whirred mechanically, beeping and flickering with red lights as it tugged violently from each vertebra. The sound of his scream was terrible enough without having to hear the horrible ripping of his skin and popping of his spine. Ivory covered her ears and closed her eyes. With another forceful pull, the whole device was torn from Dovian's body from the base of his skull all the way to his tail bone. The Sorcēarian gasped loudly, his body shaking and twitching. The metallic clatter of his apparatus being tossed onto the ground beside him echoed loudly within the chamber. Dovian's eyes suddenly lost their vibrancy, fading into a milky-white.

"Dovian...." Ivory quickly covered her mouth.

Sapphire turned to the woman. Her black eyes returned to normal. She smiled at Ivory. "How about you two take a walk outside? Get some fresh air. I'm sure Dovian has lots to show you and many stories to tell. After all, I need you two to spend lots of time together."

Ivory stared at the man on the floor. His body was unmoving. Blood pooled around him. His face was pale; the light in his eyes was extinguished. Dovian was dead.

"You killed him," Ivory whispered.

Sapphire looked over her shoulder at the Sorcēarian. She giggled and shrugged. "So what if I did? He'll be back in a little while. Remember, he can't die...at least, not permanently."

Ivory whimpered. What was the difference? Right now, Dovian was dead. So what if he would wake up later? It didn't make the matter any less tragic or atrocious.

"Go help him. It'll probably take a while to heal from that. Once he's awake, have him take you somewhere nice and romantic. I need Sorcēarian babies. We've got a war to win." The black vortex reopened, and a loud gushing of wind sounded, blowing the girl's hair in every direction. In a roar, the distortion surrounded her small body and ate her, filling the space with her disappearance and the typical visual plane.

The room was silent. Ivory lowered to her knees, her eyes locked onto the man's wounds. Slowly, she crawled toward him. Her readings told her that the floor was cold, her hands were cold, Dovian's body was quickly dropping in temperature, and he had lost a lot of blood. No pulse was detected.

"Dovian," Ivory squeaked.

He didn't move.

"Dovian," she repeated, placing a delicate hand on his shoulder.

His blood soaked her gossamer dress. Carefully, she felt his forehead. It was cool and clammy; his hair was wet with sweat. Wrinkling her nose, she gave a quiet sob.

"I'm sorry," she stammered, her shoulders shaking. "I know there's nothing we can do. There's nothing at all we can do, but we have to figure something out. She'll just keep killing you, and who's to say she'll ever stop? Is that the kind of life you want, Dovian? A life of constant death and unhappiness?"

The man did not respond. Ivory's face fell into an ugly frown as she cried.

"Dovian, wake up!" she wailed, lowering her face to his shoulder as she held him in a small hug around his torso.

"AH!" The man gasped and lifted his head.

Ivory jumped and made a similar sound. "Dovian! Are you alright? Are you okay?" she frantically asked as she placed a hand on his cheek and looked into his pale eyes that were slowly regaining their glowing attributes.

"I-Ivory," he sputtered, grabbing her hand.

"I'm so sorry," she whispered as she helped him sit up.

"Not…not your fault," he gasped again, reaching for his staff.

Ivory quickly snagged the item and placed it in his hands.

"Are you alright?" he asked. His breaths were labored as he worked to heal himself.

"I'm fine. I'm just worried about you." Ivory waited as he worked his spell, the blue energy flowing from his staff to his body. She leaned to the side, watching the gruesomely torn flesh and meaty muscle ripple and close over the exposed bone and nerves on Dovian's back.

Once fresh skin had closed over the wounds, he let out a tired sigh and dropped the weapon. "Well?" he asked, panting.

Ivory tapped him lightly against his spine, poking in different places on his back and shoulder blades. He shivered beneath her touch.

"Does it hurt?" she quietly asked. Her hand rested on the back of his neck. She gazed at his pale face, watching the color slowly return.

"Not anymore," he quietly replied.

They stared at one another for a moment. Ivory looked petrified. Tears stained her cheeks with streaks of dark eye makeup. Her fingers dug into his silvery hair. Dovian also appeared fearful. He was nervous about the future and what dangers may come to not only the human race but him and Ivory. As much as the apparatus removal was horrifyingly unpleasant, Dovian couldn't help but worry about the blonde woman sitting beside him. She couldn't heal herself, and she couldn't come back to life. If anything happened to her, she wouldn't be able to recover. It would be different if she were just a robot, but Ivory wasn't. Robots simply don't cry.

Dovian wiped away a stray tear from Ivory's cheek with his thumb. She shivered, her eyes blinking wildly as she looked at the now living Dovian. Giving a quiet squeak, she wrapped her arms around him, hugging him tightly. The Sorcēarian lightly placed his arms around her in return.

Whatever was going to happen in the near future, they were going to go through together. It was best he and Ivory worked to strengthen their bond. Not for Sapphire, but for their sake. So he held her. He even ran his hand over her back, trying his best to comfort her as he allowed himself some time to finish healing.

"So," he mumbled after a few minutes, "how would you like to go out for a little walk?"

"Get the hell out of here?" she grumbled, finally releasing her hold on him.

"My thoughts exactly." Slowly, he slipped on the top of his robes.

Ivory rose to her feet. She looked down at Dovian. He was staring blankly at the opposite end of the room where his apparatus lay. He unconsciously chewed the skin on his lip. It had been fifteen thousand years since his back was void of it.

"Dovian?" Ivory leaned sideways to look at him. Her blonde hair fell over one shoulder.

"Yes, dear?" Dovian murmured. He looked up at her; his sad eyes quickly flickered as he gave her a forced smile.

Ivory smiled back, holding a hand out to him. "No more bad thoughts for the day, okay?"

He took her hand and accepted her help to his feet. "Sounds like a good idea to me." He rested on his staff.

Side by side they walked together and left the chamber, but not before Dovian reached down to pick up the spinal device.

"Could we put it back on?" Ivory asked.

"It would take some time, but I'm not sure I want to go through that again if Sapphire finds out." He gave her a crooked smirk, making him appear youthful again.

"I don't want you to go through it again, either." She wrapped her arm around his elbow, resting her head on his shoulder.

Thankfully, the trek to the outdoors was quiet and without disturbance from Sapphire's demons. Still, Ivory's grip on Dovian's arm never loosened. It wouldn't have bothered the Sorcēarian much except Ivory wasn't an average human woman. Her android death-grip was nearly bone crunching. Dovian patted her hand, making her aware of her nerves and she immediately released.

Exiting the cave, Dovian squint his eyes, adjusting to the bright, mid-day sun. The vibrant blue of his eyes dimmed. Ivory had no trouble, her pupils shifting to the appropriate measurement to gain perfect eyesight to the outside world despite being in the dark cave for days.

"Where shall we go?" she timidly asked.

Ives was a whole expanse of fields and hills. One corner of the island contained a blue sky and large billowing clouds of white. The opposite end appeared dark; the sky was eaten away by purple and grey masses, lightning flickering on the edge. Needless to say, the opposite side didn't look very welcoming, but she wasn't very surprised when Dovian lifted a hand and pointed in the stormy direction.

"The storms are nearing, but I think we can get there before they hit."

"Does it always rain here?" Ivory asked.

Dovian hesitated, his wings sprouting from his dorsal side, the feathers fluttering in the wind. "Only when I am near," he said in a grim tone.

He twisted, lifting Ivory off the ground. She quickly complied, wrapping her arms around his neck as he cradled her.

"Is that part of your punishment?" she asked.

"No…" he muttered. "It is because I choose it to be."

Flapping his wings, they lifted into the air. In seconds, they were high and sailing away from the dreary desert cave system. Ivory deduced that the location was most likely barren because Dovian rarely visited this part of the island.

The air was cool against their skin, the sun warm in contrast. It didn't take long before Ivory was giggling, watching the landscape in awe as it moved quickly past them. The cracked land and brown pastures abruptly changed to bright plush grasslands. Spontaneous flower fields blurred, the sweet scent carried by the breeze. From afar, she could see the flapping silhouettes of flocking birds. The grass shifted near rocky areas where big lizards slipped out, their tongues wagging as their beady eyes looked up to the soaring pair. Ives was full of life. It seemed to hold all types of environments from forests to water-lands, deserts, and even snowy mountains on the far edges of the vast island. To fill them all were colorful creatures—kinds even Ivory's mind knew nothing about but were once familiar to the whole world. It was stunning.

As they neared the dead city, the vibrant colors quickly gloomed as dark thunderheads covered the sunlight. Dovian descended, avoiding the low clouds. The woman stared at the scene below. Their reflection fluttered through the silver waves of the lakes—a dark, rippling shadow with wings.

"This place is beautiful," she whispered.

"Not as it once was," Dovian murmured in her ear.

Ivory finally brought her attention to the man and caught him staring at her. He gave her a sad smile before looking straight ahead. Ivory followed his gaze, seeing the shapes of the dark city. No lights came from the windows; there were no sounds of city life, no voices, no traffic. Did Sorcēarian's even use cars?

Thunder rolled, approaching them as they neared the tall cathedral-like buildings. The temperature dropped, rushing gales flowing over the broken buildings and trees in the gardens. Ivory's smile faded as it took a moment to register that the screaming coming from the empty structures were caused only by the wind. It created a haunting effect.

"I know what will cheer you up," Dovian said, his voice laced with amusement.

He leaned to the side, turning around one massive ornate creation, his wings beating as they narrowly avoided a collision with a large cross that stood on a rooftop. As he lowered, Ivory got a closer view of the city that was once known to be bright and elegant. The colors were now grey instead of the pristine white of their former glory. The smaller institutions were overgrown with wild grass and flowered vines. In no way was the place ugly. It was still mesmerizing in its own kind of beauty. Though eerie, the city had a dreamlike quality and seemed peaceful. She looked at Dovian's face, searching for any indication of emotion. Ivory was sure he didn't find it serene but instead a constant dreadful reminder of what once was. It was a wonder how he hadn't gone completely insane, being entirely alone for so long.

"There," he said.

Spiraling in a full circle, Dovian descended into a great garden surrounded by a marble wall. The location looked maintained and not as overgrown as the rest of the city. Landing in the plot, Dovian set Ivory on her feet. She reluctantly released her hold, standing rigidly in the center of the enclosed area.

"Wait here one moment," Dovian said, rolling his shoulders.

He walked around the side of the building the garden was attached to and disappeared from view. Ivory lifted her head, taking in the sight of the tall trees and waving branches. On the inside of the wall, there were small stone planters holding large wild flowers of purple and red. The long stems arched toward the ground. The grass was fresh and green; a small cobblestone path led to a large fountain made of white marble. Tiny winged figures lined the pillar in the center, arching from the pool to the top of the spouting water. The garden was striking. By the looks of it, this one in particular was one of

Dovian's favorites.

A low growl sounded from the area where Dovian had ventured to. Ivory became stiff, her eyes looking, unblinking, at the corner of the wall. She listened. The growl called again, followed by a vicious snarl, a bark almost. Ivory barely had any time to react as the pounding of footsteps neared, and an enormous lizard rounded the corner. Its golden eyes stared at her as it trudged straight ahead. The woman gasped, lowering herself a little as she stumbled backward against the fountain.

"Dovian!" she squeaked, watching the lizard claw across the lawn at her.

The reptile slid to a halt, reared, kept eye contact with her, and warbled noisily. It stamped its feet onto the stone, huffing slightly, and its neck flaps expanded outward with brilliant colors.

"All show and no bite," Dovian chuckled as he reentered the area.

"Where were you?" Ivory yapped irritably. She quickly ran to the Sorcēarian's side, latching onto his arm.

"Well, I was retrieving...." He noticed Ivory's frightened stare. He didn't realize how terrifying the lizard could be to someone who's never seen one so large before. "Sorry. I should probably introduce you two properly," he said, running a hand over the backside of his head.

"Introduce?" Ivory asked, looking from Dovian to the lizard.

"Oh, yes. This isn't just your typical lizard." Dovian walked away from the woman. With grandeur, he held out his arms, displaying the massive frilled monitor for Ivory to see. "Ivory, I introduce to you, the great...."

The lizard flicked its tongue, straightening its posture to look all the more impressive as Dovian spoke. It gave a small, proud bark. Ivory watched the creature in awe. Its golden eyes were mesmerizing yet frightening.

"The majestic," Dovian continued, "King Petey!" He gave a short bow beside the lizard.

Petey stomped his feet again, his tail curling around his body as he noisily honked with pride. Ivory's fearful expression quickly lifted into one of amusement. A high-pitched giggle slipped past her lips.

"King Petey?!" she asked, laughing.

Dovian lifted his head, giving her a feigned look of shock.

"Yes, King Petey. King of all the frilled monitors, the largest lizard since the dinosaurs, the largest beast ever created by the Sorcēarians, a creature most fierce and not to be taken lightly." He gave her a wink.

Ivory quickly bobbed her head. "A name most deserving of a king."

"A mighty king." Dovian lifted his eyebrows, looking at Petey out the corner of his eye. The lizard was enjoying the boastful speech, looking as grandiose as possible in the comparatively small garden. "Though he may be a bit fat," Dovian added.

Petey squawked an unflattering sound that caused dribble to spill from the side of his chops. Ivory laughed again, watching the lizard with more ease.

"Aw, it just gives him more to love, Dovian," Ivory said, approaching the king lizard. "And frilled monitors need lots of love, don't they?"

Petey loosened his posture, lowering his head so Ivory could give him a pat on the snout. She cooed and made kissy sounds, running her hand over the creature's scales.

"Especially the big ones, they need extra love," she added in a loving tone.

Petey almost purred beneath her touch, pounding his feet with joy against the stones.

"Well…I wouldn't give him too much," Dovian murmured with his arms folded over his chest. "He's spoiled enough."

"Is that jealousy I hear?" Ivory asked.

Dovian smirked, looking to the side.

"Jealous?" he asked. "Of a fat lizard?"

Petey snorted, glaring at the Sorcēarian.

"It's okay, Petey. Don't mind him; he's just a bitter, old man," she snickered.

"Old man?!" Dovian protested.

Ivory looked sideways at her companion, giving him a playful grin. He narrowed his eyes at her, letting her have her laugh.

"Have you had him this entire time?" she asked.

"No. I only discovered him the other day, after Troy and Aria escaped. If it weren't for Pete, they probably wouldn't have made it."

"Did you help them escape?" Ivory asked the reptile. Petey gave a small chirp, and she gasped, "Good boy!"

Dovian was quiet a moment, watching Ivory interact with Petey.

"I helped Pete out, too, you know," he mumbled.

"Oh? And how did you do that?" she asked.

As Ivory turned her attention to Dovian, Petey disapproved, pushing his face in front of hers to demand more pets.

"He was injured in a cave. The poor old boy had a terrible time trying to heal." Dovian looked beneath Petey's head, catching Ivory's blue gaze. "I helped out by curing him."

"Dovian, are you competing for attention?" she bluntly asked.

His mouth dropped open, and he was silent a moment. "No…how ridiculous. Why would I be competing for attention?"

"Now you are blushing." She smiled.

Dovian quickly pulled away. "I am most certainly not blushing. It must be sunburn." He pressed his fingers against his cheeks.

"No…no, I definitely think that was a blush." She nodded.

"I am a Sorcēarian and a man; I do not blush!" he sarcastically exclaimed.

"You're getting redder." She pointed at him, laughing.

The man quickly pulled his hood over his head and stomped toward the fountain. Sitting on the side of the spring's wall, he refused to make eye contact with the woman. His sudden, childish behavior was certainly a spectacle. Ivory could sense he was trying to make her feel more at ease with him.

"I think I made him mad," she playfully whispered to Petey. The lizard snorted, nodding his head. "Stay here," she said, patting him on the nose.

The woman turned, peering at the brooding Sorcēarian. He refused to acknowledge her. Ivory trotted to join Dovian's side at the fountain. He quickly turned away from her, arms folded. She giggled, leaning toward him, trying to gain sight of his glowing eyes. When she saw no glow because of his closed lids, she pouted.

"Seriously? You're going to act like this?" she asked.

He ignored her.

Feeling a bit agitated, she twisted the man to face her and tugged off his hood. He looked at her with wide eyes.

"Well, I think it's cute," she said quietly with a dazzling smile.

"What is cute?" he asked.

"You…blushing."

Dovian's frown deepened. "So now I'm cute?"

"When you blush!"

"I don't blush all the time, do I?" he asked, grimacing.

"No…most of the time you are frowning…like this." She mimicked him, jutting her jaw out, her mouth twisting into an upside down arch. It was a terrible look for her, but it proved her point.

"I'm not sure which is worse, me blushing and being cute, or me looking like that on a regular basis," he grumbled.

"The frowning is much worse." She nodded.

He gave an airy laugh.

"And that is even better," she added.

Dovian stiffened as Ivory placed her fingers on the edges of his mouth. Her fingertips pushed and forced the man into an awkward smile. Ivory certainly had no issue with personal space. Dovian forced a toothy grin, and the woman cringed.

"No, not like that! A real smile!" She pushed his face into another creepy expression, and Dovian quickly grabbed her wrists and lowered her hands from his face as he chuckled, giving her a more natural smile. Ivory merely watched, giggling with him.

"Much better." She clapped her hands together. "Do you agree?" she asked Petey.

Dovian sighed, looking at the hefty snorting lizard. At least Ivory was feeling more cheery.

"So…what happened to Petey? I mean, you said you had to heal him." She changed the subject.

Dovian relaxed, glad the topic was no longer about his smile. "He had been chased by a giant demon. He allowed Aria and Troy to ride on his back. Once the two were safe, he tried to escape the monster and leapt all the way from the top of the cavern but had fallen to the bottom. The monster and all of Petey's comrades followed after. Luckily for him, Petey can heal himself over a period. All the others," Dovian faltered, "were not so lucky. They all died."

Ivory gasped, clasping a hand over her mouth. After a second she blurted, "Poor things! Oh no! What about Hector? Was he there?"

"No, no…Hector is alright. He was able to escape. In fact, he's…." Dovian paused and turned to Ivory, a genuinely confused look on his face. "Have I ever told you about Hector?" he asked.

Ivory stopped to think a moment. "I…I don't know." She blinked slowly, staring at the garden floor and then looked over at King Petey. "I just remember Hector was a standard frilled monitor. He was smaller than others but had a big appetite for albatross eggs and jerky. He slept on a large pillow on your bedroom floor and loved the smell of orchids."

Dovian's whole body went ice cold. There was no way he ever indulged in telling Ivory so much about his pet.

"What else do you remember?" he asked.

"I remember…I remember!" she gasped. "Why do I remember things?"

Ivory quickly jumped to her feet. She held her hands against her face, looking at her surroundings, gasping quietly to herself.

"This garden…." She locked eyes with Dovian.

He nodded at her slowly but remained silent.

"This…this is *my* garden," she whispered.

WWW.ARCREBS.DEVIANTART.COM

"No Hesitation"

CHAPTER 4

Clattering raindrops musically played against the stone walls and pathways; the drips plopped into the fountain and pinged against Dovian's brass armor. A soft rumble vibrated the earth, creating a shiver down Dovian's spine as he watched the stunned woman before him. With her pale hands planted on her cheeks, her blue eyes shimmered as she took in the sight of the garden. The wet orchids, the grass, and the stone pillars that supported the opening into the side of the building that led into a vast bedroom were all familiar. It was a home; it was her home. She was in her private garden where she used to sit and play with the butterflies and birds beside the fountain. Usually, the first thing she'd do when she awoke in the morning was travel barefoot into this garden to see what the weather was like.

Ivory closed her eyes, memories flickering at light speed through her mind. It was surreal. She'd have breakfast at a small table located next to the opening in the wall. She'd practice the cello or the flute in the far corner of the room. She could see everything still in its place, right where she had left it. Her bed was neatly made with an oversized fur blanket sitting atop it–the same soft blanket that she used to lay on during the storms that Dovian loved so much. He would lay with her, hold her, and they would often make love in this room. Ivory gasped, her hands covering her face. Peeking through her fingers, she eyed the man sitting on the fountain. He was staring at her in awe. But these memories weren't hers, they were I'Lanthe's.

Ivory quickly shifted her eyes toward the ground, her hand gripping the dog tag around her neck. She shivered in the rain, feeling the taps as it washed over her body. The scent of the flowers was stronger than ever. It was a smell she shouldn't have recognized, but did. Her pink lips twitched as she gave a quiet whimper, tears welling in her eyes.

"Ivory," Dovian whispered, rising from his seat. He placed his hands on her shoulders, causing her to jump. Still, she did not look at him. "What's wrong?" His voice was gentle, but the sound only made her want to cry harder.

"No," she whispered. "These aren't my memories."

"They are," he reassured her.

"No!" She hastily shoved his arms away. "These are hers!"

Thunder above answered her shout, and she flinched.

"Ivory...I don't know what to say." He looked utterly helpless. What could he say?

"She's inside me, isn't she? Is that why you brought me here? For her memories?"

"No!" Dovian reassured her. "It isn't like that. I wanted to get you out of those caves, away from Sapphire. I wanted to bring you to a place where you would feel safe."

"By bringing me to her home? Dovian, of all the places...you brought me to your dead girlfriend's home?!"

Dovian froze, accepting Ivory's harshness.

"You could have taken me anywhere! Your home, your friend's home, a stranger's home, anywhere! But you brought me here."

"I brought you here because I am familiar with it and because I hoped you would be comfortable here as well," he spoke slowly, trying his best not to sound irritated.

"How am I supposed to feel comfortable here?" she asked.

"You remember it, don't you?"

"From her memories!"

"No, Ivory! They are your memories, too!" he argued.

"How are they mine? I'm not I'Lanthe!" she shrieked.

"Then who are you, huh?" he yelled.

Ivory gaped at Dovian with wide eyes. He quickly composed himself, wiping a hand over his face.

"See? You don't even know who you are. You may think you are Ivory, but where are your memories from that lifetime?" he questioned.

"I, I don't know," she meekly replied.

"You haven't had a single recollection of your past this entire time you've reawakened. Even when you saw your little sister, you didn't recall a single memory of her. You still haven't, have you?"

Ivory lowered her head again. "No…" she whispered.

"Listen to me." He placed his hands on her shoulders again. "I did not bring you here to have you live vicariously through my past and *dead girlfriend.*" The last two words sounded bitter as he spoke them, and Ivory regretted saying them before. "I brought you here for you, no one else, alright? If you don't want to stay here, we can go somewhere else. But, please, hear me out. You do have a connection to I'Lanthe whether you like it or not. I'm not saying you aren't you, but you are sharing a consciousness with her. Now, if I can help you to remember who this woman once was, I will. If it will help you remember your past, anybody's past, I will do it."

"Do you want me to be her?" Ivory asked quietly.

Dovian remained silent for a moment. Of course, he did. He wanted more than anything for Ivory to be I'Lanthe, but he couldn't tell her that. He couldn't ask her to be that. Ivory was more than a vessel holding I'Lanthe's soul. She had a mind of her own; it just happened to be damaged.

"I want you to be who you want to be. If you want to remain who you are now, then we can leave and go somewhere else. If you want to know more about the memories and feelings you are having, we can stay here. Develop your life the way you want to, not the way you think I want you to," he said.

Ivory sighed, looking around Dovian toward I'Lanthe's bedroom. Her despairing expression quickly melted back into a shy smile. Dovian's features softened, and he lowered his hands from her.

"She could play the flute?" she asked.

"Very well," he replied.

She met his gaze. "Do you think I'll remember how?"

Dovian shrugged. "You want to try it out?"

Ivory nodded and walked past Dovian, entering the room. He watched her, his expression holding one of worry. Was she actually interested in I'Lanthe, or was she only doing this for him? A soft snort and nudge distracted the Sorcēarian.

"You don't like the rain, Pete?" Dovian turned to the lizard. The creature huffed and pressed the top of his snout against Dovian's shoulder, pushing him toward the entrance of the home. "Okay, okay. You don't have to be so rude."

A high melody commenced and a flurry of notes raised in pitch. Dovian looked toward the corner of the room where Ivory stood blowing into the silver flute. He entered the room, slowly approaching the woman as she played various harmonies and arpeggios. Petey gave a small groan and plopped onto the stone floor just inside, wrapping his tail around his body. The lizard closed his eyes, the music lulling him into a deep sleep. Dovian listened, leaning against the wall near an ornate window-seat. The music was strangely nostalgic. It was a sound that went far too long away from his ears. He watched Ivory, who sat on the edge of the table much like I'Lanthe used to. Her gaze was straight ahead, watching the rainfall. The focused look in her eyes attracted Dovian's attention. In the darkness of the room, Ivory's eyes seemed to hold an ethereal glow. He made note of this and how they flickered when the woman shifted her attention in his direction.

A brilliant flash of light temporarily ignited the room followed by a loud crackle of thunder. Ivory's concentration diverted, and she fumbled with a few notes before the flute's music faded into a couple of breathy hoots. Apprehensively, she lowered the instrument and looked over at Dovian, her eyes back to their usual shade of blue. He smiled at her, determined to keep her spirits up.

"You play very well," he said.

Ivory looked at the flute in her hands. "I doubt I had before I died."

Dovian pushed away from the wall, his hand gripping his staff. "Stop thinking like that."

Ivory gawked at him.

"I want you to focus on one thing." He lifted a finger. "One thing, got it?"

She bobbed her head.

"These memories, the ones you say are I'Lanthe's, so what if they are?"

"They aren't mine," she squabbled.

"But does that matter? What difference does it make? Think of them as yours. You remember them, make them yours. But also realize this; you have memories from the past few weeks, correct?"

Ivory nodded again.

"Those are genuinely *your* memories, correct?" he asked.

"Right."

"Focus on those memories. So what if you remember things from the past that you think wasn't yours? Do you feel comfortable here?"

She looked over the bedroom. "Yes."

"Do you feel safe here?"

She eyed Petey. "Yes."

"With me?" he firmly asked.

She hesitated. "Yes."

"Now, take those old memories and use them to your advantage toward future memories. You know where your garden is; you know where the kitchen is?"

She affirmed.

"You know where my study is? The cathedral? The escape routes and the hidden tunnel behind my bookcase?" He watched her confirm all of these with a nod. "Good. Then...if, for some reason, we are ever attacked, you will know all the ways to escape and get to safety."

"Do you think we'll be attacked?" she asked.

"You never know. I only want you to think positively about your position. Use what you can from your memories; it doesn't matter who they belong to. And from now on, be you. Your past is your past, whether you want to think of it as lost memories from a previous life in the Underbelly or ancient memories from long ago. Think of this as a second chance. This is a new you, a new life. Think about that. Not everyone gets a second chance to start over. Make this chapter of your life the way you want it. Be who you want to be, not who you think you are. Got it?"

Ivory heaved a heavy sigh. "...Got it."

Dovian stood in front of the young woman, watching her carefully. After a moment, she finally looked to the side, staring at the rain once again.

"I'm sorry I've been such a sourpuss," she uttered timidly.

Dovian smirked. "It's expected. Remember, I'm not a very jolly fellow, either. We can't have the both of us moping around, can we?"

Ivory grinned, finally looking at the man. "No! We would make terrible company for King Petey."

"Exactly. We can't be poor influences on Pete."

The lizard was fast asleep in the corner of the room, unaware of being the topic of conversation. Ivory watched the creature. "Whose is he?"

"Petey?" Dovian asked.

"Yes. I can't remember who he belonged to. At least, not right now."

Dovian stared at Petey; his expression fell. Ivory watched his brow furrow. She could tell by the distant look in his eyes that he recalled memories from long ago. He twitched and quickly shook his head.

"Mind if we sit down?" he asked, walking toward the bed.

"We don't have to talk about it if you don't want to," she said, dropping onto the cushy mattress beside him.

"No, it's fine. I just...haven't thought about my past in a very long time. In fact, I was beginning to forget some things."

"I'm sorry," she said quietly, "if I brought up bad memories."

He shook his head. "No, I don't ever want to forget, no matter how painful. In fact, these memories aren't all that painful." Dovian abruptly gave a loud laugh. The sudden noise alerted Ivory, but then her demeanor lifted. "Actually, Petey and his owner are some of the best memories I have. If I weren't such a pessimist all the time, I wouldn't have forgotten her."

"Her?"

"Ah, Lita." Dovian gave a sideways grin. "My dear, sweet, troublemaking little cousin."

Ivory grinned. "Your little cousin?"

"Well, it was a tad bit more complicated than that. My mother's sister, Cyerys, married my grandfather. It was his second marriage; his first wife had died in an accident. He met Cyerys through my mother and father and had married her right before I was born. Age matters little in a world where you live for thousands of years. It was very common for spouses to be hundreds and thousands of years apart. This made family trees sometimes difficult to follow as Cyerys became both my aunt and my grandmother. They had Lita much later in life, making her my father's half-sister."

Dovian took a moment to activate his armband. With a flicker, a diagram popped up with a list of names connected by lines. As he spoke, he pointed to each person of topic.

"I was about five hundred years old when she was born. Because of the marriage situation, Lita was both my aunt and cousin. But, since she was so much younger than I, we simply labeled her as my cousin." Dovian paused, making sure Ivory understood. She smiled, and he continued. "Lita was the only child they had together. She was so tiny; she fit in the palm of my hand. They used to call her a runt just as I was called."

"You were small?" Ivory asked.

"Oh, yes. I was very small growing up. In fact, I'm still small. It was in my mother's genes—the reason Lita was so tiny." He paused before adding, "When I was born, they thought I wasn't going to live long. I had a multitude of complications, probably due to my mother's size. They thought I was going to grow up weak." He sounded slightly disappointed by this but carried on with his story. "My mother didn't give up on me, however. She held onto me day and night for months until one morning…I was fine. No one could explain it, but I believe it was because of her. She was a magnificent healer, one of the best in the entire kingdom. She told me that she covered me with her light for every second that I was sick, and it was because of that, I received my name."

Dovian placed his hand over the orb of one of his spaulders, the blue light flowing to his fingertips. "It means 'light' in the heavenly tongue. It's not a direct translation, but as close to what we can speak on Earth." He smiled.

"And she said it wasn't her healing light that made her decide to call me that."

"What made her decide to name you that?"

"You can't laugh at me," he chuckled, looking at Ivory with an amused expression.

"Now I'm really interested." Ivory leaned forward in anticipation.

Dovian looked off to the side, letting out an exasperated sigh. "She said that she knew I was finally safe when I opened my eyes and the room filled with light. She said it was the most beautiful thing she had ever seen…but even more so was my smile."

Ivory gave a quiet 'aw.'

Dovian grimaced at her adoring sound. "My tiny, toothless baby smile was what filled her soul with light. It was at that moment that she finally knew her purpose."

"That is so sweet." Ivory clasped her hands together.

Rubbing his forehead, Dovian grumbled, "Yes, yes….So sweet. I cannot believe I told you that. I've only told two other people that story." He suddenly wanted to pull up his hood and hide, but his nervous smile remained.

"I'Lanthe and…" Ivory guessed.

"I didn't want to tell her, but she had a way of pulling my strings…Lita." He lifted his head. "Back to the topic previously at hand."

Ivory nodded. "Right, tell me more about her."

Clearing his throat, he continued, "As I said, Lita was much younger than I. I was one of the first people she had ever seen. And, I tell you what, the first day I saw those large green eyes look into mine, I knew I was doomed." Dovian hummed a quiet laugh. "That little brat was the cutest thing I had ever seen in my life. And I never admitted to anything being cute until her. She was so small and had wild hair of silver and gold spun with the slightest hint of lavender, believe it or not. I taught her everything she knew. I taught her to speak; I taught her to walk, to hold a glass, to do cartwheels, everything I could think of. We were inseparable. She was always at my side, always asking questions. I loved how eager she was to learn, to figure out things on her own."

Ivory watched Dovian. It was the happiest she had seen the man. As he told the stories, he relived the experiences, his memories as vivid as the day they occurred.

"She would run up to me, always, with something strange in her hands. 'What is this' she would ask. 'It is a snake' I told her. She screamed and dropped it, not because of the snake itself, but because now she knew what it was called and knew that many were afraid of them. This went on for years until she knew the name of every animal, plant, and insect in the entire kingdom." There was a short moment of silence as Dovian retracted into his thoughts. Ivory waited intently, finding his stories fascinating.

"Then there was the time she was in her genetics class. She always loved her schooling but was having trouble. Of course, this happened to be a class that I was teaching, and I think she was slacking off."

"You were a teacher?" Ivory asked.

Dovian gave a small laugh. "We all had our little jobs here and there. I taught classes on genetics and hand-to-hand combat."

Ivory lifted an eyebrow. "Those seem like entirely different areas to teach in."

"Not as much as you'd think. If you know the way something works and functions, you also know how to break it down. It's a very handy knowledge to have when in combat," he explained.

"I guess that makes sense," she pondered.

All of this was news to Ivory. It devastated her as she realized she knew absolutely nothing about Dovian. He wasn't just some mystical warrior from Ives. He was so much more than that. He had a life; he had a family; he had a home. It was all gone now. Dovian was just like her. No, he was worse off. He still had his memories. He still felt the pain of a beautiful life that once was and had gone thousands of years alone, everything suddenly ripped away. Ivory couldn't remember her past life. Now, she wasn't so sure if that was a bad thing. Dovian's warm voice broke Ivory from her thoughts.

"So, at the end of each year, the students are responsible for genetically engineering their own lizard. Most of the time, they follow a basic recipe, the reason behind all the frilled monitors, but Lita was having trouble with hers. I'm not positive what she was doing wrong, but the lizards wouldn't make it past the egg stage. The darn things simply wouldn't hatch." He gave a long sigh. "Long story short, she had somehow gotten ahold of my DNA and infused it with her lizard's embryo." He looked over his shoulder at Petey. "And that's how we got Pete."

"Petey shares your DNA?" Ivory asked.

"Yes. It is the reason he has lived this long and is capable of healing himself. I also have a special connection to him. When I concentrate, I can read his thoughts. I can see through his memories. That is precisely how I was able to find out what happened to Aria and Troy."

"That's amazing. So Petey really is special."

"He certainly is."

"And what about Hector?" she asked. "Is he as old as Petey? Is he still around?"

Dovian gave her a disappointed look. "No, he's not the same Hector as back in the day. The one I have now is Hector number 228. The lizards only live about one hundred years, some more, others less."

"Oh, that's sad." Ivory frowned.

"He'll die like all the others, but there will be more. I wasn't very creative with names. I liked Hector, so I stuck with it ever since." He shrugged.

"Well, it's a good name." She smiled. "A good, tough name."

Dovian chuckled. "Hector is far from tough. He's as docile as a mouse. It's a wonder how he survived the trip to the caves."

"Is he here?"

"He is at my home in his usual bed. He hasn't left it in two days. I've had to bring eggs to him; he's so worn out."

"Poor thing." Ivory held a sympathetic expression.

"Would you like to see him?" he asked.

Ivory looked over at Petey.

"He'll be fine here by himself. Think of him as a giant guard dog." Dovian rose from the bed.

"Are you close by?" she asked, rising with him. Wringing her hands, she gave a nervous laugh. "I suddenly can't remember right now."

"Close enough. We can fly there since I live on the upper floors." He looked outside, watching the downpour. "If you don't mind getting a little wet. Perhaps it's best we just stay here for a while."

"No, I want to go. I'm interested in seeing more of this place." There was a fire in her eyes. Ivory indeed was looking entertained. Not wanting to ruin her chipper mood, Dovian agreed.

"Alright. Hop up, we're heading out," he said, his wings jolting out of his back.

Ivory eagerly hopped into his arms, wrapping her own around his neck.

"Does that hurt?" She looked over his shoulder at the magnificent wings, the feathers flickering with a light of their own.

"It did at one time, but one gets used to it. Now it simply feels like a hard pop to a joint." He looked over at Petey. "Keep the place safe, Petey. We will be back."

The lizard barely budged from his sleeping position. Ivory smiled at the creature, thinking he looked precious as he snored and kicked up little dust clouds from his nostrils near the ground.

"He seems entirely too concerned by this…" Dovian stated, his voice dripping with sarcasm.

Bending his knees, Dovian leapt, his wings taking control. He carried Ivory back toward the building they previously passed that held the giant cross. To Ivory, this particular building looked slightly different than the one they had just been. It was grand with pointed architecture and had an enormous bridge out the front entrance that expanded over the silver lakes. The windows were full of colored glass that depicted a multitude of story-based images. Many of the pictured figures had wings and halos. It reminded Ivory of the church in the Underbelly.

"You live here?" she asked.

Dovian turned, floating toward an opening on one side with a balcony.

"It is my family's church. My great-grandfather, Gaius, built it. He was one of the first to land on Earth and reclaim Ives from below the ocean."

Swooping, Dovian gracefully landed inside his home. Ivory easily dismounted his grasp and turned to look over the balcony. The view was breathtaking. She could see a vast majority of Ives from where she stood.

"You're from an important lineage," she murmured.

"You could say that." He drifted slowly toward a bookcase, looking at nothing in particular as his wings folded comfortably behind his back.

She looked over her shoulder at the man. "Did that give you a lot of pressure?"

Dovian scoffed. "To be the great-grandson of the almighty Gaius—the angel that protested God's will and gave up his salvation in order to give the humans a second chance? To be the grandson of the fierce Gaius II—the one who single-handedly ended the first Great War the humans fought since the Sorcēarian Empire started? And to be the son of Gaius III—one of the most brilliant warriors of our time? He was a weapons master, a genius architect, geneticist, and an amazing agriculturist. He made the Sorcēarian lifestyle simple. So simple, in fact, that the humans swore we were sorcerers and magicians." He finally returned Ivory's stare. "I don't think pressure is a good enough word to use."

"You make it sound like you're not as worthy as they are." She frowned.

"I don't think I was expected to last as long as I had," Dovian muttered. "I don't think my father wanted to risk his name on another child like me."

"Another?" Ivory asked, shocked by this revelation.

Dovian lowered his head. "I had a brother."

Lightning flashed, casting strange shadows across the room. The following thunder was startling. Dovian watched the rain outside; his forehead wrinkled as he traced his memory.

"He was born and dead before I ever came into this world. Gaius IV…killed in battle. He was tall, handsome, and strong…like his lineage. It was just some terrible accident. He had swooped down to try and protect a human soldier and took the brunt of the blast. He wasn't a healer, was buried under the debris. The man he had tried to rescue had died…and I think he gave up. I never heard much about him, but apparently he was always hard on himself. He wanted to save everyone. He could save a thousand, and if one died, he would beat himself up over it. Oh, yes…following the Gaius lineage puts a lot of pressure on you." Dovian looked down at his marble desk and rapped his knuckles casually against the surface. "And I appeared fragile. I don't think there was a lot of faith put into my existence. It was known that the Gaius lineage would eventually become cursed. We were an easy target for darkness. My father thought I was meant to die. He distanced himself from me after my mother had passed."

"But…why?" Ivory whispered. "He should have been there for you."

"Oh, he wasn't entirely neglecting by any means. We just didn't share the same bond as he did with his father…or first son. I was quite different than the Gaius types." Dovian shrugged. "Sorcēarian men are *great* beings. You saw Euclid; he was frail compared to the others."

The woman's jaw dropped. "But Euclid was a whole head taller than you."

"And my father was an entire chest." He gave a short laugh, but Ivory could tell he wasn't amused. "At least at one time I was grand to the humans. Now, you all are a foot taller than you once were."

"Foot?" Ivory asked. "You mean *approximately thirty and a half centimeters?*" she giggled, remembering the conversation about the standard and metric system at Aria's apartment. Her smile faltered. That day seemed so long ago.

Dovian cocked his head to the side and smirked as he quietly chuckled. "Of course," he whispered.

"You are still tall compared to humans." Ivory looked up at him.

"Not by much." He slowly approached Ivory, setting his chin on the top of her head. He stood still for a second, staring at the scenery of Ives. The woman closed her eyes, avoiding the desire to wrap her arms around him. "You are almost the same height as an average Sorcēarian woman," he said.

Standing rigidly beneath the man with her cheek against the crook of his neck, she asked with apprehension, "Am I as tall as I'Lanthe?"

Dovian looked down at Ivory, his eyes searching her face. "She was slightly taller. Her forehead reached my lips."

Suddenly feeling ill at ease, Dovian stepped away, strolling toward the desk in the center of the room. He eyed the door on the floor. It had become unhinged during the attack when he first met Aria and Troy. Now, even his home held a memory of their presence–another reminder of what was to come. Sighing, he held out his palm. Blue light surged from his staff, and the broken gate lifted, quaking as it locked back into place within the confines of the wall.

"Just tidying up," he said, trying to ease the awkward tension.

A hushed hiss answered him from behind. He brought his attention to the small pillowed bed on the floor beside the desk.

"And you are finally awake?" he asked.

Lying on the puffy mass was a blanketed Hector. Dovian waved Ivory toward him. With the tapping of footsteps, she eagerly approached the man and his pet.

"Oh, look. He has a teddy bear," she giggled as she kneeled.

"I told you they are all spoiled." Dovian gave a sheepish laugh, lifting up the small knitted toy.

Ivory eyed the piece. "You made that?"

Dovian was silent a moment, an uneasy expression on his face. "I did."

"You can knit?"

"I've been alone for thousands of years. I can do pretty much anything…except sing. I can't do that." He smirked. "And I won't try."

Ivory ran her fingers over Hector's head. The lizard's golden eyes quickly closed, his tongue flickering out to taste her. She smelled like orchids and rain.

"You're just full of surprises, aren't you?" she asked, standing.

Dovian remained low on the floor, mending a broken seam in the doll caused by Hector's claws.

"And you have a lot of books," she said. "I imagine you've read them all."

"Over and over again."

"Do you have any memorized?" She fingered the bindings, slowly reading the titles.

"The Bible and the Secondary Judgment of God," he said with amusement. "But, we were all required to memorize His words."

"Besides those," Ivory said.

The room was silent for a few minutes. Ivory didn't press the man but continued looking. Gusting winds would roll by, the calm rumble of thunder vibrating the windows. Every so often she would pull a book from its place, eye the back, and then return it.

"What is happiness?" Dovian started.

Ivory glanced at him, unsure of what to say. She noticed he wasn't looking at her, put staring at the furthest wall as if deep in thought.

"Is it a laugh? Is it a smile? Or a warm hug on a cold winter's day?" He paused. "Is it a tear? Is it a cry? Or a word of comfort in a dark time?"

Ivory leaned on the balcony, watching him.

He continued, "What is love? Is it a kiss? Is it a touch? Or is it a breathless scene of beauty? Is it a pain? Is it a want? Or an act of the ultimate sacrifice?" He lowered his head, his fingers trailing through the dust on the floor.

Ivory interjected with her voice in a lower tone. "And what are happiness and love if we do not experience pain and sadness?"

Dovian lifted his head. His face held a look of shock.

She continued, her eyes sparkling in the darkness. "Because one without the other cannot exist. Would love be any more precious or rare if everyone felt it and everyone gave it? Would sadness be any more painful if the love did not exist in the first place? What is it that makes us feel things the way we do? Is it a kiss? Is it a touch? Or is it a breathless scene of beauty?"

"Is it a pain? Is it a want? Or an act of the ultimate sacrifice?" Dovian returned, gaping at Ivory in awe.

Her eyes brightened as she held a coy smile upon her face, and she spoke, "In the end, it's a delicate balance."

He stood, his heart pounding in his chest. Quietly, he continued, "In the end, it's your choice and your way that decides."

The two stared at one another. Dovian became a statue, his eyes like gems glistening in the storm, his hair shimmering in a dull halo of light. He didn't dare move.

Ivory lowered her head and gave a small laugh. "Tadhg Rioradahn...my favorite writer," she said. "You memorized his work?"

"Every word of every page," he replied, his throat suddenly feeling dry.

Dovian found it hard to breathe, his chest rising and falling at irregular intervals. He had heard her voice many times before from Ivory, but this time she was showing awareness. She was looking at him with blazing blue eyes. The smile on her face was even the same as I'Lanthe would wear it. Her whole posture was different. Standing proud and tall, she pressed her shoulders back and lifted her chin ever-so-slightly, giving her the regal presence those of high status once had.

'Move. Move, damn it, before she is gone again,' his mind instructed.

Strutting forward, Dovian was next to her in a few strides, his hands cupping her face.

"I'Lanthe," he stuttered her name, his voice showing uncertainty.

"Dovian," she replied frankly with her calm voice coated in a Legacy accent. She appeared amused despite the distress the other's countenance held.

Dovian allowed the woman to tug him down, her arms wrapping around his neck as she met him with a firm kiss. He quickly submitted. With his large hands clasping around her lower back, he held her as close as possible against his body. They remained that way, embracing one another. Dovian's brow furrowed as the thought of her leaving again plagued his mind. He didn't want to let her go, risk losing her again. Why couldn't she stay this way? Why at any possible moment would she fade away, returning back into the quiet, timid Ivory? It was a selfish thought, one that he knew was cruel, but after so long, why couldn't he be granted one moment of happiness?

She pulled away, and Dovian's breath came to a halt.

"You look so sad," she whispered. Her fingers trailed over the tattoo on his cheekbone.

Dovian closed his eyes, laying his forehead against hers, pleased to know she was still with him at that moment. "One thing is for sure…" he whispered. "Before, I thought I knew of pain and sadness, love and happiness…until I lost it all."

"Dovian…" I'Lanthe's voice flowed from Ivory's lips. She looked at the man with pity.

"And now that I've felt the worst there was, I am in love now more than I ever thought possible." He kissed her again. "And I'm not letting you go. I'm never letting anything happen to you ever again."

Ivory lowered her hands, running her fingertips down his chest. "What happened in the past is not your fault."

Dovian shook his head. "I killed them, I'Lanthe. I killed them all."

"It wasn't your fault," she repeated.

"Whose is it, then?" he growled. "If I wasn't locked up in that damn cell. If I could have broken loose just one minute sooner." His lower lip quaked as he struggled to keep his composure.

"But you didn't."

"Because I hesitated!"

Ivory shook her head and rested a hand on his cheek, not liking the troubled look on his face. She tried to speak, but he wouldn't let her.

"And because I hesitated, you died. Everyone. Karter, Orin, Quentin…and Lita!" He clenched his jaw. Now was not a good time to have a breakdown, but this was the first time in fifteen thousand years that he was able to talk to anyone who would know and understand the severity of his loss.

"Oh, Lita…" she whispered. "Dovian, you can't keep blaming yourself."

"No, no I can. Not only that, but I'm responsible for everyone else's death. I killed them. I killed them all! There were no survivors. I'm the only one." He caught his breath, becoming eerily calm. "And none of that has hurt me more than finding out that, after all of this time, you were damned."

Ivory looked down, avoiding his eye contact.

"Why were you in Hell? Was everyone else? Lita, too?!" He grabbed her shoulders.

"No, not Lita! She's safe and at peace. Not everyone was damned. There are some, but not all."

"Karter?" he stammered.

"No."

Dovian sighed with some relief.

"Most are those who teamed up with Euclid," she explained.

Dovian caught her gaze, lifting her chin. "But that does not explain why _you_ were there, why you are in this body right now."

She remained silent.

"I'Lanthe!"

"I, I can't tell you." She tore her eyes away.

He gawked at her, his look turning severe. "What do you mean, you _can't?_"

"No. Please, Dovian, I can't remember. Things are still hazy. I'm stuck between two lives right now; it's hard to tell what happened."

"You're lying to me," he grumbled.

"I don't have enough time to explain." She winced then, her hand delicately touching the side of her head.

"No, don't leave me." Dovian became frantic.

"Don't worry. I'll be here by your side. But I may not always be aware."

"Is there something I can do? Something we can do?" he asked.

Her expression softened, her eyes holding sadness. "Dovian, I cannot force Ivory out of her own body."

"But is it even her inside?" he asked in a hushed voice.

"What difference does it make? Didn't you just ask her that?"

"You can hear our conversations?"

She wrinkled her brow. "It's foggy. Sometimes it's as if I'm watching the two of you, but I can do nothing. Other times, it's like I'm asleep, dreaming, or I'm in darkness and the voices or ideas keep pulling in and out." She smiled. "But I can feel what she feels, Dovian."

The man stared past her head, not wanting to make eye contact. "What does she feel?" he asked nervously.

Her grin widened. "She is desperately in love with you, Dovian."

He sighed. "But she said those were your feelings."

"She still feels them herself, does she not? Love is love. I could tell a stranger all kinds of stories about you, and I wouldn't be surprised one bit if they fell in love with you without even having the pleasure of meeting you."

Dovian lowered his head. "You hold me at far too high a regard."

"And your humbleness is what makes you so wonderful. Stay true to yourself Dovian. Don't let this war bring you down. It never ended with us. It's been going on this entire time. But it'll be coming to a close soon, and I need you to do what you think is right."

"What aren't you telling me?" he asked.

She groaned again, her hand holding the side of her head.

"I'Lanthe!" he shouted, holding her up against her weakening knees.

"Love her, Dovian. She deserves it. Show her love just as you showed it to me," she said quietly.

"But she isn't you," he muttered.

"You already have feelings for her; you just don't know it yet."

"Don't be stubborn with me," he lectured.

"The same to you…." She gasped for air, her body becoming heavy. "Show her happiness…in this small world she's lived in; don't let the darkness consume her. Do it for me."

Fully understanding I'Lanthe's persistence, Dovian sighed in defeat. "I'll try," he said after a moment.

"That's what I like to hear." She gave him a weak smile before closing her eyes, letting herself fall into unconsciousness.

Dovian kneeled. He numbly held Ivory's body in his arms as he waited for her to awaken again. In a flash of light, the whole city was trembling in an explosive thunder, the rain gushing over the side rails of the study's balcony. Ivory jumped, her eyes opening wide. A loud shout sounded from her as the blast frightened her out of her sleep.

"What happened?!" she gasped.

Dovian didn't say anything. He only stared at the woman in his arms with an unreadable expression. Ivory tensed, feeling a dark energy exude from the Sorcēarian.

"She was here, wasn't she?" she shyly asked.

He turned his face away, frowning.

"I, I'm sorry, Dovian. I'm sorry if I interrupted your time together. If I could, I would just let her have my body so the two of you can be together," she said quietly, tears stinging her eyes.

Seeing her grief, Dovian mentally slapped himself for being so self-centered. He quickly grabbed her hand, running his thumb over her knuckles.

"I don't want that from you," he said in a hushed tone. "Don't ever think you are any less worthy than anyone else, understand?"

She quickly nodded.

"Are you tired?" he asked, worried about her mental fatigue.

"I'm exhausted," she answered quickly.

"Come, let's get you to bed."

He picked her up with ease and stepped onto the railing, his wingspan widening as he slipped over the ledge. Dovian returned Ivory to I'Lanthe's room. As he flapped inside, Petey didn't move a muscle. The Sorcēarian's cold eyes dropped to the lizard.

"Some guard dog you are," he said dryly.

Ivory quickly slipped from Dovian's arms. She remained by his side, staring at his face, looking for any indication of what he was thinking or feeling at that moment. He didn't acknowledge her but gaped at the tiles on the stone floor.

"Well, I suppose I should let you have some time alone," he muttered. Glancing at the wet floor and their soaked clothing, he unconsciously shivered. "There's a shower...."

"Around the corner," Ivory pointed to a corner of the room near the bed.

"Yes." He cleared his throat. "I'll gather something for you to change into."

Ivory looked down at herself and noticed how worn and discolored her once beautiful gown was. She twisted her feet, her boots squeaking against the wet marble. The gossamer dress was burnt and torn, cutting off below her knees rather than the floor as it once had. The bottom and a few splatters across her torso were dark with Dovian's blood.

"That would be kind of nice," she said, removing the one glove that covered her arm.

Dovian gave a slight nod and turned toward the back of the room. Ivory watched him momentarily before rounding the corner into the small bathroom. She noticed how sour the man was feeling and couldn't help but feel responsible for it. Approaching a mirror on the wall, Ivory gaped at her reflection. Her makeup was smudged, creating dark circles around her eyes. Her usually fluffy, curly hair was now a matted mess. Dirt and soot dotted her hands, arms, and neck. To say the least, she looked horrible.

"I look like death," she whispered, leaning closer to the mirror, peering into her irises.

'We both look like death,' a thought interjected in the woman's mind.

Pulling away from the mirror, Ivory gasped aloud. The woman in the mirror was not herself, but another. The reflection looked at Ivory with a kind expression on her face. Her eyes were a glowing violet. Her hair, too, was wet and matted. The long loose curls of brunette stuck to the sides of her neck. An ornate hair clip held up the rest of her curls on the back of her head. Despite looking a little worn from the weather, she looked breathtakingly beautiful.

"Everything alright?" Dovian's voice called out.

Ivory turned her head to look toward the entrance of the bathroom and then back to the mirror where she saw only herself in the reflection.

"F, fine," she stammered.

"Do you need any help?" he asked.

"What? With what?" she rambled.

"...With anything?"

Ivory stared at the mirror. "Uh, no. No, I'm fine; thank you."

"I will leave these clothes for you on the bed," he stated quietly.

Ivory caught her breath, looking down at herself and her reflection again. Hearing Dovian's soft footsteps trail further away, she ran to the entryway of the bedroom.

"Dovian!" she called out.

He paused, his hand resting against a stone pillar as he watched the rain.

"Good night," she spat out.

The man looked over his shoulder at her and fed her a gentle smile. "Good night."

With a whoosh, his wings spread, and the man departed. Ivory remained in the doorway, watching the fountain's water wave in the storm. Dropping her sight to her bed, she noticed the robes of black and gold and an overcoat much like Dovian's that was a stunning shade of purple with golden details lining the sleeves. In addition, on the pillow was a very familiar headpiece. She recognized the ornate crown from the reflection in the mirror. These were I'Lanthe's clothes.

Ivory swallowed thickly. She had a choice to make. It was time she had decided if she was going to continue being the naïve, helpless Ivory or become the strong woman her memories and feelings once belonged to–the woman that Dovian needed.

WWW.ARCREBS.DEVIANTART.COM

"What Is Happiness?"

CHAPTER 5

Leaves of green and gold clattered against the dirt trail as the trees swayed gently in the breeze. Aria tightened the laces of her neon-colored running shoes, looking up at the flickering sunlight that slipped past the full branches overhead. Taking a deep breath, she stretched her arms over her head. Singing sparrows flitted from tree to tree, their bitty onyx eyes looking down curiously at the woman. The little chubby birds developed a pattern as they traveled–hopping, staring, and giving a little tweet before sputtering away. A squirrel or two would dash through the branches. A butterfly lazily fluttered down the path. Rolling her ankle, the woman flexed the muscles of her calf, testing its strength and mobility. Deciding it was as good as ever, she pushed forward to jog through the track. The swishing trees and musical birds were relaxing but not motivating as her feet pounded against the ground.

"Music," she called out between breaths.

"Playlist?" a small voice echoed in her mind.

"Workout," she replied, eyes straight ahead on the woodsy landscape.

A sudden pulsating beat drummed in her mind as a series of electrical instruments thumped in time with her running pace. She smiled. Now she was motivated to move.

"Much better," she panted.

Following the dips and small inclines to the path, Aria kept a decent pace. It had been weeks since she was able to go for a run or workout. Though her recent missions didn't leave her sedentary by any means, it was nice to get some exercise that wasn't life threatening. And after being bedridden for four days, she was desperate for some time alone and some movement in her legs.

Taking another deep breath, she closed her eyes. She listened to the music, her imagination taking her to other places, other times, and other scenarios. Aria was a woman whose brain never stopped, not even for a minute. To only listen to music and pretend to be somewhere else was a type of vacation. It was more encouraging than sitting in the present dwelling on the unavoidable. She remained that way, running through the trees as if she had memorized the trail's twists and turns. After a few minutes, she couldn't shrug the strange feeling that she was being watched. Given a chill down her spine, her green eyes popped open, and she gave a shout as she was face-to-face with another person.

"Damn it, Troy!" she gasped, her hand pressing against her chest.

She stopped running, taking a wide stance, but the trail kept moving. Troy stood in front of her, his body levitating over the scene. He gave her a crooked smile and spoke, but his words were inaudible.

"Pause music," Aria huffed. "Stop training session."

Silence engulfed the area; the trees and sunlight faded into a white sterile room. Aria stood atop a running platform, her feet on either side of the track that was slowly winding down. She eyed the man standing in front of her, looking a bit irritated for being interrupted.

"What?" she asked. Her hands went to her hips, her bare stomach flexing with each heavy breath. She unconsciously messed with the straps of her black and blue sports bra.

"I said your name a few times, but you didn't respond." He shrugged.

"So you stand in front of me and stare at my face like a big creeper?" she asked incredulously. "Scared the shit out of me."

He gave a small chuckle. "Sorry, couldn't help myself."

"No, you never can," she muttered, stepping over the track and snatching up the bottle of water on the floor beside her. "So, what's up? You come in here just to scare me?"

He handed over a digital parchment. "They're finally releasing us."

"'Bout damn time," she grumbled, swiping her finger across the screen into a messy signature of Courtney Clarke. She then grabbed her matching lightweight exercise jacket from the rack beside the door and slipped it on, leaving it unzipped.

"They said we've both healed 'amazingly' well. And we've both passed our psychiatric evaluations." He clapped his hands together as he gave a small, cheerful 'yay.'

Aria glared at the man but not in anger at him. "That test pissed me off."

After their small argument with the nurse, the two soldiers were required to take separate evaluations to ensure they didn't suffer from PTSD or any other type of psychological distress. Some of the questions were routine, a few others more subjected toward the mention of hallucinations and hearing voices. As much as Aria wanted to purposefully botch-up the whole thing, she kept her mouth shut and gave the expected answers. At that point, she was ready to do anything to get checked out of the clinic.

"Everything pisses you off." Troy walked toward the exit. "You seemed to be doing well during your run, though. Everything feel alright?"

Aria nodded, sipping her water. "A little stiff here and there and wobbly in the ankles, but nothing a bit more exercising can't fix." She eyed her shins, taking in the large scar that traveled up her leg. "Can't say much about that scar, though."

"Makes you look tough. Besides, the doctor said it'd fade in a few months." Troy flipped through the pages on the screen. "I like those pants, by the way," he muttered.

Aria looked down at her tight cropped grey running pants. Her multi-colored sneakers highlighted against the dull color.

"Really shows off your ass," he said quickly, passing through the gym's door as he read the file in his hands.

Aria puffed a sigh, following the man into the rehabilitation wing of the hospital. Ignoring his comment, she looked him over from head to toe. He wore his camo pants, boots, and typical black muscle shirt. Troy rarely wore anything different unless he was attending parties or funerals. A sudden shuffle in his movement made Aria notice Troy had a slight hobble to his gait.

"And your leg?" she asked.

"Hm, almost healed completely. I lied a bit on the pain test, but I'm not sitting in here any longer. As long as I wear my full gear on the field, I should be fine." He shook the bottle in his hands. "Got me some drugs to help with the pain. Most of it is in my hip, but damned if I'm going to be using a cane!"

"Should you be using a cane?" Aria asked. "I can tell you're in pain."

"Naw, I'm good," he said quickly, shoving the medication into the pocket of his military pants. "I can play old man once this war's done and over with."

"And what did they say about your heart?" she asked, giving him the typical stare-down which always made him uncomfortable.

"Uh…." Troy looked up from the screen in his hands and then grinned. "Well, there he is!"

Aria turned her attention to where Troy's was. Aren was standing next to the front desk. His dark hair—streaked with hints of orange—was slicked back. He wore his military slacks and boots and wore a sports T-shirt with his leather pilot jacket over the top. Large sunglasses rested on his collar. A couple suitcases sat on the floor beside him. The young pilot smiled at the approaching two.

"Sir, Ma'am." He nodded, giving a quick handshake to Troy. "Was wondering when they were going to let you out of this place."

"Same here." Troy handed the digital parchment to the woman at the front desk. She then passed it to her robotic secretary which scanned the item before placing it in the large filing system inside the wall. "Was beginning to feel a bit too much like home."

Aria glanced at Troy, not believing he suddenly forgot the question she just asked him. His sight darted to her and back to Aren.

"Ms. Clarke?" the receptionist asked. "I've got one more thing I need you to do before you leave."

Aria apprehensively looked toward the woman. "Yeah? What is it?"

The lady eagerly held out a small metal box with a hole in the side. "Please place your finger inside. The lab has requested another blood sample from you. They detected something strange in the last sample."

"Strange?" Aria muttered. "It's probably the nanomites. I had a major blood transfusion many years ago, so my nano count is high."

Aria stuck her finger into the box and waited for the sharp prick of the needle that drew out her blood. After a quiet chime, she removed herself.

"I'm not sure what it is. They didn't specify, but they would like to double-check," the woman replied. After she had passed the sample over to the robot secretary, the woman flipped through her list and then nodded. "Okay! You're good to go! We'll give you a call if we find anything unusual or need anything else."

Aria gave the woman an awkward half-smile and then turned toward Troy, pushing him forward. She just wanted to leave already.

"Well, I've got the car ready outside," Aren said, lifting the two bags. He led the way toward the exit, pulling on his sunglasses. "Bright and sunny out today."

Troy snagged a suitcase from Aren's hand. "I can carry my own luggage, man."

Aria kept walking, allowing the young man to take hers. He looked at her in anticipation and then smiled, gladly lugging it for her.

"Where's the rest of our belongings?" she asked.

They stepped out of the hospital, the world suddenly loud and vibrant with fast-paced vehicles, chiming food vendors, and flashing advertisements. It made the woman cringe. It was an awful contrast to the replica forest she had been running in only a few minutes before.

"They allowed me to take the armor and the rest of your belongings home the day they admitted you," Aren said, loading the case into the back of the car. "I have it all packed up nicely back here."

Closing the trunk of the car, he rushed to the side, opening the door for the woman. She slipped inside, making herself comfortable on the leather seat. Troy opened the other door and dropped in beside her. Aren happily took the passenger seat in the front. The driver of the car was an automated drone—a high-end model. It gleefully chimed a 'welcome' to the group before gripping the steering wheel with two long skinny clamps. Then it merged into traffic.

"Oh, this is Franklin," Aren introduced the bot in the driver's seat.

Aria didn't trust automated vehicles too much. They may have had perfect driving records offensively, but they didn't always come equipped with the best defensive modules. If a human driver made one error, sometimes the bots didn't respond quick enough. Her eyes fell to the model type on the back of the floating spherical drone. 'Elixis-Guard Plus' was scrawled into the metal. At least it was the best the world had to offer. Aren must've dropped a year's worth of wages for the technology.

"We aren't going home?" she asked.

"Can't risk it. I have a hotel booked for us to stay in."

"Us?" she asked.

"Erm…well, I figured it was a good idea if I stuck around, you know?" the man stammered. "I mean…we're like a team now, right?"

Aria eyed him cautiously and then looked over at Troy, who was giving her a disapproving look.

"I know I'm not Gavin, b-but I figured that maybe I could help you guys out. I-I know I'm not a soldier, but I know a lot in the tech department…" he said anxiously.

"Hey, man! Of course, we're a team!" Troy stated, leaning forward in his seat. "You've helped us out a bunch so far."

Aria glared at Troy. He returned her a similar look of his own.

"Besides, we need you to fix our DNAISs." He shook a wrist.

Aren laughed nervously as he scratched the top of his head. "Yeah, yeah, sorry about that. It's the best I could do before turning you over to the doctors."

"How'd you know about Courtney Clarke?" Aria asked.

"Uh, well…" Aren stammered. "While you guys were off getting smashed to pieces, I had some time to go over the data you copied into my DNAIS. I copied some of Troy's data, too. It took some geeking and re-programming, but I was able to do it. From there, I could access some medical history information. I found out a lot about your father through some of the files you saved," he said to Troy. He looked at Aria. "And…well, I couldn't find anything from your lineage, and I couldn't use your data, so I used Courtney's. I…um did some digging through your private files in order to find that information."

"You read my diary?!" Aria growled.

"I had no choice!" Aren held up his hands defensively. "I was short on time. I was searching, and I found some connections between you and Mr. Clarke, and from there I was able to dig up more information in the Bio-Tech Identification Systems and pulled up her medical files. A little plug here and there, and I changed your identity."

Despite how peeved the woman was to know that the young man had gone through her personal data, she was impressed by his abilities to gather information from encrypted sources. And he acted like it was nothing. He actually was a valuable asset.

"I know someone you should meet," Troy murmured, glancing out the window. Aren had a common interest with a member of Delta Team Phoenix codenamed 'Nerd.'

"How much did you read?" Aria asked.

"Not much! I was just scanning for names, anything that would give me something to work with." Aren cleared his throat. "Don't worry. All your secrets are safe with me." His eyes darted to Troy. The other man noticed, and he eyed Aria suspiciously.

The woman lunged forward in her seat. Snarling, she grabbed Aren's head and pulled him into a headlock.

"Damn right they are!" she yelled. "Cuz if they ever leave your skull, I'm cracking it open, you hear me?"

"Ow, ow! Okay! Okay!" Aren whimpered, tapping her on the shoulder.

Aria quickly removed her death-grip from the man's neck and dropped back into her seat, folding her arms. Troy was laughing, shaking his head. The woman was silent a moment, fuming. Then, she noisily growled.

"And you went through my personal things!" She pointed toward the back of the car where the suitcases were kept. The thought of Aren digging through her underwear drawer was not only infuriating but embarrassing. She was sure she still had a pair or two that had tiny animal and star prints.

Aren rubbed his neck, wincing. "You'll be glad I did! Trust me; I know how a woman thinks!"

Troy eyed Aren; his mouth dropped. *'My God, he is a flamboyant...'* he thought. Now, the role was reversed. Aren went through his things, too. *'He dug through my underwear drawer!'*

Troy palmed his forehead, mentally groaning. He had a few pairs of women's panties in his drawers that he had kept as trophies. How did Aren view that? He looked up, catching an amused stare from Aren. *'Damn it!'*

Aria caught Troy's despairing look. It had taken a moment before she registered what her partner must've been thinking. She laughed out loud.

"Shut up, woman!" he swore at her, mentally.

Aria ignored him, laughing louder just to spite. Troy was ready to throttle her, to do anything to get her to quiet her guffawing. As he glared at her, he noticed the nearing Bio-Tech Military Corporation building. Something caught his eye, and he leaned over Aria, looking out her window.

"W-What are you doing?" she asked, pressing back into her seat.

Rushing out the side entrance of the corporation was Dr. Camery. Over one shoulder slung a medical bag, the nervous doctor shoving supplies and old paperwork into the sack. He suspiciously looked over his shoulders before boarding a sleek vehicle with blacked-out windows.

"Where the hell are you going, Camery?" Troy asked aloud, pointing a finger against the glass.

Aren and Aria watched, their heads twisting as they passed by Camery and the building.

"Follow him," Aria ordered.

Aren fumbled about, grabbing the bot and disengaging it from the steering wheel. The system gave a few alerts as Aren clumsily climbed into the driver's seat and took control. He pressed a few buttons on the dash, the center panel opening up to reveal the manual override system. Popping the center handle and looking into the rearview mirror, he slowed down and pulled into an old agricultural warehouse. He waited until Camery's vehicle sped past them.

"He's in a hurry," Troy said, looking through his side window.

Aren slammed the car into reverse, darting out into traffic and across three lanes. The other vehicles whizzed by, some honking their horns, many centimeters away from crashing into them. Wheeling the vehicle around, Aren manually shifted the car back forward facing and raced after Camery's car.

"Holy shit, I thought we were going to die," Aria murmured, her nails digging into Troy's shoulder.

"Think I'm a good pilot?" Aren asked. "I drove cars long before I learned how to fly."

"Just keep it on the road, please," Aria whined.

Within seconds, Aren was near Camery. He kept his distance, being sure to stay inconspicuous as he trailed behind. He soon grew nervous, however, noticing the skyscrapers drop to smaller heights, the rail systems lowering in number, and the massive traffic packs dissipating.

"This may not be good," he said, pulling further away from the car.

"What?" Aria asked.

"I think he plans on leaving town," Aren said, looking over his shoulder before merging into a side lane.

"Why would he leave the city? What's out there?" Aria leaned to gain a better view out the front window.

"Not sure." Aren shrugged.

"Wherever he's going, I'm sure Walten's nearby," Troy stated.

"Should I follow?" Aren asked.

"Yes, keep following." Aria opened the middle seat compartment between her and Troy. "You pack our weapons?" she asked.

"Yeah. Why?" Aren sputtered.

Aria ducked into the compartment, her rear-end in the air as she searched the trunk for her gun. Troy stared at the woman's backside with wide eyes, giving Aren a thumbs-up. The pilot gave a quiet laugh as he saw the gesture through the rearview mirror but then locked his eyes back to the car ahead.

"Got it," she groaned, backing out.

She sat on her knees, loading a cartridge into the front of her Fernstall 300. She was surprised Aren packed this weapon. She usually hid it under her bed, which meant he did a *lot* of snooping through her apartment. Still, she couldn't be angry. He brought her trace planters. Opening the side window, Aria leaned out the vehicle and looked down her scope, eyeing the license plate of Camery's car. She took one shot, and the trace clipped onto the plate, a tiny beep ringing from her weapon.

"Aren," she called out, sitting back into the vehicle. "Give me your wrist."

Aren awkwardly twisted an arm back toward her. Aria gripped his hand, eyed it, and threw his arm back at him.

"Other wrist, dumbass," she spat.

He reached over his head and showed the woman his wrist that contained his DNAIS. Aria pulled a thin wire from the side of her firearm; a tiny needle poked from the tip, and she plugged it into his chip. Another quiet beep sounded, and Aria detached the weapon from Aren. She pushed against his wrist, pulling up his system, and activated the tracer's data. A red blinking light oscillated above the man's hand before she let go.

"Alright, you can have your arm back." Making herself comfortable, she returned the weapon to the trunk of the car. "You can back away from them. Keep following, but I don't want them to be able to detect you. Once we're out of the city, there's only one interstate. They'll be able to see you for miles in this flat landscape."

"Roger that," Aren said, slowing the vehicle as he pulled onto a side ramp that lead to the desolate countryside.

Away from the silvers and blacks and the flashing vibrant lights of the city, the landscape fell into browns and blues. Wispy, stretching streaks of white stained the sky. The car hummed quietly, its large tires treading against the old pavement, bumping every so often as it pumped over a crack. They traveled for kilometers, for what felt like hours. Aria lounged lazily; her blank stare held to the sunroof above her. Troy fiddled with the GPS system on the screen behind Aren's chair. The car sputtered, and Aria hoped that they had enough fuel to make it to where they needed to go.

After traveling at almost top speed for so long, once the car slowed, the force nearly pulled Aria and Troy out of their seats. The sun had already moved across the sky and had lowered on the horizon, the temperature dropping on the outside. From what Aria could tell, they were far west of their territory, mountains stretching on the horizon.

"They've turned off the road," Aren murmured. The beeping of the homing device quickened as they neared Camery's position.

"Where?" Aria asked.

"Here," Troy joined in, pointing at the GPS map.

Aren slowed to a halt. "They've stopped," he informed.

Aria leaned to the side, inspecting the map. From where they were, a mile up ahead was a small mountain range. From the looks of it, Camery had pulled onto one of the sides of the mountains.

"That's not right. There are no functioning cities out here. Why would he come here?" she questioned.

"Bathroom break?" Aren suggested.

"Quite the turn off for a bathroom break. I say we go in," Troy suggested to Aria.

She was silent a moment, checking their surroundings. "Get your weapon ready. We have no idea what we can be walking into. Aren, pull as close as you can to their location, but stay out of sight. We'll walk the rest of the way and search the area."

Aren pulled forward, turning off the road toward the mountainside where Camery had traveled to. He kept his car straight, planting his tire tracks over the others. As they climbed the mountainside, the scenery changed to one of green grass and tall trees. The path became muddy, the car jostling as it ran over rocks and branches.

"Never seen anything like it…." Troy gaped out the window. "Not in real life, I mean, on the outside."

"Look, snow on the mountaintops." Aria pointed. "The water must flow just right where the sun doesn't dry it out. Looks like this area gets lots of water."

"Makes you wonder how many places in the world aren't actually dead," Aren said, glancing through the windshield at the mountaintops above.

"Looks like the running trails," Aria said, being reminded of her afternoon jog at the rehabilitation center.

The car neared a bend. The tracer alarm called out. They were close.

"Park it here. We'll get out and take a look," she instructed.

Aren stopped the car, the engine rumbling to silence. Aria exited first with her Fernstal in hand. She pressed against the rocky mountainside next to the vehicle, waiting for Troy to join her side. He soon was with her, gripping his newly released Sub-Fernstal P20. His secondary mag was equipped with SABO grenades. She glanced at him and held up a fist, eyeing Aren as he dropped low next to Troy with his Air Force issued handgun with auto-aim.

Aria opened her mouth to speak, but Aren interrupted. "I'm not waiting in the car. I need to see what you see. If anything happens, I'll be backup."

"Don't get yourself killed," Aria whispered harshly.

With a press against her mental chip, an optical retina materialized over Aria's right eye. She tilted her gun; the camera on the tip projected the image from around the corner into her line of sight.

"I can see the car. It's parked outside…a house. At least, it looks like a house," she said quietly.

"Any watches?" Troy asked.

"No, none detected. I'm going to switch to thermal view." She pressed on the tip of the weapon, changing the sight to thermal detection. "No one on the outside. I can see some figures on the inside, though. There appears to be three heat signatures. One is vague, perhaps in another room." Aria continued watching. "Three male."

Troy lifted his gun over her head, catching a sight of his own.

"There's a side entry to the right. We won't have to cross any windows," Troy murmured.

"Any security devices?" Aren asked.

Aria glanced at the young man. Looking through her camera, she set off an Electronic-Sonar detector. There was a small hum, and multiple blips showed up in her vision. "Two to the left, one to the right. Another at the front door."

"Camery is a bit paranoid," Troy said.

"Or is it Walten?" Aria asked.

The woman pulled her weapon to her side. Kneeling, she dug into Troy's pocket, the man not caring much as it was something she always did when she needed more ammo. Pulling out a few concussive rounds, she loaded the gun and aimed around the corner again, firing and shooting out the cameras. Her optical viewer switched back to thermal, and she could see the three men inside the home move into alerted states.

"Damn it, I think they noticed," Aria heaved a heavy sigh. "Moving to the right. Cover me. Aren, stay low."

She rounded the corner in a crouching position. The three heat signatures quickly faded.

"I think they've moved into hiding. Stay alert. Could be an ambush," Aria spoke through her mental chip.

Staying close to the rock wall, Aria and Troy neared the door on the side of the house. Aren stayed behind a boulder, keeping a watchful eye on the front door with his weapon at the ready. Giving a couple of hand signals, Aria leaned against the house, crouching. Troy quietly opened the screen door and heaved forward, his foot crushing against the wooden entry. He rolled to the side as Aria took point with her Fernstal aimed. The two rushed through the home, Troy checking the side room, Aria searching the kitchen. There wasn't a sound, and the house was in pitch-black. Aria turned one corner into the main living room and was blinded by a bright light, a loud siren disorienting her. Someone crashed into her, flipping her onto her stomach. She groaned, pushing against the man that held her firmly in place. The feeling of the cold barrel of a weapon pressed against her temple made her freeze.

"Move one inch, and you'll be staining the carpet with your brains," a harsh voice hissed in her ear.

"Same goes for you," Troy said, pressing the barrel of his weapon at the back of the other man's head.

"How about nobody moves, and nobody dies?" yet another voice sounded along with the cocking of a handgun's slide, this time from behind Troy.

Troy frowned, debating his situation.

"Why doesn't everybody just lower their damn weapons and we can avoid a potential massacre?" Aren called out. Aria could see the young man's silhouette in the entryway of the home though her vision was moving in all directions thanks to the disorienting frag. "Come on, no one's in a winning position. Why don't we settle this over a cup of coffee or something, huh?"

"Just do what the boy says!" A frightened voice called out; this one was clearly Camery. "I don't want any more people dying."

There was a long pause before anybody dared to move. After a few grueling seconds, a small lamp illuminated the living area. Troy lowered his weapon first, raising a hand. Turning slowly, he eyed the man holding him up from behind.

"Grayson?!" Troy shouted.

The man in the black dress suit quickly lowered and holstered his handgun. At the same time, the man holding Aria hostage quickly released her.

"Aria?! Dear God! I almost killed you!" James Clarke dropped his weapon, helping the woman to her feet. She held onto his shoulders, trying to regain her balance.

"J, James?" she asked, trying to focus on his face.

"I thought you were dead!" he sputtered, pulling her into a tight hug.

Aria gave a muffled groan.

Aren quickly lowered his weapon, watching the baffling scene before him.

"We were banged-up pretty good," Troy said. "We've been in the hospital all week."

"I ran searches in all the databases trying to find you. I couldn't get any hits on your DNAISs. There was no sign of you," James said, finally releasing his squeeze on the woman.

"I had to burn them out for their protection," Aren interjected. Clarke brought his attention to the young man. "Uh, Aren Hagar, sir." He held out his hand.

"James Clarke. You're the pilot I sent to Roma," James said, gratefully returning the gesture.

"Yes, sir. It's a pleasure meeting you, sir." Aren eagerly shook his hand.

"I assumed you were dead as well. There was a KIA file placed on you," James said.

"My doing, sir."

Aria watched the pilot. He certainly was good at covering his tracks.

"You have my deepest gratitude for watching out for these two. When I read your papers, I knew you'd be perfect for them." Clarke patted Aren on the shoulder.

The President seemed slightly troubled, sweat lining his brow. He gave Aria a once-over and frowned. "And what are you wearing?" he asked in his fatherly tone.

Aria folded her arms, glaring at the man. "It's called a sports bra."

"Right, a bra. You're running around in a bra, and it's freezing out! Not to mention it's not very tactical," he lectured her.

Aria rolled her eyes. "With the right man, it could pose as a distraction," she grumbled, gently tugging on her jacket sleeves.

"Troy, you let her walk around like this?" Clarke asked, looking over at the other man.

Troy shrugged, "Well, I…we…."

"Of course you do. You would let her gallivant around naked if she would," James grumbled.

"I believe there is something more important to talk about than my attire, James," Aria said in a seething tone. She noticed a bead of sweat drip from his forehead. "Are you alright?" she asked with a bit more concern.

"Fine, fine," James stuttered.

"Sir, you should sit down and let Dr. Camery look at your wounds," Grayson suggested.

"Wounds? You're still not healed?" Aria asked.

Camery rushed to the President's side, guiding him to sit upon an old lumpy ginger-colored sofa.

"No, he isn't. He's been running from place to place and not getting any rest. I brought him here a couple days ago so he could rest safely and beat the infection," Camery explained, opening up Clarke's shirt. "I was able to pull out a few more fragments, but the wounds had been untreated for too long. I needed more medical supplies. He left the hospital far too soon. Not to mention that little fall he took reopened all the wounds."

"I had no other choice," Clarke groaned. "It was either that or let that Sorcēarian and his dogs kill me."

Camery pulled back the wrappings on James' chest. It took some effort to remove the cloth; the blood and puss clung to the fibers. Reaching into his medical pack, the doctor quickly acquired and sprayed a disinfectant on the wound, the skin bubbling in effect. James grimaced in pain but allowed Camery to continue without much fuss.

"Speaking of Sorcēarian…" James began, "where are Dovian and Ivory?"

Aria and Troy exchanged nervous glances. "They are still in Ives."

"Alive?" James asked, not sounding too surprised.

"Not positive, but I believe they are," Aria said. "I'd like to go back for them at some point."

"Not without a unit." The President shook his head.

"And how do you suppose we go about that?" she asked. "I don't know how much you've heard, but Feyette has the entire military out of Fountains. Walten has declared war on Cherno, Roma, and Saray. To top it off, we're still *public enemy number one*, remember?"

"I've not forgotten that. I've got some friends trying to pull some strings. Once I hear from them, I'll let you know. For now, we've got to work on regrouping and pull ourselves together."

James gave a shout as Camery stapled a few of the larger wounds closed. He then smeared a transparent gel across some wide white bandages and carefully placed them over the wounds.

"Will he be alright?" Aria asked.

"I believe so if he stays here and remains under bed rest for a few days. I can't imagine his tackle earlier helped in any way," Camery stammered. A shaking hand brushed some graying hair out of his eyes.

"What is this place?" Troy asked, looking over the antique furniture.

Camery looked up at the man. "It is my family's vacation home. It's belonged to us for hundreds of years. A bit rough around the edges, but we've been able to maintain it. I haven't been here in years." The scientist buttoned James' shirt and sat back on the sofa. "No one knows about it. It was built by one of my many greats-grandfathers. It's a nice, quiet place to get away from the buzz of the city."

"Walten doesn't know of it?" Aria asked.

"No. At least, I can't see how he would know. He's never shown any interest in me until lately," Camery said, his hands fidgeting on his lap.

"Why take care of James?" she pried.

"Well, because…" Camery lowered his head, "because I want to make up for some of the trouble I've caused. It's not like I'm on Walten's side."

"No, but you did seem to equip him and Feyette's team with some excellent gear," Troy joined the discussion.

"I did the same for you!" Camery raised his voice. "Faze Shields, the ECRG weaponry, the upgraded armor! If it wasn't for Walten wanting that Sorcēarian's blood samples, you and Troy's suits wouldn't have been equipped with such fine medical enhancements."

"Medical enhancements? You're talking about the morphine in the suit?" Troy asked.

Camery scratched the bridge of his nose. "Not morphine...Sorcēarian DNA."

"You mean you enhanced the suit with Dovian's DNA? Is that how we survived?" Aria asked, shocked.

"I'd reckon so. Every step of the way, I wanted to counteract Walten's movements. It was the only thing I could think of–enhancing your suits to better the chances of your survival," Camery explained. "Sorcēarians have a fascinating technology within their weapons."

"Speaking of...." Aria walked to the edge of the living room. There was something about the home that she didn't like. Something felt off. "You know that frequency tuner that you provided us? Something that only a Sorcēarian would know how to use?"

"N-Now wait...I can explain that!" Camery stuttered. He seemed nervous as Aria edged toward the opposite end of the room.

She eyed him suspiciously. "Can you? Please, explain to all of us how you came across the ancient technology." Aria looked down the hall. She noticed Camery's gaze drifting to the same spot.

The room was quiet. Grayson stood with his hands clasped at his waist in front of the other exit to the room. Aren remained by the side entryway to the house just inside the kitchen area. Aria watched Troy as he sidestepped toward the front door; his eyes locked onto the back of Camery's head. He firmly gripped his weapon. James stayed in his seat, looking upon Camery with interest.

"What's down the hallway, Camery?" Aria asked.

"N-Nothing. There's nothing. Just some bedrooms."

"Just some bedrooms?" She turned to look with a hand on her waist. "So you wouldn't mind if I took a look around?"

"I, I'd rather you wouldn't," the doctor whispered.

"You hiding something?" she asked tenaciously.

"It's just...I have an important project I'm working on. I can't risk contamination." He tugged on his hands, one foot bouncing against the dirty carpet.

Aria lifted her weapon. "How about I go ahead and take a look around?"

"No!" Camery lifted from his seat but was abruptly tugged back down by James.

"Don't worry. I'll be sure I'm careful around your science project." She walked slowly down the dark hall, switching on the mag light on the front of her weapon.

"No, please!" Camery pleaded, holding his hands before his face.

Troy rounded the couch, taking his place at the corner of the hall, watching Aria's back. She carefully twisted the knob to one closed room, looking over her shoulder to see Dr. Camery's reaction. He looked as if he were about to have a nervous breakdown. Frowning, she shoved the door open, aiming her weapon inside. There was a small candle on the countertop next to the sink beside the toilet and ancient bathtub. Aria slipped out, moving further down the hall.

"You can't," Camery whispered, tears welling in his eyes.

"Watch him, Troy," Aria said with a stern inflection.

Carefully making her way to the second door, she pushed it open in a similar fashion. Another set of candles revealed an old bed with ornate pillows and blankets. Aria looked closely, shining her light on the closet and a small suitcase on the floor. Taking an uneasy breath, she moved back out into the hall.

"Just stop!" Camery rose from the couch, hurrying toward the hall.

Grayson was the first to the doctor, grabbing his arm. Camery shouted and flung his body in a crazed fashion. He certainly fit the mad scientist stereotype, his outgrown hair messing in front of his unshaven face. Aria moved to the end of the hall where long flowing curtains swayed in the howling wind from the open window. The scent of dead flowers wafted toward her from an old bouquet in a blue vase that sat upon a small wooden table. She gazed at the flowers, looking at the open expanse to her right. The dining room was full of elaborate china cabinets and a chandelier. The room connected back with the entryway that became the kitchen Aren had occupied. Her sight returned to the left where the last room of the house was still unchecked, and her eyes dropped to the eerie blue-green glow pulsing from beneath the crack in the door.

Aria looked at Troy, signaling for him to be on alert. Camery's shouts were becoming more frantic as Aria grabbed the metal doorknob. Locked. Frowning, she glanced at the small tabletop with the blue vase once again. There was a tiny drawer. Aria tugged the drawer open and eyed the small decorative key sitting inside. Grabbing the item, she shoved it into the doorknob, twisting it with a loud click. The knob squeaked as she turned it. As she gave it a sharp push, the door gave a haunting moan. Aria halted. She aimed her weapon, her eyes wide as a strange light consumed her body.

"TROY!" she screamed.

Aria couldn't hear Troy's approaching footsteps or Camery's terrible cries as her heart pounded noisily within her chest, the blood pumping in her ears. Directly before her was the most unexpected sight she could have imagined. Clones: yes, she expected that. Androids: sure, why not? Demons being researched and experimented on: that was believable. But in no way did Aria imagine that the massive test-tube in the center of the back bedroom would contain the body of a little girl. No less, it was a little girl with a white dress, dirty-blonde hair, and pale dead skin. But it was not just any little girl; this was Sapphire.

"Think I'm A Good Pilot?"

CHAPTER 6

In three steps, Troy was by Aria's side. He twisted his torso, aiming high over her head and halted. His trigger finger twitched, nearly giving off a round. Gaping, jaw unhinged, the male slowly lowered his weapon as he stared at the young girl inside the placental container in the cramped lab.

"What...what the hell is this?" he whispered.

"I'm not entirely sure, but someone has a *lot* of explaining to do," Aria said between the gnashing of her teeth.

"Aria?" President Clarke worriedly called down the hall.

Grayson had managed to keep Dr. Camery under control, but since the secret was revealed, the previously crazed scientist seemed defeated. Aria felt no pity for the man, however, trudging down the hall as she shouldered her weapon.

"What in the *hell* is going on?!" Aria shrieked.

Grabbing fistfuls of Camery's shirt, she pulled the older man out of Grayson's grasp. Camery fumbled over his steps as the woman tugged him down the hall. Troy immediately joined her side, gripping the man's arm. Roughly, he slammed Camery against the doorway. The doctor's pale eyes promptly fled to the little girl.

"You want to explain this to us, Dr. Camery?" Troy hissed. "You want to explain why this little girl shares an eerie resemblance to the same little girl that tried to kill us?"

Clarke and Grayson were by their side in an instant, Aren following behind. Clarke's expression of curiosity and alert changed to one of shock.

"Kill you?" Clarke asked. "What do you mean she tried to kill you?"

"This girl," Aria shoved Camery inside the room, "is the one who is behind everything. The demons, Euclid, everything."

"A-Aria…" Clarke muttered, walking up toward the pale child. "This is…." He looked to Camery, a saddened frown taking over.

Camery sighed, resting his hand against the glass near the child's face. "You are one of the few in the entire corporation that even noticed the photograph on my desk," he whispered.

"Who is this?" Aria asked.

"My daughter," Camery spoke dismally. "Sapphire is my daughter."

"But…she…what?" Troy stammered, running his palm across his forehead.

"It's kind of complicated," Camery murmured.

"We've got all night," Aria said, sitting on the edge of a power generator. Her green eyes narrowed on the doctor, flickering between him and his daughter in the tube. Just the sight of her made the woman feel uneasy.

Camery fidgeted uncomfortably, his hands shaking. Giving an exasperated moan, he took a seat on a small work table beside the container. He rubbed his face, his fingers pressing against his eyelids. It appeared as though he hadn't slept for a long time.

"Well," he dropped his arms, fingers clasping in his lap, "where shall I begin?" He glanced over his shoulder at Sapphire. "Sapphire is my dearest only child. She is no longer alive…hasn't been for nearly twenty years."

Aria looked upon the child, noticing how one of her legs was missing outside of a few thin wires and scraps of dangling metal.

"She was on her way home from school one day when tragedy struck. The bus she was supposed to take was running late. For some reason, she boarded the wrong one out of desperation. I imagine it was because she was scared, worried that she would miss dinner or something. I never liked her riding those things, but as busy as her mother and I were, we couldn't always pick her up. She had her automated drone with her; I could only assume that its logistics system had a reason for allowing her onto that bus."

Camery paused, staring at his shoes. "The bus route went through the Nex-Text business district."

"Twenty years ago? That was during the False Syndicate War," Troy said, looking to Aria.

"Their biggest competitor, Browning Smith, decided to take out their competition in a rather unorthodox way." Camery's laced fingers tightened together, his nails digging into his flesh.

"We know all about that," Aria grumbled. "The amount of explosives they used took out an entire city block."

Camery nodded. "And the bus that Sapphire was riding…of all the buses…." He gave a haggard sigh. "Of all the days…she had to ride the one bus that drove through that district right when the bombs went off. She was killed. Her mother and I were devastated, of course. The little light in our world had been extinguished. We were never the same. I drowned myself in work. My wife spent most of her time in the Underbelly with her sister. We had a small funeral for Sapphire, but what I had kept secret from my wife was the fact that Sapphire's ashes weren't actually in her urn. I had taken the body back to the lab."

"For what purpose?" Aria asked.

Camery looked up, his face holding an expression of surprise. "To start my Biomechanical Research and Development program, of course."

"You wanted to clone your daughter?" Aria asked.

"I wanted my daughter back!" the doctor shouted. "I wanted my little girl who was so ruthlessly taken from me! You cannot tell me that she was fated to go out that day! She was not meant to die in such a cruel way." Camery quickly composed himself. "And I knew my wife wanted Sapphire back as desperately as I did. I wanted my original girl back, so I did not clone her. Instead, I repaired her internal organs with mechanical parts. Her brain had suffered severely from massive hemorrhaging. I had to replace parts of it. It took lots of time, lots of trial and error, but, once it was complete, my daughter was alive again! When her blue eyes opened, I burst into tears of joy." Camery paused, his face falling. "But she wasn't the little girl that she was before. I had replaced too much of her mind with crystal core computerization. She could see me, but she did not recognize me. Her eyes were empty. She had…no soul."

Aria watched Camery; her angry demeanor faded.

"It was no longer my daughter but a machine. Still, I had hoped that we could retrain her. She would just have to relearn who I was and who her mother was. Simple, right? When a baby is born, it knows nothing of the world. Sapphire was just a newborn again. So, I brought my wife into the lab to see her. It was a surprise. I wanted to see her cry tears of joy at seeing her baby girl once again. Only…it didn't work out that way. And…my wife…she screamed. I never saw her so angry. She had thought I created a monster. It was not our little girl. It was an empty machine." Camery nodded slowly. "It was the worst mistake of my life. My wife immediately packed up her things and moved in with her sister in the Underbelly. So I stayed in my lab, working on duplicating DNA. Walten granted me permission to use dead soldiers' bodies for experimentation."

Noticing the other's looks of trepidation, Camery raised a hand. "They were orphans or without any living family members." Aria narrowed her eyes. He said it as if that made it all the more acceptable to experiment on their dead bodies. "And that's how I was able to gather my resources to create my biomechanical androids and clones. All was going well. I had enough prototypes to send out onto the battlefield. One after another, the bodies filtered in. It was easy to repair them, to replicate them. They were like a renewable resource. Every android created had an average of three life cycles. Think of the numbers of lives we could save."

Camery noticed the disgusted stares coming from Aria and Troy. "And that was the moral debate that caused my operation to be shut down. At least…that's what I thought had happened. It turns out Walten had other plans for them all along."

"So you have nothing to do with the fact that the clones have been relocated to Ives?" Aria questioned.

"It wasn't until later that I realized the clones hadn't been exterminated, once I heard a woman named Ivory was brought back with you along with the Sorcēarian."

"You know something about Ivory?" President Clarke spoke up.

Camery laughed. He laughed loud and hard. The doctor appeared to be at his wits end. "Of course I know Ivory. She's my niece!"

"What?!" Troy and Aria sounded in unison.

He sighed. "My sister-in-law was Ivory's mother. After my wife had left me to live with her sister in the Underbelly, there was another incident. The two women were later murdered while they were out late one night. They were twins, oddities you could say. Sure, I was devastated, but it had been years since I had even seen or heard from her at that point. It wasn't until Ivory's body came into my lab nearly a year ago that the full brunt of the pain hit me. Her pale skin, her blue eyes, and her blonde hair….She was a spitting image of her mother, the same as my wife. It was like looking at my young wife's corpse…and that left me wondering if Sapphire would have grown to look like that."

Aria glanced at Sapphire's body. It was beginning to make sense. Now that Camery mentioned it, Sapphire and Ivory did share a resemblance to one another, each one apparently holding their mother's traits.

"But you said the only bodies that ended up in your laboratory were soldiers. Ivory was not a soldier," Aria said.

"And that's when I found out that Walten had been lying to me. Not only had he no regard for soldiers' bodies, but he thought of the Underbelly as a wasteland full of potential soldiers he could use. They filled all the urns of the dead from the Underbelly with dust and brought the bodies to me so they could be used for my experiments. I couldn't say anything at this point. It was my biggest and most profitable project. I had to do simply what I thought best for the bodies. I made them stronger, more deadly. Next to Sapphire, Ivory is my most dangerous creation. I've equipped her with an Amasser Particle Beam. This weapon pulls in particles and amasses them into a high-density beam. Its blast can penetrate through nearly anything; its heat and pressure can turn matter into glass, sometimes diamonds. Only Ivory can withstand the temperature and force it takes to operate a weapon like that. There's no wonder why Walten wants her. She's perfect for destruction."

"But you said Ivory is only the second deadliest next to Sapphire. What is Sapphire equipped with?" Aria asked.

Camery's eyes locked onto Aria's. He casually entwined his hands before his face. "A nuclear warhead."

James shouted, "You equipped her with a nuclear warhead?!"

Troy took a step back, nervously eyeing the little girl in the tube.

"You have to understand. When I operated on Sapphire, I had only one goal in mind–revenge," Camery simply stated.

"You were going to destroy Browning Smith," Aria said with wide eyes.

"Actually, destroy the entire city-state since they owned nearly 75% of all the corporations," Camery muttered.

"These are some serious war crimes, Camery," James sternly said.

"And you think I really care?" the professor growled. "I lost everything because of them! I would have done it without hesitation if Team Phoenix hadn't beaten me to the punch."

"Sorry, we stole your thunder…" Troy mumbled sarcastically, running a hand through his hair. He gave a frustrated growl. "Am I the only one still missing something?" The group stared at Troy, waiting for him to work things out in his head. "If that girl in that tube is the real Sapphire…and you never cloned her, then who in the hell is the girl we saw on Ives?"

All the attention returned to Camery. The professor narrowed his eyes; his hands shook before his face. "That *thing* is not my daughter," he hissed. "That *thing* is the goddamned devil!"

Aria peered at Troy, her blood running cold. The male soldier returned her fearful look. Even if he had his doubts, Camery's conclusion was chilling enough, especially when he had previously seemed so skeptical about the idea of the creatures having any biblical connections.

"You…you mean you think that girl in the cave is…" Troy started.

"Don't even utter his name! You have no idea what he is capable of!" Camery shouted. "I don't know how…I don't know why, but that thing is projecting an image of innocence for all to see. He has chosen my daughter to hide behind. He's locked between dimensions and is desperate for a way out. He thinks that he can use Sapphire's body as a vessel. If he inhabits that body, he will have full access to her nuclear warhead. That damn Walten has no idea what he's unleashed."

"How did Walten even do this?!" Troy asked in amazement. Sarcastically, he continued, "Hmm…I'm feeling a bit bored today. Think I'll do some corporate trading, buyout a small city-state, and somewhere between lunch and dinner unleash Hell on Earth! Why is he even doing this?"

Aria twisted her mouth into a forced frown, trying to maintain a serious disposition.

"Believe it or not, but this whole operation was started by Walten's father. Right before he died, it was rumored he became fanatically religious. He had hopes of breaking the barrier between dimensions. He had thought he could bring Heaven to Earth this way. He wanted the Creator to come back. It was all nonsense. He was a sick man. No one took anything he said seriously," Camery explained.

"Obviously his bastard son did," Aria replied.

Camery nodded slowly. "Young Walten had grown up listening to his father's ludicrous ramblings. After his father had died, he followed in his footsteps and continued the project by having a mining team tunnel beneath Fountains. The miners discovered a high-frequency point below the Earth's crust. Walten believed it to be a gateway point. Due to the electrostatic frequencies and vibrations caused by the miner's drill and an ancient frequency tuner, they had somehow cracked it. That's when…the thing crossed over. *He* cannot enter our world without a vessel. *He* wants Sapphire."

"And what's his goal after he receives the body?" Aria asked.

"Global domination. The details are vague on my end. Walten and Sapphire…no, the *thing*, do not share much with me. *It's* angry with me."

"Why?" Aria pried.

"Because I will not share the location of Sapphire's body. Sapphire was originally supposed to be in the disposal container along with the other clones. I was unaware at the time what was going on, and I did not want her to be destroyed, so I stowed her away here in an emergency vehicle." Camery looked over at the small girl. "I imagine it's only a matter of time before they find me, however. I mean…you found me easy enough."

There was a noise outside, the sound of glass crunching underfoot. Aria instantly pieced it together–the sound of the security cameras they had shot out left shards all over the ground surrounding the home. They had already been discovered.

"Get down!" Aria gave a harsh whisper just as the power went out, the generator rumbling to silence. The room dimmed into darkness.

All was quiet until the placental container kicked on, its backup system starting up while the generator recalibrated itself. The tube containing Sapphire's body cast a sickly glow around the room once again, creating long dark shadows. Troy was crouched beside the doorway, Grayson opposite of him. James was behind a side table, a hand gripping his shoulder. He didn't look too good, sweat covering his forehead. A shuffling sound alerted her to Aren's position safely behind her. Camery was on his hands and knees beside the tube. He caught Aria's intense stare and moved, his hand slamming against a button on the side. The cylinder vibrated against its holding clamps.

"What are you doing? You'll alert them of our location!" Aria hissed.

"I'm not letting them get her," Camery whispered desperately.

The container sank into the floor, lowering inch by inch just as the front door of the home was kicked in, the wood giving a splintering crunch. Before they could move, the hallway lit up in a bright flash, setting off an alarming blast of noise. Aria and Troy activated their mental chips, blocking out the shriek, their optical retinas shielding their eyes from the harsh light. James and Camery hunkered down, trying to protect their ears. A low groan came from the pilot as he covered his head. Grayson remained unfazed, being the enigmatic badass that he was.

Troy rounded the corner low and fired while Grayson provided cover, and the gunfight began. Sprinkles of colored light flickered down the hall, the enemies' ignition rounds bursting in sprays as they hit the doorways, furniture, and walls. Aria immediately moved to where Troy's previous position was. As he fired down the hall with Grayson, she caught the shadows moving behind Troy through the window. Aria shot, the rounds splintering through the wall. The eruption of noise from the gunfight was too loud to hear if any enemy soldiers were hit, but her thermal optics easily revealed the jerking forms on the other side of the wall.

Troy glided into the dining room, his attention on the soldiers within that space and the kitchen. He took cover behind the chairs, giving a sharp push to knock the heavy wooden table on its side to form a barricade. All around him were crackles of light, shards of liquid fire burrowing deep into the walls and his cover. The centuries-old china within the cabinets was shattering to pieces, giving high-pitched tings amongst the warring sounds. The enemy gunfire was relentless. There were too many of them.

Lifting his barrel over his head, Troy fired above the table, his optic camera feeding him a clean view. He easily took down three men, but the shadows kept filing in through the kitchen door and windows as others came from the living room. His eyes were stuck to the front; he hoped his partner had his back. Just then, a warning message popped into his senses. Aria's mental chip was alerting Troy of an enemy that had slipped through the window at the end of the hall behind him. She had shot him, but he was in full body Goliath armor and was aiming directly at Troy. He processed the info within a split-second. Troy spun around the left of the table, his finger on the trigger as he shot horizontally across the room. His spreading fire took out a couple men in the kitchen area. While the others dove for cover, it provided Troy enough time to roll back to the opposite side of the flipped table to face his approaching armored enemy. Troy slid, his foot kicking the rifle from the Goliath's hands, and then he fired a whole clip into the enemy's armor. The large soldier stumbled back a few steps, colliding with the wall.

'*Shit*,' Troy mentally grumbled.

Goliath armor was highly shielded. Even in close range, the bullets barely dented the surface. As if the armor wasn't bad enough, the man wearing it was huge. He was even taller than Troy. And though the thick armor covered him, Troy could tell the man was nothing but muscle. He briefly wished this giant of a man was a Brawler instead.

A low, angry growl sounded from the armored soldier, and he pushed off the wall, crashing into Troy and knocking his weapon loose. A loud shout erupted from Troy as the two collided with one of the china cabinets. The sharp, cool sensation in Troy's left shoulder blade confirmed that he received a nasty laceration from the broken glass. He tangled with the other soldier, pushing against the cupboard while ignition rounds blasted from the wall beside their heads. There wasn't going to be anything left of the house before long. Troy twisted and pulled to switch places, allowing the splatter of gunfire to erupt into the Goliath's back. The armored man was pushed forward by the force of the bullets, the liquid fire slowly eating through his armor. The tactic could have worked, if only the Goliath hadn't head-butted Troy in the face and then tossed him like he weighed nothing.

Troy flew back, landing on the edge of the sideways table. He and the furniture tipped over. Troy gritted his teeth; the impact caused a searing pain in his already injured hip. He lay on the ground, hand gripping his back. He didn't have time to move before the Goliath had his arms wrapped around his neck in a chokehold. Troy gasped, his hands wrapping around the other man's arms. He groaned, kicking and writhing about, trying to loosen the bulky man's hold. Both of them were easy targets, bullets flying everywhere. The other man had the upper hand, however. He could be shot multiple times without repercussion thanks to his armor. Troy, on the other hand, had nothing.

"Gah!" Troy gasped, feeling lightheaded. The man was an ox. Troy wasn't weak by any means, but this man was an anomaly. Troy closed his eyes, sending a mental chip image to Aria, hoping it was enough to let her know what was up on his end of things.

'What would she do?' he thought.

Aria was feisty, even when up against opponents twice her size. She'd bite and claw her way out of a fight if she had to. Troy glanced at the ground. He may not be able to bite through that armor, but he could certainly dig in his claws.

Letting out his breath, Troy went lax in the soldier's arms, his hands dropping to the floor. The Goliath immediately loosened his grip, his heaving breaths revealing that Troy had certainly put up a tiring fight. It only took a second before Troy had his hand around a broken shard of glass. He elbowed the man against his face shield, taking him by surprise, his head tilting back and showing the chink in his armor. Troy followed through with the broken blade of glass and shoved the shard into the man's neck right between the armor plates. The man gave a gurgling growl, his hand tightly gripping Troy's neck in response. Troy grimaced, pulling out the shard and stabbing the man a second time in the throat. Removing the piece once again, the Goliath's grip loosened, and he fell back, thudding against the wooden floor. Troy wheezed, rubbing his neck. Fighting the past month against monsters, he had momentarily forgotten what it was like to battle humans.

Aria's roaring scream alerted Troy of her position. He watched her get crushed against the wall by a different man in Goliath armor. Troy hurriedly scrambled to his feet, looking for his gun. Aria continued shouting as she repeatedly smashed her fist against the man's faceplate, her legs kicking wildly to press against his chest. He clamped a giant hand around her throat, pulled her away from the wall, and slammed her back into place. Troy lifted his rifle and aimed at the back of the man's head. As he prepared to fire, another blast ignited against the side of the Goliath's helmet, knocking the enemy off center and causing him to drop Aria onto the ground. Another howl sounded, and Aren was leaping onto the man, his pilot's issued military knife drawn. He stabbed the armored man in the neck and gave a sharp tug across his throat as he pulled out. Standing, his chest heaving, the pilot looked over his shoulder at Troy with wild eyes. Troy eyed the bloody knife in the young man's hands and nodded at him, taking his aim off the pilot. Aren quickly reached down for Aria's hand. She gave him a smirk and patted him on the shoulder before retrieving her weapon. It seemed the back of the house was clear, but gunfire continued in the living room area.

"Grayson," Aria muttered, moving forward. Troy signaled to her, going the opposite way to cut through the kitchen while she and Aren took the hall to the front.

Aria slipped into the bathroom, Aren taking cover in the second bedroom. From her view, she could pick off a few of the soldiers who had their attention on Troy. She effortlessly took them down and then placed her gun around the corner, getting sight of Grayson's opponents. His large 50 cal. Liberty Eagle was putting holes into Feyette's men. The blast was enough to knock a Goliath back through the front window, the bulky individual stumbling ungracefully head first into a pile of bushes outside.

Running across the expanse of the living room, Troy grabbed a flash grenade from one of the dead soldiers and tossed it on top of the Goliath that had fallen outside. Troy pressed against the wall as the blast erupted. It may not have killed the man, but it definitely burst his eardrums.

Troy eyed another dead Goliath in the center of the room; his armored vest held an assortment of grenades. He waited a moment for Aria and Grayson to pick off the last two enemies in the room before he darted to the corpse and snatched up a large grenade. Aria signaled, her thermals picking up multiple targets on the other side of the wall near Troy. He caught the images on his optic retina and dove behind the couch just as the side wall cracked open from an explosion. With the pin already pulled, Troy stepped onto the back of the sofa, leaped, grabbed the first Goliath he could find, and jammed the explosive between the soldier's neck armor and helmet. Panicked, the Goliath gave an unsure yell as Troy dropkicked him backward through the hole in the wall and into the group of soldiers who were filing into the room behind him. The Goliath staggered, knocking the other soldiers back as the grenade detonated, setting off all the others on his vest, obliterating the men around him. Troy rolled to his feet, picking off the lingering men and the injured. He eyed one soldier whose legs had been destroyed. The wailing man was pulling himself across the lawn, reaching out with a shaking hand toward the back of the house. Troy frowned, took aim, and fired one shot into the back of his skull.

"Sorry, man," he whispered as he lowered his rifle.

These were men who worked for his company, Bio-Tech. These men should have been his and Aria's comrades. They had most likely fought side by side at one time in the past wars. Now, Walten was ruining that. He had turned lifelong partners into enemies. Troy suddenly didn't feel too well, his high from the battle diminishing as he overlooked the bodies strewn all over the lawn and inside the house. He looked at Aria. She was digging through one soldier's vest, telling Aren to pocket a few of the items she found to her liking. She caught Troy's gaze. His thoughts must've been obvious through his expression because Aria immediately stopped her scavenging.

"They aren't our comrades anymore, Troy. They were given orders and followed them," she said, her tone a little sour. Of course, she felt the same as Troy did, she just didn't want to seem like she gave a damn. "They're on Walten's side," she added.

Troy shook the thoughts from his head. Actually, Aria probably didn't give a damn at all. She never was much of a people person.

Another loud crunch sounded from the back of the house. Aria, Aren, and Troy took formation and moved to the back. Grayson was in the lead, already firing his Liberty Eagle at multiple targets. He rushed in, pulling President Clarke from Sapphire's room. Aria eyed James momentarily as Grayson continued moving him to safety. She couldn't tell if James was injured or not. She and Troy pushed through the doorframe into the small lab.

The whole wall had been wrenched open, pulled away from the side of the house by Feyette's carrier. The soldiers had Camery, forcing the frightened man onto the aircraft.

"Fire!" she shouted.

Aria and Troy shot, picking off men here and there as the others filed into the aircraft that was lifting off the ground. Feyette's unit had left a few men behind, one of them running after the jet, arms waving in the air. Its thrusters lit up and ignited, blasting the man behind it with its heat as Troy and Aria took down the last remaining pair. Turning on her thermal optics, she turned in a circle, Troy doing the same.

"I don't detect anymore," she said.

"Same," Troy muttered.

"There are no more," Grayson's low voice called from the dining area.

"Camery?" James' voice called out. He sounded weak.

Aria and Troy rushed to the other room. Aren followed closely behind.

"They took him," Troy replied.

"James," Aria whispered, kneeling beside him. "You look like hell."

"As I feel…" James mumbled. "Just a bit too much excitement, that's all."

"Looks much worse than that. We need to get you to the hospital," she said.

"Not necessary. I can't risk any of you. Walten will be looking for me. It's a miracle you weren't discovered while hospitalized," James sighed, leaning against the kneeling Grayson.

"I took them to a private hospital closer to the edge of town, one that wouldn't ask questions. I simply told them that the military hospitals were all full," Aren said. He shrugged. "They understood with the amount of causalities from the attacks, so they didn't really harass me much."

"Still, the amount of luck you had…I doubt we'll be as lucky this time around," James moaned. He looked up at Grayson. The bodyguard watched James from behind dark shades, not saying anything. "I got Grayson to take care of me. We'll find a good place to hide, and he can patch me up."

James coughed. The sound was an awful rattling in his chest. The fit continued, and Grayson reached into his pocket, pulling out a handkerchief. James gratefully accepted the article, nearly vomiting into it. Aria watched; a frightened expression spread over her face.

"James…you're not coughing up blood are you?" she asked.

"Lungs are just a little banged up from the shards of the ignition rounds. They'll push out eventually," he said, hiding the handkerchief.

"Not sure that's a good thing," Aren added. "They could get into the blood stream or cause an infection. Judging by the looks of you, I'd say you already have one."

James Clarke fed the young pilot a bitter look. "Bit too smart for your own good."

Aren cleared his throat. "Get told that a lot…."

"James, we've got to do something," Aria muttered.

Aren looked at his DNAIS. "We've got more to worry about than the President's wounds." Pulling up a digital map, he revealed a blinking red light moving toward their position. "Feyette's got reinforcements on the way. We need to bust ass out of here."

"Damn it," Aria cursed.

Troy and she immediately lifted their rifles.

"We've got to get him to the car," Aria huffed, following Aren as he led the way to the front door. Aria firmly grabbed his shoulder. He froze, allowing her to take the lead, and then fell back to the rear to provide cover.

The group crossed the front lawn, Troy and Aria taking either side, checking through their optics for any life signs while Grayson supported Clarke.

"Shit," Troy hissed.

Aria joined him, running her hand through her hair. The car had been shot to shit, the tires were deflated and barely holding onto the rim. Aren continued fiddling with his DNAIS.

"What the hell do we do now?" Aria growled. "There's the basement….At least, I assume there's one where Sapphire's being kept."

"And that's what they are coming back for, I imagine," Troy added. "Probably not a good idea to hide in there. We don't have enough ammo to last another fight like that."

Aren opened the trunk of the car, pulling out the luggage and extra ammunition.

"Maybe we can go by foot, hide in the mountains until things clear up," Aria suggested. She looked at Grayson. James was standing, but his head was hanging low, eyes closed. She frowned, matching Grayson's expression.

"Or you can help me unload the car," Aren grumbled.

"We can't carry all of that," Aria barked.

"You're going to carry it once my Hawk shows up," Aren snapped back, matching her sassy tone. Everyone stared at him silently. "I calibrated it to have auto-start through my DNAIS. Called it about five minutes ago. Should be here any minute," he explained nonchalantly, feeling on the spot under all their scrutiny.

Aria stomped up to the man, grabbing the sides of his face. "I could kiss you right now," she said, shaking him.

"…Um," Aren fumbled for words as Aria released him and walked into a clearing, eyes to the sky.

"I can see it," she said. She looked back at the others, her enthusiasm quickly diminishing. "And I see Feyette's team! We need to scramble."

In seconds, the Hawk that was kilometers away was already pulling to a stop, morphing into copter mode above the house. It circled into the lawn, and the small group moved. Aria and Troy lugged their gear, Aren digging through his car for his auto-drone. Once everyone boarded, Grayson safely buckled James into his chair before rushing to get the med-kit. Aren jumped into the Hawk, plopping his bot heavily into the seat beside him. He flicked a number of switches, the doors closing in as they lifted into the air. His drone gave a high-pitched whine as it kick-started, levitating in its seat, its pinching hands clamping open and closed while it bleeped and looked at its master.

"You're functioning as auto-pilot. I may need you to man the battle station," Aren said to the bot.

The drone gave another beep and gripped one of the joysticks on the instrument panel. The Hawk jolted as it converted into its jet form.

"Battle station?" Troy asked.

Aren looked back at his occupants. Giving a crooked smirk, he replied, "Yeah. Feyette will no doubt want a fight. Now that we're out of the house, there's nothing stopping him from destroying us."

"You're going to dogfight with us still on the Hawk?!" Aria asked, already feeling her stomach churn.

"I would let you jump out, but then you'd be caught in the middle of the desert all alone. Besides, there's not enough parachutes for all of you," Aren said. Boy, his confidence sure was rising.

"I don't like the sound of that at all…" Aria said.

"And since there aren't enough parachutes for the whole lot, then I had just better get our damn asses out of this mess in one piece," the pilot added.

"Aren," Aria said in a low tone, "if you kill us…I'm killing you."

"At least I'll take your secrets to the grave with me," he said, laughing. He gave her a wink.

Aria folded her arms. The young pilot seemed entirely too reckless, but he had already saved their lives before. She would simply have to maintain her faith in him. His humor at least helped ease the tension. Gavin's traits were apparent in the pilot.

"He'll get us out," Troy said, looking out the window. He seemed a bit distant, but in the reflection of the glass, he caught her stare and gave a lopsided grin in return.

Aria sighed, awaiting the inevitable.

A red alarm chimed, alerting the crew that something had locked onto the Hawk.

Aren pulled up a multitude of data readings on his panel. "We have two bogies. Franklin, engage."

"ENGAGE," the bot droned.

Aria gripped the arms of her chair as the dogfight began.

The Hawk swooped to the side, a missile already skimming past their wings. Feyette's team wasted no time. Aren drove forward, heading directly toward the enemy jet. His round robot clamped tightly around its joystick, the other clamp pressing various buttons in lightning speed. A clunk sounded, and the Hawk's turrets dropped; beads of light pelted toward the enemy ship. Feyette's craft sprayed its deterrent shield, the frequencies taking multiple hits. Aren's panel lit up with scattered red alerts; high-pitched alarms sounded from all directions. They were about to collide. Another missile ejected from the enemy aircraft, a burst of light spraying out the back, and Aren pulled up, passing right over the top of the other vehicle. There was a rumble that shook the Hawk. The front window revealed a rearview image of the other ship igniting into pieces. The enemy projectile had backtracked, chasing Aren's tail, and had inadvertently collided with its own craft. Thanks to Franklin's spray of gunfire, the shields were temporarily damaged just enough to allow the full force of the missile to impact the other jet.

"Holy shit! That was close!" Troy shouted; a laugh erupted as he looked out his passenger window.

"Bogie one down," Aren said, pulling the Hawk into a near barrel-roll as he dodged yet another missile. He looked to the side, his face hard and sober. "Onto bogie two."

The other aircraft kept a safe distance away from Aren, pulling back and darting to the sides as Franklin repeatedly fired. Aren mimicked the other craft's movements.

"Gonna have to try something new, Frank…" he muttered.

Franklin gave an enthusiastic squeal and Aren looked at him with a wide grin on his face. "And I had nearly forgotten! I've been waiting to try this baby out."

Franklin beeped again, and the Hawk gave a grind as a secondary weapon pulled out from the nose of the vehicle.

"What is that?" Troy asked, lifting his head as high as he could to try and get an eyeful of the massive barrel that was winding up.

"Jes somethin' I was able to snatch up from the black-market," Aren said proudly.

"How do you get the money for this stuff?!" Aria asked.

Aren gave a sheepish laugh. "Eh…mommy and daddy have a lot of money. Really, more than they can even manage."

"Must be rough," Aria grumbled.

"Hey…it's saving your ass, is it not?" Aren shot her a look.

"Yeah, Aren's just sharing his toys, Aria," Troy said.

Aria twisted her mouth into a pout.

"Fire away!" Aren called out.

Franklin gave another chime, and the turret was at max speed, whirling as it pulled in energy. The whole Hawk quaked. Blast after blast, the thundering weapon sent out pulsing bursts nearly half as wide as the enemy craft. It was an ominous noise–*Boom, Chunk, Boom, Chunk.*

"Try to dodge that, bastards." Aren pulled the Hawk to the side, matching the other's pattern to where they couldn't escape.

The first shot went wide, the second colliding with the shield. The force of the shield being obliterated knocked the other craft's trajectory off course. It momentarily fell out of the sky, and Aren had to dip, more bursts following after it.

They were facing the ground, falling fast. The blasts that missed the other aircraft sunk into the earth, balls of light and dust exploded into the air. Franklin kept shooting, and Aren kept flying down.

Aria gripped Troy's shoulder, her other hand holding onto her safety belt. Sure, Gavin had to get them out of fights before, but nothing like this. At any moment, they could smash into the ground. Aria closed her eyes. Thoughts of Gavin's Hawk exploding into the ground and the silhouette of his freefalling body following close after invaded her mind. She felt Troy grab her hand, pulling her back to reality, and then the Hawk pulled up. The enemy jet caught its bearings right before it hit the ground and began to rise, but Aren's bursts knocked it off course once again. One giant blast ripped off the right wing and then the second. The craft spiraled in a circle before it collided with the ground. Aren lifted higher, going immediately into full stealth mode.

It was silent a moment.

"Bogie two down." Aren's voice was quiet.

Aria's caught breath finally released.

"Fun, right?" Aren looked to the group in the cabin. His smile fell as he saw his crew.

Aria looked pale; Troy's hand was gripping his chest, James Clarke didn't seem conscious, and Grayson remained unfazed, his attention on the President.

"How in the hell did you get one of those guns?!" Aria shouted.

"I told you, black-market," Aren replied. "While you guys were in the hospital, I did some shopping around in the Underbelly. I was able to get the sucker installed down in the mine shafts beneath the city. People down there are a little rough, but there isn't anything they wouldn't do to make a unit. Besides, after Feyette's men took out most of the population, they were more than eager to help. Figured after that incident in Ives, I needed some heavier weaponry."

Aria gawked at the pilot.

Troy's eyes enlarged. "Aren…I like you!" He pointed at the young man.

Aren scratched his head nervously. "Uh…thanks?"

"We need to get the President somewhere safe," Grayson interrupted. He was in the process of changing Clarke's bandages.

"Is he okay?" Aria asked.

"Heart rate has increased; fever has set in," Grayson monotonously stated.

"Where should we go?" Aria asked.

"Definitely not back to Fountains," Troy replied.

Aren added, "We're not entirely alone in this world. We've got allies, right?"

"Suppose we do now," Aria said. She leaned forward, grabbing one of the radio coms strapped to the side of the Hawk. She hesitated and then gave a scoff of a laugh. Dialling a signal, she plugged the connector into her mental chip.

"Who you callin'?" Troy asked.

Aria gave another large smile before cheerfully speaking. "Kovacevic…how are you, sweetie? Miss me?" Her face deadpanned. "You miss my tits…."

Troy laughed.

"Taking On Goliath"

CHAPTER 7

The sound of screaming tore Dovian from his slumber. As his eyes shot open, the luminescence of his pupils adjusted to the sunlight that poured through the stained-glass window. Looking about his room, he heaved a heavy sigh. He was in Ives, in his bedroom. Hector wasn't in his pillow-fluffed bed. He was most likely out and about scrounging for jerky or soup. Dovian slowly sat up, rubbing his right temple. He was home. The shrieking he heard was most likely from the wind that spiraled through the broken and twisted metal of the surrounding buildings, just as it always did.

The scream came again. Dovian's eyes widened, his heart leaping in his chest. What was he doing? Yes, he was in Ives, but what about the past couple weeks? It had been the first time he had slept since the night after the battle in Saray. Dovian had wished the current events were nothing more than a nightmare, just some terrible dream that would disappear as soon as he had awoken, but no. This was real life and everything since the day he met Aria and Troy had actually happened. He was in Ives; Sapphire and her monsters weren't too far away in the caves, which meant the screams he was hearing were also very real.

"Ivory!" Dovian shouted, jumping out of bed.

His bare feet pounded against the stone floor as he darted through the halls while shouting Ivory's name. The shriek came again, sending adrenaline through his veins, and Dovian pushed open a window and prepared to climb onto the ledge but halted. Another sound followed her screams–laughter. Dovian's panicked breaths slowed into a deep exhale. He rested a hand against the frame of the window and watched.

Behind the cathedral was a large plot of green grass. The yard rolled over a hill that plunged into a small lake where he and his friends used to swim. Surrounding the pool was an assortment of debris. Large chunks of stone and metal were overrun with vines and flowers; some of the cracks had sprouted thin trees, giving the garden a unique appearance. Bright sunlight sparkled rays between the rolling clouds in the sky, making the landscape dance with flickers of alternating contrasts of light and dark. A gentle breeze swayed, carrying the scent of orchids and grass to his nostrils. In the center of it all was a wandering figure dressed in black and plum, yellow hair sprouting in all directions.

Ivory darted from each hiding place–behind a lump of moss-covered concrete to a large piece of warped metal surrounded by a spiraling tree trunk that held branches full of thick leaves. As she ran, a loud giggle erupted from the woman. She pressed herself against the nearest surface, her excited breath holding in her lungs as she waited. A loud thumping commenced, and King Petey lurched from behind one massive chunk, giving an eager growl as he jumped to the side, looking at Ivory from his peripheral. Petey's antics sent Ivory into a fit of screams and laughs as she rushed to another hiding place, the lizard giving chase. Hector ran from side to side, watching the scene and participating by giving a honk now and then. Ivory took her place behind an enormous rock of sorts. She looked around one side as Petey hid the best he could behind a tree. His face squeezed between the branches, the foliage giving him a prickly green mane. His large rear-end stuck out to the side of the tree as his tail excitedly flopped against the ground. Ivory snickered and hid behind her spot again. Petey lunged to the other side, hiding opposite of her. The two proceeded to play a game of peek-a-boo around the corners, alternating left and right.

Dovian gave a laugh, the sound making him self-aware again. He stepped up onto the windowsill, hanging out the side as he inspected the terrain. There were no enemies in sight. He and Ivory were safe. Giving another exhale, he jumped from the height of the cathedral–dropping a number of stories–and landed with a solid plant before casually walking forward with his hands in the pockets of his pants. Hector noticed him first, giving a short bark before making a quick lizard-run in Dovian's direction. It took another second of Ivory and Petey running around in circles before the massive lizard gave a snort and stopped, looking at Dovian with sparkling gold eyes. Ivory giggled, grabbed Petey's neck, and hugged him. Noticing the lizard's solid stance, she fearfully looked over her shoulder at Dovian. She relaxed when she realized who had snuck up on them.

"Having fun?" he asked.

Ivory's grin dropped. "I'm sorry...did we wake you?"

Dovian gave her a reassuring smile, patting Hector on the head as he passed him.

"It was quite a start to wake up to the sound of screaming," he said. He lazily stood with his shoulders sagging and hips drooping forward.

"Sorry," she murmured quietly.

"But it was quite a pleasant sight to discover you having so much fun with these scoundrels," he chuckled.

Ivory's expression lightened, and she ran her hands up and down Petey's neck. He quite liked her touch, tilting his head to the side as he gave a quiet, growling purr.

"When I woke up, Petey seemed eager to get outside the walls of my," she hesitated, "garden. So I took him out for a walk. This seemed like a good place to get some fresh air, and he acted as if he had been here before. He was very excited. Hector must've overheard us because it wasn't long before he showed up to play some games."

Dovian watched Ivory, unconscious of the smirk on his face. She had done her hair just as I'Lanthe used to. A few of her spiraling curls dipped from the top of her head, draping around her long neck. The black robes were a tad long but seemed to fit well everywhere else, and the purple overcoat hugged her curves, tightly pulled in by a metal and leather corset belt. The ornate threading throughout the garment glimmered in the sunlight. She looked perfect, just as any other Sorcēarian would look.

He caught her gaze upon him and noticed a slight unease as she kept tearing her eyes away, a coy smile covering her features.

"It appears I startled you out of bed too quickly. You didn't have time to dress," she said with a nervous giggle.

Dovian looked down at himself. He was shirtless but was wearing loose-fitting pants.

"I admit...it is a bit odd not seeing you in your robes." She eyed him again, her hand running up and down Petey's side.

"I don't usually wear the robes in my sleep. I have pajamas," he said as he pulled the pant legs out to the side.

"You have pajama *pants*," she corrected.

"It's warm." He shrugged, holding out his arms as he felt the sun's warmth against his pale skin. He closed his eyes, breathing in the fresh air.

Ivory took the moment to examine him. He was as fit as she imagined, chiseled like the statues in Roma. She titled her head to the side, looking at the tattoos that spread over the length of his upper arms. Dovian's eyes opened and immediately locked onto hers. He peered at his shoulder to see what she was so interested in, twisting his arm as he inspected the tattoo.

"I wouldn't have imagined you to be the tattoo type," Ivory said. "I mean, besides the ones you're supposed to receive."

Dovian turned to the side, allowing her a view of the work of art. The wings started along his scapula, spreading across his arm, making a point at the elbow. He held his arms to the side and then lifted them into the air. The tattoo moved, mimicking flapping.

"Very neat," Ivory whispered. Before she knew it, she was touching the detailed lines.

"Karter did it," Dovian softly spoke.

"Karter," she whispered, trying to gather a memory of the man.

"He was very skilled in the art. He had a passion for tattoos and had discovered the art form from a group of humans he had met at a nightclub," Dovian explained.

"Nightclub?" Ivory asked, intrigued.

Dovian chuckled. "Lita would drag the poor man all over the world. She was obsessed with human lifestyles. Karter had seen a man whose body was tattooed over every inch. He said it transformed the man—gave him an inhuman appeal. So he delved into it himself, practicing on me and others who happened to cross his path long enough for him to scribble the lines onto their skin."

"I find it fascinating that he was so interested in the humans. I'd assume it would have been the other way around." Ivory ran her fingers along Dovian's bicep, her light touch making him shiver.

"Just as we enthralled the humans, we were just the same by them. We learned from each other." Dovian lowered his arm, looking at the lake before them. "Karter made these in this very spot. Just with the tracing of his fingers, he made these lines. As painless as a mere touch." He ran his fingers over the back of Ivory's hand. They locked eyes once again. It was quite amusing. Ivory always looked bewildered when she made eye contact with Dovian.

"Here?" she asked, lowering her hand.

"Yes. I was here for a swim with Lita and a few others…and you." He stopped.

"I was here?" she asked.

Dovian looked for any indication whether or not his statement upset her.

She didn't seem bothered being associated with I'Lanthe, so he continued. "We were here quite often. The water is always warm. We'd gather for picnics and talk all day about nothing in particular." He gave a scoff. "It was also a way for the boys to talk the girls into getting in their swimsuits…or…undergarments." He rolled his eyes, laughing low at the memory of Lita in her underwear. She had nearly given Karter a heart attack that day.

Ivory laughed. "What's the difference?" she asked.

Dovian eyed her; a large grin plastered on his face.

"Oh! I remember that!" she exclaimed, turning to him.

"You do?" he asked; his face lit up.

She nodded enthusiastically. "Lita just tore her robes off and shouted, 'what's the difference' and jumped into the water!"

Dovian laughed with his hand on his stomach. "Oh, I will never forget the look on Karter's face!"

"From what I remember, she may as well have been naked!" Ivory giggled; her delicate hand placed against her collarbone in a similar fashion as I'Lanthe. After a moment, her smile faded. "I don't remember anything else."

Dovian's grin twisted off kilter. "It's alright. I had nearly forgotten as well."

He walked up to the water and crouched, his fingers swirling in the lake.

"Still warm!" he shouted over his shoulder.

Without warning, the man stood and tugged down his pants. Ivory gasped and spun away, her hands covering her face.

"You are naked!" she shrieked.

There was a loud splash behind her followed by silence. Ivory put her hands on her hips, looking at the sky. The swishing of water sounded as Dovian swam toward the center of the pool.

"What's the difference?" he shouted back.

She folded her arms. "Is this how you take your morning baths?"

"Sometimes," he nonchalantly replied. "Care to join me?"

Ivory shook her head. "Not in these robes."

"Take them off," he daringly stated.

"You just want to see me naked!" she cried out.

She couldn't see Dovian's laid-back shrug. "As if I haven't seen you naked before."

Ivory tensed. Indeed, when Dovian and the others had found her, she was completely nude.

"I can wait all day," he taunted her.

Ivory remained in her place, weighing her options. She was stuck on this island, and Dovian was her only companion.

"Come on in!" his deep voice called out. He sounded thoroughly amused as he swam in a wide half-circle.

Petey gave an excited honk and tore off in the direction of the lake. Ivory spun, watching as the large creature trotted into the water, Dovian waving his arms in the air in protest.

"N-n-no, no, no!" the Sorcēarian stammered. "I didn't mean you...."

Petey reached the deeper part of the lake and jumped, his large body crashing next to Dovian, sending a massive wave over the man. Dovian sank as he was pushed to the side. He came to the surface, gasping for air, his shimmering hair soaked and pressed against the sides of his face. Petey continued swimming out toward the center with a large lizardly smile spread over his scaly face. The reptile seemed rather pleased with himself. Dovian shot a glare at Petey and looked back toward the shore where Ivory stood laughing. Hector scattered to the edge of the water, staying in the shallow end, eating minnows and anything else he found that floated beside him.

Dovian backstroked casually. He eyed the creatures in the water with him. Holding his hands out, he teased, "Three against one, my dear." Ivory remained atop the hill, arms folded. She gave him a blushing glare. "Peer pressure," he said with a wink.

The woman looked from Dovian to Petey and then to Hector. They all three appeared to be having fun. She heaved an aggravated sigh.

"I'm beginning to figure out how you work, Dovian." Slowly, she unclasped her belt and dropped it onto the lawn. Dovian's smile widened as she turned her back to him, undoing the violet overcoat. "Turn around!" She quickly pointed at him.

"Turn around?" he protested.

"Yes! And cover your eyes!" she hissed.

Dovian reluctantly did as he was told. He waited a couple moments and then quickly looked over his shoulder, parting his fingers to get a quick look as Ivory dropped her black ceremonial dress. She was wearing a charcoal-grey set of underwear. As she bent forward, kicking off the robes, Ivory was nothing but legs. Dovian gave a silent laugh and moved back into position.

"I'm leaving my *undergarments* on!" she yelled.

After a few more seconds, Dovian heard rapid splashes as Ivory ran into the water. He tried to turn around, but she shouted at him again.

"Not until I get in the water!"

"What's the big deal?" he asked. "*I'm* naked."

"That was your decision…" she replied.

Dovian shivered as he felt her hands plant against the back of his shoulders. He spun, catching her just as she tried to drop beneath the surface, nearly pulling him under with her.

"Oh! Guess I can't swim…" she sputtered, her hands slipping as she tried to gain a firm grip on the man's body. "It's deep in this part."

Dovian grabbed her waist, and she squealed, kicking her legs.

"What are you doing?" she frantically asked.

Dovian pulled her in close, pressing her against his body. The water was warm, as was his skin. He shook his head fast, his wet hair messing into spikes in all directions. Ivory held her breath as she matched his tense gaze.

"Teaching you to swim," he said. "It could save your life someday." He gently pushed Ivory backward, and she sank. Spitting and coughing, she stood up once her feet made contact with the floor of the lake. "We should start in shallow water," he added.

"Thanks for the heads up," she sourly spat as she rubbed her eyes. She felt like a fool, swimming up to Dovian and getting locked in his smoldering gaze, letting her feelings get in the way. "I thought this was supposed to be fun."

"Before you and I can have any *fun* in this water…" Dovian began, swimming behind her. He placed a hand on her hip and whispered in her ear, "You'll have to learn to swim."

Ivory's breath hitched. His flirtations were a bit unfair. Why was he toying with her? She wasn't I'Lanthe. Was he only acting this way to be nice?

"Stay out of your head, Ivory," he murmured. Holding her tightly, he lifted her gently so that her feet didn't touch the sandy bottom.

He called her Ivory. She wasn't sure if that was good or not, but it at least allowed her to believe that he didn't think she was I'Lanthe. Perhaps it was because I'Lanthe could swim.

"I thought you couldn't read my thoughts," Ivory grumbled.

"It's obvious in your face. Remember, I'm supposed to be the sourpuss, got it?" he said.

Ivory gave a small smile. "You're not so sour today."

Chuckling, he replied, "Guess I woke up on the right side of the bed this morning."

Dovian suddenly moved his leg between Ivory's. She gave a quiet yelp, and he steadied her. "Let's start with treading water…" he instructed.

The majority of the day had been spent on the lake with Dovian patiently teaching Ivory the basics. It didn't take long for her to pick up on the exercise. No doubt the parts of her computerized brain were equipped with survival instincts. The robotic side of Ivory had no issues with learning to swim. The organic side, however, created conflicts due to emotion and lack of confidence. Whereas the first time Dovian asked her to try something, and she performed the task perfectly, Ivory developed issues performing over and again. He knew what part of the problem was, but there was nothing he could do about it since *he* was the issue. After a few trials and errors, Ivory soon became an adept swimmer, even taking it upon herself to swim out to the center of the lake to climb on Petey's back.

Eventually, they took to floating about lazily. Ivory lounged on Petey, her hand trailing through the water. A low rumble came from above, and she wrinkled her brow, watching as the clouds darkened and plumed overhead. Her gaze remained on the sky as the final tendrils of light were eaten away, the bright colors fading to dark shades with an orangey hue overlaying the landscape. Another dull thunder sounded in the air, and a wet speck plopped against her cheek.

"Dovian?" she called out, looking to the side to search for the man. Ivory gave a gasp as she noticed he was looking upward, his back to her. He was nearly out of the water, standing nude in the open without much care about anything. It had been a while since he had spoken, and Ivory had assumed he was peacefully lounging as she was. Though she couldn't see his face, Ivory could tell he was sinking into one of his moods. "Petey...go to Dovian," she whispered.

Petey complied, swimming with grace toward the Sorcēarian. The lizard only gave a few strides before Ivory patted him on the head and jumped into the water.

"Wait here," she said to Petey, her fingers scratching his nose.

Slowly turning to face Dovian, Ivory tensed and held her breath. He had lowered his head, and a hand rested against his forehead with fingers tangled in his hair. He appeared to be greatly distressed about something. Still, he did not acknowledge the woman behind him.

The thunder roared this time, and the rain began to pelt at random intervals. Ivory eyed her beautiful robes on the grass. She hoped they weren't getting too wet in this quickly approaching storm. She tugged on her hands, unsure of what to do exactly. An abrupt exhale sounded from Dovian, his body bending forward as he struggled inside.

"Dovian," Ivory whispered.

He groaned, his hand gripping his hair tighter. Lightning brightened the land in a white flash, the buzz of its current audible. An explosion of noise followed, jolting Ivory.

"Dovian!" she exclaimed. "Why is it raining?"

He straightened a little, his hand lowering from his head. He did not look at her. "I-Ivory?"

"Why is it raining, Dovian? I thought we were having fun," she quietly spoke.

Dovian didn't say anything. He stared at his hand, unmoving. Where was he? Where had his mind taken him to?

Ivory gathered her courage. What would I'Lanthe do? Apparently she was strong and capable of handling Dovian with ease. Taking a breath, she reached out and gently touched Dovian's shoulder. The man finally looked straight ahead; his gaze set on nothing. He did not protest to her touch, did not utter a word, and remained statuesque before her. She carefully wrapped her arms around his chest, pulling him against her. His tense muscles relaxed, and she felt his weight lean back against her for support.

"Dovian…why is it raining?" she softly asked.

"Is it?" he muttered dryly, looking back up at the sky.

"Yes, it is," she whispered. "We were swimming and enjoying the warm sun."

Dovian placed his hands over hers. "My apologies. I'm so used to it; I didn't notice." His voice was void of emotion.

"The rain is beautiful, Dovian, but I think we should get out of the water. I don't want to be fried by lightning," she said with a hint of amusement.

"That would not do well; I know what that feels like…." Word by word, his usual temperament resurfaced.

"You've been struck by lightning?" she asked.

Ivory continued holding Dovian from behind; her cheek pressed against his back. It was comforting to her. The wind had picked up, causing her to shiver in response.

"Three times to be exact. Not fun," he muttered. "You are cold."

"Hmm." She nodded. "You are warm."

Dovian roughly sighed. "Come; let's go inside. It's past lunchtime anyway." He finally looked at her. "And I need my pants," he added.

Ivory laughed. "Well, go get them!" She pushed the man, and he stumbled away from her.

Ivory then turned to Petey, letting the Sorcēarian get dressed. The rain was beginning to fall harder. The sound was like grinding gravel as the droplets pelted against the waves around her. After a moment, she turned toward the shore and led Petey out of the water. Hector, lying in a patch of overgrown grass, made snorting noises as he awoke from his slumber. Dovian snatched up Ivory's robes and helped her get dressed as the lizards darted for the double doors of the cathedral, eager to get inside and out of the rain. Another roar of thunder sounded, and Ivory shrieked as she ran to the entrance. Dovian lazily followed, motioning the doors to open. They all gathered inside. Petey struggled to squeeze through the frame, causing the wood to splinter and crack.

"Dear God, Pete...I'm starting you on a diet," Dovian grumbled as he watched the giant creature waddle into the grand foyer of the church.

Petey snorted as he walked away from the Sorcēarian and followed Hector into the corridor that led to one of the kitchens.

"Seems they know what time it is," Ivory said cheerfully. She tightened the brace around her waist, fiddling with the strings behind her back, and then tugged her hair up and secured it with I'Lanthe's clip.

"To a frilled monitor, every minute of the day is lunchtime," Dovian quipped.

He led the way to the kitchen area, halting at the doorway. Lost in thought, he looked back at the woman, and she awkwardly tried to avoid his stare.

'Be confident. Be calm.' Ivory told herself.

She lifted her chin. "You look at me as if I'm food, Dovian." She inwardly grimaced at her phrase. What did that even mean?

Dovian smirked, running a hand through his hair again. "You make it easy to stare; that's all," he murmured. "Tea?"

Ivory tilted her head. "Tea? Oh, yes! Tea! Sounds good." She pondered momentarily, fidgeting uncontrollably. "Have I had tea?"

Dovian chuckled, heading into the kitchen to prepare a kettle. "You've always loved tea. If you didn't have it with your morning breakfast, it was best to avoid you until you did."

Ivory smiled.

"As of late, I don't recall you ever having the pleasure of drinking any." He heated up some water in a ceramic pot with minimal effort within the palm of his hand. "Perhaps that is why you've been grumpy." He gave her a wink.

Ivory placed her hands on her hips. "Perhaps you should start drinking tea more often if that's the case."

Dovian's smile faltered. "About earlier...." He shook his head as he brewed the tea.

Ivory took a seat on one of the stools beside the island. She ran her hand across the smooth marble surface. The kitchen was a little worn, but she could tell it used to be something magnificent. Eyeing the man, she frowned. She pitied him greatly, but she didn't want him to think that she perceived him to be weak.

"Don't worry about it, Dovian," she whispered. "I can't imagine all the things you've been through. I don't think anyone in this world can ever understand what you've gone through and what you are currently going through. But I want you to know...I'm here for you. I want you to talk to me, alright? Don't keep secrets from me. Don't bottle things up."

She stared at the colorful blobs intertwined in the countertop and gave a small shiver as her wet undergarments chilled her. A porcelain cup gently slipped in-between her hands, the warmth calming her. Funny, she didn't feel the cold or the heat as if she were a regular human. Instead, her readings created a false sensation within her. Was she capable of feeling anything at all or was it merely artificial stimulation and response?

Dovian sat on a stool beside her. "And I want you to do the same," he said.

Ivory lifted her head. He gave her a tired look. She wondered if maintaining any emotional stability was draining for the man.

"I'm trying my best," she said. "I want to be here for you."

"I appreciate it, Ivory. I know I must be rough company. Being alone for thousands of years has only made things more difficult to deal with, especially when being thrown into social situations once again. Not that it is unpleasant. I sometimes get lost in my thoughts. Imagination and memory were the only comforts I had all this time." Dovian sipped his tea.

Hector waddled up to him, planting his head on Dovian's foot. The man pulled open a side drawer and grabbed something wrapped in parchment paper. Ivory watched as Dovian spoke. He instinctively undid the wrapping around the treat and handed it to the reptile. He only paused a moment to tell Hector to share the dried meat with Petey, which the lizard did, but with reluctance.

"As I get lost, I find it hard to pull myself out of the pit of darkness. It consumes all. Sometimes I'm locked into it like a trance, and I don't realize I've barely moved, eaten, or said anything for days. Though who to talk to other than myself and Hector? If I'm not talking to myself, then there is something certainly wrong." His cockeyed grin formed; his youthful face returned. He was trying, and Ivory appreciated the gesture.

She grabbed his hand. Dovian flinched at the touch at first, but the tense muscles in his chest and neck finally relaxed, and he ran his thumb over her knuckles. It had been so long since he even shared casual contact with another person's skin. Physical contact was once an ordinary, everyday thing for Dovian. Hugs and kisses shared with family and friends were a constant. Chatting and giggling was common practice. Interaction was a necessity. Everyone shared everything whether it was words, laughter, tears, or just simple, unspoken company.

"Don't despair, Dovian," Ivory spoke softly.

He looked hurt, fighting within himself to keep calm.

"I've lost it all…" he whispered. His eyes glistened in the pale light of the lit lanterns above them.

'*Oh dear, don't cry,*' Ivory thought. She didn't think she could handle seeing Dovian cry. It was already taking all she had not to give in and hold him and cry with him.

"I had it all, and then I lost it all," he mumbled, a single tear falling from his eye. "My paradise…." Dovian quickly palmed the wet stain on his cheek. "And I still cry about it as if I'm a child," he grumbled bitterly.

"There's nothing wrong with that!" she said quickly. "Dovian, you are strong. You have lasted this long, and despite everything you've been through, you hold yourself together fairly well."

He scoffed. "Hardly."

"You had fun with Petey, Hector, and I today, did you not?" she asked.

Dovian nodded. "It was fun."

"So what got you sucked in?"

Dovian looked at his cup, watching the tea swirl in a circular pattern. "I was thinking about happier times. Days where there was no impending doom lingering on the doorstep. Days where my biggest worry was whether or not my students will turn in their homework. Days where I wondered if I could gather the courage to hold a conversation with I'Lanthe without looking like a fool. Simple days. A time that no longer exists."

"We could make it that way," Ivory suggested.

Dovian lifted his gaze. "As much as I want to, I can't help but blame myself for this whole mess. You don't belong here, Ivory. This whole world is on the verge of destruction, and I am doing nothing about it. I'm sitting in a kitchen drinking tea and…playing house."

Ivory's face fell. He was absolutely right. Still, his words hurt for some reason. She was at a loss for what to do. Could she ease his pain, or was she only hurting him more? If the world did end up the way Sapphire wanted it, would the two of them even be able to live with one another? Could they accept their fate as being cowards who allowed the world to be consumed by Hell? How could they live with themselves?

"I'm sorry, Dovian."

He was silent.

"I wish I could bring all of that back for you, change the past, and prevent the future. I wish I could send you back to a time where you were happy and lock you there for an eternity. You don't deserve any of this," she said.

"You owe me nothing, Ivory," he murmured.

"I owe you everything! You've saved me numerous times, showed me kindness, and filled me with hope..." she hesitated. Love. He also filled her with love, but she couldn't say that. Those were words that he needed to hear from I'Lanthe, not her.

"Hope for what, Ivory?" Dovian stood from his seat. He dug through the cupboards, pulling out random spices and jars of liquids. He gathered an assortment of vegetables from what appeared to be a refrigeration device. Sorcēarian technology was strange but seemed to last through the ages.

"Hope for the future, Dovian. Not Sapphire's future, but our future," she said. Ivory watched him a moment. "What are you doing?"

"Making soup. It helps take my mind off of things." He began slicing some potatoes and carrots, tossing the bits into a large pot. "And what is our future, if not for Sapphire's way?"

"You, me, Hector, and Petey..." she stated hopefully. "Aria and Troy, too."

Dovian looked up at her. That actually sounded quite pleasant. It would be a good start. But what about throughout time? What would Dovian do after Aria and Troy were gone, after everyone he knew once again lived out their lives?

As if understanding Dovian's thoughts, she continued. "I'm an android...I can last. I can live in this dead world with you. We can bring it back to life," she stated with determination. A small, breathy laugh passed her lips. "I may need some repairs now and then, but I think we could make it work."

"Every relationship has its quirks," Dovian said jokingly, only it sounded more sarcastic than anything. Did he not like her idea?

"Of course...I can't replace what you've already lost," she added.

Dovian heavily dropped the knife onto the countertop. Ivory was startled by the sound. He was avoiding her stare again.

"I should learn to stop bringing it up," she whispered.

"You should," he agreed.

Her eyes cast downward to her hands.

"But not because I do not like you mentioning her. It is because when you say things like that, you are diminishing your self-worth. You are more valuable than you know, Ivory. Much better and stronger and smarter than you think. You are a stunning young woman, and you have an excellent, wonderful future ahead of you. So stop devaluing yourself. Got it? You're beautiful." He pointed the knife at her, his eyes blazing. "Say it...."

"Say what?" she asked, intrigued by his behavior.

"Say that you are beautiful."

"No!" she gasped, looking down again.

"Ivory!" he shouted.

"I..." she started.

"You are beautiful," he repeated. "You matter."

"I...I can't," she laughed sheepishly.

Dovian looked at the ceiling. "I'm beautiful!" he shouted. "I am *beautiful* and I *matter*!"

Ivory giggled.

Dovian grinned. "Ivory! I am marvelously beautiful!" He theatrically held a hand against his chest.

"You are!" She nodded, breathless from her laughing fit.

Dovian lowered his eyes, pointing the knife at her again. Ivory quickly gathered herself, staring at the tip of the blade.

"I'm..." she hesitated.

"You're what?" he asked.

"I'm beautiful," she sputtered quickly and quietly.

"Noooo..." he drawled, shaking his head.

"I'm beautiful!" she shouted. "I'm BEAUTIFUL! Okay?"

"You're beautiful!" he said it again. "And?"

"And I matter!" she yelled. Ivory laughed, covering her face in embarrassment.

"So damn beautiful," he mumbled, staring.

She eyed him carefully.

Petey squawked from the hallway as he was much too large for the kitchen, his snout sniffing the air.

"Petey is beautiful, too," Dovian muttered, stirring in some liquid to his concoction. He rolled his eyes to the ceiling and quickly added, "And Hector. Hector is gloriously beautiful."

A different, smaller squawk replied. Dovian smirked and nodded, stirring.

Ivory continued to watch the man as he prepared their soup. Every so often he would speak to himself, sometimes even argue. The lizards would chime in, and Dovian would respond as if they had actually spoken. It was an entertaining show. It calmed Ivory. Some may have thought Dovian to be an odd bird, but he was actually quite incredible. He lived life for thousands of years and had found interesting ways to cope. From how he laughed at a funny-shaped potato, to the way he spoke Legacy as he created a flame to heat the pot—everything Dovian did was interesting. As long as he had no reminder of the past, he functioned quite well and innocently enough. She wondered if it was due to his Sorcēarian genes that he remained so passive during his more private moments.

"Soup," he announced as he set the bowl down before the woman.

"Smells lovely." Ivory sniffed the food.

"Haven't heard you use that word in a while," Dovian said. He twirled his spoon in his broth.

"Haven't had much of a use for it lately. Until today, that is. Everything about today was lovely. I really enjoyed the lake outside." She tasted the soup, blowing on it first. She nodded in approval. Dovian smirked as he watched her. "You're so talented," she mumbled.

"It gets rather bland when you eat it as much as I have," Dovian replied. He cleared his throat. "Wintertime." The word threw Ivory for a loop.

"Hm?" She tilted her head.

"You'll enjoy the lake during the wintertime as well," he explained. "It freezes over."

"But then you can't swim in it," she stated.

Dovian's eyebrows rose. "No, it's best if you don't swim in a frozen lake, however…you can ice-skate."

"Ice-skate?" she curiously asked.

Dovian nodded, sipping from his bowl. "You seemed to enjoy the ice and snow while in Cherno. I think you would enjoy the winter months here even more. I can teach you to ice-skate." He noticed Ivory's lost look. "It's a form of…dancing one might say…but with blades on your feet."

"Blades on their feet?" Ivory wrinkled her nose at the thought.

"Like knives. You balance on them atop the ice, and then you skate across it–dancing, twirling, or falling on your backside…whichever you're best at," he elaborated.

"I can imagine you are a flawless skater."

"Oh…not at first."

"You fell?" Her eyes enlarged.

"Of course; everyone falls." He folded his arms. "I just happened to fall a lot."

"Who taught you?" She immediately regretted asking questions about his past.

"My mother," Dovian said quietly. "She taught me, and then I taught Lita. Lita taught I'Lanthe."

"Was I'Lanthe any good?"

"What do you think?" His tone told her everything.

"She was perfect, wasn't she?" The woman chopped a bit of potato into smaller pieces.

"In my eyes she was," he replied softly.

Ivory sighed. How could she even compare?

"But that was a long time ago," he added.

"You don't have to push her memory aside for me, Dovian. It is what it is. She was an important part of your life."

"I wouldn't be half of who I was without her," Dovian whispered.

"Was?"

Lowering his gaze to the lumps of vegetables in his bowl, he replied in a low voice, "I died that day. A large part of me left with her and never returned. Not sure if I'll ever retrieve it again, but there's certainly room to grow. Love doesn't simply end. It transforms, turns into something new."

"Do you still love, Dovian?"

The man was silent. He looked genuinely perplexed as if he hadn't thought about it before. "Not for a very long time." His youthful visage now appeared mature and hard. The light in his eyes dimmed, and he looked at the woman next to him. "And not until recently."

Ivory took a deep breath. He apparently did feel something for her and the others, there was no doubt about it. Still, she wondered about his motives. "What will you do?" she asked.

"I will do what is right."

"Which is?"

Now the big question was at hand. What was Dovian doing? What was he going to do? Would he allow the annihilation of his friends and the entire world?

"I will know when the time arrives." He abruptly stood and gathered his bowl.

Ivory snatched his wrist. "Dovian. Don't leave me in the dark on this. I need to be ready for whatever is to come." She was becoming more severe in tone, her eyes hardening as she trapped him for once in her icy stare.

"I'm playing this all by ear." He swallowed hard.

"That's not good enough," she said in a harsh whisper.

"Who…who's talking to me?" Dovian clenched his teeth together, looking at the floor.

"You can't leave us in the dark. You have to tell us what is going on," Ivory said, her voice translating into Legacy. Dovian nearly didn't recognize the language.

"If we speak in Legacy, she won't understand," Dovian replied, watching Ivory carefully.

The woman shook her head, sighing. "It's hard remembering the other languages after all this time," she said, her voice flowing back into English.

"Lanthe?" Dovian questioned slowly.

"Who do you think?" She lifted her head, giving him an eyebrow raise.

Dropping his bowl onto the counter, Dovian rushed to her, gripping the sides of her face and kissing her. Every moment with her was pure gold. He wasn't going to waste it, no matter whose body she was occupying. His hands ran down her sides, gripping her hips tightly. His kisses moved from her lips to her jaw, traveling to her earlobe and neck.

"Dovian," she gasped.

"I need you," he hissed.

"Not like this," she said.

Dovian halted, holding her firmly against him. Her hands ran through his hair; her nails lightly trailed down his neck and shoulders.

"Please," he begged.

"Not like this," she calmly whispered.

"You have no idea…."

"I do," she reassured him. "This is hard for me, too, but we can't do this."

"Why do you leave me?" He held her tightly, nearly squeezing the air out of her. Their foreheads pressed together.

"I can't help it. I'm working on it, but I can't just take over her whole mind. It's broken, Dovian. I can't be whole."

Dovian lifted his head, growling at the ceiling above them. "Why?" He closed his eyes.

She planted a soft kiss beneath his chin. "Patience. Just keep doing what you are doing. You will have me soon enough. Until then, remain strong. Follow the path that will lead you in the right direction."

"And what is the right direction?" he asked, resting his forehead on her shoulder.

"You know the answer to that," she whispered, running her hand through his hair. She held him, gently swaying back and forth.

"Tell me...."

"I won't," she denied him.

"Stay with me...."

She could barely manage a whisper. "I can't."

"Lanthe," he started, tying his hands around her waist.

"Shh," she shushed him. "Just rest."

Dovian obeyed, allowing her to hold him. He had no idea how long he had stayed that way. In fact, he had drifted into a light sleep for a while. When he awoke, he gave a twitch, lifting his head a little from the woman's shoulder. They were still standing, swaying. Dovian wrapped his arms around her torso, hugging her.

"*I love* you," he whispered.

The woman abruptly stopped moving. He could feel shaking hands on his shoulders and the tremble of her body against his.

"She...she's gone," Ivory whispered, her voice cracking.

Dovian quickly pulled and turned away, his fingers tightly gripping the sides of the countertop.

Ivory stared at his back. "I'm sorry," she said. Her voice quivered, threatening to break her resolve.

Dovian didn't have to turn to know there were tears in her eyes. In fact, he heard her heart break as he remained silent. The sound was a high-pitched gasp—the struggling sound of Ivory trying to regain air in her lungs. He knew that feeling. It was the sensation of a sinking heart that caused the chest to deflate, making it impossible to breathe. It was a soul-crushing pain that felt as if there would never be any relief. He didn't mean for this. He didn't mean for any of this to happen. Ivory did not deserve this kind of treatment.

"No, I'm sorry," he managed to get out between his shuddering breaths.

He was met with silence. Dovian turned, staring at the dark doorway that led into the halls. Ivory was gone. The swinging of the double doors took her place, banging against the stone walls of the cathedral. A moaning wind howled, sweeping cold air into the kitchen. Dovian slammed his fist against the marble countertop, sending cracks down the side. He held his head.

Thunder rolled.

"Conflicted"

CHAPTER 8

Dovian leaned on the island of the kitchen, his hands gripping the sides of his head. How could he have screwed up so badly? How could he have hurt Ivory like he just did? What was he going to do about this whole situation? He wanted I'Lanthe. Now that she was awakening more frequently and was showing awareness, Dovian wanted her more than ever. But what about Ivory? What was he going to do about her? He had developed a trust for the blonde, and she had done the same for him. Still he managed, despite all his efforts, to break her heart. The day had been going so well, too. For the first time in nearly a week, he had felt a small amount of joy. Yes, he did enjoy her company. He liked the sound of her laugh and getting caught in her lingering gazes and bright smiles. She was beautiful, but how could he love her? Especially with I'Lanthe trapped inside her mind?

It was entirely his fault. He had plenty of time in his life to prevent these events. He had plenty of time to secure the future of humanity, yet he stood by and did nothing. Living out his days in a fit of misery and self-pity, Dovian did absolutely nothing to preserve mankind, to preserve his race. Now, he was running out of time. If he didn't make things right, he would undoubtedly see the ruin of everything for which he sacrificed his race. Would the death of his friends and family be in vain? Would he be able to live with himself in a world full of regret and pain?

The questions, once again, were too many. Dovian had no answers, and he had no idea which route to take. Had everything he done so far lead up to this point for a reason? Was it supposed to be like this? Perhaps humanity was destined for destruction and this whole time spent alone was Dovian's punishment for going against the order of things. Maybe this was the time to make things right, to wipe the planet of its disease and allow his race to reign supreme and create a perfect world. Except that wasn't Sapphire's actual plans; Dovian knew that. How could she promise him a new world like the one he had nearly fifteen thousand years ago? No. Sorcēarians would not reign supreme. The world would be consumed by the souls of the damned, by Sapphire's demons, and the empty vessels of the biomechanical androids would be inhabited by those who were no longer allowed into the heavens.

Dovian lurched forward, feeling sick to his stomach. He hadn't felt pain like this in a while. Groaning, he fought with himself to contain his anger, his frustration, and his sadness. He wanted to tear Ives down brick by brick, burn the yards, and scorch the sky with his pain. After a few minutes of spiraling through his mental illusions of destruction, Dovian centered himself and brought his awareness back to the kitchen where he was idly standing. Why was he feeling like this?

He gasped, his eyes widening. Of course. His back apparatus was gone. There was no filtration to his energies. What had been created when Dovian was a mere child could become his downfall. Sure, the device had saved him countless times from releasing his boiling rage and had prevented the destruction of many civilizations, but what had it trained him to do? Dovian spent his life with a crutch, something to help support him through his rough days and emotional breakdowns. Now he was a danger not only to himself, but to everyone around him. There was no telling what Dovian would do, what he was capable of doing.

A small hiss sounded from the corner of the room. Dovian looked over his shoulder to find Hector slipping backward into the hall, his golden eyes narrowing, his pupils dilating. Petey stood, allowing Hector to cower beneath him. A low guttural snarl rumbled inside the giant lizard's chest. Dovian furrowed his brow, looking the opposite way to gain sight of what had their attention and sent them into a state of alert. The silhouette that occupied the doorway of the kitchen stilled Dovian. Pushing away from the counter, he took a firm stance, pulling his shoulders back.

Lightning flashed, revealing the foyer outside the kitchen. Beside the doorframe was a tall slender form covered in golden sleek scales. The creature gave a hissing growl, its jagged teeth parting to allow a strand of drool to fall onto the floor. The yellow glow cast from the lanterns in the kitchen caused a glittering dance of light to creep across its skin, giving it the appearance of being made of fire. Black eyes watched Dovian. It didn't move to attack but remained still and fearsome in its position.

"What do you want?" Dovian murmured.

The creature couldn't speak but lifted its jaw slightly, letting out a breathy sound. The room was humming from its presence. A dark energy flowed from the creature. Dovian's hands balled into fists. He could feel that the monster had not necessarily come to cause him harm, but rather was a type of message—Sapphire's calling card.

In another flash of lightning, the creature was gone, the doors slamming against the wall. Dovian's skin crawled with goosebumps. He hated the demons. The longer he stared at the absence of the creature's presence, the more he wished he had taken out some of his pent-up anger on the beast. It wasn't like Sapphire couldn't find another one. He would just have to do that later once he arrived in her cave. For now, he needed to put on his robes and get on with his life. No more playing house. Dovian had a mission. It was time to stop dragging his feet.

"Pete, Hector," Dovian said in a harsh tone.

The two lizards stood at alert, watching Dovian with anxious eyes.

"Find Ivory. Go to her. Protect her. Do not let a single beast near her," he commanded. He looked over his shoulder at the reptiles; his eyes glimmered like the sun, heat emanating from the orbs. "She will not be harmed."

With a loud grunt, Petey trudged forward, his long talons digging into the marble. Hector followed closely behind, his tail wagging from side to side. Petey crashed through the double doors, nearly breaking the whole wall. The loud thuds of his footsteps pounded with the thunder as he valiantly moved toward the grand building housing Ivory.

Dovian moved after them, his black wings sprouting from his back.

The noise of warfare rumbled, the booms vibrating the rundown hospital. Aria looked out the window. She could see Kovacevic's men backing slowly toward their city walls. Feyette's army was relentless. They weren't going to last long. She heaved a loud sigh, unknowingly the tenth time she had done it in the last five minutes.

"Will you quit doing that?" Troy asked, annoyed.

Aria looked back toward the man seated across the room from her. He sat in a cushioned chair, looking a little worn. His arms crossed over his chest; his eyelids were heavy as he fed her an irritated glare.

"Stop what?" she asked with a huff, air passing through her nostrils.

"That!" he said. He ran his hands through his hair, his biceps flexing. "You've been making that damn breathing noise nonstop since we got here!"

Aria glowered. "So I can't breathe?"

"You can breathe! Just do it…I dunno…more quietly?" he asked, gritting his teeth.

Aria returned her attention to the battle, giving a groaning growl instead. She was unusually irritable today. "I hate sitting in this stupid hospital while Kovacevic's men are out there getting slaughtered."

"He told us to stay here," Troy said. "So we're staying here."

She raised her hand toward the window. "They are dying, Troy!" Aria griped as her hand dropped into her lap.

"And you want to just run out there and die with them?" he asked.

She folded her arms, her fingers tapping against her skin.

"Look at you. You haven't even changed your clothes!" he said.

"Neither have you," she fussed.

"Eh, well…I have clothes ON!"

Aria glanced down at herself. She was still wearing her workout gear from the previous day. She had at one time been wearing her matching jacket, but the heat of Saray seemed to be burning through the hospital. Since Euclid stole the reactor, Saray had to rely on its natural reserves for energy, but it was only to be used sparingly. Thus, the only things cooling the hospital patients were thin fans in the ceiling.

"He's right you know," James called out.

Aria's eyes widened; she scooted forward, pulling her chair with her so she could sit next to the bed James was laying on. His body was hooked to an assortment of wires and machines. One unit was feeding oxygen into his lungs; another was dripping fluids, and a third was filtering his blood. He had a raging blood infection, and if they had waited any longer, many of his vital organs could have shut down. Needless to say, James Clarke looked like death would take him anytime soon. Still, his caramel-brown eyes glistened in the light. He was a fighter. He wasn't going to let something like a fragmented incendiary burst take him down. It didn't help calm Aria's nerves though. She worried about him. He wasn't young anymore.

Aria grabbed his hand. "Why do you always take his side?" she asked.

Clarke smiled; the tubes in his nose moved slightly as he gave a nasally laugh. "Because he sometimes takes my side."

"Only when he's lecturing me," she pouted.

"Hey! You lecture me nonstop! Let me give it while I can," Troy interjected.

Aria gave the younger man an ugly face, sticking out her tongue.

"Attractive…" James muttered, pinching her cheek.

Aria smiled.

"You do look tired." James squeezed her hand.

"I didn't want to leave your side until I knew for sure you were alright," Aria said softly. She gave a loud yawn, trying to hide behind the back of her other hand.

"I don't need you to be risking your health for an old man like me," he huffed.

"You would do the same for me." She shrugged.

"Well, now that I am awake and appear to be fine…why don't you get yourself cleaned up and settle into that rather uncomfortable looking chair for a nap?" He gave a weak laugh, the sound rattling in his chest. It caused him to have a harsh coughing fit, his hand flying to his mouth.

"James! Don't…don't laugh." Aria stood and filled a cup with water.

James quickly composed himself, his white face turning red. After a few slow deep breaths, he had the fit under control. He accepted the offered glass of water and quickly downed the contents.

"I will have to remember to remain serious until I recover," he grumbled.

"Just don't say anything. I don't want you to tear anything. Your lungs are damaged enough; we can't have you coughing like that. Just rest." Aria filled up his glass again before heavily dropping into the seat beside the bed.

"Aria. Go shower and take a nap," Troy grumped.

She glared at him.

"Grayson and I will watch over James." He gestured toward the bodyguard standing in the corner of the room. "Seriously…you need both desperately!" He plugged his nose.

Aria's whole body tensed. "I do not!"

"Oh yeah, your attitude and body odor both stink!" He made a face.

Troy knew Aria all too well. He could tell she was exhausted, and who knew how much longer they'd have to rest before they were called to action. She was also prissy when it came to certain things like her appearance and hygiene. Despite spending most of her life in the military, Aria's root behaviors were greatly influenced by the first nine years of her childhood living as an elitist civilian. She had proper tendencies that Troy often made fun of her for.

Aria self-consciously sniffed herself, wrinkling her nose. She eyed Troy, and he gave her a quick nod.

"Gah! I hate you!" She quickly stood from the chair and snagged her luggage.

James gave a smile of approval at Troy, trying not to chuckle.

"I'll be right back! You come find me if anything happens!" she sassed.

Troy turned in his chair, watching her head for the hallway. "Eh, I could come with you…help you out. Ya know…in case you drop the shampoo or something."

Aria gave a loud laugh, not even looking back at the man.

Troy cringed, momentarily forgetting James was in the room. He slowly locked eyes with the older man. To his surprise, James looked humored by Troy's response.

"If you two don't stop with your antics, I'm going to start laughing, and then you'll have to find me some new lungs," James rasped.

"Sorry, sir. I'll be sure to keep my mouth shut," Troy murmured sheepishly.

"Ha!" James coughed. "That's funny."

Aria smiled as she walked through the sterile hospital. James seemed to be in good spirits, and that was enough to make her giddy. She gave another deep sigh and frowned at herself. The sound *was* annoying.

Thanks, Troy, for making me aware of that,' she thought.

Aria entered the ladies' washroom, lazily heaving her luggage onto a bench inside one of the private showers. She groaned, rubbing her tense shoulders as she closed the door of her section with the swing of the hip. Yes, a warm shower sounded very nice.

Snapping open her suitcase, she rifled through the things–sweaters, tank tops, jeans, shorts, bras, underwear…even the lacy kind, and a swimsuit. Sure enough, Aren had packed as if she were going on an extended vacation. Aria dug out her toothbrush and her comb; she even found a bottle of her favorite perfume. Aren had thought of everything. Pawing through the case a couple moments longer, Aria scoffed. Well, almost everything. Aren forgot one basic necessity for a woman–her feminine products. Aria pondered a few seconds. What the hell day was it? How long was it since the last time? She shrugged. Despite Troy's belief that Aria was a bit prissy, she didn't have a knack for womanly things such as makeup, fancy hairdos, or something as simple as a mental calendar to remember 'that time of the month.' Oh well, it wasn't as if she needed them now, but when the time came, she'd be sure to send Troy and Aren to the market to pick up some of the essential items. The thought made her laugh.

Removing her clothing, Aria shivered in the cold. She quickly started the shower, picking at a few of the buttons and switches on the wall panel to select her preferred shampoo, body soap, and lotion. Once the water was at the right temperature, she slid under the pelting fall. She gave a moan. The water was warm and gave her a light massage. Oh yes, she could get used to this. Taking a mental note of the brand name scrawled across the selection panel, Aria thought about how she'd like to remodel her bathroom to make room for something as luxurious as this. It surprised her Saray even had a facility like this inside the hospital. Outside, the whole city seemed rather rundown. Her thoughts traveled to Kovacevic and how dirty he looked upon their arrival. Perhaps fancy showers were considered to be a necessity in a land full of sandstorms and endless war that covered the city in a cloud of dust and debris. Aria shuddered. Why the hell was she thinking about Kovacevic while she was in the shower? She could almost hear his sinister chuckle.

Aria's brow furrowed.

'Wait a minute…' she thought.

Aria pulled her head to the side away from the gushing water. Sure enough, she could hear whispering and quiet laughter. She spun around, catching a head dart down behind the privacy of her shower door. She gasped, covering herself.

"Kovacevic!" she snarled.

Stamping forward, Aria wrenched open the door, not caring to cover herself up.

"Is this what you wanted to see, you pervy old man?!" she growled. She gave another gasp as she heard another man shriek. "A-Aren?!"

Standing in front of her was Kovacevic waggling his eyebrows as he chomped on a cigar. Beside him was Aren; his back quickly turned to her as a hand covered his eyes. Aria grabbed Kovacevic's arm, pulling him around into a headlock, covering his eyes with her hands. The man gave a small laugh, relishing in the feel of her wet chest against his back.

"Miss…Miss…Aria!" Aren stuttered. "My, my apologies, ma'am! We have an important meeting to attend ASAP, and Troy said you were in the showers. We, I…we, uh…." Aren looked over his shoulder and made another squeak as he saw Aria still standing in the nude, using Kovacevic as cover. He quickly shielded his eyes. "I tried to stop him. I really did."

"Uh huh," she muttered doubtfully. Giving Kovacevic a rough shove toward Aren, Aria slid back into her shower room, slamming the door behind her. "Give me a few more minutes; I'm almost finished," she called over the sound of the rushing water.

"Y-Yes, ma'am," Aren meekly said.

"Need any hel–" Kovacevic started.

"No! Get out!" Aria screamed.

She could hear the loud shuffling of the men's boots as they ran out of the bathroom, their whispers and laughs echoing against the walls.

"Last time I listen to you," Kovacevic grumbled. Aren's protests were cut short by the closing doors.

Aria rolled her eyes, heaving another one of her irritated sighs.

Although the shower was warm and inviting, and Aria's relaxation was cut short, she couldn't wait to go back out on the field. She could primp and prime herself once the war was over.

Turning the shower off, Aria quickly dried herself under the heating unit. Warm air whooshed around her, blowing through her hair. She threw on her typical military garb, ran a brush through her locks, and frowned at her reflection in the mirror. The heating element had fluffed her hair out like a wild mane. After a few failed attempts at smoothing the black and blue tresses, Aria gave up and gathered her luggage, stomping out the door.

She and Troy were caravanned to city hall where Aren and Kovacevic were already in the process of having the large vid coms setup, a video crew running back and forth to prepare for an emergency broadcast. Aria eyed the nervous Aren atop the stage. He was fidgeting while Kovacevic rambled to one of the personnel. The auditorium was full to the brim with civilians and military alike, all murmuring to themselves in curiosity. Whatever Kovacevic had planned, it was big.

"Aria! Troy!" Aren called out, waving the two militants over.

"What is going on?" she asked, feeling scrutinized beneath everyone's stare.

"We're about to go live. Kovacevic is going to give a full report…and the feed will be worldwide!" Aren said. His eyes were bugging out.

"What?" Troy asked, amazed. "We're going to be broadcast all around the world?"

Aren nodded. "Yup! And you and Aria are going to be doing most of the talking."

"Wha-?! I…I ain't…I can't…" Troy stammered.

Aria put a hand on the man's shoulder. "Easy, Troy. Guess that means I'm doing the talking."

"Kovacevic has released tons of video evidence of the attack on Saray. He plans on letting the entire world know about Walten's involvement with the demons. He thinks that if we can reveal the truth, he can stop the wars between our allies and Feyette's armies," Aren explained.

Aria took a deep breath. "It's a good idea. I hope it works. Too bad I don't have the data on my DNAIS."

Aren tapped his wrist. "Don't worry about it! I got that all handled. I copied everything, remember? And not only that, but I was able to tap into the security feed in the Underbelly. I've got a lot of friends down there. Know the right names and you can get anything. I've got the airport feed; the church was still broadcasting when the attacks began, and we even have photographs from the local newspaper! A lot of people died, but those that survived are hiding out in the mines beneath the city. We not only have footage of Feyette's men killing innocent people, but we have proof that his team was working together with Sapphire's monsters! It's too good an opportunity to pass up!" The pilot pulled out a pamphlet from his back pocket. "Also, I was able to work up something with those printing presses in the lower city. We got *tons* of pamphlets made that reveal the truth about Walten's involvement. I took what I could from your DNAIS and wrote out a brief explanation of the events starting with the 66th I.R.B. up to the point where I saved your asses from that giant on Ives. It's been printing for days on end; the sheet's being mailed to every residence in the City of Fountains. If we can't convince the world, perhaps we can start an uprising against Walten."

"That's great, Aren!" Aria exclaimed. She shook his shoulders. "You are the greatest!"

Troy nodded with a stupid smile on his face. "You're just too good to be true, man."

Aren rubbed the back of his head; an awkward grin formed. "Um…thanks!"

"'Ey! You kids going to stand there all day?" Kovacevic shouted. "We're getting ready to broadcast! Git yer asses up 'ere!"

Aria and Troy quickly hopped up onto the stage. Aria took Kovacevic's side. He gave her an eye up and down and chuckled quietly. The man behind one of the recording devices started the countdown before they went live.

"Just as I imagined them to be," Kovacevic muttered lowly. His eyes flickered to Aria's chest.

"Better remember it, cuz it ain't happenin' ever again," Aria said through closed teeth as she faked a smile.

"Let me buy you a drink later, and perhaps I can persuade you otherwise," he said, his cigar bobbing between his teeth.

Aria scoffed a laugh. "Nothing could get me drunk enough."

"We're live!" shouted the cameraman.

Kovacevic took a step forward, grabbing his cigar. "Ladies and gentlemen, General Kovacevic of Saray here! Sorry to interrupt your fag-tastic television shows about mentally-retarded celebrities, but there are more important things goin' on in the world." He puffed on his cigar, looking at the recording droid dead in its zooming eye. "Such as the violent battles threatenin' to take down the walls of Saray!"

The newsfeed was overrun by images of the war outside Saray's walls. Feyette's team relentlessly demolished hordes of Kovacevic's men and robotic soldiers.

"Those are my men out there…" Kovacevic grumbled.

The screen flickered to reveal warfare in Roma and Cherno. All around the scenes were debris and dead soldiers.

"And those are the dying soldiers of Roma and Cherno!" he added.

Images slid by one after another of screaming civilians, children lying beneath crumbled buildings, and heavy mechs destroying anyone and everything in its path.

"Looks like Feyette's men didn't get the memo on the rules of warfare. Those are innocent people out there…dying." Kovacevic stepped back, holding a hand out to Aria, Troy, and Aren. "But it's not just my men and my allies out there dying. Looks like Walten's private military also has a beef with his own people of Fountains!"

Aria took a step forward as Aren clicked away at his DNAIS, pulling up numerous projections.

Aria cleared her throat. "That's correct. Cherno had nothing to do with the attack on the Underbelly. Neither did Saray nor Roma. I was there the day the Underbelly was destroyed. In fact, Walten had sent Feyette's team on a search and destroy mission. He wanted me and Troy dead," Aria said. Troy nodded beside her. "He wanted to capture Dovian, the last Sorcēarian, to clone his DNA in order to create an invincible army to wipe out his competitors. Not only that, but Walten had plans to kidnap our friend, Ivory, who was a citizen of the Underbelly. Turns out, over the years, Walten's been stealing corpses from the Underbelly and using them to create biomechanical androids!"

The room thundered with gasps and low murmurs.

"All the people of the Underbelly have been receiving urns full of dust, not the ashes of their loved ones!" Aria shouted.

"Where's the proof?!" someone shouted from the back of the room.

Aria frowned. "You want your proof?! Here's your damn proof!" She turned to Aren, signaling to him.

The pilot expanded one of the projections, the footage revealing the Underbelly of Fountains. It started in the midst of the chaos, Feyette's men already unleashing war upon the city's civilians. Some of the citizens had their own weapons. Others were running for cover but were mercilessly gunned down. Somewhere a frag was thrown, sending the video feed into static. Aren quickly enlarged a different projection, one that revealed the area near the church. The Soldiers of God were fighting, trying to rescue as many people as possible–mostly children. A flanking group of the elite fighters were charging Feyette's team at the edge of the airport. From around one of the corners were Aria and her team filtering into the facility, the citizens of the Underbelly covering for them.

"They helped us all," Aria said quietly. "The people of the Underbelly sacrificed themselves to save us."

Aren pulled up another image. Most of the feed he hadn't gotten a chance to look over. He had caught a few critical moments and had the battle scenes prepared, but he hadn't bothered censoring or picking and choosing particular segments. Any amount of the feed was shocking enough, but this particular section hit home with him.

"At the start of it all, Feyette and his men were after us," Aria said.

The images revealed the restaurant in which Ivory had hidden after she had met her sister, Fiona, and had her mental breakdown. The cameras caught imagery of Feyette's military rushing to the front of the building. A few seconds later, thanks to Dovian's powers, the side wall had exploded outward. Something blocked one side of the camera–a sniper from the rooftops. He waited until Aria, Troy, Ivory, Fiona, and Dovian were all out of the building and then fired one blast. The round hit Fiona square in the chest, killing her instantly.

Aren made a sound, his hand flying to grip his chest. Was he being affected by the feed as well? Aria looked at him from the corner of her eye. She admitted; it was shocking seeing it all, even after living through it. But she was surprised to see tears streaming down Aren's face. It all worked out for her and her team as the auditorium filled with more sounds of fury. The recording droid moved across the stage, catching Aren's distress. He quickly wiped a sleeve across his face, hardening his demeanor.

"Feyette had Fiona killed without a moment's thought," Troy spoke up. "Turns out she was Ivory's sister, and he didn't want her interfering. That blonde woman…." He pointed as Aren quickly composed himself and zoomed in on Ivory, who was screaming. She reached out for her dead sister while Dovian tried his best to pull her away from the corpse. "That is Ivory.

She is an Underbelly citizen who was murdered a year ago. Her body was taken by Bio-Tech Military Corporation and given to Dr. Camery. He turned her into a biomechanical android!"

Aren shook his head, a frown covering his face. He looked angry now. Terminating the feed, he pulled up another one that showed Ivory sniping from the rooftops. Dovian fought in the streets below while Aria and Troy took cover. Scenes flashed as Aren pulled out bits and parts that highlighted the moments of Dovian's capture. He exposed Feyette shooting the Sorcēarian in the head, Dovian's miraculous recovery in which he fought off the surrounding soldiers and disarmed Feyette, and the general finally revealing the truth behind part of Walten's plan.

"This is where he admitted that Walten wanted to clone Dovian's DNA. At the time, we had no idea what was so special about Ivory. That wasn't revealed until much later…when we journeyed to Ives," Aria stated. "Inside the cave system of Ives are all of the biomechanical androids from Dr. Camery's program that was supposedly shut down. An entity named Sapphire is pulling the strings, using her demons and the androids to wage war against humanity."

There were a couple of laughs and scoffs across the room, but mostly hushed talking from those who were watching.

Aren diligently continued. He pulled up photos from Aria's optical camera of the clones and creatures inside the caves on Ives. He followed up with the previous feed of the Underbelly. Once Aria and her team flew away from the city, Feyette's men kept fighting. A dark portal opened, allowing a flood of demons into the city. The civilians were outmatched, and the battle did not last long. Aren quickly pulled away from the newsfeed as the crowd's screams and shouts were picking up.

"Not only did Walten give the androids to Sapphire for her use, but he also unleashed her beasts onto his own city folk. He killed countless innocent civilians–fathers, mothers, and children." Aria turned to Aren. "Do we have any of that hospital feed ready?"

Aren nodded quickly. "Yes, ma'am."

The pilot pulled up a new segment that showed Euclid with the demons inside the hospital located on the top level of Fountains.

"And to all of you who are watching right now in Fountains…to all of you on the upper side. You think you're safe? Think again," she growled. "President Clarke was shot in the midst of battle and taken to a hospital in the upper city. This is what happened during his stay, by Walten's orders."

Once again, the projection expanded, revealing a panicked Clarke inside the hospital. There was a split in the screen, the second image showing soldiers in the hallway as they were torn apart by Euclid's entourage of demons.

"Walten doesn't want anyone to stand in his way. That's why Athenia was nuked. He ordered Euclid to pull out Athenia's reactor core and use it to blow up Cherno, his competitor. Instead, the core was sent back through the portal from which it came and inadvertently destroyed Athenia and Walten's new enterprise, Elixis. And that's why Walten is after us. We accidentally nuked Athenia because we were the ones who put the reactor back where it came from."

The crowd exploded into an uproar.

"We had no choice! It was either that or allow Cherno to be nuked and potentially destroy the entire planet. Trust me, if we had known the reactor was from Athenia, we would have tried to find a different solution. We were cramped for time, and the only thing we knew to do was put that reactor back inside the portal," Troy finally joined in, stepping forward.

"I would have done the same!" Kovacevic shouted. The auditorium quickly hushed, hanging onto the general's words. "These soldiers helped save Saray. They helped unify our city-state with Roma! They saved Cherno…sadly at the expense of Athenia. They are heroes…and our allies! There are always casualties in war, but we have a decision to make! Are we going to become casualties due to one rich little prick who is angry he didn't get that new toy he wanted for Christmas?"

There was a loud roar of 'no' among the crowd, mostly Kovacevic's men.

"Hell no!" the general hollered, puffing on his cigar. "Are we going to keep up with our allies and fight until that asshole and his little demonic friends are wiped off the face of the planet?"

A meek 'yes' sounded.

"What was that, you panty-wearin' sissies?" he snarled. "Did I hear a yes?"

Now the crowd was booming in affirmation.

"That's what I like to hear!" Kovacevic gave a rumbling laugh. "And how the hell are we going to do that, eh?"

Silence.

"I tell you what…let's have us a lil fun." Kovacevic spun on his heel, signaling to Aren.

The young pilot pulled up an image of Fountains. The screen zoomed in on the largest skyscraper in the city. It zipped right up to the top floor which contained a luxurious condo with a swimming pool and an entire wall made up of glass.

"Bio-Tech satellites…finest in the world. We can see *you*," Aren muttered, twisting the view to where it caught an image of Mr. Walten standing in the middle of his living room, gaping at the massive vid screen on his wall. Good, he was watching the live feed.

"Game starts now," Kovacevic said. "This is a search and destroy mission. Anyone out there man enough to take out this little douchebag will become a rich son-of-a-bitch. Won't be hard seeing as he seated his throne atop the largest building in the City of Fountains. A god among petty men," he scoffed. "Kill him, and pillage all he's got. Keep the riches for yourself. You do know he's the richest man on the planet, right? Go git him!" Kovacevic ordered.

The sounds of the auditorium were nearly deafening. People were cheering; others were shouting obscenities and death threats, and some were people of action–already packing their gear and heading out the door to prepare their hunt.

Kovacevic held his arms out, basking in the limelight. Aria folded her arms, giving a little smirk. Anarchy, she liked it. She eyed Aren again. He was staring off into space. For some reason, she figured he'd be enjoying himself a bit more.

Static filled the hall. The audience's excitement was cutoff as the broadcast was interrupted. Aren's projections terminated, and he confusedly tapped against his DNAIS. Behind the team, above the stage, was a large vid screen. It fizzled, casting its own image.

"Now, if you're finished having your fun…" a child's voice cut in. Aria and Troy tensed, spinning to look up at the screen. "I believe it's my turn."

Sapphire stood in the center of a room that appeared to be a conference hall of some sort. Floor-to-ceiling burgundy drapes decorated the walls. Golden chandeliers spiraled glints of light throughout the room.

"It seems that Aria and the others have already ruined the fun of introducing myself and have revealed my sadistic plan of destroying the world, but I remain a girl of class," she giggled. The laugh and child's mentioning of her name made Aria's hair stand on end. Doing a little curtsy, the girl cackled again. "My name is Sapphire, future queen of the world!"

There was barely a response as everyone watched Sapphire on screen.

"Oh, the sounds of confusion are growing all around the world." She lifted her arms, closed her eyes, and pretended to listen. "Euclid? You ask. What about Euclid? That mysterious man who was luring my pets into your city-state is dead, replaced by another who is much stronger."

Sapphire looked to the side, giving a short nod. She eagerly waved someone off camera toward her; a large grin was plastered on her face. Walking onto screen was Dovian. He moved slowly; his drawn hood cast a dark shadow across his face. Aria gave a sharp intake of breath, clutching Troy's arm. He tensed at her touch. The Sorcēarian looked fearsome as his black wings expanded from his dorsal side. He was a giant of menacing evil as he stood beside the child.

"I've got myself a Dovian! Remember him? The precious Sorcēarian who was going to save humanity? The one who allowed Feyette to get away, who allowed the destruction of the Underbelly? He's mine! And he's going to follow me to the end!" Sapphire cheered.

The cries and shouts were momentous in the room, and Aria's head spun.

"No," she mumbled.

Sapphire's smile faltered. Dovian's brilliant eyes cast through the screen, drilling a hole into Aria's soul.

"You're lying! He didn't allow any of that to happen! He's been on our side! You, you trapped him! You're holding him and Ivory captive!" Aria shouted.

Troy grabbed Aria's arm, telling her to keep quiet. Even though Sapphire was merely on screen, he couldn't help but feel she was still capable of killing them.

"Trapped?" Sapphire laughed. "Dovian's a free soul. You know what he is capable of. There's nothing keeping him here other than his own freewill! Right now, if he wanted to, he could teleport and be right by your side. You know this."

Aria swallowed hard. Was Sapphire right? She locked eyes with Dovian again.

"I don't believe you," she stubbornly hissed.

Dovian lifted his head, giving her a daring look.

"He stays because of a promise. The promise to revive his people, a chance to make the world as it was supposed to be–perfect and divine! Not disease-infested and full of war as it is now. The destruction of humanity is the solution, and Dovian will see to it that my plan is fulfilled. He and Ivory will repopulate the Earth!" Sapphire gave a shrill laugh.

"Repopulate?" Aria repeated the word. She felt her heart drop, realization hitting her. She knew about Dovian's inner turmoil, his desire to have I'Lanthe and his people back. Still, she couldn't quite believe it. She tried to find his eyes again, but his head was downcast.

"God left this world. He abandoned his people. He left the world for me to rule. There are only two options. Either you give up now, surrender, and I may spare your lives. If you do not backdown; if you continue to fight, I will destroy you all," Sapphire said, her tone lowering a bit as her eyes narrowed. "Backdown. Put an end to your useless fighting."

"We will never backdown," Aria growled.

"This is humanity's fight. You'll have to destroy us all," Troy added.

"Fine. That makes my job all the easier. It's what I want anyway," Sapphire retorted. "Fight all you want, but there is no hope. There never was any hope."

Sapphire signaled once again. There was a growl from off-screen, and only a moment later did a Brawler come into view, dragging a frightened Dr. Camery behind it.

"Oh, God…they've got Camery," Aria mumbled.

The Brawler tossed Camery onto the floor beside Sapphire's feet. The older man's blue-grey eyes widened as he noticed Aria and Troy on screen.

"I…I wouldn't tell her," Camery stammered. "B-but she already knows."

Sapphire stepped forward, her hand touching the man's head. He gave a quiet yelp as she stroked his hair. "In the basement of the vacation home. Unfortunately, there's a key code I need. I could break the glass, but…." She waited for him to respond.

"But, but you would alert the security device, and the whole thing will detonate, setting off the nuclear warhead inside," Camery whimpered.

"I figured it was booby trapped. Only a father would protect something so dearly." Sapphire leaned forward, her arms wrapping around the man. "Give me the key code, daddy," she sweetly spoke. Camery sobbed, tears forming at the corners of his eyes.

"I didn't want this. I didn't want this," he chanted, shaking his head.

Sapphire pushed away. "No, but you certainly made it possible. No matter. Dovian can retrieve the code for me. He has those incredible mindreading capabilities, don't you, Dovian?"

Dovian looked at her and then down at the scientist before him. Camery remained on his knees, his head shaking back and forth.

Aria watched anxiously. Her heart pounded.

'Don't do it, Dovian,' she thought.

Dovian reached out but then hesitated only for a moment, his eyes flickering up for a split-second. Sapphire's cold eyes were upon the Sorcēarian, and Dovian planted his palm atop Camery's head. The doctor yelped and then clasped his hands together before his chest.

"Think of the last time you opened the tank," Dovian said in a calm tone.

"I…I can't remember," Camery whispered, his eyes clamped shut.

"Four," Dovian stated slowly.

"No!" Camery shouted.

"Two," he listed a second number while Camery quaked beneath him. "No…think about the number, Camery."

"I can't," the poor man whispered.

"You kept the container in a separate room away from the rest of the clones. There was a code you used that dropped it down a chute into a van that took it away to your vacation home. Once in the home, you set up the security panel. What was the code?" Dovian waited a moment. "Four, two…" he waited, "six, nine."

Camery protested once again, trying to pull away, but Dovian held him in place, his second hand gripping his shoulder. A wry smile covered Dovian's face. It was like a game.

"One more," Dovian said lowly. "Four, two, six, nine…asterisk. How creative." He quickly removed his hand from Camery's head, and the man gave a quiet whimper.

"Good, we have the numbers," Sapphire gruffly said. "Now kill him."

Camery gave a squeal, his hands covering his face. Dovian gaped at the little girl, and she gave him a glare.

"No hesitation." The girl's hands balled into fists. "No hope."

Dovian slowly placed his hand on Camery's head once again. This sent the doctor into a sobbing panic, his hands clasping again as he whispered to himself.

"Oh, I'm sorry. I'm so, so sorry! Please forgive me! I didn't mean for this to happen! I didn't want any of this to happen!" Camery pleaded; his eyes tightly closed.

"No use praying now," Sapphire chided.

Dovian closed his eyes as well, his fingers pressing against Camery's skull.

"No! Dovian, stop! You don't have to do this!" Aria shouted.

"Can it, Aria. He obviously wants to do this," Troy snarled through gritted teeth. "He's double-crossed us." He sent a green-eyed glare to the Sorcēarian on screen.

"He's not going to do it. He's not," Aria whispered.

Troy grabbed her hand, and Aria bit her lip. "Don't be surprised, Aria. He has his reasons."

Troy was right. Dovian did have his reasons. She only wondered if she would be doing the same if the future of her race depended on it. In a way, she was. In order to save her race, she and Troy were going to have to destroy Sapphire and her demons…and destroy Dovian. The question was how, and could she? Could she kill Dovian?

'No. I don't believe it. Dovian isn't like this,' she mentally argued with herself.

"Please forgive me!" Camery sobbed again.

"Do you want to be forgiven?" Dovian mentally asked the doctor, unheard by anyone else in the world.

"Yes…Yes, I do," the man chanted aloud.

"Do you believe?" Dovian asked.

"I believe. Please, forgive me," Camery wept. "I, I don't want to die." The sounds of his pleads and weeping were horrible. It was gut-wrenching to the audiences around the world.

Sapphire looked upon Dovian in question. "Kill him already!"

"Then you shall live, Camery. All will be well with you," Dovian calmly whispered into the scientist's mind.

Camery's eyes opened, and he gasped; an expression of hope spread over his face. And Dovian frowned, his eyes pulsating with light. He tightened his grip on Camery's head, and the blue energy sped forth from Dovian's optics, down the length of his arm, and into the doctor. The energy burst throughout Camery's body, causing him to stiffen barely for a second. The only sound Camery made was a sharp intake of breath, and then his eyes rolled back. Dovian immediately pulled away, and Camery limply dropped to the floor with a loud thump.

Aria was as shocked as the people surrounding her. The whole hall was full of screams. She had not realized that her nails were digging into the back of Troy's hand, drawing blood. Troy turned his eyes away from Camery, looking at the woman by his side. He figured she was going to take this hard.

"Like I said, there is no hope," Sapphire coldly stated. "Surrender or die."

Aria raised her chin; her jaw clenched tight as she looked upon Dovian with an unreadable expression. The Sorcēarian coldly stared back, his eyes glowing brilliantly.

"Surrender," his voice echoed in her mind. The tone was low, quiet, and full of sadness.

'I won't,' she mentally replied. She didn't need to use her mental chip; he could understand her just fine through her thoughts.

"Don't look for me," he added. His black wings ruffled behind his back.

Sapphire stepped closer to the screen. "Walten, I'm calling you and your friends in for a private meeting." Her blue eyes darkened into black holes, and the vid screen abruptly went to static.

The whole auditorium was in chaos. People were screaming and shouting. The camera crew struggled to save their equipment from those who were running from the building, trying to get back to the supposed safety of their homes. What a silly idea, running away to hide. As if Sapphire would spare them all. She would just kill them once they surrendered. And even then, Aria didn't feel that that was what Sapphire wanted. No, she didn't want the humans to give up. She wanted them to put up a fight. She wanted them to suffer. It made the carnage all the more fun. Watching the enemy squirm beneath your feet and struggling to survive was always more enjoyable than watching them beg relentlessly for mercy or weep to stay alive just as Camery had right before Dovian murdered him.

Dovian, the sole survivor of the Sorcēarian race, the one meant to preserve humanity, had killed Dr. Camery without so much a second thought. Would he do the same with Aria and Troy? No, Dovian was not intended to save the human race. He was the arbitrator. He was their judge. He would be their downfall if he remained on Sapphire's side. The evil little girl was right. There was no hope. There never was to begin with.

"Losing Hope"

CHAPTER 9

As soon as permission was given, Dovian turned the dial of his frequency tuner. He just wanted to get out of the rotunda and away from Sapphire as fast as possible. Once traveling through the spindle of time, Dovian allowed his wings to carry him at a bursting speed. He didn't care how fast he was going and ignored the feelings of darkness and unbearable pain and sadness that engulfed the warp around him. Dovian held his eyes clenched shut. Home, he just wanted to get home. He needed to be as far away from civilization as possible. The blackness of space swirled around him, stars and balls of light flashing about as he traveled in the alternate dimension. The journey was much faster than he had expected. Once he was near his desired location, he twisted his frequency tuner again, appearing in Ives far off in the plush fields outside the desolate city.

Dovian frowned, trying to gather his bearings. He was too upset; he couldn't even travel properly. Shaking his wings in frustration, he pushed off the ground and burst into high speed toward his cathedral, a roar sounding from his movement. The plants flattened to the earth behind him as he propelled forward. Splashes painfully pelting against his skin, the rain threatened to cut Dovian to pieces as he sped toward the city. He didn't care. Faster, he needed to go faster. The cathedral was in sight, and Dovian covered his face as he prepared for the impact. He was too hasty. There was no time to slow, and the Sorcēarian crashed through the side of the building, bricks and marble shattering to dust. He tumbled and rolled, coming to a halt against the wall on the opposite side of the room. The impact crushed all the air out of the man's lungs.

Dovian moaned. Despite the violent entry into his home, he quickly pushed to his feet. Dust fogged around him as he stumbled into the hallway, trying not to give in to the lurching of his stomach. Dovian searched with nervous eyes as he tried to still the shaking of his hands and keep from throwing up his lunch.

Making his way into a small bathroom, Dovian halted at the sight of his reflection in the mirror. His eyes were glowing so brightly he could barely see himself within the darkness of the room. Covered in grey dust, he looked like a ghost. The man grumbled and quickly shook out his hair and robes. Turning on the hot water, Dovian hurriedly washed himself. He harshly ran his hands over his face repeatedly. When he looked into the mirror again, he cried out, seeing blood smeared all over himself rather than the wet powder from the collision. He heaved, gagging. Cupping the water with his hands, he rinsed out his mouth and continued his fanatical cleansing.

'Blood, blood everywhere. It's everywhere.'

He looked over his shoulder and shuddered, seeing dead bodies spread throughout the halls and scattered across the bathroom floor. Dovian blinked, trying to force the images away.

'They are all dead.'

From afar, he could hear the screams of the women and children, the moans from the people on the battlefield. He could feel the sting in his back from the removal of his apparatus. He could feel the pain of his dying friends; he could hear the sobs from those who were dragging themselves toward their loved ones, crying out their names.

Dovian shook his head, washing his face again.

'Not real. It's not real.'

Dropping his hands roughly onto the edge of the sink, Dovian leaned forward, staring at his white pupils.

"That happened a long time ago," he murmured to his reflection.

He caught movement out of the corner of his eye. Turning toward the doorway, Dovian instantly became a statue of ice. He erupted with a loud scream, falling backward into the old shower, hitting the back of his head against the stone wall. His eyes swirled with double vision as he made out the body of I'Lanthe standing in the doorway. She beckoned to the man, her hand waving him toward her. Her eyes were white with death. Her dark-brown curls stuck to the sides of her neck and shoulders due to the rain that soaked her body. Blood seeped through her purple robes. Dovian closed his eyes, trying to blink the vision away.

'It's not real,' he thought. Had he lost control over his powers? Were his illusions being brought to life by his own mind, torturing himself?

"Go to her," I'Lanthe's voice whispered.

Opening his eyes once again, Dovian shuddered as the woman was still there, her death stare upon him.

"She needs you," the woman's voice called again through her closed lips.

He ran his hands over his face, and as he looked back at the doorway, he felt a mixture of relief and fright wash over him. The ghastly vision vanished, but the voice called out once more.

"You need her," it said one last time.

Dovian sat in the shower, his long legs stretched out on the sides of the raised step. Silence consumed him and the room. He remained there, staring, trying to gather his breath.

Ivory was located only a couple of buildings away. She had heard the boom of Dovian crashing into his cathedral. Frightened, she rushed to one of the windows of the upper floors. From where she was, she could see a dust cloud billowing from one side of his home. The woman tightened her grip on the windowsill, the roaring thunder and gusting winds scaring her all the more. She wasn't sure what had happened, and she wasn't sure whether or not to go check up on the man. Was he alright? Perhaps he was attacked by some of Sapphire's monsters. Ivory wasn't positive, but the way the lightning flashed and crackled made her push away from the window. A loud huff alerted her, and she turned to find Petey in the dark room with her. Ivory heavily exhaled. The lizard looked a little perturbed at her for leaving the safety of her bedroom.

"I'm sorry, Petey," Ivory whispered, running her hand along the massive creature's neck.

Hector came sauntering in, rubbing against her ankles. She also gave him a pet behind his fringe.

"I'll try not to run off again," she said.

Feeling a bit tired, she sat on the ground beside the smaller lizard. He quickly curled beside her, trying to gather some body heat. Ivory frowned. She wished she could provide better warmth. Instead, she was a cold robot. Her body was full of icy steel and fancy alloys, wires, and churning hydraulic fluid.

"I'm a robot," she sniffled, trailing her hands up and down Hector's fringe. "How can I even compare to someone like I'Lanthe? How does an empty vessel like me compare to something as magnificent as a Sorcēarian? A beautiful Sorcēarian that Dovian loved on top of that. I...I can't." She shook her head. "I just can't."

Petey groaned and rested on the floor beside her. She leaned against the creature, her thoughts spiraling through her mind. After a small mental debate, tossing and turning over the memories that belonged to her and those that were I'Lanthe's, Ivory came to a simple solution. Why dwell on the issue? Her choice was easy. Clearly, she had feelings for Dovian. She wasn't going to help herself or Dovian if she continued on her clueless path of being Ivory, the girl with amnesia. She had to be I'Lanthe.

"I've made up my mind," Ivory whispered.

"And which mind is that?" Dovian's voice came from down the hall.

Ivory gave a gasp, jumping to her feet. A delicate hand rested against her chest.

Dovian walked into the room, running his shoulder against the wall as he came to a stop against the doorframe. He hid behind his hood, but his frosty gaze remained visible. Ivory swallowed hard, feeling a bit frightened by his presence. Was he injured? She didn't like the glare he was feeding her, nor the wrinkle in his brow. Placing a shaky hand against the frame, he straightened his posture.

"Dovian..." she spoke slowly, "are you okay?"

A menacing, quivering laugh fell past the Sorcēarian's lips. It gave her chills.

"I killed a man today," he casually stated. He held his hands out to the side, shrugging.

Ivory's eyes were like saucers. "Wha...what?"

"Dr. Camery. I killed Dr. Camery." Dovian inched toward Ivory. The lizards quickly scuttled out of the way.

"Why?" she asked, her voice high-pitched. "Why would you do that?"

Dovian scoffed. "Sapphire's orders."

Ivory held her breath as Dovian approached her. Gingerly, he touched her shoulders as he peered down at her.

"Oh, Dovian," Ivory whispered. She knew what that meant. He wasn't given a choice.

Placing his hands on Ivory's hips, Dovian pulled her against him. She nervously locked eyes with him.

"I saw Aria and Troy," he grumbled.

Ivory caught her breath.

"They are in Saray. They are not going to surrender," he explained.

She shivered under his touch. "What, what does that mean?"

Dovian kept his eyes on her face, making her uncomfortable. "I'll have to kill them later…whenever our paths cross again."

"No." She shook her head.

"Yes," he replied.

Ivory inhaled deeply. She glared at the man standing before her. "I won't let you."

"Fight with me all you want, but Sapphire will have her way."

"I don't care about Sapphire. I don't care about her stupid demons either. I care about you and Troy and Aria. I care about keeping our friends alive, keeping our relationship alive," she said as boldly as she could.

"I have to do as she says, to keep the war as far away as possible from you," Dovian murmured.

"Don't worry about me! I'm not worth the destruction of the world, and you know it."

Dovian narrowed his gaze. "I can't let you die."

"No…it probably would be best if I don't die, but I am more than capable of protecting myself. As I said, I'm not worried about myself; I'm worried about you." She wrapped her arms around him in return.

Dovian's grip on her waist loosened. He tried to retract from her, put she held him firmly in place.

"If I'm gone…who will make sure you make the right decision?" Ivory questioned.

Dovian remained silent.

"I need to be here by your side to make sure you make all the right choices. You are *not* allowed to destroy the world. You are *not* allowed to kill Aria and Troy, you understand?" she sternly stated.

Dovian stared at the dusty marble floor.

"You're a good man, Dovian. Don't let Euclid or Sapphire make you feel otherwise. That's what they want," she added.

"I'm not a good man. I've run away from humanity. I've tried killing myself over and again just to end the pain. I allowed the destruction of our race…my race. I've broken every rule. I'm cursed," he said.

"You're not cursed." She grabbed his face, forcing him to look at her. "Dovian, has it ever occurred to you that you are alive because you are meant to be? This isn't a curse. It's an opportunity."

He remained silent.

"You cannot allow Hell on this plane. I won't let you," she said in a low tone.

"And how do you plan on stopping me?" Dovian asked, his eyes returning to her in a daring glare.

"By reminding you why you didn't allow Euclid to go through with his plans before," she said. Ivory's voice dipped into I'Lanthe's vocals, and Dovian's grip tightened on her once again. She pulled his forehead against hers. "By reminding you of the most important thing we were brought up to believe in."

Dovian swallowed thickly, his pulse becoming erratic. "Which is?" he asked, almost testing her.

Ivory giggled. "Always the teacher…." She ran her hands through his hair and stepped onto her tiptoes. With her lips grazing his, she whispered. "Love."

Dovian didn't need any more of an invitation before he kissed her. She breathed in deeply, reveling in the feel of Dovian's lips against hers. Apparently Ivory's imitation of I'Lanthe was convincing enough as Dovian's hands were all over her, his kisses full of need. He pulled her hips against his, and she gave another moan.

"Dovian…" she muttered, feeling countless memories and emotions flooding through her.

She couldn't keep her breath. Quick gasps erupted from her as Dovian took to her neck, kissing and breathing near her ear. His hands fumbled for her belted corset, and Ivory grabbed the front of his robes, gathering his attention. He gave her a feral look, and she didn't waste any time for fear of him catching her lie.

"Bedroom," she moaned, the word sounding more seductive than she had intended.

Dovian made a similar sound and grabbed her hand, hurriedly leading her to the lower level where I'Lanthe's room was located. Ivory ran with him, trying to keep up. Her free hand was on her chest; butterflies fluttered in her stomach. She knew she was going to regret this decision, especially if Dovian found out that she was imitating I'Lanthe. Still, Ivory had to. He needed her to be strong for him, to be the woman he wanted. Ivory wasn't going to help him, but I'Lanthe could. And seeing and hearing the desperation in his eyes and voice was enough to break her heart. He needed her.

Rounding the corner into I'Lanthe's old room, Dovian immediately twirled Ivory into his arms, kissing her all over as he gently guided her backward onto the bed. She fell back onto the mattress and tried her best not to appear weak or nervous. But as he removed his robes and climbed atop her and met her with a kiss, Ivory's anxiety melted away.

She would hold up her front as best as she could…for Dovian's sake. Besides, she needed it, too.

Mr. Walten staggered into the hall, trying his best to finish tying his tie. He eyed the tall slender beauty next to him. She had a manicured hand on his shoulder as she led him. Despite her long dark hair, mocha skin, and fitted skirt suit, Walten was not captivated by her. In fact, he was deathly afraid of this woman. Her pink lips formed into a tight, suspicious smile. Bright caramel-colored eyes watched Walten as he struggled to smooth out his hair. He had to appear his best during this meeting. He wore his most expensive suit, his favorite exotic cologne, and had his checkbook with him. He was prepared for anything.

'Who the hell are you kidding?' he thought.

As if Sapphire gave a damn about anything he had to offer. He screwed up, and he screwed up badly. Not only had he upset the satanic child, but he was sure the rest of the world's elitists were fed up with his crap. Now that the truth was out, there was no one that Walten could trust. For all he knew, there could be a team of assassins waiting for him as soon as he passed through that rich mahogany door.

Eyeing the eerie beauty beside him, Walten nervously cleared his throat. He could tell this lady wasn't just an ordinary woman. She was sent by Sapphire to pick him up and bring him to the important gathering. There was something about her that was off, however. He shivered again as she smiled even wider, her white teeth glimmering in the light.

"You act like you've seen a *ghost*, Mr. Walten," her silky voice purred.

"I've just never seen you before, is all," he answered.

Catching her eyebrow raise and hearing the quiet scoff pass through her nose; Walten chewed on the inside of his cheek. This chick was an android, he just knew it. And by the way she was looking at him with her facetious smile and making little quips about ghosts, he was sure she was inhabited by one of Sapphire's demons. The thought was enough to give him chills.

"Well, sir…." She halted before the door, turning to face Walten. Walking to the man, she tightened his tie with a rough jerk, pulling his head up to look into her shimmering eyes. "Are you ready for your meeting?" she asked as she pulled away and grabbed the knob to the mahogany door.

Walten stood rigidly in his place, staring blankly at the door before him. Something was off. The whole room seemed to be exuding a negative energy. No, not negative, something evil. That door, with the woman's polished hand upon its golden knob, was an ominous entryway into the depths of

Hell. Walten was so screwed.

Clearing his throat and adjusting his vest, the young CEO nodded. The seductress smiled and twisted the knob.

"After you," she said.

With a hand spread across the wooden surface, the woman simultaneously pushed the door open and guided Walten inside. He looked upon her face, staring into her eyes as they seemed to flicker with amusement. She left an unsettling feeling within his gut. Nope, he did not trust her one bit.

Looking straight ahead, Walten was appalled by the ghastly sight; his heart nearly burst from his chest. It took a moment to register what he saw as he took a couple more slow steps, his eyes widening, his breathing coming to a halt.

"Wha...what is this?" he asked, deathly frightened.

He was in the usual rotunda where all of the elitists would gather, except the interior was remarkably different this time around. The rich wood-paneled walls were covered in gore. Mushy entrails were scattered and smashed against the walls, the dark reds blending in with the scarlet curtains that covered the floor-to-ceiling windows. There were stains all over the cream carpets, the once pristine color was marred with streaks of blood and crunchy bits of bone intermixed with what looked like brain matter. Covering the tabletop were strips of human skin. The chandeliers were swinging back and forth by the weight of the limbs dangling from the lights. Eyes, there were eyes randomly scattered throughout the room. Walten stared at the floor beneath his feet, lifting up one shoe from the blood-soaked carpet. The man swallowed back the bile rising in his throat.

"How do you like the new interior decoration?" Sapphire's voice called out from the front of the room. Walten's gaze tore to the black leather chair at the head of the conference table. It swiveled around, revealing the child. She nearly glowed beneath the golden light of the room with her white dress, pale skin, and blonde hair. The red surrounded her. As she spoke, it seemed the walls moved like red waves in the ocean. "My designers were very creative. They come from very far away, but their taste is rather charming, don't you think? I just love the color red."

Walten gagged, trying to keep his eyes from darting to the horrifying sights surrounding him.

"Where...where are the others?" Walten asked, holding a hand over his mouth.

Sapphire laughed. It was a piercing sound. "Why, they are part of the centerpiece! Rather lovely, I think. I finally found a use for those useless pieces of meat."

Walten glimpsed the gory chandeliers and fleshy debris on the tabletop. She had killed them all, slaughtered them like animals. Oh no, far worse than animals. They appeared to have been torn to pieces and blended up. Walten gagged, trying to walk toward the door.

He felt the tall, mysterious woman place her hands on his shoulders, steadying him.

"What's wrong, boss? Do you not like the new decorations? We worked so hard on them," she said in a mockingly sad tone.

"Let…let me go," Walten stammered.

"You're not going anywhere," Sapphire stated coolly.

The CEO's eyes darted back to the child. Clicking his thumb against his silver ring on his finger, Walten put in a distress call to Feyette and his team. He had no idea where Feyette was, but he needed his personal bodyguard right now.

"Wh-what do you want from me?" Walten asked.

"What do I want from you? Are you seriously asking me that question?" Sapphire was annoyed. "You have yet to withhold your part of the bargain, Mr. Walten. Why are President Clarke and his soldiers still running about?"

"I, I have tried my best. I've done everything I could! It's that Sorcēarian! He's gotten in the way of all my plans!" Walten explained.

Sapphire rolled her eyes. "I hate excuses, Walten. You couldn't even kill Clarke when he was lying in a hospital. You couldn't retrieve my body yourself. You couldn't destroy any of the other militaries. Instead, you allowed Elixis to be destroyed by your own people. That set my plans back by weeks. I could already have the world by now if it weren't for that little *misunderstanding*."

"What, what about Euclid? He failed on his part, too, and so did your demons!" Walten growled, his anger growing. "I've funded your entire war; I've given you all the tools you've needed, and yet you've done nothing for me!"

Sapphire stood from her chair, her body flashing to the edge of the table directly in front of Walten, her eyes black as night. The CEO jumped back, running into the door behind him. Sapphire stared at him, her dark aura making him feel physically ill. Red stained her white shoes.

"You have used me for your fame and fortune; you wanted your never-ending life of riches." The girl's tone was flat and dark like the day Walten had first met the black shadow that crept from the cavernous hole within the mines beneath Fountains. The voice creaked like metal as she spoke, her blonde hair blowing wildly about her face. "You didn't hold up your part of the bargain. I've given you more than enough chances."

Walten froze under her stare. "You…you promised us salvation. You said that God would bring his sight upon us once again if you were released. You said that once you started the war, He would return and cleanse the world and bring all of us to salvation."

A quaking laugh roared from deep within Sapphire. "As if He would come back to this miserable planet! When will you humans realize that He left you long ago? You're a disease. He doesn't want you. He never wanted you."

Walten's mouth opened and closed, trying to form words. Tears stung his eyes. "But…but you said He would come back for us. The plan was for you to merge the realms and allow your demons passage onto this plane. You said that God would come back for us. You said that you wanted a second chance. You were going to strike a deal with Him. You said you wanted salvation; you wanted forgiveness."

Sapphire's demeanor remained menacing, squeals and screams flooding from her form in a musical shriek. Walten cringed at the sound.

"Why should I give up what I want to go back to that place? He's had more than enough time to come to this world. He's not here. He's not been here for lifetimes. You've been forsaken. The precious, weak humans have been forsaken. Now, I'm taking back what is rightfully mine. I'm taking back my planet. This will be my home. This will become the home of the damned, and your race will be our cattle," a deep voice resonated from within the child.

Walten's lower lip trembled as he felt dozens of hands upon him. "I only wanted salvation," he whimpered.

"I AM YOUR SAVIOR. DON'T WORRY, WALTEN. THERE'S A SPECIAL PLACE IN HELL FOR YOU," the voice rang out.

Walten flinched at the sound of Sapphire's sinister laughter. He couldn't move, couldn't speak, and couldn't do a thing as his body pulled apart in all directions. His eyes were wide, locked onto the sight of the horrible little girl, his view spinning in circles as his head dropped onto the carpet and rolled beneath the table. The sound of his own death echoed in his ears, merging with the sound of Hell flowing from Sapphire's body. Walten stared at his mangled body parts scattered across the floor, his blood seeping into the carpet and curtains. He was tired and numb, no longer feeling anything for this world. Slowly, everything faded to black.

"The Meeting"

CHAPTER 10

Aria, Troy, and Aren occupied one of the rooftops of Kovacevic's military compound, watching the battle between Saray and Feyette's men. Things were beginning to look bleak. Aria stood while Aren and Troy sat beside one another, their legs dangling over the side. The two men were chatting casually, Aren digging into the hole in Troy's wrist where the DNAIS was located. The male soldier remained unfazed; his hand involuntarily twitched now and again as Aren poked and prodded the new chip he had embedded into Troy's skin.

Aria watched the battlefield, her jaw locked tight. One stray bullet from far off in the distance, a sniper round, exploded near her head. A blue burst of light erupted beside the woman, the invisible disrupter field sizzling upon the bullet's impact. She diverted her attention to the rippling electric wave only for a second before she eyed the battlefield again, her optic camera locking onto her target. The sniper was sitting atop one of Feyette's two-legged mechs. The machine heaved from side to side as it walked forward, its massive gun turrets blasting against Kovacevic's mechs. The woman highlighted the form of the sniper's heat signature and made a call to Kovacevic's men. Only a moment later did an automated drone speed above the enemy and drop a hefty bomb atop it, obliterating both the man and machine.

"Take that, you bastard," the woman grumbled.

"Aria," Troy called out.

She turned to look at her partner. He was leaning back, looking around

Aren to catch her green stare.

"Will you quit worrying about them? Kovacevic has it under control," Troy said, unconsciously scratching the forearm occupying Aren's attention.

"Don't scratch!" Aren shouted. "I'm almost done."

Troy muttered a 'sorry' as he gazed at his wrist.

"Doesn't mean I can't help a little," Aria grumbled. She turned her attention back to the fight.

Aren reached into his pack, digging through the mess of items inside. After a couple of minutes, he gave an irritated growl. "Gah! I can't find my capacitors."

Aria walked up to the pilot, taking a glance at the bag, her hands on her hips. "Want me to go check below? I bet Kovacevic has some lying around."

"Yeah; the quicker I can get these done, the better. Who knows how long we'll have before we have to move out," Aren said, still sifting through his stuff.

"I'll be right back," Aria said. She patted the boy on the shoulder and headed for the entry to the building.

"She seems a bit on edge," Aren mumbled.

Troy shrugged. "That's Aria. She's always on edge."

"I bet that the broadcast was unsettling, though, you know?" Aren directed his eyes to Troy's only for a moment. "Seeing Dovian kill Camery like that. Even I wasn't expecting it, and I barely knew the guy."

Troy's mouth twisted into a frown. "Yeah...I think that unsettled everyone."

"Were you expecting it?" the pilot asked. He grabbed Troy's hand, pushing on different pressure points.

"To be honest–Ow–" his hand involuntarily flexed, "I wasn't expecting it. I mean, Dovian and I had butted heads a little, but even then...I never expected him to do something like that."

"Do you think he really wanted to? He was with you guys this whole time. Did he do anything at all to make you believe he'd double-cross you like that?" the pilot asked.

Troy was quiet a moment. After giving an agitated sigh, he replied, "No...I did not suspect a thing. Well, I did have moments where I didn't trust him, but that was mostly because I was, well, kind of jealous of the guy."

Aren's eyes bugged. "Jealous?" He smiled.

Troy rolled his eyes. "Yeeeesss," he drawled.

"Fighting for Aria's attention, eh?" Aren asked with a little laugh.

Troy scoffed. "Who cares?! That's not the point. In the end, we thought he was our friend, and he evidently was lying to us the whole time!"

"That's pretty cold. I mean, he seemed convincing enough, I guess."

"Yeah. He was real convincing," Troy muttered.

The soldier was at a crossroads with his feelings on the subject. In the beginning, he didn't trust Dovian. He had even suggested that the Sorcēarian was on the other side, but he didn't actually believe his own accusations. Dovian was their friend. They laughed and joked despite his brooding behavior. Troy had drinks and cigarettes with the man. The two had even shared a hotel room, which they played cards and told dirty jokes all night while the women were asleep down the hall. Dovian was an okay guy–a bit odd–but tolerable. Not to mention, he had saved them countless times. He had healed Troy and had saved Aria's life when Troy couldn't. Truthfully, Troy had not expected Dovian to trade sides. Deep down in his gut, however, he still believed that Dovian didn't want to become a traitor. Surely there was a reason for his behavior.

"Don't know what to tell you," Troy began. "There were many times he could have double-crossed us. He could have left us for dead in the Underbelly. Instead, he got us out of there, even foiled Feyette's plan. It just doesn't make sense."

Aren's face fell. "Yeah…a lot of people died down there."

Troy watched the pilot, noticing his sudden distress.

"You knew a lot of people in the Underbelly, didn't you?" the male soldier asked.

Aren nodded slowly. "Originally I had enlisted in the army. I wanted to be in Delta like you and Aria. You guys were heroes!" he exclaimed. His expression quickly lost its cheer. "I went through basic and everything, and then my girlfriend begged me not to go."

"Girlfriend?!" Troy stuttered. He couldn't help sounding shocked by the revelation. He quickly corrected himself, Aren feeding him a questionable look. "I, um, you never mentioned having a girlfriend." He tried to do damage control, but he could tell Aren had caught Troy's surprise at the announcement of him having a girlfriend.

'Damn it, Dovian,' Troy mentally cursed the Sorcēarian for planting the idea in his head that Aren was gay.

"Yeah, girlfriend," Aren said slowly. "Damn it! You thought I was gay, didn't you?!"

"I, well…there was a rumor." Troy scratched the back of his head nervously.

Aren gave an aggravated growl. "That was one time! Jeez! How does everyone know about that?! I totally thought he was a chick!"

Troy's eyes lit up. "Sounds like you had a run-in with Lola and her she-male posse."

"I was drunk, going through a rough time, she…he…took advantage of me. I got out of there quick once I realized!" Aren stumbled over his words.

Troy laughed. He was ecstatic there was an actual rumor he could use as cover. "It's alright. Happens to the best of us."

"Lola is a scary…woman…man," Aren murmured.

"That she is!" Troy chuckled. "But what about your girlfriend? Lola didn't encroach on any of that did she? She knows better than to mess with taken men."

Aren shook his head. "Was during a time my girlfriend and I had momentarily split. She wasn't sure about my life choices. Said she didn't want to be with a guy who could potentially get killed at any minute of the day. In the end, she talked me into being a pilot instead. Sure, it's just as dangerous, but she felt better knowing I was in the skies instead of on the ground."

"That's a smart girl you have there," Troy said.

"Had…" Aren replied with a quiet scoff. "She was killed during the attack in the Underbelly."

Troy quickly lowered his head, giving a defeated sigh.

"God! You know how hard I tried to protect her?!" Aren shouted. "I supported her all through school. The kids were so mean to her, and I never understood why. She was beautiful! And she had a personality to match. Girl wouldn't even hurt a fly. But she was different…had blonde hair and blue eyes. She was even attacked once! Shot even! Why does that happen?" Aren fell silent, gathering his thoughts. "I joined the military because of her. I wanted to make a difference you know? Protect her somehow. And, in the end, I still couldn't save her. My own company killed her and covered it up with lies! And I wasn't there with her! I just think, if only I were there…."

"You can't think like that, man," Troy said. "Once you start doing that, thinking what if and blaming yourself, you lose not only as a soldier but as a man…as a human being. There are always casualties in war, and there's nothing you can do about it. You can just do your best at bringing down the bastards that caused the pain in the first place, the evil bastards that try to screw everything up for everybody else. Like Walten."

Aren nodded. Silently, he pulled on a chain wrapped around his neck. Hidden inside his shirt was a locket. Aren popped open the cover and a holographic image blipped. The girl in the picture had a large, bright smile.

She was beautiful. Her blonde curls framed her face. Even her blue eyes seemed to sparkle with life.

"That's her. I'll keep fighting for her," Aren said. "At least…at least you guys were with her in the end."

Troy gasped, grabbing Aren's locket, tugging the boy forward. He gaped in awe at the photo, nearly running his face into the image. The young woman was none other than Fiona, Ivory's sister.

"Holy shit!" Troy yelled.

"Holy shit, what?" Aria asked, walking toward the two men, a small box of capacitors in her hand. She eyed the photo Troy was scrutinizing. Her face quickly fell as she recognized the woman.

"I hadn't realized until I saw the security feed this afternoon that Ivory was the same Ivory that I once knew." Aren's eyes were bloodshot, tears trying to form in the corners. He quickly sniffed, fighting back his emotions.

"The security feed…" Troy groaned. "You saw her…." He didn't want to say more, but Aren nodded. "I'm sorry, man. If I had known Fiona was your girlfriend…I…we wouldn't have let you show that video."

Aria frowned. Now she knew why Aren seemed so upset during the huge reveal of Walten's plans. They just displayed Fiona's gruesome death to the whole world.

"No, it's alright. I knew she was killed. Just wasn't sure how," Aren said, the image disappearing back into his locket as he snapped it closed. "And I'm glad we showed the footage. It just strengthens my hate for Walten and that stupid little girl."

Aria took a seat beside the young man. She placed a hand on his shoulder, giving him a little shake. He fed her a weak smile. "We'll get 'em," she whispered as she handed over the small box.

Aren nodded, and within a couple seconds, he was back to work on Troy's wrist. Using little tweezers, he placed the tiny capacitor inside the hole in the soldier's wrist. A moment later, Troy's DNAIS popped up, recalibrating itself.

"Good as new!" Aren clapped his hands together.

Troy smiled, flicking through his items. "Ah! Even my little black book of numbers is still there!"

Aria scowled at him. She flung her arm across Aren's lap. "My turn?" she asked.

Aren grabbed her wrist, readjusting his micro-optics and zoomed in on her, trying to locate the pinpoint hole in her skin. "You two are slave drivers…" he grumbled.

"Welcome to Delta," Aria said with a cheerful smile.

"Welcome to Team Phoenix," Troy added as he stood up, watching the battlefield from afar.

Aria looked up at the man and then over to Aren, who had an open-mouthed expression. "Since you've already faked your death...." She nodded at him, and he gave a stupid grin.

"Cool," Aren said. That was one more thing to scratch off his bucket list. Never had he imagined he'd be working side by side with Aria and Troy of Bio-Tech Military Corporation and be considered one of their team members.

As Aren plugged away at Aria's DNAIS, Troy kept watch over the battlefield, keeping track of the numbers. He narrowed his eyes and cocked his head to the side. One of Feyette's massive shuttles was pulling back, calling in his soldiers. They were retreating.

"Hey! Check it out!" Troy pointed. "Feyette's pulling out his men!"

Aria watched as the rest of the shuttles pulled back, soldiers scurrying and rushing for escape. Kovacevic's men didn't relent. They kept pushing forward, hitting Feyette with the hard stuff. They brought down two of the large vessels; the rotors sputtered with sparks and explosions before the vehicles crashed onto the ground. Troy tallied up the death tolls. Five hundred and sixty-two were killed on Kovacevic's side, two hundred and eighty-four on Feyette's. Not too bad. Most of Kovacevic's military was still standing. His army had lost a lot of drones though.

Within minutes, the booming battlefield was nearly silent, and Feyette's unit was only a few flying dots on the horizon. A couple of shots would ring out here and there as Kovacevic cleaned up the combat zone, ridding the area of the enemy soldiers. He didn't bother taking any prisoners. At this point, Aria wasn't sure if she would have either.

"Wonder why they pulled back?" Aren asked. "You think we got to Walten? Think he called off the war?"

Aria's expression twisted. She was unsure. "I wouldn't ever think Walten would be the man to back down, especially when teamed up with Sapphire. I don't think she'd want him to retreat either. I dunno. Doesn't feel right. Something's up."

Just then, Aren put his finger to his ear. He looked deep in thought, nodding to himself. Aria watched him. After only a couple of seconds, he lowered his hand and diligently continued his work on her DNAIS.

"Clarke just called. He says there's an urgent call on his end. He wants us to meet up with him ASAP," the young man said. He held Aria firmly in place, not allowing her to tug away. "Almost done, just give me a sec."

He poked her pressure points, asking if everything felt alright. She quickly nodded as she tested out her elbow and digits. Aren pinched a capacitor between his tweezers.

"Just let me place this, and you'll be all set," he said in a strained voice as he concentrated on inserting the itty-bitty piece into Aria's chip. With a tiny click, Aria flinched as the item charged up. "Done!"

Aren and Aria stood; Troy had already gathered the scattered tools and dropped them into the pilot's bag. Together they marched downstairs to catch a ride in one of Kovacevic's buggies to the hospital, Aria tugging the war-hungry general along.

At the hospital, Aria was relieved to see that James Clarke appeared much healthier. He had color to his face, and his eyes looked less weary. Grayson was still in the corner, right where they had left him. He stood straight as a board, eyes locked on the doorway. He nodded at Aria and her group as they entered the room.

"What's up?" Aria asked, plopping into the seat next to Clarke's bed.

"I have an unusual call on the line. I figured you would want to be here for this conversation," Clarke said. He didn't seem amused, but there was something about the look in his eye that proved things were getting a bit odd.

"Who's on the line?" she asked, sincerely interested.

Clarke clicked onto his DNAIS, a projection hovering above the bed. A giant face fluttered on screen.

"Feyette!" Aria shouted.

The man on the screen jumped a bit at the sound of her voice. He looked in her direction, and Aria noticed his tear-streaked face. Had Feyette been crying? Now things were getting weird. Clarke let Aria do all the talking. Most likely, he already knew the details of what was going on.

"Ms. Ivanov," Feyette responded, his baritone voice quaking with nervousness.

"I noticed you pulled out your men. Dare I ask why?" she asked.

Feyette's twitchy gaze fled from Aria to the others gathered around her. "It's...Mr. Walten. He...he's been murdered."

Aria's eyes widened. She couldn't help the twitch of her smile. "Oh, really?" she asked, sounding more pleased than intended. "Did he have a run-in with some rogue assassin while he was drinking champagne on the rooftop of his castle?"

Feyette's glare typically could cut through anybody's soul, but it did nothing to hinder Aria's resolve. "I know you are enjoying this, *ma'am*, but perhaps you'd like the details before you start your celebrations."

Aria rolled her eyes, folding her arms across her chest. She waited, listening intently to what Feyette had to say.

"As much as you are apparently enjoying the news of Walten's death, I'd like to make it clear that it was not a rogue assassin, vigilante, or mercenary who had taken his head as a trophy." Feyette fiddled with his own DNAIS, pulling up a second screen. "It was Sapphire," he said in a haunted tone.

Aria stiffened at the sight of the security feed of the rotunda where the elitists held their meetings. The room was covered in human remains. Sapphire stood atop a large wooden table, her eyes locked on a frightened Walten. In a burst of red, the CEO was killed, his body ripped apart. Clarke gave an audible gasp, as did Aren.

"As you can see…it was a little savage." Feyette quickly terminated the security video.

The room was silent. The weight of the situation was nearly suffocating. Humans no longer had to fear each other. There was a greater threat– Sapphire.

"How does it feel, Feyette, to see the death of Mr. Walten?" Aria asked.

Feyette glowered at the woman.

"Aria!" Clarke reprimanded her.

She kept her stare locked onto Feyette's. "You killed a lot of innocent people, Feyette."

"By Walten's orders," Feyette replied.

"You know the rules! Walten or not, what you did was wrong!" she shouted.

"As his bodyguard and general to his army, I had to follow his orders," he quarreled.

"Ethics and morality go out the window when a rich kid doesn't get his way, huh?" she remarked.

Aria knew about Feyette's history. In the beginning, he was a respected soldier from the Underbelly. He had served and protected for many years beneath Walten's father. Feyette quickly became a general and had a world-renowned reputation for being a great and honest man. After the death of Walten Sr., and ownership of the company fell onto his thirteen-year-old son's lap, Feyette's reputation quickly tarnished. He followed all orders from the boy without hesitation. What began as a father and son relationship between the two had quickly turned into a disgusting display of power-hungry madness. The young Walten's requests for reign had given Feyette too much power. So much that Feyette had forgotten his roots. The day the

Underbelly was destroyed was the day the world lost all respect for General Jeron Feyette.

"I don't deny that the actions I've made these past few weeks have been less than acceptable by the guidelines of war. In the end, it is still war. And if I had refused, what would have happened to Bio-Tech? You all know very well what it's like to be branded as traitors," Feyette said.

"By Walten's false accusations! He was pushing the blame on us!" she shouted.

Clarke finally interrupted the little feud. "Arguing won't solve a thing. Aria, we all know Feyette is a piece of shit; can we move on to something else?"

Feyette looked to the President, his dark eyes widening. After a pause, the general nodded. Aria huffed and sat back in her chair, glaring at the projection.

"So, Walten's dead. What the hell do you want from us?" she asked.

"An alliance," he replied.

"What?! You want an alliance?! After everything you've put us through?" Aria asked, bewildered. "You've killed your own people, allowed Sapphire's demons to destroy the city you grew up in, and have started unjust wars all over the world!"

"And Fiona. He killed Fiona," Aren added.

"You ordered Ivory's sister to be killed," Aria stated in a deathly tone.

Feyette's expression made no change. He remained numb to her scathing words. "I'm tired, ma'am. I really am. I've had enough of all the fightin'. I'm tired of being a ghost. I've lost everything. And all by my own hands. Bio-Tech was my home. Fightin' was all I knew. Walten, well he was the son I never had. Sure, he was spoiled as hell, but it was my responsibility to make sure he grew up into the fine elitist that he was. I know he was a monster, but I would say that's because he was greatly misguided by his father's dying words. In the end, Walten was only trying to bring the Creator back to this world. He had plans to bring Heaven to us. As backward as his methods were, he undoubtedly has gathered some attention. He was only following through with his father's ideas. It was a dark plan planted in the boy's head when he was too young to understand how the world worked."

Feyette's tone lowered. "I know it isn't an excuse, but I've lost everything. Allow me to make up for the years I've done wrong in my duties. I've already sent out a peace signal to all city-states. I've got my higher-ups trying to negotiate alliances as we speak."

"And if we ally with you, what do you have to offer us?" Aria asked.

"My military. You have my army at your disposal," he offered.

Aria leaned forward. "You will take orders from me."

"I didn't think it'd be any other way, ma'am," Feyette agreed.

"What? We're actually allying with him?" Aren grumbled.

Troy grabbed Aren's shoulder. He nodded at the young man, his face dead serious. As much as the pilot hated the idea of it, he knew it was an invaluable option. They needed the whole world on their side.

"Is that all?" Aria asked.

Feyette lifted his chin, looking down at her. "Plans."

"Plans?" she repeated.

"I know what Sapphire plans to do next."

Aria clamped her hands together, a wry smile covering her face. Perhaps the man could prove useful to them. "And what is that, exactly?"

Feyette returned her crooked smirk. He pulled up a map for them to view. The southern part of the United Americas highlighted in red. As the map zoomed in, a circle marked around the Amazonian Desert, home to the largest resource of Earth's natural water. The Amazonian Desert also housed the giant water spigots that sprayed hundreds of millions of gallons of ocean water into the atmosphere each day as a way to tame the harsh solar radiation from the sun.

"Oh, shit…" Aria mumbled.

"I get that you understand what this means," Feyette said.

"Yup. I would guess that she not only wants to destroy our natural water supply, but she also wants to cook us slowly." The woman grimaced at the thought.

"Hmm…barbecue," Troy added his two cents.

"I…I don't want to be a hotdog," Aren muttered.

Kovacevic slapped the two men upside their heads, causing them both to groan.

"Sounds about right," Feyette continued. "I'm not completely up to date on the details. She usually kept her meetings private with Walten. As far as I know, she's more than capable of causing some damage down there. Not only that, but Camery had fashioned together a rather hefty Faze Shield of sorts, something capable of disrupting energy fields by at least fifty meters."

"Holy crap, what would she want with that?" Troy asked, rubbing the back of his head.

"All I know is…she's got more friends she wants to bring to this party. I don't know how many nor how big, but this is about to get messy," Feyette said.

"Sounds like fun." Aria stood from her chair. "Anything else we need to know?"

"If you want to stop her, you'd better plan on moving out soon. She plans on attacking first thing in the morning," he advised.

Aria set the watch's timer on her DNAIS. "Never a dull moment."

"I will have all of my men regroup at Bio-Tech. I will be announcing to the world in a moment the death of Walten and our agreed upon alliance." Feyette then looked over to Kovacevic. "Do I have your alliance as well?"

"Aw, shit…seeing as you killed a good number of my men today…" the general of Saray puffed on his cigar, "why the hell not?" He shrugged. "As long as you agree to keep the alliance permanent between us. I'm gettin' too old for this shit."

"Then it is agreed. From this day forward, Bio-Tech Military Corporation vows to cease all militaristic attacks against all other city-states and has joined an alliance with Saray. Do I have a concurrence with this statement?" Feyette looked to Clarke.

Clarke sat up in his bed. "I, President James Clarke of Bio-Tech Military Corporation, agree upon the alliance between Bio-Tech and Saray."

"And of those present in this room?" Feyette looked to Aria.

"It is agreed," she stated firmly.

"It is agreed," Troy followed. He eyed Aren.

"Uh…it's agreed," the pilot quietly replied.

"It is agreed," sounded Grayson from the corner of the room.

Feyette looked toward Kovacevic. "And does Saray agree?"

Kovacevic straightened his posture. "Seeing as, uh, Alijah Dizdarevic ain't around, and I'm the head of Saray's military, and it's been my men you've been killing, then I'll act like the man in charge. It is agreed."

"It is agreed," Feyette echoed. "I will follow up with peace negotiations between the other states and will get back with you afterward. My men are to regroup in Fountains and depart for the Amazonian Desert at 0500 this following morning. We will await orders upon your arrival." Feyette saluted.

Aria gave him a quick salute in return, and the call terminated. She silently remained in her place as she stared out the large window of the hospital room. So many people had died today, and just like that, the tables had turned. Seeing Mr. Walten's death on camera was a little unsettling and not simply because of how gruesome it was. It revealed that Sapphire wasn't playing by any specific rules. Her plan was still her plan, and now that nothing was holding her back, Aria feared the worst for humanity.

"Well…today has been an interesting day." She heaved a tired sigh. The sound grated on Troy's nerves.

"Damn it, woman! I thought I told you to stop making that noise!" He ran his hand across his forehead.

"Defending Saray"

CHAPTER 11

The sound of morning birds stirred Dovian from his slumber. Taking a deep inhale, the sweet scent of wet orchids and honeysuckle tickled his nostrils. The man sprawled across the mattress on his back; a warm blanket lay diagonally across his naked form. With his arm pinned, he turned to look down at Ivory, who was sound asleep. A tiny hand lay on his chest beside her squished cheek. Blonde curls coiled about her face and scattered across his torso. He couldn't help but give a smile. His arm was wrapped around her, his hand resting on the small of her back. She looked peaceful in her sleep; he didn't want to leave her side. Pulling the covers over her bare shoulders, he placed a gentle kiss atop her head.

Ivory made a little groan, twisting and pulling the covers with her, unveiling Dovian. He gave a hushed laugh and pulled his arm away, stretching. He had no idea how long he had slept, but he felt very chipper and at ease for a change. Taking another deep breath, he sat up in bed, scratched his head, and gave a low yawn. The blonde beside him did not move. He watched her for a moment, wondering if she was capable of sleeping and if she even had dreams. As memories of the night passed him by, Dovian's guilt returned. Had he pushed himself on the woman, or had she actually wanted him? He knew Ivory had feelings for him, but was she giving herself to him in an attempt to appease him in some way? Dovian gave a small scoff through his smile. Whether she was Ivory or I'Lanthe in her mind, it was certainly something he both needed and wanted. Ivory was as gorgeous as anyone could get, and her innocent behaviors were quite adorable. She would never have to ask twice to get Dovian into bed with her.

He scowled as he felt a bit repulsed by the idea, but then shrugged it off. Who cared? He spent long enough without having the company of a woman. He deserved a night or two of fun after all he'd been through. Selfish or not, he wasn't going to regret last night.

His stomach gave a gurgle, reminding him of how famished he was. The idea of breakfast in bed sounded rather pleasant. And as he thought of surprising Ivory with pancakes and watching her eat them while covered in a bed sheet, he grinned. Oh, she would believe it would be lovely.

Dovian slid off the bed and swept up his scarlet coat, pulling it around him like a bathrobe. Tiptoeing, he cautiously stepped around the sleeping Hector and Petey. As Dovian made his way toward the kitchen, soaking in the rays of sunlight that shimmered between the broken panes of stained-glass, he thought over the cupboard's inventory. Did he still have that old bottle of maple syrup he found inside the vacation home? As he strode into the kitchen, Dovian's simple, thoughtless smirk fell from his face. There was an intruder.

"Who the hell are you?" Dovian asked.

There was a woman sitting on the center island of the kitchen. She had a cup of tea in her hands, dipping a tiny bag up and down repeatedly. Her chocolate eyes flickered with amusement, her pink smile widening.

"Well, good morning to you, too," she said with a velvety voice.

Dovian glared at the woman. Her hair flowed to her waist like a black waterfall, half the strands dropping over the front of one shoulder. Her skin was of a darker shade. Tall and with an hourglass figure, she was exotic in appearance. The clothing she wore was like a glaring neon sign that read, "open for business." And her body posture only enhanced her sexual presence as she arched her back to stick out her full chest. The force of her bust pressed against the red and purple bustier pushed an ample amount of cleavage up toward her collarbone. She swung a long leg over the other; glossy leather with tall black heeled boots only completed the look of the whole costume.

"I'm not asking again," Dovian murmured.

The woman narrowed her dark eyes at him. With a clink, she set down the porcelain cup before hopping off the countertop. Her heels clacked against the marble floor. Dovian eyed her warily as she swirled her dark hair with a manicured finger.

"My name is Lilith," she said, wetting her lips. She kept her mouth parted slightly as she walked toward Dovian.

"How fitting," Dovian grumbled, not amused. "I assume you are one of Sapphire's pets."

"I'm one of her favorites," she said. "I guess you could say we are like sisters."

Dovian took a step back. The presence of the woman made him exceedingly uncomfortable. All he wanted was pancakes. Why couldn't he just make some damn pancakes and be left alone?

The woman laid a hand on his shoulder. Casually, she slung her other hand around his neck. She smelled like flowers and death.

"And if I'm Sapphire's sister…" she pressed into him, her hips grinding against his, "then I guess that makes you my daddy." Chocolate eyes full of lust peered over Dovian's face.

Dovian was locked in her gaze. She had nearly pressed her lips against his, her hand slipping low into his robes, when he stepped away and tightened his coat. He was pleased by her perturbed look.

"You don't want me?" she asked.

Dovian gave a rumbling chuckle as he stepped around the woman. "Lilith, there's nothing you can give me that I would actually want." Searching through the cupboards, he added, "And a venereal disease is something I would rather not risk at the moment."

As he reached for a bowl, the seductress snatched his hand. He eyed her cautiously; she had moved the whole expanse of the kitchen within a blink of an eye. The light in her eyes appeared void for only a moment; then they flickered back to life.

"Ah…you're a bionic. Figured as much," he said calmly.

Lilith pulled and twisted Dovian, slamming him back against the countertop. She firmly held his hands in place; her eyes were wild.

"I could make you my bitch, Dovian, so don't even try pissing me off," she snarled.

Dovian fed her an even glare.

"And I could decimate you without a moment's thought," he returned.

Her grip tightened so not to allow Dovian to wriggle away.

"You won't do that. As I said, I'm Sapphire's favorite. You destroy me, I'm sure she won't hesitate to do the same to you," Lilith said. The whole time she spoke, she moved against Dovian, trying to lure him into a lustful state.

"She can't kill me," Dovian said, attempting to ignore the way her body felt against his.

"No, she can, but only momentarily. Just because you'll come back again doesn't mean she won't try." She slipped her leg between his.

Dovian swallowed hard. Now that was true. Sapphire had already torn off his apparatus.

Reaching up again, pressing her full pink lips against his jaw, Lilith gave a breathy moan.

"Oh, come on, Dovian. Give me what I want," she pleaded.

"You weren't human before, were you?" he asked.

Lilith leaned back, eyeing him. "No," she replied quickly.

"So what do you affiliate yourself with? Succubus?" He paused, raising an eyebrow. "Incubus?"

The woman fluttered her eyelashes, digging her nails into the back of his hands. "What do you want me to be?" she asked near his ear.

"I want you to be out of my kitchen so I can make pancakes," he grumbled.

"Pancakes," she scoffed, "are much too sweet. I have something else you can eat."

Dovian rested his head back against the cupboard, closing his eyes in irritation.

"Come on, Dovian. I've always wondered what the real thing would feel like. Living in the depths for so long…you can only imagine the want and need I have for someone like you," she hissed.

"Not happening," he said.

"I've got the information you want. How about we trade?"

"There's nothing you can tell me that I would find valuable."

She gave him a mischievous look. "Not even about I'Lanthe, and why she was in the pit for the last seventeen thousand years?"

Dovian opened his eyes, nervously looking at the woman before him.

She gave a sinister laugh. "Oh, now I've got your interest."

"I'm sure nothing you say will be the truth," he muttered.

"Why was she *down* there, Dovian?" Lilith asked, sinking low. "Deception? Lies?"

As soon as she crouched and tried to open his coat, Dovian grabbed her by the arms and hauled her back up, glaring at her.

"I'm through with these games," he growled. "Get the hell out of my kitchen."

"Why does that blonde little whore get you? Why can't I have my turn?" Lilith scowled.

Dovian's grip tightened on the woman's arms. He did not appreciate her calling Ivory a whore. "You call her a whore again and you won't have a head left to do any sexual favors."

"Dovian?" Ivory's voice rang out in the kitchen.

Lilith grabbed Dovian, kissing him in his momentary distraction. Ivory entered the room, wrapped up in a bed sheet. She came to a halt in the doorway, her blue eyes widening. A quick gasp sounded from her. Dovian frantically shoved Lilith backward, the woman running into the island behind her. His eyes were crackling with electricity. Lifting his head, he looked at Ivory, a hard frown set on his face.

"Who, who is this?" Ivory asked quietly; her thin hands lifted toward her mouth.

Lilith straightened her top, tugging it down to where she nearly exposed herself. She sauntered toward Ivory and held out her hand.

"Lilith," she said with a sneer. Dovian abruptly slapped the seductress' hand away from Ivory's.

"Don't even touch her." Dovian glowered.

Ivory's shocked face turned into a glare of her own. Walking in on Dovian kissing another woman was shocking, and the sight hurt her, but clearly that was not of Dovian's doing. The blonde looked Lilith up and down.

"Don't know why Sapphire chose her anyway. She said I could have whatever I wanted. Why can't I have you?" The mocha-skinned woman returned Ivory's stare. "Just an empty vessel with a broken mind," she scoffed.

Ivory's hands balled into fists. "I'll show you broken!"

Dovian quickly slipped between the two. He took a slow, deep breath. "Leave, now." Lilith opened her mouth to say more, but Dovian wouldn't hear it. "Now!" he boomed.

Lilith clicked her tongue, eyeing Ivory and then Dovian. She spun and made her way out of the kitchen as she called over her shoulder, "Sapphire wants you to report to the throne room ASAP. We have work to do."

Dovian waited until the woman was out of sight before he relaxed his tense muscles. "Damn it." He exhaled gruffly.

"I don't like her," Ivory said quietly.

Dovian looked at her with a sad expression. "Sorry you saw that. She's a bit promiscuous."

Ivory shrugged. "I could tell you really liked it," she replied sarcastically. She stepped around Dovian, eyeing the tea Lilith had been drinking.

"Hardly," he said, clearing his throat.

Ivory's blonde curls were untamed, springing in all directions. She had a severe case of bed-head. Dovian smirked at his handiwork.

"So, you're heading out?" she asked timidly, pulling the sheet tighter around her body.

Dovian hung his head, nodding slowly.

She approached him again, capturing his face. "Please don't kill anyone."

"I don't have much control over that."

"Sure you do," she argued.

"Not if it's Sapphire's orders."

"Find a way around it." She planted a quick soft kiss on his nose.

Dovian grabbed her waist. "Would much rather stay in bed with you," he said with a husky voice.

Ivory felt a tingle at his words. "Oh, yeah?" she asked with a shy laugh.

He gave a little chuckle, swaying back and forth with her. "Oh, yeah."

It seemed pancakes would have to wait. Dovian hadn't mentioned anything to Ivory about the child's plans. Instead, he wanted to keep her in the dark. She was having enough trouble worrying about him; he didn't want her to worry about humanity as well, particularly Aria and Troy.

"I've got work to do," he said.

He gently let her go and turned away.

"Dovian?" She took a step toward him.

He looked over his shoulder, his eyes emitting piercing light. The sight was unnerving. He was already preparing for war.

"Please, be careful," she whispered.

He gave her a quick nod and entered the darkness of the hall.

The sun beat down its searing rays of light upon the Amazonian desert. The heat was intense, seemingly drying out every part of moisture in the surrounding lands. Troy opened the face shield of his helmet and wiped a bead of sweat from his brow. He could feel his skin baking inside the metal of his body armor. Though the suit was climate controlled, the desert's raging temperature was enough to make him want to peel off his protection. That would be a stupid mistake, as the spigots that spouted raging water currents blasted the atmosphere above and magnified the sun's radioactive waves.

On top of the sweltering heat and blasting rays, the humidity was still high. Unfortunately, the environment was a vicious cycle of scorched earth and humid air, leaving nothing for plant life to grow on the surface. Beneath, however, was an entirely different story. Far beneath the cavernous cracks and crevices sat a vast gorge of fresh water–Earth's largest supply. Among the waters was a plush ecosystem of moss and strange vines and saplings. The Amazonian desert was one of Earth's most protected sites. It was the final location that still held some resemblance to the ancient world.

"Well?" Troy asked, turning his head to gaze at Aria.

Aria narrowed her eyes, staring over the dead land. She found it hard to imagine trees and animals in a place like this. Though they were supposed to be waiting for the arrival of Sapphire's army, the landscape remained barren. She and Troy had been holding position for hours.

"Well," she responded, "either we're blind or Feyette's intel was wrong," she huffed.

"Why would he lie about the enemy's location?" The man rubbed the knotted muscle on the back of his neck.

"Who knows. Maybe it's a setup. A trap or something." She frowned and crouched. Her delicate fingers poked at the dusty earth. A rock crumbled beneath her touch.

Troy kicked at a pebble. "I dunno. It seems pretty quiet to me."

"That's cause you're an idiot," the woman harshly spat.

"Someone's in a good mood today." He rolled his olive eyes in response. "So what do you think, then?"

Aria glanced over her shoulder. "Can't you feel it?"

"Feel what?"

"The tension. Everybody's so quiet." She nodded toward the enormous army waiting nervously behind them. Troy followed her gaze. He had almost forgotten about the cavalry. Behind Aria and Troy stood nearly five thousand troops, a whole battalion of andronic-mechanized soldiers and mobile tanks from Saray, and a small air fleet that consisted of Feyette's best fighter jets. Overkill? Aria didn't think so. Not even close. But it was all she could gather in the short amount of time.

"It's like everyone's waiting for something big to happen. We can all feel it…well, everyone but *you*," Aria said.

"The only thing I feel is a yawn coming on." Troy opened his mouth and let out an obnoxiously loud moan.

"And that, my lovely friend, is why I am the one in command." Aria stood erect and patted the man on the shoulder.

"Cause you kiss a–" A sudden rumble quickly hushed him.

On the horizon was a flicker of distortion. The air pulsed and spun inward like static. There was a whooshing noise, and the disturbance blipped into a pin-sized hole of black and then flashed outward with a strange, high-pitched whistle. The ground unexpectedly convulsed. Aria stabled herself with a hand on Troy's shoulder. He quickly snaked an arm around her waist and held on. There was a thunderous sound nearly four hundred meters from the small army as the ground splintered and cracked, dark scars staining the surface. Aria's eyes flitted from crack to crack. With a sudden drop, the distant landscape sank and then exploded outwards, sending chunks of rock into the sky.

"Everybody on guard!" Aria mentally shouted her orders.

The land glimmered from its wound with red bubbling magma and steaming flames. It gushed as boulders and rocks were strewn about. There was a hum, the same familiar hum that Aria and Troy now associated with the sound of approaching death. A massive appendage flew from the gaping hole. It was a nightmarish scene, something they were all unprepared for. Giant fingers dug into the desert surface, the phalanges treating the rocky ground like it was clay.

"Holy…." Troy gaped at the scene.

There was an ominous vibrating sound; it was low, had two different tones, and was unlike anything the humans had ever heard. Aria and Troy watched in horror as an enormous being climbed from the hole, rock and magma pouring down its body like water. The creature screamed again. It had beady black eyes on a bald skeletal head. It had a level nose with flaring nostrils and a giant flat forced grin on its face caused by tight, almost transparent, skin. Slowly, the body rose from what was apparently Hell until its towering form stomped into the earth. The thing had to be at least thirty meters tall. It watched Aria and Troy with darker-than-black eyes and gave an enormous roar which echoed across the land.

"Look!" Troy pointed at the beast.

At first it appeared the massive creature had a small wing sprouting from one shoulder, but as the flame and debris slowly faded away, its silhouette revealed a much more shocking scene. Standing on the creature's shoulder was Dovian.

"Dovian!" Aria screamed. She tore away from Troy's grasp and darted toward the monster.

"Wait!" The male tugged her backward. "Look at him…."

Black scaly wings sprouted from the Sorcēarian's back. Shackles bound his wrists together, and what appeared to be a metallic collar was strapped around his neck, a large chain dangling from the back. A woman reclined on the monster's opposite shoulder. She grinned and laughed hysterically. Dressed in rather revealing garb, the strange woman eyed Troy as she traveled a decorated hand through her long dark hair, down her chest, and left it to rest upon a curvaceous hip. She opened her mouth slightly as she tugged on the chain in her hand, pulling Dovian slightly to the side.

"Uh, why don't you let me handle her?" Troy gave a cockeyed grin.

"Look at the way she handled Dovian…" Aria muttered.

Aria brought her glare up to meet Dovian's. Even at this distance, his defiant stare chilled her to the bone. But something was amiss. His characteristic pale-blue eyes now held a red glint. Dovian gave a flap of his ebony wings. The staring contest continued. Aria and Troy gazed upon the enemies ahead. The soldiers behind the two were anxious. Nervous whispers and the shifting of bodies and weapons sounded from every direction. Dovian looked over the army. He peered down at his ex-comrades and fed them a spiteful grin.

"Target number one," Aria said through her mental chip, *"…the Sorcēarian."*

She saw Dovian's amused smile widen. A shiver ran down her spine. The typical Dovian was nowhere in sight. This man before her was not the Sorcēarian she knew.

"What?!" Troy gripped his battle rifle tightly. "Are you insane?!"

"He chose his side, Troy," Aria grumbled through gritted teeth.

"Yeah, but–" He began but Aria shoved him roughly to the side as she took aim with her electrically charged rail gun with multi-grenade launcher.

"I'm bored…" Lilith groaned. Licking her lips, she tugged on Dovian's chain once again.

"Pleasure's mine." Dovian stated mindlessly.

The succubus of a woman sauntered across the monster's shoulders over to Dovian's side. She wrapped her arms around him, smiling as she unclasped the bindings at his wrists and neck. He gave her a sour look as she handed him something and patted his shoulder once, giving him permission to leave. With fists clenched tightly, Dovian's wings lifted him high into the air. He was fast, spiraling swiftly into the sunlight, his black silhouette casting a shadow across the desert floor. Aria and Troy shielded their eyes from the blinding light. Dovian wasn't wasting any time making the first move.

"Fire! Fire, fire, fire!" Aria shouted.

Bullets soared into the air, the sound deafening to ears all around. Dovian pressed forward as ammunition, EMPs, an assortment of projectiles, and even heat-seeking missiles missed their target. Aria and Troy frantically shouted commands through their mental chips. They had seen what Dovian could do and knew what he was capable of. Aria reassured herself that he was brainwashed. He would never do this. But there was something in the back of her mind that also told her that she shouldn't be so surprised.

Fa-boom!

The sound barrier broke as Dovian took off down toward the army. Aria froze, goosebumps chilling her as Dovian came right between her and Troy like a bursting gust of wind and annihilated the entire force behind them in one fiery inferno. Aria didn't have to look behind her to see the destruction. The deadly silence told her enough that it was best to keep looking forward. She shivered, suddenly feeling cold as Dovian floated ever so gracefully before her. With one quick movement, he grabbed her, tugged off her helmet, and snatched her chin forcefully to look up at him. Tears stung her eyes. Just like that. One move and they were defeated. They really were helpless fools.

"Hey!" Troy stomped forward. Dovian's hand went to the soldier's throat, and then he shoved him back.

"You want to defeat Sapphire?" Dovian shouted. Aria's lips sealed tight as she gazed fearfully at the Sorcēarian. "You have to destroy me first."

Dovian thrust something into Aria's hands, and he finally released his harsh grip on her jaw.

"They have Ivory…" Dovian said in a quiet tone. He looked to Troy. "Find a place deep underground. Find a way to kill me before we kill you." He gave one fleeting look at Aria and frowned. She was chewing on her lip, her mind repeatedly refusing him. Giving a moment to close his eyes, to force out the voice of her mental turmoil, he took a deep breath. "This is a warning for mankind." With that being said, he lifted from the ground and returned to the beast in the distance.

Aria watched as Dovian was shackled once again. The creature began to sink back into the Hell it had escaped. All the while, Dovian kept his eyes on the ground. Slowly, ash and liquid fire erupted from the opening until the monster and its riders were swallowed whole. Aria didn't notice the tears that slowly fell from her eyes. She gripped the item in her hands tightly, trying to console herself. Her sight fell onto what Dovian had given her.

"His back apparatus," she murmured. "It's been removed. That means he has no control over the power he can unleash."

Troy stared at the metallic spinal cord replica. The edges were covered in blood. It seemed to have been forcibly removed from his back. The thought made the soldier cringe.

"His warning was serious." Aria sniffled, turning to see the destruction behind her. A quick sigh of relief escaped her lips.

Dovian had merely managed to injure the humans but had destroyed the entire mechanical fleet, barely leaving any remains.

Aria felt Troy place a hand on her shoulder. She shivered beneath his touch and gave a whisper, "Just a warning...."

Another quake occurred; the tumultuous sound of creaking metal and groaning blended with thunderous rumbles. Aria and Troy spun around once again, looking to the giant water spigots that touched the sky. Each massive cylindrical spout began twisting and vibrating, ready to rupture. One far off in the distance burst, hundreds of thousands of gallons of water gushing back toward the earth, mixed with the sulfuric fire from the lower depths of the planet.

"Everybody move!" Aria screamed. She snatched up her helmet and placed it back on.

Waving and shouting, she and Troy called for the army's retreat. In minutes, the whole lands would be flooding with water and molten lava.

"*Aren!*" she mentally called.

"*On my way, ma'am,*" the pilot responded. The thumping of the Hawk's propellers was already nearing Aria's ears.

Another explosion of noise sounded followed by a second. Two more spigots were destroyed, the water rushing toward the militants like massive tidal waves. Aria and Troy kept pushing their men back, telling them to evacuate. One after another, black ropes dropped from the sky from the reinforcements that were waiting on-call in case of an emergency such as this. A few of the carriers lowered to the ground, taking in multitudes of soldiers from both Feyette and Kovacevic's armies. Aria and Troy each snagged their rope from Aren's copter. The water was already hitting their feet as they were lifted into the air. Only a couple seconds later and the land below was full, swirling with muddy waves of blue and red and black. Trillions of units of military technology and weaponry were destroyed.

Amongst the crashing waves, a large chunk of debris caught Aria's rope. Pushed by the fierce current, the enormous piece tugged at the cord, jolting her to the side. The Hawk revved as the weight pulled the aircraft.

"Aria!" Troy shouted as he reached out for her.

"Shit!" the woman cursed aloud, her hands slipping.

Troy clipped himself to his rope, lowered, and snatched the woman's waist, pulling her toward him.

"Hold onto me!" he shouted.

Aria grabbed Troy's cord, buckled herself securely, and wrapped her legs around his waist for extra measure. With one swipe, Troy drew out his military knife and cut through Aria's cable, finally freeing the Hawk. Aren overcompensated, and the copter violently shifted in the opposite direction, pulling Aria and Troy quickly behind. The swift tug jolted the couple, and Troy's buckle snapped. Detached, the man dropped, his hands gripping Aria's legs.

"Holy shit!" Aria groaned, locking her ankles around him.

"Damn cheap Bio-Tech merchandise!" Troy groaned, maintaining his death-grip on the woman's legs.

Beneath them, the Amazonian desert became an ocean; wild rapids and churning riptides swirled with deadly debris of broken metal and sizzling molten rock. Aria gripped her belt's nodules, starting up the fast-gear. With a buzzing whine, Aria and Troy sped up into the Hawk. The two clumsily fell inside, tripping over one another as they tried to untangle themselves from the ropes. Once free, Troy leaned out the side, looking at the chaos below. The sky was full of multiple silhouettes of fighter jets and hawks alike. It appeared that most of the men were able to get out before things got too messy, but as Troy squinted at the water below, a hard line set on his face. There were bodies floating and banging against the sharp debris.

"Well, there goes our water supply," he grumbled.

"Hopefully it's not completely destroyed," Aria matched his tone.

"Everyone alright?" Aren's voice called out.

"Peachy," Aria puffed, giving a wave to the pilot as she dropped into one of the chairs.

"You know…I never really got that expression," Troy said, plopping into the seat beside her.

Aria watched him a moment. His posture was lax, drooping in the chair. The armor looked heavy, and the way his helmeted head sagged, Troy looked exhausted. He took a deep breath, his hand resting against his chest.

"You feeling okay?" she asked.

Troy straightened up. "Yeah. *Peachy.*" He gave her a thumbs-up.

Aria leaned forward pointing at him. "How's your hip?"

"Fine," he sassily replied.

"Troy," she said in a motherly tone. She had a way with words where all she had to do was mention his name and the sound gave him a full lecture.

"Fiiiine-nuh." He folded his arms.

"Your heart?" she asked.

Troy exhaled in exasperation. "Woman," he growled.

"Hey, I just want to make sure you're fit for action. If your heart can't handle the stress or anxiety, I don't want you out there," she explained.

Troy suddenly stood, wiggling his fingers and waving his hands in the air.

He did a strange twist with his hips and a small cha-cha dance. "Fine! I'm fine! Dexterity, flexibility, stamina…I feel fantastic despite nearly being killed by raging waters and molten lava!" He dropped into his seat again. "Groovy, 'kay?"

Aria sulked in her chair, folding her arms this time. She didn't believe him, but he was as bull-headed as she was. "Fine. But if you die on me on the battlefield, I'm going to give you so much hell."

Troy gave a snort. "Like it'd matter; I'd be dead."

Aria gave him an even glare through her helmet that he couldn't see. "Dead or not, it'd matter, *Troy.*"

He frowned. "Okay, okay. I'll let you know if I ever have a problem, but it's no big deal. Really."

He fidgeted uncomfortably in his seat. He had to admit; things were a tad-bit weird between Aria and him since the events at Roma. She had been particularly moody, but also overly protective of him. He also had caught himself more than once touching and holding her when it would otherwise be unnecessary. But instead of shrugging him off as she usually did, she would reciprocate. Perhaps he was only now noticing their bond. They had grown up together, been partners since they were in their teens. But something else was up, and things were only getting more intense since their near-fatal departure from Ives. He shook his head. Obviously things would be different. Aria had a connection with Dovian. She was close to him and just like that; he betrayed them and left. As much as Aria wouldn't admit it, Troy knew she had quickly taken a liking to the eccentric Sorcēarian. And as much as Troy didn't necessarily approve of their short-lived relationship, Dovian was able to comfort Aria when he could not. That was probably what stung the most about the whole ordeal.

'Stress. Stress and crazy female hormones,' he reminded himself.

A beeping came from the vid com in the middle of the aircraft. Aria swiveled in her chair, pressing for the com to activate. With a flash, the screen appeared and revealed a split screen with both Feyette and Kovacevic's faces.

"Good, yer alive," Kovacevic sounded first.

"How are your men?" Aria asked.

"Haven't been able to get an exact head count yet, but I estimated that I lost about fifty men," the general from Saray grumbled.

Feyette's dark eyes shifted between Aria and Troy. "I estimate a total of seventy."

Kovacevic snorted. Feyette gave a glare, most likely directed at the other general.

"Sorry," Kovacevic started, "it's just…less than twenty-four hours ago, you were attacking my city."

"Well, now we are a bit more even," Feyette said in a flat tone.

Aria palmed her forehead. She forgot she was wearing a helmet and her armored hand made a loud clap when she smacked herself. "Can we just get past this? We have real enemies to deal with; we can't be competing with each other."

"Yes, ma'am," Kovacevic and Feyette sounded at the same time.

"So…what in the hell do we do now?" Aria asked.

Kovacevic and Feyette fumbled for a solution, looking every which way as if the answer would come from thin air.

"Great," she deadpanned. "Let's just meet up in Fountains. Kovacevic, your men can stay in our facilities. We've lost so many, I'm sure there will be room enough. Feyette, I expect your men to get along well with our guests. We're all humans here, fighting for the same rights."

"The right to live!" Troy cheered, throwing his fist in the air.

Aria looked over her shoulder and glared at the man.

"I'll put in a call to Clarke. We'll be sure everything is prepared for all soldiers and that a hot meal will be ready. We've all been fighting nonstop for weeks. Let's focus on boosting morale for the time being. Let the boys have some fun while we formulate a plan of action. Feyette, you will be giving us a full debriefing of everything. I want to know all about Walten and Sapphire's negotiations, all about Camery's work and his new devices he's created."

"Yes, ma'am." Feyette nodded.

"Good. We'll meet back at HQ. Call me when you're ready, and we'll meet at the President's office," Aria advised.

Troy waved his hand back and forth like a child in school.

"What?!" she snapped.

Troy slowly lowered his hand. "Um…President's office was destroyed by Euclid, remember?"

Aria groaned. "Just call me when you're set up, and we'll meet in the cafeteria or something! We'll play it by ear!"

"Yes, ma'am," both Kovacevic and Feyette agreed.

With a beep, the screen dissipated. Aria spun in her chair. Her posture gave away everything. She was glaring at Troy, and he was smiling back.

"You're a goddamn child," she growled.

"Colossus"

CHAPTER 12

The zipping of traffic lights was hypnotic. The trails of yellow blended with the shimmering flashes of neon lights throughout the expanse of the city. Aria's eyes were set on the landscape though focused on nothing. The scene was a blurry haze of colors, a smudged canvas. Despite the chaos of her life and the events that had occurred over the past month, humanity carried on as if nothing had happened. The fast-food joint on the corner was still selling cheap greasy burgers. Tiny mobile shops scattered to their various locations, knocking on windows and making their sales. A bike would sporadically speed by—either a civilian enjoying the crisp, chill air of the mild winter or a pizza delivery man on a mission with a stack of boxes. Even the parks were occupied with chatting couples and during the day were full of laughing children. No one had any idea what was going on. If they did, they surely didn't care.

Bio-Tech will handle it. Bio-Tech always handled everything, even in the roughest of times. Too much trust was placed in the hands of the corporations. So much that the corporations themselves had become the enemy, the ones who invited the evil into the world. Aria wasn't entirely surprised. She knew something would happen someday, just not necessarily to the extent that it had.

Sighing, the woman lifted her mug of coffee to her lips, sipping the brew. She couldn't help but think of the chipper Ivory. Aria didn't think she would ever have a cup of coffee without thinking about the other woman and her addiction to the caffeine. It made her gloomy. Why should she care? She hadn't known Ivory and Dovian for long. If anything did happen to the two, why should it bother her so much? Sure, they had spent nearly every minute of every day together in the short time they had known each other, but had she really grown so attached to them? Aria never got attached to people. Well, except for her Team Phoenix, but that was a given. They were partners; they were in it for life. Even though Aria and Troy rarely did missions together with their initial team anymore, they still met up occasionally for cheap Chinese food and beer. But this felt a bit different. Ivory seemed like a lifelong friend, like a sister. And Dovian…well, Aria felt close to Dovian, too.

She eyed the two pink boxes on her countertop that once held the chocolate truffles from Saray. One of the boxes was shared between the four, the other a "get well" gift from Dovian while she was in the hospital. Was he only toying with her, or was he trying to tell her something? Did he have a plan, or was he actually falling in line with Sapphire's orders? Would Dovian take part in humanity's annihilation? Did he even care about Aria and Troy?

"Not going to make a damn difference in the end…" she grumbled into her mug.

Taking another slow sip, she didn't flinch when she heard the familiar beep at her front door followed by the sound of the door sliding open and closing quietly. Aria only risked a glance at the silhouette that entered her dark apartment. She stayed at her table beneath the dim glow of the kitchen light, moving her attention back to the outside world. Rotating the second mug across from her, she handed it over to her guest.

"Was expecting me?" Troy asked, accepting the mug.

"I just wanted to be prepared. I know you like to be alone after missions, but I had a feeling you'd show up," she simply stated.

She eyed the man. He was dressed in civilian clothing for a change. Instead of his typical black military trench, he was wearing his dark leather jacket. With it, he wore a basic t-shirt and jeans. After weeks of nonstop fighting, Troy's beard had grown out a bit, but she noticed he finally took the time to groom himself. Despite the clean look, he appeared exhausted.

"Know me well, eh?" he scoffed, tapping his fingers against the porcelain.

Troy turned and sifted through Aria's cupboard, pulling out a small packet of caramel powder. There was one thing Aria would never learn about Troy, and that was how he liked his coffee. Nearly every day he drank it differently. Sometimes he wanted it black, other times with hot cocoa, occasionally with caramel, and now and then with only sugar or milk. Once he had put whipped cream into the brew, and more than a few times she had seen him use the soft serve machine in the cafeteria to mix things up. Aria figured it was his daily use of creativity. While she enjoyed the occasional painting, Troy enjoyed creating strange concoctions with his morning drink.

After pouring the powder into his mug, he snagged a cookie from one of her jars and dropped into a metal chair across from her. "You always have the best stuff…" he hummed as he dunked the treat and shoved it into his mouth.

"Gotta fatten you up somehow," she muttered, watching him.

They sat for a while in silence. Aria cocked her head to the side, bringing her attention to the cars that flew by in the night. It was like the times Gavin would visit her. Of course, she and Troy had hung out alone countless times before in her apartment, but the visits were usually loud, rambunctious, and often involved alcohol rather than coffee. Now he seemed quiet and slightly disheartened compared to his usual obnoxious self. Despite the change in Troy's behavior, Aria felt at ease in his presence. In fact, she was pleased to share a quiet moment with the man. Life had been a rollercoaster, and she was ready to get off.

"You often do this?" he asked.

Aria darted her stare to the man. She shrugged. "Hmm, I guess so."

"It's so quiet…and dark." He looked over his shoulder. "You like this lonely atmosphere?"

She inspected her surroundings, giving a little nod. "Yeah. It's peaceful. No noise, no chaos, no violence. Just quiet and everyday life."

Troy twisted his gaze back out the window. An advertisement for beer popped up on the glass before him. He frowned and canceled it out.

"I hate those things," she complained. "Supposed to stay in the corners of the windows but have been popping up everywhere lately. I've also been receiving these weird static streaks sometimes that distort the view." Just as she said it, the window flickered.

"Disturbance, huh?" Troy touched the glass. Deep in thought, he wrinkled his brow.

"I thought it was just our building, you know, because of the attack, but then I noticed it happens all over the city, too." She pointed a finger in the direction of one of the neighboring conglomerates. From the top to bottom the whole building flickered.

"Weird." Troy watched with interest. The entire city seemed to give an occasional shiver.

"The lights sometimes flicker, too. I can only assume it has to do with Sapphire and her meddling with the dimensional planes. I wonder if there have been a lot of static frequencies disrupting any other mechanical feeds."

"Would make sense." Troy gulped his coffee.

Aria stared into her cup, mesmerized by the swirls. Troy drank again, eyeing her curiously.

"You alright?" he asked.

Aria gave a hum, looking to him.

"You've seemed spacey lately." He waved a hand around his head.

"Oh...haven't noticed. Perhaps."

"You also look a bit pale. You feeling alright?" he pried.

She twisted her expression. "Yeah. Maybe just a little tired. Been having trouble sleeping." As if being reminded, she gave a loud yawn.

"Maybe you should go to bed instead of drinking coffee all night long."

"I can't sleep. I toss and turn all night. No matter what I do, I can't seem to get comfortable. One minute I'm cold, the next I'm hot. If I do fall asleep, I have strange dreams."

Troy leaned forward. "Also noticed you're not eating much."

"Not been hungry. I mean, I get hungry, but everything makes me nauseous. I think I'm just stressed the hell out, ya know?" She shook her head. "Haven't felt like this since the False Syndicate."

"Same here. Worse even. Eh, I can't sleep either. It's just...I handle it better than you do." He swirled his mug. "Stress I mean."

"Handle it better?" she snapped. "What do you mean you handle it better?"

Troy gave a loud laugh. "You're a stress ball! A little black furry ball of stress that growls and bites!" he exclaimed. "You're a frail little thing and stress doesn't help."

Aria looked down at herself. "I'm not...frail!"

"Aria, you get sick constantly. You may be able to hold up in battle and get shit done, but you are destroying your body at the same time. You need to find a way to relax. And it's not just your physical health. I worry about your...you know...mental stability."

Aria's jaw tightened. "Is that why you are here? James asked you to check up on me?" She scowled.

"What? No! I'm just discussing my concerns for you!" he explained.

"Well, why don't you just throw me in a straightjacket and lock me away already?" she snarled.

"That's not what I meant!" Aggravated, he ran his hands through his hair. "Gah! You're so moody!"

Aria stood, rinsing her mug out in the sink. There was a loud groan from the pipes, and the water abruptly shut off.

"Shit," Aria hissed. "Looks like Sapphire's work in the Amazonian desert paid off. Water shortage." She dropped the cup into the sink, spun, and leaned against the counter, folding her arms.

"It's not like I wanted this," she whispered after a minute. "Any of this."

Troy lowered his head. "No, Aria. It's not like I wanted it, either."

"Really? You wouldn't have become a soldier like your father?" she scoffed. "I can't imagine that you would have made too many different choices."

"What's that supposed to mean?" Troy twisted in his chair, looking up at her in disbelief.

"It's just who you are, Troy. There's nothing wrong with it, but seriously…what the hell am *I* doing?" she asked quietly.

"What is this? What's with you questioning your life lately?" Troy raised an eyebrow.

Aria gave a growl, her fingers slipping through her black hair. "Damn it, Troy! I'm fifty-two! I wasn't even born in this city! I was born in Cherno! I had a wealthy mother and father who were of high status! Now, I'm not bashing soldiers or our lifestyle, but this isn't what I was meant to be. Look at me! I'm supposed to be running my own company, wearing a business suit and shouting orders to scared interns. Or I should have my own gallery…or multiple galleries across the world. I'm supposed to be married with children, snuggled in bed reading bedtime stories. Instead, I'm living in a nightmare, fighting and killing people…killing monsters." She rubbed her forehead. What was the point of telling him this? All it would do is anger him.

"No, Aria, you weren't born for this. But you know what? You *are* in this. You don't have immunity to the rest of the world. No one does. Sure, you're a classy gal…when you want to be, but that isn't you. Maybe when you were tiny…but not now. You aren't that little girl from Cherno. You're the strong and brave Aria of today," Troy stated.

"Don't be a hypocrite. You just called me frail a minute ago," she sassed.

"Come on! You know what I mean! I worry about you because you are far too hard on yourself. Look at you. You're worried about the life you no longer have. A life you never really had to begin with. This is your life, Aria. I know you had parents, and they seemed really great, but you've got to realize that *this* is your family. James, Team Phoenix…me. We're in this together and always have been." He looked a bit hurt as he spoke, and Aria shared a similar expression. She didn't mean to dismiss Troy and the others. She only wished she could have lived a different lifestyle with them all. Troy continued, sitting sideways in his chair. "You can't dwell on living a double life; there's just no room for that, but there's no reason you can't start a family. You're not old. You're far from it. Someday you can have all that. You can boss scared interns around, submit your paintings to that rich, fancy place down the street, get out and meet some intelligent guy. Not at a bar, but at some classy place. Resign from your position at Bio-Tech, and get yourself knocked-up. There's plenty of time for that. Just…don't let it cloud your vision. We're dealing with a life changing event here. I can't have you losing your mind worrying about things that never happened. Last thing I need is you dying on the battlefield because your head is stuck in a world that doesn't exist."

"So I'm just supposed to ignore everything and worry only about the bodies in my crosshairs?" she quipped.

Troy's face fell. "Yeah. Just forget everything, Aria. Become a mindless drone and shoot and kill…because that's all we do. Soldiers don't feel anything at all, right? We're just a bunch of stupid grunts," he muttered sarcastically.

"So what are you telling me?!" she shouted.

"I don't know! Stop worrying about everything you can't control! Why are you worrying about babies and art galleries and getting married at a time like this?" He finally stood from his chair.

"Because, Troy, at any moment you and I could be dead! And what will we have to show for it? What have we done with our lives?" she asked.

He gaped at her in wonder. She was thoroughly upset. How long had she been dwelling on these ideas?

"Do you really want to bring a child into this world, Aria? Look around you. People are dying everywhere! Civilians are constantly killed by warfare; your parents are proof of that. Sapphire is out there right now letting her creatures maul children to death. Would you really be happy knowing that you could die at any moment and leave a child behind to live the same miserable life you lived?" He placed his hands on his hips, giving her a stern look.

Aria lowered her head. "I'm just scared, alright. So many what-ifs…buts…." She chewed on her lip.

"Can't worry about it. It'll only distract you from things that are important," he said a bit more gently.

"And what is important? What are we fighting for?" she asked.

Troy gazed at the light above him, thinking a moment. "Uhhhh…I dunno. What are we fighting for?" Truthfully, he rarely thought about it. Outside of the obvious reasons, Troy only fought because it was all he knew how to do. He didn't necessarily enjoy killing people, but he also couldn't see himself doing anything else, especially flipping pancakes at a place like the Syrup House. What exactly was he fighting for? Humanity? Was that specific enough for him?

Aria lifted her head and locked eyes with Troy. "Dovian and Ivory."

Troy smirked. "Fighting for our friends?"

"We're going to bring them back." She was dead serious.

Troy watched her for a while, his mind mulling over the thought. "Kidnap them from the devil-child and bring them back here?" he asked.

"Damn straight. We're bringing our friends home," she replied.

"You believe Dovian hasn't traded sides?" he asked.

"I think he's only trying to scare us." She hesitated. "What do you think?"

The man exhaled slowly, giving a shrug. "My gut is telling me that he wouldn't really do the things he's doing, but he's still doing them."

"You always believe in your gut." She pointed.

Troy shoved his hands into his pockets, taking a deep breath. "Yeah...I always do." Giving a slow nod, he added, "Okay. When do we start?"

Aria gave an eager smile. "First thing in the morning."

The morning rain had done nothing to help with the overwhelming heat of the day but, rather, had intensified it with thick muggy air. Dovian wiped at his forehead, feeling sticky and uncomfortable. Though the cold pool behind his home was rather inviting, he had no intention of hopping in and enjoying himself for one moment. He didn't deserve that. Still, his robes and armor were constricting, but he'd continue to wear them. There was no telling when Sapphire would need him again. Her requests were becoming more arduous, and he had spent the better half of the day overlooking the progress of the Roman soldiers and avoiding the luring advances from Lilith.

He hadn't seen Ivory. In fact, he hadn't made much of a thought towards the woman. Dovian assumed she was safe and sound with Petey and Hector swimming in the lake, or she was possibly sitting by the fountain in her garden. The more the hours passed, the more she behaved like I'Lanthe. Dovian had to admit; it was a little unsettling, but he wasn't sure why. Soon he would have to make an appearance for the woman. Undoubtedly, she was still uneasy about being left alone.

Inhaling deeply, taking in the scent of old paper and stale dust, Dovian closed the large book in his hands and gently set the item on the desk before him. The lantern cast a white light around him but dimmed somewhat by his will as he lifted his head, listening. One footstep into the room would have been utterly silent to human ears, but he could place the gentle pressure of the ball of the foot sinking quietly onto the stone floor. Boots. The change in airflow altered slightly as the body entered the room.

"I would say that I'm surprised you came, but that wouldn't necessarily be true," Dovian uttered in a hushed tone.

There was the cocking of a weapon, the body movement becoming a bit more careless. One foot twisted over the other, and Dovian slowly turned to face his guest.

"You know everything, don't you?" Aria asked. Her glare fixed upon his dull expression.

"Not quite, but close enough," he replied. After a pause, he continued, "I thought I told you to hide."

"As if you thought I actually would," she scoffed.

"I had hoped you would have at least considered it. Instead, you show up not much more than twenty-four hours later in my home. Rather stupid, don't you think?" he asked.

Aria kept her weapon aimed at the Sorcēarian. He didn't seem bothered by it.

"If you think fighting to save my friends is stupid, then yeah. Pretty damn stupid." Her voice dripped with bitterness. She was not happy with him, but he did not expect her to be.

Dovian was silent, his mouth twisting into a frown.

"But there's nothing you can do about it. Whether you're coming or not, we've got Ivory." Aria moved to the side, keeping her aim on the man.

Dovian's eyes narrowed into slits of shimmering light. "Do you want to die?" he asked. The sound was a little alarming, but Aria held her resolve.

"Do you want Ivory to die?" she asked.

He gave her a questioning look.

"She's safer with us. You'll only get her killed leaving her here alone with Sapphire and the demons while you are out destroying the world," she said sourly.

"And you will only put her in harm's way if you take her. Sapphire will personally hunt you down," he rumbled.

"Goin' to die either way, right? So what does it matter what I do?" The words were sarcastic and only annoyed Dovian further.

"She's safer here with me…with the demons nearby."

"That doesn't even make sense!" Her attitude worsened.

186

"You don't even know the half of it!" he boomed.

Aria swallowed, meeting his glare evenly.

"I'm taking her," she said defiantly.

Dovian lowered his head, his hood shrouding his face in darkness. "You're not going anywhere."

"Then kill me already!" Aria finally lowered her weapon and held her hands out to the side. "What in the hell are you waiting for?!"

Dovian's hands balled into fists as his mouth set into a firm line. Aria was so infuriatingly stubborn.

"Huh?" she asked. "Look at you Dovian. Can't even deal with one human woman. Why is that?"

He avoided her stare.

"It's cuz you're full of shit." She shouldered her weapon. "Now, are you coming with me or not?"

Dovian gave a short laugh. "Go with you? Do you really think that would work?"

"Then what are you doing? Are you going to destroy the world? You're really going to forsake everything you've ever done and been through just because of Sapphire? That isn't you, Dovian." Aria folded her arms, shaking her head.

"As if you know a damned thing about me, Aria," he said through gritted teeth. "You think I'm some angel, some protector of the human race. I'm none of that."

"No, I don't think you're anything like that. But I do know that the darkness isn't you. You aren't evil, Dovian. You never were, and you never will be."

"I destroyed my race..." he began.

Aria shook her head. "I don't believe you."

She looked at his bookshelf, trying to read the Sorcēarian titles. She twisted her mouth, finding it odd that some of them translated just fine in her head. Perhaps it was some strange magic the books contained.

"I think it's a scare tactic," she continued. "You just want people to believe you're some big, bad Sorcēarian with magical powers. I think you're nothing more than a person of circumstance. You were forced onto a path where bad decisions were made, where things happened that you couldn't control. And you blame yourself. That's why you said you killed them all."

"Now you can read minds?" he asked. Giving a menacing chuckle, he walked toward the woman, but she didn't bother meeting his eyes. "You have no idea what you are talking about," he whispered near her ear.

"No?" Aria asked, spinning to face him. She lifted a book. "Because every evil Sorcēarian enjoys reading a book full of poetry about love."

Dovian snatched the item from her hand and shoved it back onto the shelf. He glared at her, but she smiled in return.

"I can read you like a book, Dovian." She sauntered over to his desk, looking down at the handwriting scrawled across the parchment of what appeared to be a journal.

"I killed them all. It is my fault. I killed *everyone*." He faced the bookshelf. Aria watched him, not reacting to his words. "All of my friends, my family, the elders, everyone."

Dovian flinched as Aria suddenly grabbed his hand. She gently ran her thumb across his knuckles. For some reason, the gesture was entirely soothing to him, and he wasn't sure why. He let out a quick breath, relaxing into the touch.

"Not I'Lanthe," she whispered. "I know you didn't kill her. You wouldn't."

Dovian turned toward Aria. Despite the comfort she was giving him, he knew it was only going to cause more trouble for him. He needed her to leave, and he needed her to leave now. Any weakness he showed her was going to make her stay. And the longer she lingered in his home, the closer she was to meeting death by Sapphire's hands.

Dovian held onto her hand, squeezing it.

"Aria…" he spoke slowly.

"Come with us, Dovian."

Her voice held pity, was full of need. Her thoughts were running rampant, and her emotions were dancing around him like a fog. It was intoxicating. He hadn't noticed that the storms outside had kicked up again, and the sunlight was fading. Rain pelted against the marble sides of his cathedral.

She spoke softly, "Please." It was a simple word, but it held all kinds of desperation.

He locked eyes with her finally, and he felt his walls crumbling apart on the inside. Everything he had done was to preserve the human race. It was for people like Aria. She was not helping the situation. In fact, she was only making everything more complicated. He needed her to hate him, to desire him no longer.

Dovian roughly grabbed her by the arms, jolting her. "Leave!" he boomed.

She gave a sharp gasp. "N-No!"

"I killed every single member of my race in order to save humanity. Don't think for one second that I won't destroy your entire race to bring back what I lost." He ground his teeth together, fighting to keep from reading her thoughts. There was something off about her. Perhaps it was his overload of energy detecting it, but she seemed to have a firm hold on him with her emotions. "Don't think for one second I won't kill you and Troy because I won't hesitate."

"You've already hesitated. Many times," she corrected him.

"No more. Not any longer," he spat out.

"Let me take Ivory…then I'll leave. I'll leave, and you can continue to live a lonely and miserable life all by yourself with Sapphire and her monsters. Try all you want, but we aren't going down without a fight, and we aren't going down without making sure Ivory is safe."

"She will be safer here with me; you'll only get her killed," Dovian grumbled. His hands were still tightly wrapped around Aria's upper arms.

"And how is she safe here?" she argued.

"TRUST ME!" he shouted. "She needs to be here. She needs to be by my side! If you take her, you are all doomed. Sapphire will only have you killed in an instant, and Ivory will be brought right back here. Nothing will be solved."

"But that saves you from having to do it yourself, right?" Aria pulled away from him.

Dovian gave her a heated stare. "If anyone in this world is going to kill you, it had better be me," he muttered.

Aria was stunned by his remark. In a way, it made sense. He didn't think they had a single chance at survival. Dovian thought that by being the one to kill Aria and Troy, he'd be merciful. Aria didn't doubt that. He'd most likely make it quick and painless. Sapphire and her pets would be sure to make it slow and excruciating. She'd do things to Aria and Troy that were more horrifying than anything Euclid could ever imagine.

Aria turned her gaze back to the book on the table. "So why don't you just do it now, then?" she asked quietly.

"Because when it comes down to it, I want Sapphire to see it," he said. "And if you don't leave soon, she'll be here. She's most likely already sensed your presence before you even entered my home. If she sees you, she'll have you killed on the spot. She will have far too much fun ripping the flesh off your bones while you are still alive."

Aria picked up the massive journal on the table beside her. Dovian eyed her anxiously. "Fine. I'll leave right now, and I'll allow Ivory to stay with you. But…I'm taking this with me."

"That is nothing more than drivel. Useless words of an old, depressed man." He gave a shrug.

She gave a short, mocking laugh as she ran a hand over the cover. "Depressed. You forget something important, Dovian. Wings or not, you were born on this earth. You're just as human as I am." She walked past him and halted in the doorway. "You better promise me that you'll keep her safe. No matter what."

Dovian's face revealed no doubt. "I promise."

Aria nodded slowly, chewing on her lower lip. "But not only her. You keep yourself safe, Dovian."

He lifted his head, trying to give her a chilly stare, but failed as the corner of his mouth turned upward. Aria couldn't help but give a similar gesture and shook her head.

'Liar,' she mentally accused.

Aria took off in a run. Her boots echoed along the corridors, the gushing of the nearing storm sending bursts of air into the building, ruffling her hair and clothing. She gripped her Fernstal tightly, her optic camera watching for any lingering shadows. When she had first arrived, the sun was shining brightly, and the heat was nearly unbearable. Now it was like night, but it was only mid-afternoon. A grumble of thunder roared, and Aria shoved past the heavy doors–the same doors she and Troy had walked through when they first met Dovian. Pushing harder, she sprinted down the charcoal-stained bridge connecting the front of Dovian's church to the green pastures ahead where the Hawk 90 was waiting. Aria could see Troy outside the copter, Ivory standing awfully close to him.

More thunder boomed, and Aria saw a floating shadow cast from above. Looking up, she caught sight of Dovian with his wings spread outward. Tightening her grip on the book and her gun, Aria called out to her partner, "Troy! Let her go! We have to let her go!"

The male soldier looked confused. Ivory shuffled her feet. As Aria neared them, she noticed how different the blonde appeared. Her hair was pulled up in an ornate clip. She looked like a full-bred Sorcēarian in her violet and black robes. Not only that, but her posture was more confident. She didn't seem as childish as she once was.

'Is this what I'Lanthe looked like?' Aria mentally wondered.

"I told you he wouldn't be happy! I could tell by the storms!" Ivory shouted.

Aria slowed up, catching her breath. "We have to let her go."

"What? No way! We're taking her with us," Troy argued.

Aria shook her head. She tossed the journal into the cabin of the Hawk and spun to look upward at Dovian as he circled overhead.

"He won't let us. We have to let her go," Aria explained.

"But after all this? You're just going to let her go? We could've died coming out here! I'm not leaving empty handed!" Troy shouted.

"He…he didn't want to leave this place?" Ivory asked. "He really does want to stay here?"

Aria turned to the blonde, her serious expression falling into one of joy. Without much thought, she wrapped her arms around Ivory. "I promised him I would let you go. He says you'll be safer here."

Ivory gratefully returned the hug. "I figured he'd say something like that. Still…I wish I could go with you, but I can't leave without him, either. If he stays, I'm staying."

"They hell you are!" Troy barked. He grabbed Ivory's arm and tugged her away from Aria. "There are monsters out there! I'm not letting you risk your life for this madman! He'll only kill you, too, in the end."

Ivory gave a yelp as Troy shouldered his rifle and pulled out his pistol. He held her against him and quickly put the barrel of the gun against her head just as Dovian drove hard into the ground. Stone cracked beneath his weight.

"You promised to release her!" Dovian's voice was like thunder, his eyes like lightning. He was a living storm, and he was about to unleash his energy upon the male soldier.

"Stay the hell back!" Troy shouted.

"Troy! Let her go! What in the hell are you doing?" Aria stood to the side, her weapon not aimed at anybody in particular. "I told Dovian I would let her go. She'll be safer with him."

Troy shook his head. Dovian took one step closer, and the soldier pulled back the hammer of the weapon. "Stay! I swear, Dovian. I will not hesitate to blow her computerized parts all over the ground!"

Dovian's whole body went rigid, his face wrinkling into a scowl.

"If she can't come with us, then I'll kill her right now. It's better than letting her stay with you and eventually get torn apart by those monsters you command." Troy didn't dare even blink.

"We had a deal, Aria," Dovian said lowly.

"Troy…let her go," Aria calmly said.

Her partner tightened his lips, refusing to budge.

"Now! It's an order!" she hollered, aiming at him.

Troy wrinkled his nose in disgust. He waited one more second and then lowered his weapon, still maintaining eye contact with the Sorcēarian.

"You, you were going to shoot me?" Ivory timidly asked.

Troy holstered his sidearm and gave Ivory a gentle shake. "No...of course not. I'm not some heartless *killer*." The words weren't necessarily meant for Ivory as much as they were for Dovian.

The Sorcēarian's expression loosened as he held out a hand for Ivory.

"Go on," Troy said, pushing Ivory toward the other man.

Ivory gave a look over her shoulder at Troy and then to Aria.

"Thanks for trying," she squeaked.

The two soldiers looked defeated. They had gotten nowhere with this escapade.

"Shoulda threw her in the copter and flew up to get you. Coulda been gone in seconds," Troy murmured to Aria.

She squeezed his shoulder. "Looks like we'll have to play everything by ear from here on out. There's no telling what's going to happen."

Ivory didn't take Dovian's offered hand but walked right past him. He gaped at her in shock, his hand dropping to his side. "Leave," he grumbled, glaring at Aria and Troy.

Aria rolled her eyes and spun on her heel, jumping into the copter. Troy followed in after her, still feeding Dovian an unpleasant look.

"Uh, a little help, maybe?" the woman asked, gesturing toward the sky. Her eyebrow rose as she waited for the Sorcēarian's response.

Dovian lifted his palms. After a moment, he directed his attention upward, closing his eyes. He took a deep breath, and the clouds began to dissipate, moving to opposite corners of Ives. Troy moved between Aria and the door, slamming it shut. Aren wasted no time lifting off.

"So what the hell do we get in exchange for letting Ivory go?" Troy muttered, glancing at the heavy book on the floor. "Something for your new book collection?"

"It's Dovian's journal," Aria replied.

"Why the hell–?" He gave her a wondrous, exasperated sigh.

"It'll give me more insight into his motives and who he is as a person. I will be able to tell if he's serious or not about killing us, about destroying humanity. I will also be able to figure out the truth about his past. I don't believe he killed everyone." Aria picked up the book, glancing at Dovian through the small cabin window. He was fading away into a small black dot when something caught his eye, causing him to look in the opposite direction.

"Fly fast!" his voice rang out loud in Aria's mind.

The woman looked in the direction of the cave systems. There was a shadow on the horizon, and her breath caught in her throat. An entire fleet of Sapphire's army was waiting for them to near.

"He ratted us out!" Troy yelled.

"No! He wouldn't do that!" Aria looked back to where Dovian was. His flying silhouette was already entering the cathedral. He wasn't going to help this time around. "Shit."

"Hold on tight!" Aren called over the intercom. "I'm taking it into jet mode."

Aria and Troy quickly buckled into their chairs, the Hawk jolting from the momentum of the copter blades transforming into solid wings. Aria watched the massive cross atop Dovian's home. She wondered what his punishment would be for letting them go once again.

"Oh, shit!" Aren shouted from the cockpit.

"What?" Aria and Troy simultaneously cried.

They were answered by a violent jerk of the copter. The Hawk spun, sinking lower and lower as sirens blared.

"We're hit! I repeat: we're hit! Bail! Bail now!" Aren called out.

The force of the spinning copter pressed Aria and Troy back into their seats. There was another jostle, and the right side of the jet tore off, fire and sparks flying in all directions. An assortment of gear was sucked out of the craft. Aria reached, trying to keep Dovian's journal from flying out, but another tug ripped off the second wing, and the book was gone, leaving a trail of paper behind. As it tumbled, the Hawk's warning siren screamed. Aren's drone called out in warning, and within seconds they were crashing into the ground. The sound was like the crunching of ice. Aria's harness tugged hard against her body; something slammed against her head, and everything cut to a dark silence.

The sound of the wreck reached Dovian and Ivory's ears. The two ran to the window, gaping wide-eyed at the smoke on the horizon. Ivory was already whimpering. Dovian's hands gripped the windowsill tightly, his knuckles turning white. He knew, deep down, he shouldn't have let Aria and Troy go. He should have taken care of them right then and there. Now, who knew what had happened to them. Were they crushed in the wreckage? For their sake, he hoped so. If not, Sapphire would surely have more terrifying plans for their demise.

A sudden bursting hum sent Dovian's hair on end. Terrifying shrieks sounded in the back of his mind. The darkness was in the room behind him. He had no time to react as he was smashed sideways into the wall. His ears rang from the impact, the sound mixing with Ivory's horrified scream.

Dovian reached toward the spinning three silhouettes of the blonde.

"I hope they are still alive, Dovian. It's time you make up for your constant mistakes!" Sapphire's shrill voice echoed in the dark room. "And I thought Euclid was useless. Perhaps I was wrong in letting you destroy him!"

Dovian groaned, slowly rising to his feet. Another force slammed into him, and he spiraled backward onto the floor. "They...they were going to take Ivory," he sputtered.

"So? What does that have to do with the fact that you let them escape?" Sapphire hollered.

Dovian held a hand to his head, and he quickly blinked his eyes. "They...they were going to kill her. Troy had a gun. He was going to shoot her in the head. He was holding her hostage."

"So?" the child asked again with aggravation.

"So I exchanged their lives for hers! I figured you would want her alive, am I correct? Having Ivory dead wouldn't make the sex all that great," he grumbled sarcastically.

He finally focused on Sapphire's black eyes. She didn't look amused.

Dovian continued. "It would make the whole reproduction thing a lot more complicated, too."

Sapphire walked toward him, her small hands gripping her white dress. "Are you finished?" she snarled. "You could have still killed them with ease!"

Dovian brought his attention to Ivory and then back to the child. "Ivory had begged me to spare them," he said.

Sapphire quickly looked over her shoulder at the blonde. Ivory quickly nodded.

"I don't care what she did, Dovian. I have strictly said over and again that you are to kill Aria and Troy on sight!" Sapphire crouched before the man.

She allowed Dovian to sit up. He casually ran his hand through his hair, yawning. The gesture only irritated the child more. "I am to mate with this woman. Don't you think it would be a good idea if I try to appease her best I can?"

An invisible hand clenched around Dovian's throat. He grimaced, trying to pry himself free. "I don't care if you have to rape her. Your job is to impregnate her and kill the humans, understand?" Sapphire asked.

Giving a quick nod, Dovian was promptly released. He gasped for air, staring at the dusty floor. Sapphire stood upright, moving toward the timid Ivory.

"I can't punish her in the way I would like without killing her. Well...I could sever a limb or break something." Sapphire looked over her shoulder at the man. "You could always heal her."

Dovian scrambled to his feet. "No! Don't you dare harm her!"

The act of Dovian telling the child 'no' was infuriating. It only fed more fuel to the fire. "She's not pregnant yet, so I can still deal some damage for now."

Before Dovian could respond, a glass shard on the floor lifted into the air and sped directly at Ivory, embedding deep into her lower abdomen. The poor woman had no time to react. A quick yelp erupted past her pink lips; her frightened expression alone was pitiful outside of the twitch she gave. Ivory's pale hands covered the wound, and she gently lowered to the floor. Dovian rushed forward but was carelessly knocked back again. This time his knee bent backward as Sapphire broke one of his legs.

"I'm not playing games, Dovian. If you can't do your duties, I will punish you. Seeing as your past punishments haven't been enough, the next time you fail me, I'll retaliate against her. Got it?" Sapphire snapped. "She doesn't need arms or legs. I can do what I can to make both your and her life a living hell. Don't tempt me; it's hard enough not tearing the two of you apart."

Dovian cried out in pain as he quickly mended his broken appendage. He glared at the child, livid.

"If you want her safe, Dovian, impregnate her and kill those bastard soldiers." Sapphire opened up her portal. "Finish healing, and get to the wreckage. There's work to be done." The black mass swallowed the child whole, leaving the couple to themselves.

Ivory was on her knees now, trying to dig out the glass deep inside her body. "I'm sorry! I'm so sorry!" she sobbed.

Dovian scooted toward her, pulling her into his arms. "Don't touch it!" He smacked her hands away.

"Dovian! I'm sorry!" The woman repeatedly chanted the words.

Dovian called his staff to him. Somewhere from the darkness, the sound of metal grating against stone commenced. Within moments, the pole was flying into the room and firmly into Dovian's hand. Pulling blue light from the orb set between the wing tips of the weapon, he placed his palm over the wound.

"It's not your fault, Ivory. Don't ever think it's your fault," he murmured, slowly pulling the glass shard from her insides. "Does it hurt?" he quickly asked.

Ivory shook her head from side to side. "No…just feels a bit funny."

Dovian pulled out the glass and frowned. There was blood. Ivory's eyes glossed over.

"That…is that blood?" she whimpered.

Dovian nodded slowly. "Appears you really do have some of your original organs…."

Ivory gave a moan, clenching tightly onto Dovian's scarlet coat, and buried her face into his chest.

"You'll be okay," he whispered. "You're already healed."

He continued to pull blue light over the wound, easily closing it up. Once finished, he pulled his bloodied palm to his face. Before, in Saray, when Ivory was fatally wounded, the blades from the Brawler must have barely missed her reproductive system. She was lucky. If she had been impaled any lower, she could have died. Ivory wasn't just a machine. She *was* still human. Her body still contained all of the essential components to house life. For some reason, the realization finally hit home to Dovian. Ivory could die. She could be injured beyond saving or repair. All it would take is something as simple as a strategically placed shard of glass. Dovian held onto the blonde tightly, running his hand through her hair.

"I'm so sorry, Ivory. I should've let you go with them. Aria's right. I can't keep you safe." His voice was shaky, and his skin was clammy.

Ivory pressed her forehead against his. "No. I wouldn't go, either. I have to stay, Dovian. Someone has to keep you safe."

He gave a weak smile. How absurd of her to think of him in a moment like this. His amusement faded, however, as he made another realization. Sapphire was a mere projection and had no physical body. She couldn't be destroyed. In order to keep Ivory safe, he had to kill Aria and Troy. There was no way around it. And by Sapphire's current orders, the time was now.

Gently releasing the woman, Dovian slowly pushed to his feet. He stared out the window at the pluming smoke from the wreckage. Though his hard visage gave away nothing, Dovian was dying on the inside. It was time to do what he had been avoiding all this time.

"What are you doing?" Ivory asked, pulling the man from his thoughts.

As he looked down at her, Ivory's body tensed. His smoldering eyes made her uneasy. "I'm going to kill Aria and Troy now."

"What?! No!" Ivory lurched forward but was far too late as Dovian twisted the dial of his frequency tuner and disappeared, leaving the woman alone in the dark.

Ivory looked out the window and dropped to her knees. Resting her arms on the frame, she covered her head, crying.

When Aria awoke, the world was trembling all around her. The sounds of screeching metal rang in her ears, and soon she was being pulled violently from the wreckage. Dazed, she tried to gather her surroundings. She was in what appeared to be a desert, the sun shining brightly in her eyes from between dark clouds. Aria lurched forward, trying not to pass out. Blood dripped in random intervals against the cracked land beneath her dragging feet, indicating that she was wounded. No doubt her medical bills were going to be through the roof over the next few months. A pungent smell nearly made the woman vomit as she was dropped carelessly onto the ground. There was a multitude of sounds around her, but she couldn't make out any words. Her head was still spinning. That was when she realized there was blood dripping from her nose. A sharp, searing pain erupted from the top of her head down to her left eyebrow.

The woman was roughly tugged to her feet. She caught a glimpse of Dovian, his blue eyes shining through the delirious haze of her vision. Sputtering, she tried to reach toward him, mumbling some unintelligible version of the Sorcēarian's name. Dovian gently pushed her hand away, and Aria's vision slowly came into focus.

"Wha...what happened?" she managed to speak.

Her head lowered, but she was finally recognizing that she was being held up by two sets of hands. Aria limply tilted her head, catching sight of two strangers on either side of her. They didn't seem concerned for her. In fact, their faces were expressionless.

"Who? Who the hell are you?" she moaned.

Aria moved her sight toward the wreckage a couple meters away. The Hawk was completely demolished. It was a wonder how she survived the impact at all. That was when Aria's awareness began to come forward.

"T-Troy!" she tried to shout.

Aria's eyes darted, looking at the strangers around her and the awfully eerie sight of Sapphire glaring at her. She and the others were surrounded by a circling of Sapphire's beasts. From the side, another two of Sapphire's cronies drug Troy from the wreckage just the same as they had Aria. She tried to wrench free, her knees buckling beneath her weight. Still, the hands did not release her. Troy noticed Aria, his glazed eyes widening as he became aware.

"And what of the pilot?" Sapphire asked, gathering Troy's attention.

"Dead," one of the strangers responded.

Aria's eyes burned with tears as she looked over to the destroyed Hawk. The whole front of the craft was smashed. There was no way Aren had survived the impact. "Aren…" she whimpered.

"Aria!" Troy called out to her. He was struggling, trying to push with his feet to gain leverage. Blood covered his uniform from a deep gash on his forehead. One of his hands was bent to hell, broken fingers splayed in all directions.

"Troy!" Aria responded. The act of shouting took too much energy. Dark spots floated before her eyes as she struggled to keep consciousness. "Let him go," she ground out.

"Don't waste your breath. I need you to be alert for the next few minutes." Dovian's voice invaded the woman's ears.

Aria rolled her eyes in his direction. "Help…help us, Dovian." The sound was pathetic.

Dovian cupped Aria's face. He healed her just enough to bring her consciousness forward. The sensation was soothing, and Aria nearly begged for him to continue.

"There's no more help for you, Aria," he whispered. "You've had plenty of opportunities. You have had many chances to live your life."

Aria's lower lip trembled. "No," she fought back her tears, comprehending her precarious situation.

"Yes." He nodded. "Time is now. Are you ready?" he asked in a calm, yet eerie tone.

Aria looked between him and the others surrounding her. She assumed the other people were biomechanical androids housed by demon souls. Gaining some strength, she locked eyes with Troy. He was terrified; he appeared completely frightened out of his mind. Aria had never seen him like that before, and it alarmed her even more.

She groaned, trying to free herself from the icy hands that held her in place. Dovian put a palm on her head. The woman gnashed her teeth together, trying not to show weakness, trying not to show Dovian that she was scared. She failed miserably.

"Nice and quick. Just like Dr. Camery," Dovian spoke in a calm tone. It did nothing to relieve her anxiety.

"No!" Troy shouted.

Dovian slowly pulled away from Aria, looking back toward Troy. The male soldier was squirming. His skin was nearly white from blood loss. The shaking of his hands had put his whole body into tremors. Shock was going to set in soon.

"Don't touch her. Kill me. Kill me first. Just…just don't hurt her. She doesn't need to die," he choked on his words. "It's all me. It was all my idea.

She wanted to hide. She was going to hide, stay away from Ives; she was gonna stay away from Sapphire. She was going to give up, try to live a nice, quiet life." He coughed, spitting out blood. "Ya know how she is. She cares too much, right? All I had to do was suggest the idea to her, and she was in. Just kill me. Send her back home, and it'll be like she never existed."

Sapphire watched the spectacle, waiting to see what Dovian would do.

Troy looked about uneasily, giving a nervous laugh. "Come on, man. What can one woman do, really? Look at her. She's such…a *weak,* little thing. She can barely keep herself alive. I mean, how many times did you have to save her?"

Dovian observed the male soldier. He didn't say anything but kept staring in interest.

"A lot, right?" Troy asked. "It's not like she could do much on her own. I'm the one you want. I'm the one who has caused all the trouble for you."

Aria screamed, "Shut up, Troy!"

Dovian turned to Aria, his mouth open in amusement. "You know…I think he's right."

Aria shook her head. A metallic taste coated her tongue from a bloody cut on her lip.

Dovian laughed, picking up an item from off the ground. Tugging off his hood, he gave Aria a cheerful smile as he waved an Air Force issued pistol in front of her face. "Maybe I should kill him first." He winked.

"Don't you dare!" she spat.

Dovian smirked at Troy's fierce expression. "You know what, Aria, my dear? I think we have a hero in our midst. What do you think?" the Sorcēarian asked with delight.

The gun in Dovian's hand made her incredibly anxious. "Drop the weapon…" she weakly ordered.

Dovian ignored her. "And I think the best heroes are always the ones who die, am I right? They're the ones who have the courage to put themselves on the frontlines. They're the type of people who wouldn't think twice about courageously jumping in front of stray bullets to save their comrades. Don't you agree? The best heroes are always the dead ones."

Dovian then turned and aimed the gun directly at Troy's head. Aria screamed, and without much thought, kicked upwards and knocked Dovian's aim off kilter. His arm moved to the side, and the weapon fired. Hard hands shoved Aria onto her knees. In all the commotion, she didn't get a good look of how Troy was hit, but she didn't need to see much to know that her efforts were futile. Blood spurt in all directions around his head, and then the man was lying on his back on the ground, motionless. She couldn't see his face. She needed to see his face! Aria twisted, trying to gain sight of Troy's head, but her position prevented a good view. However, the massive puddle of blood that poured around him was a harsh indicator. He'd bleed out soon if he didn't receive medical attention. That is if he wasn't dead already.

"TROY!" Aria howled. She had been shouting his name repeatedly since Dovian shot the weapon. Pitching forward, she jumped to her feet and tried to pull away, but the enemy refused to release her. It all had happened so fast. One second Troy was looking at her with frightened eyes; the next, blood was pooling around his head. In a flash, Dovian was in front of her, grabbing her face roughly and threatening to tear her head off with his death-grip. Like a wildfire, his eyes pierced her soul.

"You really are trying *hard* to screw things up, aren't you?!" he roared.

"Is he dead? Is he dead?!" she shrieked.

"I've no clue! You knocked me off balance!"

Aria's face was stained with blood and tears. Her hair was matted with her own gore. Despite her weakened state, her eyes were nearly glowing from her hate and anger. Adrenaline. It was known to keep people alive much longer than considered normal.

Aria stopped fighting as she watched Dovian shove away from her. Peering down at Troy, he kicked at the soldier's boot. Troy gave a strangled cry, and his body began shaking. A gasp thrust from Aria's throat, and she stared with dread as Dovian threw his hands into the air in exasperation.

"Congratulations, Aria. You've caused him to suffer." The robed man crouched beside Troy. Holding out a hand, Dovian sent a beam of light from his fingertips onto Troy's body, starting with his head on down. In one burst, the soldier stopped moving.

A loud wail erupted from Aria. "What did you do?! What did you do?!" she screamed.

Dovian was near her in an instant, grabbing her by the back of her neck. "Killed him, Aria! What in the hell do you think?"

The cry had come from her again only for a split-second before she composed herself. Aria went back and forth between having a complete breakdown and gaining self-control multiple times before she settled on forcing her eyes to lock onto Dovian's.

'I hate you,' she hissed in her mind.

"As you should." Dovian's eyes were cold. He wasn't revealing anything to her. *"I warned you…."*

Aria looked down at Troy once more. Her eyes turned to slits as giant tears fell down her face. Sobbing, she barely managed to form the question, "Is he really dead?"

Dovian frowned, nodding slowly. "Yeah."

"No." She refused to believe him.

"Yeah. He is." He reconfirmed.

"No….No…" she cried. Finally, her ragged words became moans as Aria bawled.

Dovian watched her cry. It was shocking how much he was intrigued by her tears, by her pain. Now she knew what it was like to see the world crumble around her. Not just her parents, not just Gavin, but Troy, too. He saw the hope drain from her eyes, felt it pour from her soul. Even if he allowed her to live, there'd be no life left for her. She'd be an empty shell. She was human, after all. Humans always had a breaking point.

After an excruciating minute, Dovian gathered Aria's face into his hands once again. "Aria…" he spoke slowly. She tried to pull away. "Aria!" he shouted.

Giving a few short gasps and chokes, she finally gave him her attention. "You ready?" he asked her.

She shook her head, trying to wring her wrists free. After another moment, she stopped moving. "You gonna make it fast?" she asked. It was a silly question. After all she had done in her life, killing men and women all around the world, fighting battles for bastards like Walten, the last thing she deserved was a quick death. Still, she didn't make people suffer. She always made sure to eliminate her targets quickly. She had just hoped that her death would come the same way.

Dovian shook his head. "No. No, Aria. Not now. I'm not going to make it fast."

"But you said…" she started.

Dovian then nodded, placing his forehead against hers. "I know. I know I said I would, but after what you made me do to Troy, it's only fair I do the same to you."

He was a maniac. Dovian had lost his mind. The way he talked to her, the way he seemed to enjoy the whole ordeal, made Aria want to vomit.

"Then do it already!" she snarled, her glare returning in full force.

Aria felt the barrel of the weapon press against her stomach right beneath the ribcage.

Boom!

The violent blast pushed all of the air out of her lungs. She felt like she was suffocating. A fierce vibration shuddered up and down her body. Finally, her hands were released, and she immediately moved them to Dovian's shoulders, her fingers gathering up the scarlet cloth. Aria opened her mouth, trying to form words.

"Hate me," he whispered harshly. "Hate me with everything you've got."

A quiet croak sounded from the woman, and she began to sink. Dovian held onto her a moment longer.

"Do me a favor, my dear…" he said in a soothing tone. Aria's eyes struggled to focus on his face. She reached up, smearing her blood-soaked fingers across the tattoo on his face, her fingernails digging into his skin. Now he struggled, a small tremble crossing over his lips. Pulling her hands away, he suspended her. With his face nearly against hers, he whispered, "Stay down."

He released her. Aria's body fell back with a weighty thud. A sputtering emitted from her, blood crawling past her teeth, dripping down the side of her chin. She was cold despite the heat of the desert. The dust that whirled around her didn't bother her. She couldn't feel it pelt against her face or worsen her failing intake of breath. This was it. She was dying, and it felt just as cold and lonely as she had always imagined it would be. Nails scratching against the dirt; she tried to reach for Troy. At least she had gotten part of what she always wanted. She had wanted to die by his side. Sounds churned around her—the clattering of flame from the wreckage, dust spiraling around her ears, and the gurgling noises of her suffering.

"Quite the show," Sapphire said. For the first time, the child sounded pleased.

Dovian didn't move. He stared at Aria, watching her shiver in the heat.

"No, really. I'm impressed. I didn't think you were that sadistic. To do something like that….I've come across countless murderers, rapists, pedophiles, anything and everything you can think of. That was pretty harsh. I loved it!" she cheered. "One of the best shows I've seen! I almost felt sorry for them."

"I've learned from the best," Dovian murmured, watching Aria's eyes flutter closed.

Sapphire leaned forward, smiling and listening intently.

"Humans. They are the worst of all evils," he added.

"See? I told you so!" Sapphire pointed and giggled. "Alright! Let's bring in the dogs! We'll let them snack on their bodies!" The various creatures that surrounded the scene lunged forward.

Dovian lifted his head. "No."

Sapphire's enthused expression fell. He raised a hand, easing her anger.

"You said we could do things my way. This is how I want to do them. Leave them out here. Let the sun dry them out." Dovian looked over the bodies. He noticed Sapphire still didn't seem enthused by the idea. "What? You don't get it?"

"Get what?" she seethed.

Dovian hummed a laugh. "In this harsh sunlight, their skin will turn into leather. I'll use their hide...to form my new set of armor."

Sapphire gave a massive intake of breath, clapping her hands together. "What a fantastic idea!" The laughter that erupted from the child was ear-splitting.

"If there's anything left over, perhaps we can make you a new dress, hat, or shoes," Dovian suggested with a sideways smile.

Sapphire only applauded more.

"For now, let's leave them out here to dry." He looked at Aria again.

The little girl nodded her head energetically. She was ultimately pleased with the idea.

Given permission, the bionics quickly dismissed themselves, teleporting back to the cave systems. The creatures followed their actions, and Sapphire twirled and danced around the bodies a couple of moments longer before finally deciding to return to her throne room to plan out the design of her new dress. She left Dovian to himself.

The Sorcēarian stood for a while between Aria and Troy, staring at the wreckage. Finally, as if something snapped, he fell to his knees. His hands gripped the rocky dirt, his nails grinding against the hard stone beneath. A lingering moan resonated within his chest. Giving a quick shout, Dovian sent his hands to his hair. He tugged on the silver strands and fell forward, slamming his forehead against the ground. He remained motionless, fighting with all of his strength.

"Father...forgive me," he whispered. "Allow them all to forgive me."

"Unforgivable"

CHAPTER 13

As soon as Dovian made it back into his home he dropped to his knees with one hand clutching his frequency tuner and the other slapping against the stone floor. He let out a quaking breath, his stomach threatening to turn inside out. Shaking his head, he tried to erase the image of Troy and Aria from his mind. It took a few minutes for him to gather his bearings and calm himself enough to recognize the other presence in the room. Slowly turning his head to the side, he looked up at the fiery blonde whose eyes were radiating sparks. Ivory stood rigidly in the corner of the room. Dovian tore his eyes away, steadying his breath. For the first time, he was afraid of her.

"What did you do?" she asked in a harsh tone. Her voice was low but still was her own.

Dovian didn't say anything. What could he say? What should he tell her? The truth? How could he possibly make her understand?

"Tell me!" she screamed.

He took in another haggard breath and held it.

Ivory didn't need him to speak. She knew exactly what had happened, and the details would only break her heart even more.

"You actually did it, didn't you?" she asked. The silence was unbearable. "Dovian! The least you can do is stand and look in me in the eye after doing what you've done!"

The Sorcēarian tightened his fists and abruptly pushed to his feet. As much as he tried to appear cold and collected, his wrinkled brow gave away all of his fears. He stared at Ivory; his mouth parted as his mind reeled for an explanation. He didn't know where to start. No words came forth. In fact, the act of speaking threatened to cause him to vomit.

He couldn't handle the fierce look she gave him. It only spoke volumes of his character, the truth that he was a monster. All the faith she had held for the Sorcēarian was now shattered, falling to pieces around her like a glass wall. He had disappointed her. No, disappointed wasn't a good enough word. Dovian had failed Ivory, had failed everyone. There wasn't anything left to do or say. He had finally buried himself in a hole so deep the darkness would forever consume him. How could he think for one moment that she would ever forgive him if he were incapable of forgiving himself?

She marched up to him, whipped her hand back as far as she could, and whipped it across Dovian's face. It was one of the hardest hits he had ever taken, and despite trying his best to hold his ground, he toppled over onto the floor. A hit like that would have taken off a human head. It proved to Dovian that Ivory undoubtedly didn't feel concerned about possibly killing him. She had seen him die and suffer a few times now, and the threat of injuring him at that moment was not on her list of things to be worried about. And it was then that Dovian wished he could die.

Holding a hand to his red-streaked face, he didn't bother healing his broken cheekbone. Instead, he gaped at the woman as she gripped the sides of her robes in anger. Tears bubbled out the corners of her eyes as she yelled as loud as she possibly could.

"YOU ARE A MONSTER!"

The words echoed in his mind, bouncing off the walls of his never-ending hole of darkness. His throat was parched; his eyes burned; his hands and body ached with pins and needles. He wasn't sure what caused it–his fractured cheekbone and vertebrae or Ivory's words. Images and sounds invaded his mind, telling stories of hate and pain, whispering cries of death from not just his world but Aria and Troy's. The hiss of Ivory's disgust filled his heart, and Dovian felt like dying. He simply wanted to die. It was all he had wanted for thousands of years, but he didn't even deserve that, especially after what he had just done.

Ivory spun and darted out of the room, thunder roaring at what seemed like her command. The stained-glass window above Dovian shattered into a thousand pieces, coating his body. He sat in misery, his whole life flashing through his mind in a hurricane of murky, despairing emotions. There would be no mercy for him.

"RUNNING DIAGNOSTICS…COMPLETE. 25 ERRORS."

"REPAIR…COMPLETE."

"RUN VITALS SCAN…COMPLETE. 4 FRACTURES, 3 BROKEN BONES, HEAD TRAUMA, CARDIAC INSTABILITY, MASSIVE BLOOD LOSS."

"INITIATING LIFE SUPPORT SYSTEM…ADMINISTERING SHOCK THERAPY."

ZIP!

"CARDIAC RHYTHM STABLE…ADMINISTERING ADRENALINE…"

A prickly puncture in Aren's chest tore him out of his comatose state. He awoke with a sharp intake of breath, his lungs feeling as if they were being torn to shreds. The young man's heart pounded furiously, his hands shaking uncontrollably. The world was spinning, making the nerves in his stomach heave. Taking slow, steady breaths, Aren tried to calm himself.

"Damnit…" he groaned.

The act of speaking sent a splintering pain throughout his entire body. Aren's form stiffened as he sharply sucked in air.

'Don't move,' he thought. *'Don't move at all.'*

"READING VITALS…STABLE."

Aren tried to look up, but the pain shot through his body once again. Moving his sight down, Aren noticed a jagged piece of metal had blown through the cabin and impaled him through the left side of his chest.

"Oh shit," he mumbled, beginning to pass out.

The pilot closed his eyes a moment, focusing on his breathing.

"BLOOD PRESSURE LOW…"

Aren moved his eyes upward, tilting his head only a bit so not to hurt himself. "Franklin," he moaned. "Are you alright?"

"In operable condition," the robot replied.

"And…" Aren paused, "what is my condition?"

"You were pronounced dead for 35.3 seconds, but are now stable," the robot chimed.

"Oh…well, that's good, right?" Aren muttered.

"For next 45 minutes. Blood loss at rapid rate. Must slow bleeding."

Aren swallowed hard. "Med kit?" he asked hopefully.

"Cannot retrieve," Franklin replied, his pincers snapping in response.

Aren gained enough strength to look around him. How he had survived the impact was nothing short of a miracle. When in training, it was always advised to duck and cover when collision with earth was imminent. Aren could have ejected with his pilot's chair, but then he would have abandoned his comrades, and he would never do that. Besides, the attack from Sapphire's squad had occurred too fast. There wasn't much time to eject before the Hawk crashed into the ground. Instead, the only thing Aren could do was dive beneath the reinforced instrument panel.

All Hawks were equipped with what was called a safety cage. The safety cage was like a little black box of refuge. Due to being made of reinforced graphene, the safety cage was capable of providing some protection during cataclysmic impacts. Initially, the graphene boxes were used at the front of the Hawk, not as a form of shelter for crashes, but to house and conduct the magnetic force fields that protected the Hawks when in battle. Because of the metal's strength and electro-thermal conductivity, the field allowed the aircraft to receive multiple hits from lasers and missiles before breaking down and also provided protection from impact. When exposed to molecules containing carbon, the hexagonal fields were capable of repairing themselves. Thus, the best tactic to bringing down a craft was simultaneous hits within the same radius to prevent proper repair, allowing for artillery to pass through and directly collide with the ship. Due to the field's shrinking when heated, the hexagons tightened, concentrating its energies further. This protected the Hawk from heat and radiation upon entering or exiting the atmosphere, provided similar resistance against nuclear-based war, and offered protection from flash fires often caused by collisions or explosions. Needless to say, the cage saved countless lives.

The Hawk may have been destroyed, but Aren's life was saved for the time being. He struggled to contain his laugh at the thought of Walten's industry losing trillions of units at the expense of the vehicle in exchange for his life.

'Eat that,' he thought.

"Must prioritize method of transport to medical facility," Franklin chimed.

Aren nodded slowly. "Right. Uh, any way you can disengage? Get out of here?"

Franklin was quiet but made droning sounds as he twisted and twirled, gathering information.

"Ejection seat," the robot replied.

"This is going to hurt." Aren cringed as Franklin promptly ejected himself from the Hawk's rubble. It wasn't a very sneaky escape and most likely would attract the attention of Sapphire's monsters.

Aren waited a few moments, his consciousness fading in and out as thumping and bumping occurred behind him in what was left of the cabin of the copter. It was dark, nightfall had arrived, which meant Aren had been out for quite a while. The pilot gasped, trying to maintain composure.

"Hey!" he shouted, grimacing in pain as he did so. "Franklin! Any survivors? Where are Aria and Troy?"

"Negative," Franklin called out.

His blood ran cold. "What?"

"Negative."

"Ugh! What…what do you mean?!" Aren tried to gain sight of the cabin, but the metal in his torso disallowed his movement. "AH! Franklin! Where are Aria and Troy?!"

"MEDICAL KIT RETRIEVED…SCANNING…ALL ITEMS CLEAR." Franklin ran his proper functions.

"I don't care about that right now!" Aren cursed. "Get…get over here!"

With a loud clatter, the drone zipped into the front of the cabin from its newly created hole. A high-pitched whine sounded, and Aren gave a shocked cry as Franklin poked him with a needle.

"MORPHINE ADMINISTERED."

Tingles and chills covered Aren's body, and his mind flurried into a daze.

"Franklin…" he slurred, reaching toward the bot with his right hand. "Get me the hell out of here."

"Protocol requires stabilization of patient. Blood levels dangerously low. Must stop bleeding."

The young pilot watched in fear as Franklin's chomping clamp arm disappeared into his round body and returned with a plasma cutter replacement.

"Oh, shit," Aren whimpered. "Get that thing away from me!"

Franklin ignored Aren's request and zipped forward, cutting into the metal bar embedded in the man's shoulder. The whir and grind of the cutter mixed with the sound of Aren's panicked screams. After only a few seconds, Franklin had the scrap dislodged from the front. The drone investigated a bit more and found that it had gone completely through the pilot and into the chair behind him. Aren's screams had faded into moans, and he shakily wiped sweat from his brow.

"You are like baby," Franklin said.

Aren groaned, glowering at the bot. "The hell did you say?" He flung his arm in the robot's direction.

"That was easy part." Franklin replaced his cutter with his clamp and positioned to the front of the man.

"Easy?! Hey, you listen here you little SHIIIT!" Aren screamed as Franklin clamped down on both shoulders and thrust backward. The spherical drone pulled and pulled, encouraging Aren to move forward, but the pilot hadn't the strength, and the pain was only making things more difficult. If Aren wasn't going to help, then Franklin would simply pull harder. So the little bot revved his tiny motors and tugged with an astonishing force. Franklin's master gave another shriek of pain just as he was completely unpinned. Satisfied with the result, Franklin let go. Aren dropped to the side, giving an exhausted groan.

"READING VITALS...DANGER."

Franklin floated above the man, tugging and pulling an assortment of items out of the medical kit. After a second of searching, the droid gave an aggravated tone and dumped everything atop the boy.

"I'm going to punt you..." Aren whispered harshly.

"Touchdown!" Franklin gave a cheer as he lifted a hefty amount of gauze and gel ointment.

The robot's antics did not amuse Aren. Whereas he would argue with the machine on a regular day, the pilot didn't protest. He knew that this was Franklin's job. Hell, it was worth the ridiculous amount of money. But when Franklin pulled out his plasma again, Aren couldn't help but question the machine's motives.

"Now what?" Aren stuttered.

"CAUTERIZATION COMMENCING..."

The young man's eyes doubled in size. "Wha-AHHHHHHH!"

Franklin pressed the heated tip against Aren's chest. After a few moments, he roughly turned the young man and cauterized the hole in his back. Once finished, Franklin rotated his master onto his back again and did another read of his vitals.

"READING VITALS...STABLE."

Franklin beeped in satisfaction. The droid then smeared gel across Aren's wounds and tightly gauzed him up. "Chance of survival has risen 45%." Franklin mimicked the motions of clapping his hands. "Dr. Franklin has successfully completed first medical emergency."

Aren, gathering the last bit of his strength, called out to his bot. "Franklin...run search for nearest ally. Preferably someone with Bio-Tech connections."

Franklin buzzed. "SCANNING..."

Aren lay on the floor, his hazel eyes dropping to the blood-soaked locket before him. Carefully, he opened it. The hologram blipped, revealing a beautiful image of Fiona. A wavering smile crossed Aren's face.

"You were right…only gonna get myself killed." He ran his thumb over the surface of the jewelry. "I'm sorry I couldn't be there for you, Fee. If…if I don't make it out of this war alive, wait for me. I'll be searching for you."

Aren faded fast while Franklin worked. Sleep pulled him into a dream world, sending him to his old home on the top side of Fountains where he grew up.

A soft breeze filtered in from a vent beside the window seat he was lounging on. From above, he watched the green trees swaying in the city park. A stone pathway led through the plush lawn, branching off to different seating areas adorned with fountains and bronze statues. He took a deep breath, inhaling the scent of leaves and freshly cut grass. It was an artificial smell, but it was all the same to Aren. He didn't know any better, and he affiliated the scent with the outdoors, which was just as relaxing as being there in person. Giving a yawn, he thumbed a digital page of his most recent book, reading the title of the latest chapter, *"Civilization Lost."* He grinned and set the book down so he could stretch out his aching muscles. Lounging at the window all day was sometimes worse than sitting in the cockpit for hours on end. Turning his attention to his bed, Aren felt his heart swell.

Amused blue eyes watched him from under the covers. A mischievous giggle sounded, and the blankets wiggled. Aren quickly dropped to the floor, crawling on his hands and knees toward the bed. The excitable laughter rose in volume, getting more anxious as he neared.

"What's beneath the covers?" Aren asked playfully. More squealing giggles answered him.

The bed quaked as the body beneath the blankets slithered to the opposite side. Aren readied to pounce but was sent reeling back when the girl on the bed lifted. She opened the blanket wide between her hands and jumped.

"It's the Fee monster!" she shouted and collided with Aren, sending them both toppling to the floor.

Aren feigned a frightened scream, trying to hold back his laughter as he proceeded to attack the girl atop him by digging his fingers into her sides. She shrieked and wriggled; the blanket covered her form. He continued relentlessly, tickling her sides as he pretended to bite her neck.

"No fair! No fair! I'm a monster! I'm supposed to eat you!" she cackled.

Aren snarled as he rolled over and pinned the young woman to the floor, gnawing on her some more.

"Self-defense," he replied casually, turning his bites into soft kisses.

He brushed a hand through her blonde curls. Her giggles halted, and she tilted her head to allow him better access. A quiet purr sounded from the young woman as she wrapped her arms around him, her fingers raking through his orange-streaked hair.

"Seems I've tamed the Fee monster," he growled into her ear, biting her earlobe.

"Hmm. Keep that up, mister, and you'll feel the full wrath of the Fee monster." Wrapping a leg around his, she ground her hips beneath him.

"Oh, come on, Fiona…you can't tease me unless you're actually going to follow through," he moaned against her shoulder.

She gave another laugh and held onto him, her eyes watching the ceiling fan.

"I wish we could stay like this forever," she whispered.

Aren pulled away to look at her face. He shrugged. "Why can't we?" he asked, giving her a wide smile.

"Because," she pouted, "you have to go to work."

"Oh…well, we can always just continue where we left off," he murmured.

Fiona's smile faltered. "Unless something happens…."

Aren sat up, running his hand through his hair. "It's just an exercise, Fee. I'm only going to be doing simulations. No one has ever died during a simulation."

Fiona rose, wrapped her blanket around her, and created a small hood that pressed her blonde curls against her face. "I'm not talking about tomorrow. I'm talking about in the future."

"Why do you worry about the future so much?" he asked, confused.

"I'm just afraid something bad will happen to you!" Fiona was too sensitive. The mere thought of Aren getting hurt or dying would bring tears to her eyes.

"Come on, now. I'm a pilot. I'm not a ground soldier, alright? I changed that for you. There's no better place for me. I like the Air Force; it pays well." Aren looked about his bedroom. "Someday I'll be able to buy us a house like this. You and I can sit at the window all day long; we can take our kids to the park and have a picnic. Things like that."

Fiona's eyes lit up. "Kids?" she cheeped.

Aren pulled her into his lap, giving her a charming smile. "Yeah, our kids! What do you think?"

Fiona laughed. "You've not even proposed to me, silly, and you're talking about kids."

Aren mockingly gasped. "Oh, gosh! You're absolutely right, Fee! I knew I forgot something!" Reaching into his pocket, he pulled out a silver orb. Holding the item before Fiona's face, he opened it. "Can't start a family without popping the question, right?" he chuckled.

Fiona's eyes sparkled in the light, her chest heaving as she gave the loudest gasp ever. "Whaaaaaat?!" She eyed the beautiful ring inside the orb container. It twisted with black platinum, cobalt gems sparkling in the light of the window. Fiona liked out of the ordinary things, and when Aren spotted the ring, he knew it would be something she'd adore.

As he removed the item from the container, he grabbed her hand. "Well?" he asked. "What do ya say? Want to be my gal forever and ever?"

Fiona bobbed her head up and down. "YES! Of course!"

Aren smirked and slipped the ring on her finger. Fiona nearly broke him when she hugged him.

"You're serious?" she asked, still surprised.

Aren laughed. "Of course I am. What kind of cruel joke would that be?"

Fiona shook her head. "I just...wow." She stared at the jewels. "This is the most beautiful thing I've ever seen, Aren!"

"Figured you'd like it," he said, watching her adoringly.

Fiona cupped his face, placing her forehead against his. "I love it," she whispered.

"I love you," he replied, kissing her.

It was in these types of moments that Aren wished he could pause time. He didn't want to get old; he didn't want to wake up the next morning and move on with his day-to-day life; he wanted to stay here forever and never change a thing. He would never admit it, but he worried just as much as Fiona did.

Fiona living in the Underbelly was nerve-wracking to him. Every day there was the chance she could be attacked or worse–killed. The Underbelly wasn't meant for sweet, beautiful young women. It was a place for the worst of humanity. It was for murderers, thieves, rapists, and other criminals. Fiona was a diamond amongst the trash, and Aren had every intention of snatching her up.

"As soon as we get married, I'm taking you away from the Underbelly. We'll get ourselves a nice apartment together. Sound good?" he asked.

Fiona sucked on her lower lip, acting hesitant toward the idea.

"What? What's wrong?" he asked.

Feeding him a gentle smile, the woman shrugged. "Just a huge jump, ya know?"

Aren nodded slowly. He understood. Leaving the Underbelly would mean leaving her past behind. As much as Aren knew it was a bad idea for her to continue to live alone in the Underbelly, he found it hard to tell her to pack up and leave. Her entire life had been spent in the dank lower city. And even though there technically wasn't anything left for her down there, he still couldn't tell her to grab her urns and say it would be good as new up top where the sun shined.

"I know it's silly," Fiona breathed a laugh. "It's just hard. I can't imagine living anywhere else."

"I know. We can take as long as you want," Aren whispered.

Fiona became teary-eyed once again. "I'm getting married."

Aren gave a small smile. "Yeah, that's right."

Fiona sniffled. "I just wish Dad and Ivory could be here."

Aren hugged her. "Yeah, that'd be nice."

Straightening herself, Fiona gave Aren a charismatic grin. "As long as our apartment has lots of windows! And there has to be a mantle where I can place the urns nearby. Ivory always liked to look out the window."

Aren agreed with her request. "Most definitely."

Fiona eyed her new ring once again, twisting her hips side to side as she sat on her knees. "So…you're just gonna whisk me away from the dark city and take me to your castle in the sky?"

The pilot grabbed her hips, steadying them. "That's the plan," he said in a husky voice.

Fiona gave a quiet chortle. "My hero."

BWEEP!

Franklin gave a chime, tearing Aren roughly from his slumbers.

"FOUND…AFFILIATION: BIO-TECH…"

Aren, with his eyes locked on Fiona's portrait, mumbled, "Great. Send a distress signal…requesting backup and possibly a search and rescue. List all parties in the transmission. I'm sure they will realize the severity of the situation."

He eyed the second necklace that had pulled out from the safety of the inside of his shirt. Fiona's ring sparkled in the reflection of her photo. Sadly, Aren never got a chance to pop the question to Fiona. He had planned on making an event out of it the day of their anniversary, but was called into action once the recent attacks stirred up around the world. Unfortunately, he had to cancel their date. The next day the Underbelly was attacked, and Fiona was murdered. Aren swallowed his anger. The company he worked for hadn't succeeded in killing him, but had killed Fiona. Even though he knew it wasn't his fault, Aren still couldn't stop blaming himself.

"SENDING REQUEST…COMPLETE," Franklin sounded.

"ETA?" Aren shakily asked.

"LOCATION: BRITAINIA CONGO…ETA APPROXIMATELY 65 MINUTES UPON APPROVAL OF REQUEST."

His lids were still heavy, but Aren needed one more bit of information before he gave up and lost consciousness once again. "Team name?" he lazily asked.

Franklin whirred excitably. "TEAM NAME: PHOENIX."

Aren gave a short chuckle. "Holy shit," he whispered and closed his eyes.

"*Distress Call*"

CHAPTER 14

Michelle crouched behind an ammunitions crate, waiting and listening for the monster to approach her hiding place. Breathing quietly through her nose, she pushed the muzzle of her enormous automatic rifle out from behind the crate, the tip low to the ground. The camera on the end projected an image over her optics, revealing a massive shadow on the far wall at the end of the hallway. Flickering and swaying, the shattered fluorescents made the various shadows of the building dance; the crackling snap and pop of severed lines and destroyed electronics created a fitting soundtrack to the eerie setting. A gurgling growl warbled throughout the building. It was one of the big ones.

"Damn it," she shakily whispered.

Running a hand through her dark hair, she mentally cursed herself for forgetting her hair tie. A bead of sweat dripped down the side of her neck, a feeling like that of spider legs. She shivered, wiping the droplet away. The Britainia Congo was one of her least favorite places. It was hot and humid despite being surrounded by nothing but sand, and the bugs were atrocious—the spiders and scorpions being the worst. Most of the insects were the size of her hand and could make her scream like a little girl. But now, bugs were the least of her problems. These foreign monsters had attacked the Chadian I.R.B. nearly a month ago, and her team was sent in to investigate. Unfortunately, the constant blow of EMPs had done a number on her and her squad's DNAIS systems. The reach to call out for help was very limited, especially once the primary satellite had gone offline, making it nearly impossible to keep up communications with her company, Bio-Tech.

The technician of the squad, Nerd, had been working tirelessly for a week when he was able to bring in a signal to one of the main comps that hadn't been destroyed in the facility. That was when they realized Bio-Tech had gone down. President Clarke was missing along with the CEO, Walten. No one knew for sure what exactly was going on, but the live feed that had transmitted all around the world a few days ago was a mixed blessing. For the first time, her team had confirmation that Aria and Troy were still alive. Unfortunately, it seemed the two of them were directly involved with the horrors going on. Michelle had no idea who the strange little girl was, and she wasn't sure *what* in the hell the man in the scarlet robes was either, but it left a terrible feeling deep within her gut. Judging by Aria's reactions, there seemed to be a direct link between them all, and apparently things had gotten very bad. Despite all of the bad news, Michelle's group leaders were alive, and that kept her going.

Carefully, she silently checked her ammo count. She was low. A frown covered her face.

"Where you at, Spoofy?" Nerd's voice cut in through her mental chip, causing the woman to jump.

Michelle's code name was Spoofy. It was an odd name but referenced an old inside joke between Aria and her. Despite its mysterious meaning, the word registered well enough through mental communication and stuck.

Pressing against her nodule behind her ear, she replied, *"East wing. Got separated from the others when one of the big ones burst through the wall."*

"Christ! How the hell did ya get that far so fast?" he asked.

Nerd was a funny guy. He had a bit of Scotty in him but was raised in the Americas. Outside of the plaid tweed cap he always wore, one couldn't tell Nerd was a Scotty except for times where he was excited or angry. That was when his accent came to the surface.

"I ran…" she sarcastically replied, *"fast."*

"Well shit, Spoofy-gal, are ya goin' ta be able ta make it?" he asked. *"We're clear on the opposite side of the compound."*

Michelle gave an unsure groan to herself, keeping her eye on the angry beast that was now turning the corner. The massive creature sniffed the air, its golden eyes narrowing into slits. It was at a crossroads but turned its proportionately undersized head in her direction, giving another menacing growl. Boiling liquid dripped from its jaws. As it stepped forward with two stumpy legs, the monster had to duck just to fit inside the building. Rolling smoke filtered in behind its giant form, indicating that fire was close behind.

"Uh, will have to get back to you on that. Looks like the enemy has possibly spotted me," Michelle quickly stated.

Watching as the beast purposefully moved forward with its eyes locked on her hiding place, she readied her grenade mag. Sabo hadn't worked; basic grenades didn't seem to do much against it, perhaps she could fight fire with fire. Slamming an incendiary into the front of her weapon, she prepared to move.

"Yup, it's definitely spotted me," she said.

"Get yer ass outta there. I don't want any Spoofy barbecue, hear me?" Nerd called out.

"Moving!" she replied.

"I've got yer signal on my radar. I'll be sendin' reinforcements. Keep as straight a path as ya can."

"Shit. Easier said than done." She looked over her shoulder. The hallway stretched for nearly two hundred meters before a door blocked it. She had no idea what lay on the other side of that entry, but she would have to take her chances as the creature was already nearing her position. *"Send me schematics!"*

"Roger."

Pushing to her feet, Michelle fired one incendiary grenade toward the towering beast and tore off in the opposite direction down the hall. By the sound of it, the flames had momentarily halted the nemesis, but it wasn't too long before she heard the thumping steps as it progressed further and picked up speed. It only encouraged her to move faster. Slamming against the door blocking her path, Spoofy jiggled the handle a couple of times.

'Great...locked. Of course,' she thought.

Glancing back to check on her nearing enemy, she grabbed the handle with her left mechanized arm. Wrenching the handle off the door and giving a hard shove with her shoulder, she burst through and continued on her path straight down toward the second door.

At first, Spoofy was devastated when she had lost her arm during the False Syndicate War, but since then it had proven to be a blessing in disguise. She was retrofitted with a mechanized prosthetic that cupped over her left shoulder. Having the option to receive a more accurate and proportionate fitting had Spoofy shaking her head. Why choose a weak design? She wanted something that would be more accommodating to her lifestyle. Instead, the woman had a high-end mechanized-soldier arm attached. It was bulky and sometimes got in the way, but it proved more helpful than anything, such as wrenching doors from their hinges when running away from bloodthirsty monsters. Besides, it helped her out immensely during the arm wrestling tournaments she was often drug into with the boys.

She dashed through the doors as if they were paper; the giant picked up speed and continued to gain on her. Before her eyes, a schematic of the compound appeared. The blueprint spun, fixing in on her position. She was marked in blue, her chaser in red.

"Gonna have to make some twists and turns, Nerd. This guy won't letup," she mentally called.

"Definitely approved. Get a move on."

Gritting her teeth, she pushed harder, wishing she had mechanized legs as well.

'Maybe I'll get an upgrade after dealing with all this bullshit.'

Crunching through the next door, the soldier spun to the left and darted down the hall. She immediately turned left again, backtracking in the parallel corridor as the beast crunched through the previous doorway, giving a low howl. She must've pissed it off. Hopefully it would buy her some time to gain some distance. Winding around random turns and being careful not to make too much noise, Michelle gave a triumphant smirk as she saw the flickering exit sign not far away. Running at a split in the hall, she twisted to her left and halted.

Of all the corners and all the halls of the entire complex, there had to be one of the tall, lanky creatures hanging out in front of her refuge. The creature spun at the sound of her arrival, its toothy jaws opening as it sang a little welcoming hiss. These things gave Michelle the heebie-jeebies. Though she wasn't positive what they were exactly, these types reminded her far too much of the aliens portrayed in the sci-fi movies she often watched–large black eyes, small ribcage, long arms, and horrible shrieks. They were worse than the big guy that was currently hunting her.

A symphony of airy moans and hisses sounded from behind her. Oh yes, she had turned left, but she hadn't bothered looking to her right as she ran toward what she thought was her salvation.

"Run sonar. NOW!" she ordered.

Nerd complied as the map in her optic camera revealed her blue dot, the red dot before her blocking her exit, and the dozen other dots directly behind her.

"Shit," she snarled.

Ducking and rolling back into the area she came from, she dodged the swiping hand that would have clamped over her face. She turned, firing her M28 Shredder. The gun was usually equipped to the mechs, but since the weight didn't affect her all that much, it proved to be helpful in mowing down the enemy. Equipped with .50 magnum blistering pulse rounds, the weapon could easily destroy the barriers around the creatures. Usually, these breeds weren't much of an issue outside of giving her the creeps. She only had to be wary of the ones that clung to the walls. The kick of the Shredder often threw off her aim, and when the critters began to climb and jump was when they posed a real threat.

CHUNK, CHUNK, CHUNK.

She fired relentlessly onto the pile. It only took a couple seconds to blow half of them away, but then they scattered to the sides. Not only were the beings like aliens, but they were like goddamn spiders, clinging to the ceiling and wall and scampering toward her at an unreadable speed.

Backing away, the sonar kicking off every now and again to alert her of other dangers, she kept up her fight. If she could just obliterate these things, she could make it out to the courtyard and give herself some space to fight. She had to act fast as the deafening noise from her weapon had certainly given up her position, and the gargantuan monster would be back on her tail. One, two, three, four, five bodies dropped to the floor in a shuddering heap. The piercing cries made her cringe, and she backed up, tearing through the final few. Lowering her weapon, Spoofy gave an exhausted sigh. Judging by the sonar, a single creature lurked in the shadows, waiting for her to approach her exit.

'*Smart little bastards,*' she inwardly cursed.

Aiming carefully at the corner of the hall, another burst of sonar went out, and she fired three shots. The blue pulsating light ruptured the edge of the wall, the two other rounds colliding with the body on the other side. A high-pitched shriek sounded, and steaming blood flowed around the corner. She lowered her weapon again, giving a tired laugh.

Her time to rest, however, was not now, especially as the rapidly approaching tremors told her to move. As she rolled to the side, the wall next to her exploded outward. The giant had returned. Michelle resumed the chase, leaping over the bodies of the fallen creatures. She jammed the fingers of her left hand into the wall, acting as a hinge to smoothly whip her around the corner. Her chaser sped right on past, breaking through the wall into the courtyard. Ramming against the exit door, she kept her pace straight ahead, running along a suspended walkway. Now that was unexpected. She hadn't realized there was a drop-off on that side of the building. It worked in her favor as the enemy fell a good distance, smashing into the concrete below with a loud crunch. The sound of warfare commenced, and she slowed her steps, rounding a corner on the path.

Down below was the rest of her squad. They had the creature pinned, firing relentlessly into its broken body. Michelle gave a sideways smirk.

"Yeah! Get the bastard!" she shouted.

Taking careful aim, she fired upon the bubbling orange glowing sacs lining the spinal column of the gigantic beast. The pockets exploded outward, showering the concrete with a fiery liquid.

"Woah, Spoof, a little warning next time," Monkey called out.

"What? Didn't want that hot golden shower I sent your way?" she asked.

"Not exactly the kind I was hoping for," he replied.

Firing once more at the final sac at the base of the creature's skull, she gave a warning, *"May want to back up, guys. This little firecracker is about to go off."*

"Take cover!" one of the men below shouted.

They scattered like ants as the gurgling monster boiled and expanded. A moment later, once it grew to be twice as wide, the thing exploded and sent lava-like materials all over the courtyard.

"Hot damn!" Zombie hooted, stomping out from his cover behind a wasted tank in the far corner. He straightened his cowboy hat, his typical unbalanced grin growing more crooked the longer he stared at the creature's remains. "We finally killed the bastard." His southern drawl was as apparent as ever.

Zombie was originally called Wild Bill. Born and raised in the Dallas city-state, his company had been bought out in his early twenties by Walten and merged with Bio-Tech. It was then that he was placed on Aria and Troy's Delta squad. After the deadly mission during the False Syndicate War, where the entire team was assumed dead, the group was labeled Team Phoenix. Having an unhealthy obsession with zombies and finding the relabeling of the group an opportune moment to change his personal identity once again, he changed his name from Wild Bill to Zombie. He justified it as fitting the life-after-death theme. No one questioned it, and the name stuck relatively quickly.

Leaning forward, he kicked a piece of the monster, giving a sick laugh as he did so. Indeed, Zombie was having far too much fun with the creatures. At first, his theory was that they were a type of zombie created during illegal biological experiments on humans. The others hadn't disagreed with him, but as the other forms showed up one after another, each one stronger than the last, they were beginning to think there was some other explanation for them. Aliens. Zombies. Whatever they were, there had to be a leader as they seemed organized in some way. After the team had seen the live video feed with the disturbing little girl, the theories and connections became even stranger.

Spoofy found a ladder on one side. Shouldering her weapon, she stepped over the edge of the railing and slid to the bottom. The others had circled around the mess, eyeing the debris and making cheesy comments about its burning flesh. Twisting her face in disgust, she groaned when Zombie continued poking part of the monster's fleshy hand with the pointed toe of his boot.

"Will you stop that?" She slugged him in the arm.

He let out a loud groan of pain, glaring at the woman. "Let me have my celebrations, woman."

It had been nearly a week since the fire-breathing monster appeared at the base. For the most part, the team had avoided it pretty well. Unfortunately, as they were confiscating the core crystal drive, they were ambushed by it and a pack of the "lanky ones." The group had been separated meaning the second half of their mission would have to be put on hold once again. As their DNAISs had all been temporarily offline, their communications with the rest of the military and their general had been cut-off. But, judging by the debris and unnatural silence of the compound, it seemed all hope was lost for any recovery of survivors.

"By chance run into any survivors?" Spoofy asked.

"Survivors? No," Monkey replied. "But we did run into General Hughes."

The large man scratched the back of his shaved head. Monkey was a man of mass. He was tall and strong, not overly muscular, but knew how to throw around his weight. The guy looked a bit like a gorilla, but with his lax personality and loud cackling laugh, he was dubbed Monkey instead.

"You found him?" Spoofy asked. She felt some relief, but she knew better.

"Yup. Dead. Guy didn't go out without a fight though," Monkey said as he lifted up a blood-stained dog tag. "Used every last bullet. Was backed into a corner. Seemed like the pack may have gotten to him."

"Damnit," Spoofy hissed. Aggravated, she ran her hand through her dark-brown hair, her fingers tangling in the tresses.

"Copied his DNAIS so we'll have a full report at least," Monkey added.

Spoofy shoved her hands onto her hips, nodding quickly, her mouth zipped tight. "Yeah, perfect. We've completely botched the mission."

"Hey, we took down the big critter. I'd say we done a hell of a job," Zombie spoke up.

"We're still alive. I'd say that's a win...right?" Kaino asked.

Kaino was the team medic. He did what he could on the field and was often helpful in a gunfight. He was also skilled with knives and had saved a teammate's ass a time or two. He was the perfect replacement for Viper—who had met his demise during the war—and was much more pleasant to be around. The kid, however, was no longer a kid. He had grown from the tall, scrawny, nervous recruit into a full-blown soldier. He towered over nearly everyone on the team, only coming up short on Troy. His giant red-tipped mohawk only made him all the more menacing. To add to his intimidating appearance, his brawn was awe-inspiring. For being a field medic, Kaino could take on any soldier when it came to strength. For years, the team joked about changing his name to 'Roid', but Kaino's native heritage had kept him adamant about keeping his name. Thus, no one pressed the issue.

"Always thinking on the positive, ain't ya?" Zombie muttered as he toe-poked the hand again.

"Someone's got to. You guys are all anti-zen." Kaino wiped his knife off on his pants. He was always cleaning the thing.

Spoofy twisted around, her hands on her hips. "And let me guess…you all left Nerd by himself again?"

"He's safe in the bunker," Monkey said. "Besides, you think he'd leave his girlfriend behind?"

Zombie laughed at the statement.

"You mean his drone, Bridgette?" Spoofy snorted. "Guy needs to get out more. Still, who knows what will show up next after the amount of noise we just made. We better head back." Spoofy trudged forward, heading to the side of the compound where Nerd was located in the underground bunker.

When they arrived, the whole place smelt like electrical fire. Nerd was fanning his hand over a comp device, coughing and cursing. Spoofy sauntered in, circling the table and eyeing the seemingly fried part the technician was fussing with.

"I take it that was the navigational panel we needed for the Hawk…" she murmured.

Nerd, giving an aggravated snarl, nodded. "That would be it."

"Can you use this?" Monkey asked, dropping his heavy pack onto the table.

"Jeez! Careful with that, man!" Kaino winced. "Got my health pack inside."

Nerd's eyes lit up. "Did you get it?!" he asked.

"Core crystal drive is inside along with a few other random parts we could find." Monkey smiled widely, pleased with himself. "Also found a pack of candy bars."

Nerd unzipped the bag, his fingers dancing as he peered inside. "Ohhh! Hoo hoo!" He laughed, pulling out the core drive. "Ain't she beautiful?! Look Bridgette!" Nerd heaved the drive into the air, plopping the item onto the table before the round drone. "Wish I could miniaturize the thing. Make you a pretty gem to wear." He poked the bot. It whined in response.

Zombie rubbed his brow, eyeballing Monkey humorously.

Kaino slipped between the men, snatching up a candy bar. He tossed one to Spoofy, and soon they had melted into their chairs, finally relaxing after the recent adrenaline rush. The food supply was running short, and they had minimized all water usage the past few days. If Nerd couldn't repair the Hawk soon, they'd be hoofing it to the nearest base or city-state to try and find a transport of some sort. The idea didn't seem all that enticing as the closest compound would be hundreds of kilometers in every direction. They'd most likely die first of heat exhaustion, dehydration, starvation, or by monsters.

"You think you can fix it?" Spoofy asked with her mouth full of caramel.

"What?" Nerd asked, tearing his attention to the woman. "The Hawk?" he scoffed, scratching his goatee.

She gave him an irritated nod.

"Psh! Yeah! Of course!" Nerd exclaimed. "Ain't nothin' I can't do with this baby." He slapped the side of the drive.

Spoofy clapped her hands together. "Great! Then you can get your ass in gear and get that chopper fixed before another one of those lava monsters shows up."

Nerd heaved a loud groan. "Damn pissy woman! You're such a slave driver!"

Spoofy clenched her metallic fist and waved it before her face, her eyebrow rising past her forehead. The men were always mesmerized by the eyebrow raise. The furry brow seemed to have a mind of its own as it could detach and arch much higher than anatomically seemed possible.

"Yeah, yeah. Gettin' right to it." The man waved a hand at her.

While Nerd tinkered with his supplies, making sure to finish Bridgette's upgrades first, Spoofy watched Monkey with a careful eye.

"How many of those have you had?" she asked.

"What?" Monkey replied, opening another candy bar. He heard her plain as day but was more irritated with her pointing it out.

"Is that your fifth candy bar?" she asked.

"Maybe," he grumbled, shoving the treat into his mouth.

She scowled, stood up, marched to the man, and tugged the bar from his hand.

"Hey! What the hell?!" he shouted, shocked.

"And you wonder why you're getting fat. Stop eating so much!" She waved the bar in his face before tossing it to Kaino to finish.

Monkey nearly wept at the sight of Kaino unhesitatingly scarfing down the chocolate in one bite. "But he ate as many as I did!" he protested.

Spoofy folded her arms. "He works out for hours every day; he can eat as many candy bars as he wants."

"I work out," Monkey pouted.

Zombie snorted, rolling his eyes. "You work out your jaw muscles!"

Spoofy gave a sarcastic laugh. "You told me to keep you from eating too much junk food."

"Babe! I'm starving!" Monkey whined.

"Good! Maybe your body will eat itself!" she growled, biting into her snack.

As she turned away, Monkey slapped her rear-end.

"Hey...monkey see, monkey do. Maybe you should lay off the candy bars, too," he huffed.

Nerd quickly chimed in, "You jes' rhymed."

Spoofy spun back around, readying to smack Monkey upside the head, but he caught her arm and gave a boisterous laugh. "I'm just joking!"

She tugged her arm away, glaring at him with her crazy eyebrows. She finished her candy bar and plopped back into her chair, watching Nerd work.

Monkey leaned back with his feet on the table. "Why are you women always so moody?"

"Because we're surrounded by idiot men," Spoofy snapped.

Kaino butted in this time. "Hey...I have a Ph.D."

Spoofy sat up, holding her hands out toward Kaino. "See? Brains and brawn. The perfect specimen."

Kaino gave a sheepish smile while Monkey sulked.

"I graduated high school," Nerd added as he passed by the woman.

She patted him softly on the head. "You're cute," she said in a condescending manner.

Nerd shrugged. "I try!" He looked at his bot. "Hear that Bridgette? I'm cute!"

A strange noise similar to flatulence sounded from the drone.

Nerd paced back to his workstation, holding his chin high. "I'll take that as a compliment."

Spoofy rubbed her forehead, letting out a sigh. "I feel dumber already."

"Don't ya worry, Ms. Spoofy. I'll get the Hawk into the air in no time." Nerd gave her a lovable smile, his green eyes creasing. She couldn't help but return the expression.

Nerd may have been an easy target to tease, but the man truly was a mechanical and technological genius. He was self-taught, too. Anything that had moving parts Nerd could fix. At his current age and experience, all he had to do was look at an object, and he could figure out how the whole thing operated. Not only that, but he was a master of transforming one part into another. If he didn't have the proper tool or hardware, he could jury-rig something entirely unrelated into a fully functioning part. In fact, Spoofy had seen him turn an entire M28 Shredder into a tiny motor using only a few spare parts. It all made sense to him, but it was like rocket science to her. She didn't care as long as he got things running.

After having a dinner of chocolate bars, Spoofy and the others eventually passed out from sugar overload. Nerd kept feverishly working, the candy providing more than enough fuel to keep him going. After an hour, he and Bridgette finished up reworking the navigational panel, taking a few spare chips from the crystal core. The drive provided much more useful than Nerd had hoped. Not only had he been able to fix up the navigational panel, but he was able to upgrade it and a number of other electronic parts for the Hawk. He traveled back and forth from the bunker to the helicopter, constantly looking over his shoulder as he left the tunnel each time. He couldn't help but feel like he was constantly watched. He was sure the critters were waiting for the perfect time to strike. Bridgette kept a careful watch, sending out sonar and thermal readings for Nerd while he worked. Though, the drone couldn't help but squeal every once and a while just to get a rise out of her owner.

"Damnit, Bridgette! Would ya knock it off?" Nerd shouted after the sixth time the high-pitched noise screeched.

This time the drone didn't stop but kept up the sound in even beats. A blinking light on his wrist alerted him, and he gave a quick yelp as he slammed the navigational panel back into the Hawk's motor. Twirling, the man sprinted down the tunnel back into the bunker, his DNAIS chiming in alarm.

"Spoof!" he shouted.

The woman jumped at the noise, already glancing at her wrist which was sounding off. The chimes beeped at irregular intervals between the entire team. Soon, the whole squad was awake in alarm, staring at the light. Spoofy clicked against her wrist, her DNAIS pulling up a distress beacon.

A robotic voice called out, words scattering across the holo-screen.

"SAR REQUEST. SAR REQUEST. HAWK DOWN. HAWK DOWN. BIO-TECH CLASS A-5 AND A-4 MILITARY FIGHTERS IN NEED OF ASSITANCE. INJURIES SUSTAINED. LOCATION: IVES. SURVIVORS: PILOT, AREN HAGAR. UNKNOWN: CLASS A-5 OPERATIVE, ARIA IVANOV…CLASS A-4 OPERATIVE, TROY MOREAU. REPEAT…"

The SOS repeated. Spoofy confirmed retrieval and rose from her seat.

"Nerd…you got that Hawk ready?" she eagerly asked.

All the others were already gathering their gear and cleaning up Nerd's mess.

"Yes, ma'am. Just finished 'er up." He nodded.

"Great. Get her started. We're heading out ASAP." She grabbed her bag, already having everything packed and ready beforehand. "Come on, ladies! We've got to help out our friends!"

Zombie followed quickly behind, sucking down his cigarette like it was his last. Kaino ran up to the man, multiple packs slung across his back and arms. He reached around the cowboy and tugged on the cig, throwing it to the ground. Zombie didn't protest outside of a grunt. He knew he was supposed to have quit the habit long ago, and Kaino was a constant reminder.

Following the team down the tunnel, Kaino called out to Monkey, "Hurry it up, chunky-monkey! We'll leave without you!"

Monkey finished scooping his arsenal into his knapsack, making sure not to forget the candy bars. Shoving another into his mouth, he was sure to finish the sweet before boarding the Hawk so Spoofy wouldn't notice. Kaino and Zombie no sooner tugged Monkey into the craft before Nerd had lifted it off the ground, the doors closing around them.

"Jet mode activated, ladies and gents. ETA: 65 minutes," Nerd called out over the com.

Spoofy and the others buckled themselves, all anxiously trying to settle in. They eyed one another and then took varying glances out the side window as the Britainia Congo disappeared from view.

"Never a moments rest," Monkey muttered.

"Hated that place. Hopefully, where we're going is a lot better," Zombie drawled.

Spoofy gave an unsure groan. "Don't bet on it."

"Where we goin' again?" Monkey asked.

"God! Do you ever pay attention?" Spoofy eyed him angrily. She noticed the chocolate smeared on the corner of his mouth, and her frown deepened.

"I was gathering my stuff!" he protested.

Spoofy sighed, pulling up a map on her DNAIS. She pointed to their designated destination.

"Remember that place from all those fairytales Aria used to read that we used to make fun of?" Spinning the map around for the others to see, she brushed through her hair. "Looks like that's the source of all the action. Aria and Troy are stranded in Ives. And based on the report...there's a possibility that they may not be alive."

"You think they may be dead?" Monkey asked slowly.

Spoofy shrugged. "The report said it was inconclusive. Meaning the Hawk had crashed, and their pilot has no idea whether or not they are living. If that's the case, then I can assume that they weren't at the site of the wreck. Possibilities could be endless. We're on a search and rescue mission, boys. We do not rest until Aria and Troy's bodies are found...dead or alive." Shutting down the map, she rested her chin in the palm of her hand, looking out the window while the men exchanged worried looks.

Aria and Troy were heroes. They were often the ones to rescue the rest of the team's juvenile asses. Now it appeared as though the tables had turned. It was up to Spoofy and the others to save them. At least, she hoped Aria and Troy were still living enough to be saved. Chances were if something took them down; it had to be big and bad. Spoofy hoped her gang was capable of rescuing their leaders without getting into trouble themselves. She gave a nervous exhale. Things were getting a bit scary.

'*Aria, you had better be alive,*' Spoofy thought, looking over the rest of her team. '*You can't leave me alone with these guys.*'

"Spoofy"

CHAPTER 15

The sweltering heat of the desert sun was horrendous, engulfing all that was in white light. Aria felt like she was boiling, her body being covered in sweat. Opening her eyes with a flutter, her pupils thinned into tiny dots as she focused on the bright sphere above her. She immediately clenched them shut; her sight remained white behind her lids. Licking her dry, cracked lips, she covered her face. Everything was like a fog. Her head was pounding, but the pain was quickly fading. Giving a rattling cough, she rolled to her side, her hand sticking to the tacky blood on her shirt. Hiding the sunlight behind her hand, Aria looked to her other blood-soaked one. She moved her fingers, the blood cracking like paint against her palm. At first she was confused; then realization hit her.

Giving a sharp gasp, she sat up, tugging on her shirt. Blood had soaked her clothing at one time, but now was mostly dry. She stuck a finger through the singed hole, wiggling it, and then moved the material from side to side, trying to catch a glimpse of her stomach wound. Nothing. There was nothing there but the red stain of her blood. There was no bullet wound. Placing her hand on her back, she gave a quiet whimper as she palmed the cloth. She felt no pain, felt no hole, and drew her hand back to find it dry. The longer she was awake, the better she felt, and soon she was jumping to her feet. Grabbing the opening at the front of her shirt, Aria pulled and tore the hole wider. She stared at her bare stomach, continuing to pull the shirt apart all around her lower torso. Still nothing. She was completely healed.

"How?" she whispered, checking herself repeatedly. "I...I don't get it."

She looked up, and fear stilled her. Troy lay not far away, but he appeared very dead. Aria gave a shout and sprang forward. She dropped harshly to her knees, reaching to check his vitals. Blood caked the whole right side of his face and neck. A cry erupted from Aria when she felt no pulse. Snatching his wrist, she pressed against his DNAIS, activating his vitals log. The screen blipped slowly, static streaking across it. Dovian could've fried his system, but there was a small singular beep that chimed, and the woman's eyes widened. She waited another moment, staring at the screen with her full attention.

"Come on…" she whispered. "Come on…."

She looked back down at Troy's face. He was paler than she'd ever seen, but his cheeks were red from sunburn. The blood that had poured from him was now dry and a dark shade that matched the cracks in the desert ground.

"*Please!*" she pleaded, staring at his DNAIS.

It blipped again, and Aria gave a shuddering breath. She placed a hand on Troy's face, calling out to him.

"Wake up, Troy. Please tell me you're still alive." Tears stung her eyes as her hand fell on his chest. There was a faint rumble beneath her fingertips, and the machine blipped again. Confused, Aria pressed her ear against the man's chest. Sure enough, she heard a quiet vibration, and the DNAIS called out to her once again.

"That," she looked at the display again, "…isn't right."

As she pushed against the screen, Aria's heart skipped a beat. Choking on a sobbing laugh, she felt a mixture of emotions–relief, sadness, and anger.

"Oh my God, Troy!" she growled. "You have a pacemaker?!" She hit him in the chest, causing the DNAIS to beep once again.

Of course, he would need one after the heart attacks he went through in the hospital. But what she didn't understand was why he hadn't told her. In that instant, Aria didn't care. All that mattered was that the previous heart attacks were a godsend. If it weren't for the pacemaker, he would certainly be dead. Right now, it was the only thing keeping him alive.

Aria swiped across the holographic image, clicking on a series of commands.

"Resuscitate?" she asked with a shaky breath. "Uh…yeah? Yeah, I think so." Panicked, she pressed the commanding button. She screamed and gave a jump as Troy's body jolted with electric shock from the internal defibrillator.

"Oh, God!" She covered the lower half of her face, watching in fear as his body shook a second time.

The violent tremors continued a few more times before Aria couldn't handle it anymore.

"Stop! Stop!" She slapped the screen. "Just stop!" Tears fell down her face. A couple of short sobs gushed from her followed by a small wail as a warning message popped up, bringing a new image to the forefront. Troy's brain wasn't sending or receiving signals. The EEG wasn't reading anything. In other words, he was brain-dead.

"Ohhhh," she moaned, her chest heaving with her quaking breaths. "Ohhhh, no."

Slowly, she placed a hand on Troy's head, crying out in distressing groans.

"Troy," she bawled. "My...my Troy."

Aria wrapped her arms around him, weeping like a child. A hand clutched his hair as she rocked him, her body heaving with her violent sobs.

"Why?" she asked. "Why am *I* still alive?"

She pressed the side of her cheek to his forehead, closing her eyes.

"I've got nothing now. Nothing. You were all I had, Troy. You're my everything." The words were barely formed as she spoke. "If I could, I would take your place. I would rather be dead than live a life without you."

Aria sat in silence, cradling her partner. She thought about his unresponsive brain. She imagined the emptiness that consumed his once vibrant personality. His mind was like a black room with all the light bulbs broken. As Aria held Troy, her hand tightly gripped his skull. The screen whirled and flickered to life. The model representation of his brain jostled and spun back and forth as readings scattered across the image, gathering a new set of information.

"Oh, God...please," she whispered. "I don't know what I would do without him. Don't take him. Please don't take him away from me."

Aria did the only thing she could–pray. She prayed hard and relentlessly. The more she wished she could take his place, the weaker she felt. Perhaps she was dying. On the outside, she appeared fine, but maybe she was baked on the inside. Was it possible that she was nothing more than a ghost wandering the world trying to find Troy? Was she even alive? Was this what death was really like?

A series of alarms broke out across Troy's DNAIS. Aria jerked out of her sleepy haze. She gave a quiet gasp and clicked on the screen. Troy's mind was responding. It was coming to life, and one after another the cogs fit back into place. He was receiving blood; electrical signals were reading, and neurons and synapses' were firing. The questioning for resuscitation appeared again, and she quickly accepted the request. Another electric shock went through Troy's system, followed by a second. By the third zap, a loud strangled cry exploded from the man, and his olive eyes popped open.

Aria gave a surprised scream in response. Her heart nearly shot out of her chest as the man in her arms gave a sharp intake of breath, his eyes darting all around him. A faint laugh passed Aria's lips, and she suddenly felt lightheaded. She dropped Troy and fell backward, her head slamming into the rocky ground behind her. Harshly sucking in air, she struggled to keep her eyes open as darkness consumed her.

"Aria!" his voice called out to her.

She couldn't see, but his voice was like magic, pulling her back to him. No, not now. She wasn't going to die now that he was alive. Aria lifted her hand in the air, smacking against something. Another hand held hers. Trying to gather the sight of the blackened-out silhouette of the man that kneeled over her, Aria gave an airy laugh.

"Who…who's the hero now, huh?" she stammered.

She didn't hear a response this time, but she welcomed the embrace that she received instead. She was glad he wasn't asking questions because she didn't have any answers. What had just happened was nothing short of a miracle. Aria weakly clung to the man; her eyes closed. She was exhausted, but she knew that they had to find a place to hide. They were, after all, stranded on Ives.

"Troy…are you okay?" Her hands remained clasped around his neck. She felt him nod, and for the time that was enough. "I'm so glad. We need to hide. We need to get somewhere safe," she barely whispered.

The man remained silent but responded by lifting her in his arms. She was surprised he had so much strength. Aria decided that she shouldn't question anything. They were alive, and that's all that mattered.

Tearing her head away from the man only for a moment, Aria gathered her awareness. Her optic camera still worked, giving her a familiar reading.

"Keep heading that way." She tried pointing a finger, her body bouncing against Troy's chest. "You'll come across the old vacation home. Maybe we can get some rest…for a while."

Despite desperately wanting to stay awake, Aria felt sleep creep over her. Troy encouraged her to rest, pushing her head against his chest. The sound of his heartbeat and the simple gesture of his thumb running up and down her arm soothed her.

The next time Aria's eyes opened, she found herself surrounded by darkness. Crickets chirped outside; a fresh breeze rolled by, carrying the scent of rain. There was a rumbling in the distance, and a series of quiet ticks and patters sounded. The woman sat up; her heart pounded. Where was she?

Searching her surroundings, a pale light from the moon cast the room in a blue hue. She was lying on a pile of blankets atop a makeshift bed. Her boots were missing, and the grime had been washed from her body. As she took in the sight, she found that she was alone.

"Troy!" she shouted.

A chill air enveloped her, and she wrapped a blanket around herself. There came no response.

Panicked, she looked out the window beside her. "Troy!" she cried out again.

A shuffle in the doorway alerted her, and she brought her attention to the entry of the room where a tall shadow stood. A cloud blocked out the moonlight. Aria squint her eyes, trying to gather detailing of the person. He walked forward, feet crunching against rock and dry grass. As he neared, the light appeared again, and Aria finally released her held breath. It was Troy.

He held up a hand, showing her a water canteen. He shook it lightly. That was when she realized how thirsty she was. He passed the container over, his leather glove wet. Aria took a swig, eyeing the window as the rain outside gently poured. Not wanting to hog it all, she tried passing it back to the man, but he only shook his head. Tapping on his belt, he made her notice the second bottle at his side.

Aria eyed him suspiciously. "Not in a talking mood?" she asked.

Troy hung his head, his hands shoving deep into his pant pockets. He swayed about nervously, giving a casual shrug.

"You're never like this," she pressed the issue. "Even at your worst, you're never quiet."

Scuffing the toe of his boot against some splintered wood, he gave another shrug. Aria took a drink, watching the solemn man before her. What was he thinking?

"We're alive, Troy. That's all that matters. Not all hope is completely lost. We've survived. That means something, right?" she muttered.

Air passed through the man's nose, and he nodded.

"So what's the deal?" she questioned again.

The man ran his hands over his face. There was no aggravated groan, no whine, no curse words, nothing. Troy's eyes held a hint of sadness as he forced a lackluster smile.

"What's wrong?" Aria asked. Now things were getting a bit weird.

He shook his head and dropped into a seated position beside her on the bed. The light rain filtered off and on, the clouds fighting with the light of the moon. A single ray momentarily beamed into the old house, shining across Troy's face. He had a large scar running from his ear down the side of his neck. It was a bullet wound, but somehow it had mostly healed already. Aria touched the line, gaping at the man in wonder.

"How?" she asked.

Troy shrugged.

"Damn it, Troy! Are you going to talk or not?" she hollered.

The man's face finally turned into a sour expression. With his hands flying in her face, he signed to her.

'I can't talk.'

Though sign language had no volume, Aria could see his frustration.

"What do you mean you can't talk?!" she exclaimed.

Grimacing, he signed again. *'I can't talk. Not since this.'* He ran a finger down his throat.

Aria shook her head. "No! You, you said my name when you first woke up. I heard it."

He disagreed. *'I didn't say a thing. I tried, but no sound came.'*

"Mental chip?" she questioned.

Troy turned his head, poking the back of his ear. His mental chip was damaged as well. Aria narrowed her eyes. She could swear to the moon and back that the man had called out her name. It was her sense of security as she blacked out. It was Troy, and he was alive.

"I heard your voice," she whispered.

'Impossible.'

Aria watched him carefully. His spirit was gone. Troy was defeated.

"We'll get it fixed, Troy. We'll get your voice back. Don't worry." She placed a hand on his shoulder.

He gave a harsh breath through his nostrils. *'How?'*

Aria was quiet, pondering.

'We're stranded. Hawk is destroyed. Aren is dead. We're dead. Only a matter of time.' His hands moved slowly, matching his gloomy resolve.

Aria reached and lowered his hands. Looking him directly in the eye, she spoke firmly, "We are not dead, Troy. We'll make it out of this."

Troy shook his wrist. *'DNAIS isn't reaching. Storms are blocking signals. Can't send SOS.'*

Aria abruptly looked to her wrist, trying to pull up a signal. All she received was static noise.

"Damn Ives and its storms…" she growled.

They sat in complete silence with one another. Aria's thoughts drifted to Dovian.

"Why are we still alive?" she whispered.

Troy shrugged.

"Do you think it was his doing? Do you think he somehow spared us?" she asked.

Troy lifted his shoulders again before curving in on himself, resting his elbows on his knees to cup his face.

"You were dead. I woke up, and you were dead," she spoke quietly.

Troy remained silent.

"You were brain-dead. Your vitals log told me so." A whimper sounded from her, and she covered her mouth. "And look at you now. You're alive. You appear perfectly fine. Well, except for your voice."

He didn't move.

"And why didn't you tell me you had a pacemaker?!" she shouted.

Troy pressed his face deeper into his hands.

"Damn it! You could've been killed so many times now, Troy. What would have happened if I zapped you with an EMP on accident? It could have sent you into a heart attack! You should have told me!"

"Please stop yelling. Why are you always yelling?" Troy's voice rang out in her mind.

Aria halted her lecture. "What?" she asked.

The man didn't say anything.

"Are you sure your mental chip doesn't work?" she asked.

Troy lifted his head, eyeing her carefully.

"You just spoke to me," she sputtered.

'I didn't say anything,' he hastily signed.

"I heard it." She grabbed the side of his head, inspecting the large scar.

The man turned to her, grabbing her shoulders.

"You talk so much," his voice called out again.

"There!" she shouted. "You did it again! I heard you!"

Troy irritably closed his eyes. *"I'm not saying anything! You're crazy!"*

"I am not crazy!" she snapped.

Troy's eyes opened wide. *"You heard me call you crazy?"*

She briskly bobbed her head. "Yeah. I think your chip is working."

He gave an unsure smile. *"I'm not trying to use my chip."*

She was bewildered. "Then...how?"

"I'm thinking." He paused. *"I think you can read my thoughts...."*

"That's impossible! No way."

"What am I thinking about right now?" he asked.

Aria was hesitant to answer as a swirl of noises and images passed through her mind. She shook her head, trying to sort them all out. Then she gave a quiet laugh.

"What you always think about...cheeseburgers and beer!"

Troy finally gave a crooked smirk, wishing he could share a laugh with her. After another second, Aria's face fell. Troy's feelings and thoughts were spiraling around her, revealing much more than she had ever realized about the man.

"That's really how you feel?" she asked.

The man gulped, trying to clear his thoughts. What was he thinking about in that split-second?

"Am I that unhappy all the time that it makes that much of an impression on you when I smile?" she asked.

He gave her a pitying look. *"It's always nice to see you smile."*

Aria detached herself from Troy, sinking into herself once again.

"Wish I could read your thoughts." He leaned forward, resting on his knees.

"How is this possible, Troy?" she asked. "None of this is making any sense."

Troy lifted his palms up. *"Beats the hell out of me."*

"Maybe Dovian did something. Maybe he healed me somehow. Maybe it took a lot of energy, and I'm feeling residual effects?" she suggested.

"I'd rather not think about him right now, Aria." Troy stood from the bed. *"We've got to get out of here."*

"He didn't kill us, Troy," Aria said. "We were right. He doesn't want to do the things he's doing."

"The hell he doesn't, Aria. For once, please stop justifying his actions."

Troy glared at the corner of the room, his hands curling into fists. He couldn't help but think about it, think about Dovian and Aria together in the hotel. He thought of how much she laughed when she was around the Sorcēarian. He couldn't help but think of Gavin, think of how torn up Aria was inside about his death. Troy was no comfort. He provided no security for her. And despite all of his efforts, throughout his entire life, he had done nothing but failed her. When it came down to it, Troy couldn't rescue her as Dovian heartlessly aimed at his head and fired the pistol. Troy wanted nothing more than to save Aria. He had no idea what Dovian had done to her, but judging by her shock, he had tried to kill her, too.

"We're alive when we shouldn't be, Troy. That says something. I'm not justifying him. If Dovian wanted us dead, we'd be dead. No doubt about it. How else would we be alive right now?" She stood from the bed, placing her hand on his shoulder. "I know you lost your voice. But maybe it was necessary to keep you alive."

Troy turned to her. His mouth opened as he tried to speak, but no sound came. *"Aria. Dovian didn't save me. You did."*

Aria scoffed. "That's ridiculous."

"It's true. When he sent his energy through me, I felt the last amount of life drain from my body. At that moment, I went from feeling scared to completely relaxed. He made it so easy, Aria. So easy to give up and die." Troy lowered his head, staring at the floor between their feet. *"I left you, Aria. I left you to die alone. Despite my efforts, I've only failed you."*

"You didn't fail me, Troy." She placed a hand against his cheek, but he didn't meet her gaze.

"I was gone, feeling nothing, dreaming of nothing. I was surrounded by darkness. It was like a deep sleep. For a moment, I no longer existed. Then, I heard you call. I heard you saying my name. Suddenly, I was being pulled forward. I felt…odd. Like a blast of light washed over me. There were tingles throughout my brain that went through my entire body. Next thing I knew, you were leaning over me, and I was waking up." Troy's brow wrinkled. *"You saved me, Aria. I have no idea how, but your voice was like magic. I heard strange words flow from you that I've never heard you speak, and you pulled me back."*

Aria stepped away. "You think I healed you?"

Troy rubbed the back of his head. *"Felt that way…to be honest."*

Aria looked at her hands. Perhaps Dovian had somehow transferred some power to her. In that last moment, as he held onto her, maybe he placed something inside her that she didn't feel at the time. Was she capable of temporarily housing his power? It still didn't make sense. He had told her that he could only heal someone if he physically touched them. His weapon was an extension of himself, and only he could use it. All of Dovian's power belonged to him and no one else. Then, there was the armor Camery had designed for Aria and Troy. He said he infused the armor with Dovian's DNA instead of morphine. Was it possible that his DNA was still in her body? That didn't explain why Troy couldn't heal himself.

As Aria concentrated on the idea, she saw a blue tinge to her hands. Gasping, she tugged off her leather fingerless gloves. Prickles of blue light surged over her fingertips. Holding her hands up in the shadows, she noticed that it wasn't the moon casting the glow. Aria was emitting light. Troy warily watched her.

"What's happening to me?" she whispered.

Anxiously, she wrapped her hands around Troy's neck and clenched her eyes shut. The man stiffened under her touch. Nothing happened at first, but soon an electric prickle crackled over his neck. It tickled like the fibers of a feather against his skin. The woman concentrated, her thoughts forming over a prayer. It seemed to work last time, perhaps it would work again. As she said a simple prayer, wishing for Troy to be healed, asking for assistance, blue light flowed from her palms and washed over the man's head and neck. Troy gave a deep breath, feeling a sense of peace.

Aria could mentally visualize the healing process. Troy's vocal cords reattached accordingly, nerves moved, skin cells rearranged, and soon everything shimmered with sparkling white light. Opening her eyes, Aria watched as the glow dissipated. Afraid to move, she kept her hands wrapped loosely around the soldier's neck. Timidly, Troy wrapped his hands around hers, lowering them.

"Well?" she asked apprehensively.

He gave her a mysterious look, cocking his head to the side. "I think it worked," he said in a raspy voice which sent him into a fit of coughs.

Aria gave a quick laugh and wrapped her arms around him. Troy held her against him. He cleared his throat, the sound loud in Aria's ear.

"Have you always been able to speak in tongues?" There was humor in his voice, but there was also a hint of unease.

Aria looked up at him in confusion. "Speak in tongues?"

Troy gave a sideways smirk. "Yeah. Just now…when you healed me, you weren't speaking English."

Aria's forehead wrinkled. "I thought I was."

Troy let out a slow breath. "What'd he do to you, Aria?"

She shook her head, placing her ear against his chest again. The pacemaker clicked in her ear between random heartbeats. The sound worried her.

"He didn't do anything," she muttered.

"He did something. I wasn't alive, remember? You have to tell me what he did." Troy's anger was rising suddenly, and Aria wasn't sure why.

She moved away. "He…." She was reluctant to tell Troy what happened. She honestly believed deep in her heart that Dovian wasn't a monster. Truthfully, she was frightened out of her mind while Dovian was on his psychotic rampage. She had never seen him like that, and assumed he'd never behave that way. In fact, she believed he wanted to kill her. All hope had been lost. But now she was alive. She was standing and so was Troy. Dovian had to have been responsible for that as well.

"Damn it, Aria. Did he hurt you? There was blood on you. What happened?" he asked lowly.

Aria looked down at her bare stomach. She shyly ran her hand over her skin. As she replayed the events in her head, tears filled her eyes.

"Troy…" she tried to laugh about it. "He shot me."

Her words unglued the man. Spinning away, he gripped his hair. "He shot you…." He could barely manage to say the words.

"Yeah. With the same gun he shot you with. He turned around, jammed it under my ribcage, and pulled the trigger." Her jaw was clenched tight, awaiting Troy's wrath.

The man slammed his fist down on the stone table in the corner. The booming noise caused the woman to jump. He placed his hands on either side of the surface and didn't meet Aria's eyes.

"He actually did it. He really *did* try to kill you. Despite my pleas…despite everything we've been through. He tried to kill you," Troy snarled in a harsh whisper.

"I don't think he wanted us dead, Troy. We're still alive!" Aria spoke up.

"That's not good enough! That doesn't make sense, Aria. He didn't want us alive! If he did, he would've come back with us. He would have let Ivory come with us! The man's a monster, plain and simple!" he yelled.

"How do you explain us then? Why are we standing here?" she asked.

Troy shook his head. "I have no clue, Aria, but it wasn't his doing. I know it."

"What other explanation is there?" She stepped forward. "Why are you so set on him being a monster? I thought we were past this. I thought you were over that stupid night in Saray!"

"It's not about that!" Troy shouted.

"The hell it isn't!" she quarreled.

Troy gave an exasperated sigh. "What I wouldn't give for you to lose your voice for once. It'd give me time to sort my thoughts and form some damn words!"

"Those are your thoughts, Troy! You resent Dovian. God! I have one night, one night where I let loose, and you get pissed! What about all the nights I had to babysit you, come to the rescue, or give you advice on all the different women you brought home?" Aria shouted.

"That's not what I'm upset about." Troy rolled his eyes.

"Then what in the hell are you upset about, Troy?" Her voice was like ice. "Lately it seems all you want to do it fight with me."

Giving a frustrated scream, the man tugged on his hair. "It's because I'm inadequate!" he roared.

Aria was stunned. "You…feel inadequate. So…because you feel

inadequate, you fight with me?" She sounded thoroughly confused if not slightly sarcastic, and that only made Troy more perturbed.

He sank back against the table, his palm running over his face. "No, no. I don't want to fight with you," he said in a calmer tone. "Aria, can't you see? I do enough fighting. I go out nearly every day fighting wars that don't make sense, risking my life for others I don't even know. People say I have no heart, have no soul. They define me by what they think I am. They ask me why I do this. They think I am lost. But you know what? I'm not lost."

Aria's posture loosened as she listened intently.

"Fighting in these wars, in these endless battles, they are what keep me living. I get up every day and fight. Not for glory, not for honor, but to be by your side. I do this to protect you, to watch your back, to make sure nothing happens to you. Because once you're gone, I have nothing. I *am* nothing." Troy palmed his chest. "I'll lose my heart; I'll lose my soul. I'm not lost because I fight. I'm found because I am doing it with you, for you. If anything were ever to happen to you, I would be lost, Aria. It's not what I do that defines me; it's who I do it with that defines me. And I can't think of any better definition for myself than *you*. So no, I'm not here to fight with you. I'm here because I love you."

Once again, Aria was speechless. Troy lowered his stare to his boots.

He continued, "And I feel inadequate because I have consistently allowed you to get hurt. I have allowed you to remain unhappy. And I'm tired of running away with you. I'm following in the shadow of your fears from the past. I don't want to do that anymore. I want to be here with you, in the present. I want to keep you secure for the future. So, I'm not angry because you're happy. I'm not angry because Dovian had made you laugh at one time. I'm mad because I wasn't the man who did it. I'm mad at myself for not being able to bring those smiles to your face, for not being able to comfort you in the death of our friend...Gavin. I'm mad because I allowed harm to come to you, from Dovian no less. And I'm mad that I wasn't a better friend to him, to maybe prevent him from doing what he's doing now. You know, my mind spins in circles, too. And yeah, I shut it off. I ignore my problems. Because if I dwelled on everything like you did, we'd probably not be standing here today." He rubbed his eyes, feeling awkward under her scrutiny. "So, um...yeah. That's what I was thinking."

In two large strides, Aria was against him, her arms snaking around his torso in a tight embrace. Squeezing her eyes shut, she fought back her tears. Troy didn't hate her. He never had. He loved her, and he showed his love every day since the first day they met by always fighting by her side. No matter what other options arose for him, he always stayed with her. After everything they had been through, after all the years, Troy's love never faltered but only grew stronger. And now everything in their world threatened to tear it apart. She had nearly lost him, just like she had lost Gavin. Every day they were in danger, and every day of the future their lives were going to be at risk. It scared the hell out of her.

"But...what if?" her voice wavered as she sniffled.

"What if what?" Troy asked. He gently held her away from him, trying to look at her face. "What is it you're so afraid of?"

Aria's green eyes fled to his. "What if things go wrong?"

Troy smirked. "You're always pessimistic. For once, why can't you just ask yourself, what if things go right?"

Running a hand along the side of her face, he brushed her hair behind her ear. Moonlight shimmered against the tears in her eyes, creating silver orbs. Leaning down, Troy met her lips. Aria sank against him, pulling him tightly toward her. He returned the gesture and wrapped his muscular arms around her small frame. For once, he felt whole. Aria was the missing puzzle piece. She made sense; she felt right. She was his everything, his home.

Aria parted, giving a quiet gasp for air as she fought with herself to maintain self-control. "Don't ever leave my side," she said in a shuddering whisper.

Troy held her, planting a firm kiss on her forehead. "Never," he spoke softly against her.

Aria directed him back to her lips. They had nearly died, and now they were stranded on Ives. They had no way off the island, and it was only a matter of time before they were found. It frightened her. It could be the last night of their lives together.

After another kiss, she finally reciprocated. "I love you. I love you so much, Troy."

He gave a quiet sigh. "I've waited years for you to say that," he replied with a chuckle.

Troy deepened the kiss, and soon the two could barely keep their balance as Aria pulled him with her.

"Bed," she moaned, her teeth grazing his lower lip.

He hummed a laugh against her flesh, kissing and exploring her neck. "Is that an order?"

"Yes!" she hissed.

He gave another rumbling laugh. "Waited years for you to say that, too."

Aria's passionate gasps only urged Troy to continue as he gently bit her earlobe. The woman pulled him, and he fell onto the bed. She climbed atop, straddling him. A broad grin crossed her face as she tugged off what remained of her shirt. The feel of his body beneath her was tantalizing. Troy looked thoroughly amused, his face holding a dumb smirk. He tried grabbing her chest, and she smacked his hands away, giggling. He persisted until Aria gave up and allowed him to continue his exploration. Sitting up, pulling her hips against him, he trailed kisses along her collarbone and shoulder. It wasn't long before Aria's control over him was slack, and he took the opportunity to flip her over onto the bed, a loud squeal erupting from her. She twisted her mouth in feign dissatisfaction.

"You've had plenty of years to dominate over me, Miss Ivanov." Troy pulled off his shirt. His dog tags clinked against his bare chest. "You have your areas of expertise…let me show you mine."

Aria gave a gasping laugh as the man effortlessly pulled off her pants with one tug. Troy beamed with joy, grinding his hips against her in a way that made her cover her eyes in embarrassment. The sound of her laughter was like music to his ears. Seeing her beneath him in nothing more than her underwear with a pink tinge to her face, Troy finally felt like he had won the war.

'Oh, yeah. I've waited years for this,' he thought.

Covering the woman with his body, he planted a soft kiss on her lips. He finally had her, and he was never letting go.

WWW.ARCREBS.DEVIANTART.COM

"Tired Of Waiting"

CHAPTER 16

As Ivory walked down the dilapidated halls, she trailed a thin hand along the walls. Etched markings covered the surfaces, her fingertips reading the language, translating tales into her mind of the world beyond hers that once belonged to the Sorcēarians. A shattered marble statue blocked her path, and she stepped over it with ease. She didn't know who exactly it commemorated but could guess its resemblance belonged to someone in Dovian's lineage. Exhaling an exhaustive breath, she neared one of the rooms that possibly housed the man she was looking for. Padding quietly around the corner, she halted at a doorframe. Though the room was not his, something drew her there, and to find Dovian seated on the floor was no surprise.

The room was feminine in nature. Purple and green banners and curtains decorated the room, all marred with soot and dust, some of the colors now undistinguishable. A long silver and gold bed with twisted metal posts framed the large window along one wall. A few stuffed animals crowded the pillows of the bed; some were now stained and worn beyond recognition. There were dry petals scattered across the floor, leading to an armoire that had dead flowers atop it. Ivory's eyes fell to the man seated on an ornate rug.

"I figured you'd want to be far from me," he murmured.

Ivory took that as permission to enter the room. She kept a safe distance from the man, watching his back.

"It's terribly lonely in this city. It's hard to receive comfort when there is none," she spoke quietly.

Dovian didn't budge. Keeping a seated position, he placed his hands on his knees.

"What are you doing?" she asked.

Dovian slowly opened his eyes, looking at the rumbling clouds in the far-off distance. Lightning darted from one cloud to another, the beams spreading like fire across the bubbling forms.

"Meditating," he replied.

Ivory approached the bed. It looked clean enough, so she took a seat. Dovian continued to stare out the window, his expression tense.

"Isn't meditating supposed to relax you?" she asked.

Dovian's frown deepened. "It usually helps, but I'm not necessarily trying to relax as much as I am trying to think."

"Am I interrupting?" She tugged on her fingers.

Dovian finally met her gaze. "No. You're fine."

They didn't say anything for a while, and Dovian fidgeted a few times, taking in the sights of the bedroom.

"Lita's," he stated, barely audible.

Ivory looked around.

Dovian continued, "I used to meditate out in the grass. She interrupted me when she was having troubles, which wasn't too often. Sometimes she would simply join my side."

"You two were very close," Ivory said.

Dovian closed his eyes, his face wrinkling. "Losing I'Lanthe was one thing, but losing Lita was a whole other pain. There was a bond we shared, and to have it severed in the way it had…it left me broken. I lost two parts of my soul that day."

"You didn't kill her."

He looked out the window, resuming his attention on the storm clouds in the distance. "No," he finally admitted. "I did not kill her or I'Lanthe."

Ivory straightened her posture. "You make it out to be like you're a murderer who destroyed everyone and everything."

"It's to protect others. I do not need attachment from others. I cannot have humanity depending on me. And yes, I am to blame in certain aspects, but I cannot lie anymore. I will not say I killed I'Lanthe or Lita, but I can say that I wasn't much help in the matter." He tugged on a loose strand on the rug.

"Was that something you could control?" Ivory diverted her attention out the window as well.

"Do you want the illogical or logical answer?" he questioned, halfway amused.

Ivory gave a small smile. "You blame yourself, yet you had no control over the way events played out."

Dovian lowered his head, giving a tired scoff.

"I would love to have met you in the past, Dovian. Were you always so hard or had you been entirely different?" Ivory leaned forward, resting her chin in her hands.

The man remained lost in thought, memories flooding through him that he had often forgotten about. He had pushed them into the back of his mind so not to feel the pain.

"I was always a bit of a downer, as Lita would say, but I was a different man." He tiredly rubbed his eyes. "I had some semblance of genuine happiness."

She smiled sadly. "I wish I could have known you then."

"I wish I could say that someday I will return to that naive persona. Honestly, after everything, there's no chance of that. Life will never be what it once was." He leaned back on his hands. "I wish I could give that to you, Ivory. You belong in that time, not here and now."

"I may speak of wanting to know you in the past, but there's nowhere else I'd rather be than here with you right now." She ran her hand through her curls. The humidity had made her hair unruly.

Dovian gave her an inquisitive look. "Ivory, in all right, you should loathe me and desperately want to be anywhere but here with me right now. I should have let you leave with Aria and Troy. If I had…perhaps, I wouldn't have had to do what I had done."

Ivory looked out at the storm and then back to Dovian. "I'm glad I wasn't there. Sapphire would have made you do it either way, and I would not have wanted to see that."

"I tried," Dovian whispered. "I tried everything in my power to keep them from meeting their demise. Damn it, Ivory. There were so many possibilities. Every minute of every day there is an opportunity to change the entire outcome of this nightmare, and my decisions seem to make no difference."

"What would you have done differently? And would it have worked?" she asked.

Dovian reached out as if grasping the clouds in his sight.

"At that moment, everything had become exponentially limited. The way things played out, I was left with very few options. So…I took the best route, only to have things hindered significantly by Aria's response." He ran his fingertips along his forehead.

"She fought you, didn't she?" Ivory asked, giving a fleeting grin. The thought threatened to bring tears to her eyes. Aria was so strong and determined despite her painful past.

Dovian nodded. "I could have fatally wounded them and still allowed them some chance of survival. My goal was to make it look real, give the impression that I had killed them, and then turn Sapphire's attention away from them. I found a gun...something that I could use that would play off the coldness of my act. They'd have more of a chance of survival from that than my powers. However, upon trying to injure Troy, Aria hit me. There was a little chance; few different outcomes could have arisen, and I attempted to compensate for the possibility. Troy was hit in a lethal way." He gave an aggravated groan. "She's so frustrating! It significantly reduced his rate of survival. In fact, if he had not received medical attention promptly, he would die. And seeing as there are no hospitals around...." Dovian grasped his hair. He remained silent.

Ivory frowned.

"I'm sure he's not survived. There would be no way. All because of a split-second decision on Aria's part," he said, covering his forehead. "Something I did not see at that time."

Ivory gave a smile. "It makes me happy to know that you tried, Dovian. You did what you could."

Dovian disagreed. "It wasn't enough! It's never enough! Ivory! I...." He struggled to form words, and quickly pushed everything back to maintain control of his emotions. "I had to kill him. He was suffering. I had to end him. I sent a pulse of energy to his head and stopped his brain functions. Aria went ballistic, and I gave her what I could to break her. I jammed that pistol beneath her ribcage, and I hoped for the best as I pulled the trigger. Maybe, somehow, she could survive. Maybe, by some miracle, she could live and get the hell out of here. My only regret is that I couldn't save Troy." Dovian hid his face in his hands. "I've failed," he harshly whispered.

Finally, tears fell from Ivory's pale eyes. She tried to choke back a sob. "I know you did your best. I knew you wouldn't truthfully do it."

"But I did!" he shouted. "Let's be realistic. There is no way either one survived. But I had to direct Sapphire away from wanting to tear them apart. I suggested we leave their bodies out to dry in the sun."

Ivory's eyes widened. "Why?"

"I told her it was so we could make a dress out of their skin. I knew the idea would excite her and divert her attention away from completely destroying Aria and Troy. It also gave me a false sense of hope that perhaps…if they did survive, somehow…they would have a chance of escaping this dreadful place." Dovian gestured toward the storm. "I've directed my focus over the desert. If the storms continue out there, it will prevent their bodies from drying out like Sapphire expects. The last thing I'll allow to happen is for those two to become a wardrobe. I will be sure they are respected in death."

Dovian's face fell; his shoulders sagged. Giving a moan, he covered his eyes and curled in on himself, his shoulders shaking. Ivory hopped from the bed and dropped to her knees, wrapping her arms around him.

"I didn't want this," his voice quaked.

"I know." She ran her hand through his hair, trying her best to comfort him. Relief washed over her as she came to realize that Dovian wasn't exactly a cold-blooded killer. She couldn't imagine what it would have been like to do what he had.

"I should have let you go. I should have made you leave." He straightened and grabbed her arms, looking her straight in the eye. "In fact, I'm telling you to get out of here. Leave. You are not safe here. I cannot protect you. I only did what I did to keep you safe. I was afraid that Sapphire would hurt you. And instead, I hurt you; I hurt our friends."

She shook her head. "Nope."

"I don't understand," he was almost angered by her response.

"Dovian, though what you did was astonishing and horrid on all levels…I need you to know that I still love you. I always have, and I always will. I know…" she gave a high-pitched laugh, "it doesn't make sense! But I'm confident that I'm right where I'm supposed to be. This is what I was made for. This is what I was destined to do—to be by your side when you need me the most. Whether I'm Ivory or I'Lanthe, it doesn't matter. We both feel the same thing. We are not leaving."

The man's hard visage loosened, and he let out a sharp sigh. "How on earth could either you or I'Lanthe stay with me after all I've done?"

Ivory took a deep breath, ruffling Dovian's hair. "Well, for starters, I'Lanthe has known you at your best, and I have known you at your worst. Together, we have formulated a similar opinion." Her cheerful voice soothed the man, and he watched her in wonder. "You are sweet; you are caring, and you are charming and intelligent."

He scoffed, but she went on. "You're mysterious, brooding, depressed, anxious, and moody. You're deadly; you're unpredictable, and incredibly terrifying."

"I'm a danger to you; it's why you should leave," he grumbled.

"Dovian, look at you. You are broken. Your soul is broken. A shattered vase can't put itself back together again. You need me here...so I can mend you."

"And how does one mend someone like me?" He watched her.

"With what you always preach, Dovian—love. Let me love you." For a moment, Dovian almost thought they were I'Lanthe's words, but Ivory's voice was clear as day. The two were merging together into one persona.

"It doesn't matter how much love you use to repair me; I will still have my flaws, my cracks." Dovian looked at his hands.

"And no matter how deep those cracks are, no matter how many you have, they are only a mark of how beautiful you truly are." She directed his face toward hers as she ran a thumb across the tattoo on his cheekbone. "I would be afraid, Dovian...if you did these things without effort. If you did them without regret and pain. To create darkness and not have cracks...that would be terrible. Dovian, you do the things you do out of love, not out of hate. I see it clearly in the way your eyes shine. I feel it when I'm near you. It does not excuse what you have done, but the mistakes you have made and continue to make only reveal more of who you are. Once you figure out who you are, you can begin to repair yourself in the ways that are needed. But until then, let me love you. Let me heal you in the ways that you need. I can mend you the best I can. And though a broken vase glued back together may show its cracks, it can still hold water. You're not completely broken yet, Dovian. Don't allow the darkness to pour out of you freely. That isn't who you are."

She firmly held his head and placed a gentle kiss on his cheek. Dovian winced.

"You haven't healed yourself, yet?!" she shouted, her mature demeanor fluctuating.

"I figured I deserved the pain for a while," Dovian murmured, holding the back of his neck. "That was quite a hit, by the way."

Ivory held a hand to her lips. "I did whack you pretty good, didn't I?"

He gave a crooked smirk, but she didn't find it amusing in the slightest.

"You heal yourself this instant!" she yelled.

Dovian hesitated but complied. Placing a hand on his cheek, he healed the cracked bone then moved to the fracture in his vertebrae. It only took a moment, and Ivory was relieved.

"I'm sorry I hurt you." She gently touched his cheek again, being much more delicate in her caress.

"And I'm sorry I hurt you, Ivory. I plan on making up for it...somehow. I will work on keeping my darkness at bay." He placed his head on the woman's shoulder.

She planted a soft kiss on his head, holding him. "You *are* keeping it at bay. Darkness knows no love, Dovian."

Dovian mumbled, "No, it only knows of pain and suffering."

"Perhaps darkness is like a hole. Maybe by filling it with love, the darkness would turn into light?" Ivory suggested.

Dovian pulled away and looked at her, intrigued. In that instant, they each had the same thought. What if Ivory showed love to Sapphire? Was that monster of a child capable of accepting love? Could Sapphire possibly love in return?

"Do you think she's capable of feeling love?" Ivory whispered.

Dovian opened his mouth to speak, but a sudden thumping commenced, tearing his attention away from Ivory.

"That isn't thunder." Dovian sat up, rushing to the window. He stared with anticipation at the sky. "Turn it down! Cloak yourself!" he called out.

"What is it?" Ivory asked, joining his side.

For a second, she caught the sight of a blinking light that emitted a pulsing thump. It passed them by and headed toward the site of Aria and Troy's wreckage. Then, all went silent, and the light disappeared.

"What was that?" she asked again.

Dovian's eyes were aflame. "A Hawk."

"Hawk? A hawk...oh!" She nearly fell out the window as she pressed forward to get a better view. "A helicopter!"

Dovian watched with her, trying to gather a set of data from his optical camera. His heart pounded within his chest. All kinds of 'what-ifs' traveled through his brain. For a moment, he finally had some hope. Apparently, Ivory felt the same as she hopped and slung her arms around his neck and squealed loudly, toppling the man over.

"Ladies and gentlemen! I present to you...the forbidden land of Ives!" Nerd called out over the intercom of the Hawk. He wasn't meant to be a pilot but knew enough about the vehicle that he had managed to get them safely to Ives.

Spoofy and the others leaped from their chairs, scattering to the various windows in the cabin. Though it was night, they could tell the land was lush and vibrant with life. On the horizon was a clustering storm, one that made

Nerd anxious. As they neared the city, Spoofy darted to the front of the craft.

"Nerd! Get her in stealth mode! Whatever it is that brought Aria and Troy down could still be out there! We need to make this quick and as quiet as possible." She leaned against Nerd's seat, looking out the front of the airship.

"Aye, aye, captain!" Nerd sputtered.

As they flew near an ancient rundown city, the Hawk shuddered into stealth mode. Spoofy's eyes narrowed as she watched for any sign of life. Her optics portrayed numerous life signs, but all were relatively small—most likely animals of some sort. She hoped they weren't all monsters. However, the city held no light, which comforted her somewhat. It appeared there was no surviving civilization on Ives. If there was, it had to be rather primitive as everything seemed worse for wear.

"They could be anywhere," Nerd muttered.

Spoofy pulled up her DNAIS, reading the SOS data again. There should have been a position analysis somewhere in the report, but there was none. If anything, the Hawk should have emitted a signal of some sort unless there were a type of electrical disturbance. The woman eyed the horizon where the storms flickered with life.

"Head toward the clouds. I bet they're preventing the signal." She pointed.

"But if it's providing electrical disturbance, it could take us down, too," Nerd said worriedly.

"Fly low, then. We have to find them." She patted him on the shoulder, giving him a rough shake.

Just as she spoke, the stormy weather churned, spiraling to all sides of the island. It was as if the storm was alive, granting the Hawk access to their destination. Within a few seconds, Spoofy's DNAIS chimed with the coordinates to the wreck. She quickly pushed the information onto Nerd's dash, and his windowpane lit up with blinking triangulation finders. One red beam picked up on a piece of fiery debris, highlighting it before zooming in on the crash site.

"I think we found our wreck," Nerd spoke apprehensively.

Spoofy eyed the clearing storms.

"This is kind of spooky, eh?" the pilot asked.

The men in the cabin all made murmurs of agreement as they watched the clouds.

Spoofy's mouth twisted into a frown. "Just keep on the alert. Either someone or something is helping us out, or we're walking right into a trap."

Spinning about-face, the woman trudged into the cabin, snatching up her enormous rifle. Loading the weapon, she only gave a fleeting glance to her teammates. They all moved, taking up their arms and supplies.

"Keeping up stealth. Preparing to land. I'd like to make as fast a getaway as possible," Nerd quickly stated as he lowered the invisible vehicle to the ground.

Spoofy nodded. "Stay in the copter, Nerd. We'll check out the wreckage for any survivors."

Monkey opened the door. His body seemed to materialize out of thin air as he jumped into the outside world. He aimed, taking quick steps toward the demolished Hawk a few meters away. The others filed in line behind him, checking to the left and the right for any potential ambushes.

A clattering sound came from the wreckage, and the team paused and tore their attention toward the source. Giving a shrill shriek, a spherical drone slowly rounded the corner. A digital white flag popped up over its head. Its clamps opened and closed; the large camera in the center of its face darted from side to side as it gathered data on Team Phoenix.

"Team Phoenix has arrived," the bot whined.

Spoofy moved to the front, only lowering her weapon slightly. "State your name and status."

"Franklin. A-okay!" The bot twirled. "Pilot, Aren Hagar, in critical condition. Requesting medical aid."

Spoofy looked over her shoulder at Kaino. He was already on the move, leaping over the wreckage.

"And what of Aria and Troy?" she asked the drone.

"MISSING...MISSING." Franklin twitched, searching for life signs.

"What happened to them? Why aren't they at the site of the crash? Were they with you when the Hawk went down?" Spoofy inquired.

"Aria and Troy were inside the Hawk. After crash, gone missing."

"Now how in the hell is that possible?" Zombie questioned.

Franklin moved a few meters off to the side as a green scanner searched the ground. "Rain has destroyed most evidence. But evidence reveals some form of resistance."

"Resistance?" Spoofy looked at her comrades. They all shared worried glances.

"GATHERING DNA READING. STATUS POSTULATION: ARIA AND TROY IN CRITICAL CONDITION." Franklin moved ahead.

"Hey! Wait for us!" Spoofy trotted after the bot.

"Franklin doesn't take orders from strangers," the robot beeped.

"Franklin! Stop!" A younger male voice shouted. The drone abruptly halted.

Kaino walked toward the others, supporting a staggering young man.

"You're the pilot?" Spoofy asked the injured man.

"Yes, ma'am. Aren Hagar." He offered her his hand. "Spoofy, I presume?"

"That's me." She pointed to her other teammates. "You've met Kaino; this is Zombie, Monkey."

Aren nodded toward the others. "It's an honor to meet you all. I'm a big fan." He winced, his hand gripping his bandaged shoulder.

"You going to make it?" she asked.

Sweat beaded on Aren's brow. "Uh, maybe. Surprised I'm still alive at all. Franklin patched me up pretty good though."

Kaino shook his head. "He needs medical attention ASAP. He may be alright for now, but his health is declining fast. Pretty sure he has a nasty infection."

Spoofy placed her hands on her hips. "Perhaps we should have Nerd take him to the nearest hospital and meet back up with us?"

"No!" Aren shouted. He groaned and held a hand to his head. "No. I'm not leaving. We have to find Aria and Troy as quickly as possible and get the hell out of here. You have no idea what's on this island."

Spoofy folded her arms. "Oh, I can guess."

Aren's face fell. "Sapphire's entire army is located here in the cave systems. All those monsters that have been attacking the city-states? They're all housed here! The sooner we can leave, the better, but I'm not going without Aria and Troy."

Team Phoenix once again exchanged concerned looks.

"How do they keep getting themselves into the worst kinds of trouble?" Monkey looked over each shoulder, paranoid.

"You think the monsters took them?" Spoofy asked.

Aren warily eyed Franklin. "Not sure. I'd assume so. Franklin! What data do you have on Aria and Troy?"

Franklin whirred, spinning and floating toward the pilot. "Aria and Troy have received critical injuries. DNA reading reveals movement away from crash site. Large amounts of blood lost. More DNA trails that way." The bot turned to the side and projected a beam in the southern direction of the island.

"That goes away from the cave system. Perhaps they survived and found a place to hide," Aren mumbled. Feeling lightheaded, he dropped. Kaino grabbed him, securing him to his side.

"Everyone to the Hawk! Aren, can Franklin follow the trail?" Spoofy moved slowly with the pilot and medic as the other two men jumped back inside the vehicle.

"I can have him track it as far as he can read. Follow in the Hawk. Hopefully, something will show up on radar for you. I'd suggest running a DNAIS scan to find their location," Aren said, struggling with his words.

"Franklin! Follow the trail! We'll be close behind," Spoofy hollered.

"Do as she says, Franklin!" Aren puffed.

The robot only protested with a noise before speeding away, tracking Aria and Troy.

Spoofy and Kaino hurried into the aircraft with Aren and quickly settled. Nerd lifted immediately and pushed forward, his eyes locked onto the green scanner from Franklin.

"Fast lil bugger," Nerd called out.

"Just don't lose sight of him," Aren whimpered.

Spoofy sat in front of Aren, resting her elbows on her knees. "So, what's been going on? We've been in the dark for a few weeks."

"Did you happen to see any of the live feeds recently?" he asked.

She nodded.

"Okay. Now, this all may sound a bit insane, but I'm going to say it straight out. Sapphire is that little girl that interrupted the news. She's as evil as evil can get. She's not what she appears to be. She's some otherworldly being. Some think she's the devil." Aren groaned as Kaino applied more antiseptic to his wounds. Kaino speedily made a cross over his chest in response to Aren's tale. "Those monsters are demons I guess."

Zombie and Monkey shared skeptical expressions.

"Hit yer head a little hard?" Zombie snorted. Spoofy punched him in the arm, causing him to yelp.

"I need you to believe me on this." Aren glared at the men. Lifting his wrist, he pulled up his data log. "I'll send copies of everything I know to you all. It's got my and Aria's notes in it."

"Who's the scary guy with the wings?" the woman asked.

"Dovian. He's a Sorcēarian. He was originally in our party, but things got too dangerous last we were here, and we had to pull out. He was left behind. We were trying to rescue a friend…Ivory. She has some weird connection to this place. Now she and Dovian are stuck here, and I guess Sapphire's using Dovian for his powers. Not really sure whose side he's on now." Aren frowned. "I really hope Aria and Troy are alright. Maybe Dovian had something to do with their disappearance."

After a few minutes, an alarm chimed at the front of the cabin. Nerd lowered the copter.

"Got a read on some life signs hidden in some ruins. That bot's radar is goin' through the roof!" Nerd spoke over the intercom.

Aren tilted to get a look at the windshield of the cockpit. "Aria and Troy had mentioned some ruins once. They had holed up there before. You think it's them?"

"That bot of yours is sayin' it is!" Nerd exclaimed, nearly dropping the craft in excitement.

The soldiers jumped out not much later than the skids landed in the plains. Spoofy and the others marched through the tall grass up to the damaged door of the worn cottage. Pressing against the side of the building, she held up her fingers, counting. One, two, three. Monkey put all of his weight into a kick against the door, sending the piece shattering to the floor. They all darted in, taking tactical positions with their weapons aimed. Checking out the destroyed front room, their flashlights beamed against broken furniture. Despite the home being tattered and rundown, it seemed a bit cozy. Carefully stepping over chunks of crumbled stone and splintered wood, they moved toward the back of the house. Spoofy halted near one of the bedrooms. She spun quickly around the corner, her flashlight illuminating the room.

"HA!" Spoofy blurted a laugh. Aiming her light from corner to corner, she caught sight of exactly who she was looking for. "Did I just see Troy's ass?!" she cackled.

Aria appeared only momentarily frightened before her face fell into its usual cantankerous form. She finished buttoning her pants and pulled up the straps of her bra while Troy shimmied into his trousers, nearly tripping over his boots. The team shared some enthused laughs, pleased to find the rest of their team safe and in one piece and humored at finding them in the middle of an intimate moment.

"Ever hear of knocking?" Troy yelled, dropping sideways onto the bed as he laced up a boot.

"Well…I kinda knocked," Monkey replied.

"Sounds like you burst through the door. We thought you were the enemy," Aria spoke up, tugging her torn shirt over her head.

"Speaking of enemy, what in the hell happened to you?" Spoofy asked. "We thought you were severely injured…possibly dead."

"That's a long story." Aria threw Troy his shirt, the article smacking him in the face.

"You knew the enemy was out there, and you two were in here doin' the naked dance?" Zombie drawled.

Aria and Troy fidgeted uncomfortably.

"Well...ya know...if you're gonna die, better go out with a smile!" Troy laughed, giving a half-assed salute. Aria casually shoved him to the side.

"Yeah, well...while you two were having your fun, you forgot about someone." Kaino joined the conversation. He was dragging Aren with him.

Aria and Troy's faces both held looks of horror.

"Aren?!" Aria cried out, running toward the young pilot. She squeezed between Spoofy and the doorframe and gripped the pilot's face. "You're alive? How? The whole front of the Hawk was smashed in! How did you survive?"

Aren looked a bit disgruntled. "You survived, didn't you? Not even a scratch on you. Reinforced cage, ma'am. Don't you know a thing about those copters?"

Aria hugged him, suddenly feeling a bit motherly. "I'm so sorry! The androids...they said you were dead! Troy and I...we...." Aria felt horrible. They didn't even check the wreckage.

Troy stepped up. "I'm sorry, Aren. I heard it, too. The enemy had confirmed your death."

Aren wobbled slightly against Kaino. "The graphene cage and electrostatic would have blocked any data reads on my life signs. But I understand, I suppose." He gave a weak smile. "It's a miracle I survived, but what happened to you guys? You should be messed up, but you look fine."

Troy shook his head, frowning. "They drug us from the wreckage and shot us. Left us in the desert to die. When I awoke, Aria was passed out. I grabbed her and took her here to safety. I was in panic mode."

"Shot you?" Spoofy asked.

Aria nodded. "Like I said, long story. I'll explain on the way out of here. We've got to leave now! Sapphire and the others no doubt detected you. They could already be outside waiting for us." Turning to Aren again, she directed his eyes to hers. He didn't look too good. "Aren, stay with me for just a few more minutes, okay? I'll get you patched up in no time. Let's get to the Hawk!"

Aria stayed in the middle of the formation. Having no weapon, she let Spoofy take the lead. Rushing to the front of the building, it was a relief to find no monsters were in sight, but Nerd was waving frantically from his pilot's seat. That meant bad news was coming. The entire team rushed out the small home. They quickly filed into the Hawk, Aria signaling Nerd to take off.

"We've got a whole army of blips on the radar! They're nearin' fast! We've got to get out of here!" Nerd shouted.

The doors nearly closed in on Kaino and Aren as the Hawk pulled into the air. A moment later, the craft jolted into jet mode.

"Hold on tight! Looks like those storms are back! May be in for some turbulence!" Nerd warned.

Kaino laid Aren on the floor. The boy was pale-white; his hair was wet and stuck to the sides of his face. Aria took her gaze to the window, staring at the billowing thunderheads that warped around the jet. Her brow furrowed, and she looked to Troy. He was watching, too.

"Cover?" he asked.

Aria nodded. "Dovian's watching." She gave a laugh of disbelief. "He's providing cover!"

Troy rubbed the back of his head. "I wish he would let us in on his plan."

"How in the hell did you run into a sorcerer anyway?" Spoofy asked.

"Sorcēarian," Aria corrected. Spoofy shrugged sarcastically, and Aria met her gesture. "Yeah, basically the same thing. I'll explain everything in a moment. We've got a long ride ahead of us." Her tense gaze dropped to Aren. He was shivering as his body went into shock. His vitals log was reading critical; he had lost too much blood. "I've got to help him first."

Aria slid to her knees, grabbing Aren's hand. "Look up at me, Aren." She pointed to her eyes. "Breathe nice and slow."

"What are you going to do?" Kaino asked.

He sifted through his bag, looking for an IV and some nanomites. Aren had an infection and possibly tetanus. Kaino could administer the nanomites to fight the infection that would filter the blood and fight the bacteria, but the machines wouldn't replenish the blood he had lost. The plasmabots were all gone; the case had been smashed during battle a few days before.

"I'm going to try to heal him." Aria pulled off her leather gloves.

"What? With your bare hands?" Kaino incredulously asked.

"That's right," Aria said, biting her lower lip. She eased the bandages away and grimaced at the sight. Aren was burnt, but a lot of the infection was still trapped in his shoulder. "Jesus, Franklin did a bang-up job." Her sarcasm wasn't soothing to Aren.

Tears gathered at the corners of his eyes. "I…I'm gonna die, aren't I?" Thoughts of Fiona crowded his mind, and Aria could see them all.

"No. I'm going to fix you," she whispered.

A gasping laugh sounded from the young man. "You're not Dovian."

Aria swallowed hard, placing her hands against the wound. She closed her eyes and began to mumble quietly.

"This is ridiculous! Troy! Has she lost her mind?" Kaino asked, prepping the IV. "Aria….God, woman. Move over and let me do my best, alright?"

Aria opened her eyes, green light shimmering from her pupils. Kaino's jaw dropped as goosebumps covered his skin. The large man slid backward, giving the woman room to work.

"I've already lost Gavin! I'm not losing Aren, too!" she yelled.

"Just let her work," Troy snapped.

Kaino sat back on his heels, watching Aria work her magic. Blue light flooded from her hands, and her whispering rose in volume, revealing a foreign language.

"What kind of voodoo is this?" Zombie muttered, staring intently at the black-haired woman.

"What happened to Gavin?" Spoofy whispered, nudging Troy.

Troy hung his head. "Damn it. You don't know?" he grumbled.

The other men all shook their heads. Aria made a choking noise, but she continued with her odd chants, light flooding over Aren's body.

"Gavin's dead, you guys," Troy spat out the words.

There was no gentle way of telling the others. Gavin had been their pilot for many years. He helped get them through the False Syndicate War. He was their savior many times over. The only reason Nerd learned to pilot was in cases where Phoenix got separated from their leaders. Gavin was Aria and Troy's personal pilot for their sub-missions. If Gavin wasn't with Aria and Troy, then he was with Phoenix.

"What? What do you mean? Gavin's…dead?" Monkey's face fell, his mouth hanging open.

Spoofy watched the other woman patch up Aren. She was Aria's best friend, the only person that Aria opened up to. Spoofy knew about Aria's relationship with Gavin. Really, the whole team had an inkling that something was going on, but the other female knew all the details.

"Shit," Spoofy ground her teeth together.

"I'm guessin' that happened when we were in the dark." Zombie momentarily removed his cowboy hat and bowed his head.

Kaino shook his head. "I liked that guy."

"Did I just freakin' hear you correctly?" Nerd called out over his shoulder.

Troy closed his eyes. "You heard me!"

"Christ!" Nerd cried. "What in the hell happened?"

"Will you shut up?!" Aria screamed. "I can't concentrate!"

Troy held up his hand, silencing the team.

Everyone pursed their lips tightly, leaning forward in their seats to watch Aria work. Finally, her expression relaxed. Within seconds, Aren's complexion was full of color. He took a deep breath and opened his eyes wide, staring at Aria as if she were a ghost.

"What...what did you do to me?" Aren gaped at her.

Aria finally pulled her hands away. Instead of the massive burns and the ragged hole, the skin was now unblemished. Aren's upper chest appeared to be perfectly fine. He slowly ran his fingers across his chest and shoulder, shivering beneath his own touch. The fever was gone; the chills were no longer causing his body to quake, and he didn't feel nauseous. In fact, he felt great.

Kaino jumped back, hitting the wall of the craft. "Holy sweet baby Jesus!" he stammered.

Zombie gave a boisterous laugh, slapping his hands together. "Cheese an' rice! You shittin' me?"

Monkey leaned further forward, his mouth widening enough for a strand of drool to drop out. "Holy tamale."

"The crap did you just do and how?" Spoofy asked, her eyebrows rising to unspeakable heights.

Aria stood up, reaching down for Aren. He gratefully accepted her hand, and she effortlessly tugged him to his feet. Slipping on her gloves, she gave a sheepish smile. Franklin squealed with delight and fled to the young pilot, scanning his body and confirming that all was healed.

"I fixed him," Aria stated.

"You just pulled a messiah!" Kaino sputtered.

Kaino's family was spiritual in all aspects. Kaino's beliefs extended over all religions and lifestyles. He respected everyone's views and thought anything and everything existed as one. Needless to say, he was terribly superstitious and took all things religious seriously. In fact, he was nearly afraid of anything that seemed paranormal. Kaino kept a safe distance away from Aria, watching her as she secured herself into her seat.

She rolled her eyes at the medic. "Sit your ass down, Kaino. I'm not going to bite."

Spoofy pointed at the other woman. "Okay, missy! Speak up! You've got shit-tons of explaining to do!"

Everyone gathered their attention on Aria, looking like children waiting for a campfire story.

Aria held up her hands. "Okay, okay. I'll start from the very beginning."

"Search And Rescue"

CHAPTER 17

Aria cringed at every cutting word that exploded from James Clarke's vocals. It was the angriest she had seen him in many, many years and rightfully so. She hadn't told him, Feyette, or Kovacevic of her plans to go to Ives to bring back Dovian and Ivory. Instead, she made the call and took Troy and Aren with her without the older man's permission. The woman stood rigidly with her nose wrinkled and her teeth clenched together. Clarke's mouth was moving, but she couldn't hear his words as much as she felt them. He was insufferably irate, frightened, and relieved all at once, the emotions twisting around him like a hurricane. Of course, she knew that this would happen, but it was better to have tried than not tried at all. Dovian and Ivory were worth a shot…even though the stunt had nearly gotten her and her teammates killed.

'Damn it, Aria! You're still my little girl!' Clarke's thoughts drifted as he calmed himself, his palms pressing against his desk.

Aria chewed on the side of her lip, eyeing the President cautiously. Was this what it was like to be a Sorcēarian? It was a bit overwhelming being able to hear, feel, and read people's thoughts and emotions. As soon as she was beginning to pity the man, he started back up, shouting again. Aria's back straightened as she took in the words once more. Grayson stood behind Clarke, as emotionless as ever. Feyette and Kovacevic were at a side table, timidly placing cards down in their poker game, their eyes shifting around the room. Behind Aria was the rest of her squad. Troy was seated in a leather chair, his hand rubbing his forehead. The rest of Team Phoenix was standing at attention with their hands clenched tight and their faces crinkled from the force of the President's volume. Now and then Bridgette and Franklin would chime in, squealing and twisting to look at the group. Aren and Nerd struggled to maintain their silence.

"I just wish I knew why you would do something so asinine." Clarke finally eased his vehement tone.

"I knew I couldn't tell you because you wouldn't have let us go," Aria spouted.

"Because I would have known that something like *this* would have happened! You should be dead, Aria!" he scolded.

The woman scratched her shoulder, staring off to the side. "Well…we brought back Team Phoenix!"

Clarke did not look amused.

"They had no communications with the outside world! If it weren't for the SOS beacon, they wouldn't have known to come to us. Ives was the only continent close enough for their sensors to pick up." Aria fidgeted uncomfortably in her place.

Spoofy spoke up. "Right! It's a good thing we were at the Britainia Congo; no one else would have been able to rescue them in time. Coincidence?"

Clarke ran his hands over his face. "Could have simply gotten all of you killed. If she had just stayed put in her apartment, you all could have made your trip safely home without any issue."

Aria pouted, glaring at Clarke.

"It was a wasted trip, Aria. We could have been formulating a plan this whole time. Now we are a day behind," he rebuked.

Aria folded her arms. "You couldn't make plans while I was gone? You really need me here to plan everything for you? Guess that game of poker is really important." She eyed Kovacevic and Feyette. The men stopped mid-play, gawking at her nervously.

"Don't try to push the attention on someone else, young lady." Clarke pointed accusingly at her. "We've made plans. Kovacevic's men are in the process of securing the site at the Amazonian desert to repair the broken spigots. Solar radiation has risen tenfold since the accident. Feyette's men have been in communications with the other militaries. They are currently comparing tactical notes. So while you were out on your search and rescue mission, we've been diligently at work trying to secure the future of the human race!"

Aria growled in irritation, turning away from the man.

Troy slowly raised his hand. "Hey," he mumbled.

Clarke glared at the man. He wasn't too pleased with Troy either. The President had entrusted the man with the safety of Aria, yet Troy always seemed to support her decision to get caught in dangerous situations.

"Any recent attacks in our area?" Troy asked.

Clarke was taken aback by his question. "I, uh, we…no, actually. The entire day was quiet within our region as far as I know."

Troy waved dismissively. "Guess we provided quite the distraction for the enemy, huh?"

Clarke's face turned red in anger. Aria spun, looking amused.

"Seems Sapphire's afraid of us! We kept her attention the whole time we were on Ives," she smugly stated.

Clarke puffed out his held in breath and dropped into his chair. "Where have I lost control? I no longer have a company…just an army of undisciplined renegades."

"Seriously, though." Troy rose from his chair. "Sapphire thinks Aria and I are a threat. Once she figures out we are no longer on Ives, let alone still alive, she's going to flip out. She's going to stop at nothing to take Aria and I down."

Aria nodded. "He's right. Everything she directs at us, we deflect. It's got to be infuriating to her."

Clarke finally agreed with the situation, nodding. "So, what do you propose we do?"

"Make for a final stand. Sapphire has an ego. If we challenge her and call all the shots, she's most likely to take the bait. We will have a war on our terms. We pick the location of the final battle, and that will give us the opportunity to have the upper hand for once," Aria suggested. "We can announce that we're still alive and call her out during a live feed across the world. You know she'll see it. That's when we will lay out the terms. If we list a time and day, I bet she'll agree."

"Aria, what makes you think she'll play by the rules?" Clarke asked.

Aria smirked. "Because no game is fun when there aren't any rules. Rules set guidelines. Guidelines are what makes winning great. Besides, Sapphire is a rule breaker. She'll only have more fun if she gets to break the established rules. Whatever she is, she's still got that childlike behavior. I'm betting she'd go for it. It'll be too tempting for her to resist."

"But what if she attacks us anyway? What's stopping her from attacking now?" Monkey asked.

"As much as Sapphire won't admit it, she does like games. She only likes them when they are in her favor, though. She could have killed Troy and I herself, but she wanted Dovian to do it. She wants to create a sensation of utter hopelessness. That's why I think she'll most likely play into our hands if we bring the war to us." Aria enjoyed the surprised protests around her.

"Bring the war to us? You mean to Fountains? You want her to come to Fountains? Are you nuts?" Zombie asked, chewing on a plastic straw.

Aria nodded. "Exactly. Our home ground. We know it better than anyone else. We'll set up outside the city. It'll be exactly what she wants. Destroying our city would be pleasurable for her to watch. She wants to see the hope drain from our souls, right?"

Troy agreed. "That's what she said."

Aria grinned. "She'll play by our rules. At least, until the war starts. There's no telling what she'll do in battle, but we at least can set a time and day, and she'll follow accordingly. She wants all attention on her so a time and date would be perfectly fine by her standards as the whole world will be watching. It'll give us time to thoroughly plan things out and regroup with all of our men."

"I like it!" Kovacevic added his piece to the conversation. Clarke gave him a weary stare, and the man returned to his game of cards.

"Though I really don't want our city to end up looking like Saray, you do have a good argument. We will finish up with our current briefing with the other militaries and finish forming alliances. That way we are somewhat prepared for a random attack by Sapphire in case she's not interested in playing games. We will have our live meeting with Sapphire tomorrow. For now, I suggest you all get some rest. We've got sentries set up around the perimeter sending out constant sonar bursts. If anything heads our way, we will know immediately." Clarke gave a rough salute. "Dismissed," he weakly moaned.

The others turned, giving quiet mumbles and laughs. Aria was last to reach the door.

"Aria," James called out.

The woman stopped mid-step, looking over her shoulder.

"You're grounded." James revealed a hint of a smile.

Aria fought her own grin, wrinkling her nose. "You can ground me once we defeat Sapphire." She stuck out her tongue just as she did as a child and exited the room, shutting the door behind her.

"Kids…" Kovacevic scoffed.

James merely looked upon the generals and then the cards in their hands. "They aren't the only kids in this room."

Kovacevic gave a low, rumbling laugh. He chewed on his cigar, pulled a second from his pocket, and passed it to the President. "Just get your ass over here so we can finish our game."

James chuckled and pulled up his chair. "Grayson?" He offered a hand of cards to the quiet man.

Grayson straightened his suit jacket. "Sorry, sir, but it would be no contest."

Feyette and Kovacevic eyed one another.

"Sounds like big talk to me," Feyette said.

"Awful big talk with nothing to back it up," Kovacevic added, turning his stare toward Grayson.

The silent, well-dressed man had kept his position only a moment longer before he grabbed a chair, scooting in-between Feyette and Clarke.

"Placing bets?" Grayson coolly asked.

The morning sun cascaded a hue of orange across Dovian's face. He meditated, sitting on the same rug within Lita's bedroom. After dealing with the negative emotions and taxing actions from the day before, the Sorcēarian believed a long night of prayer was in need. Truthfully, it had been far too long since he had participated in what should have been his morning routine. The ways of his people were long lost even with the scarlet warrior still alive. He had forsaken not only the humans, but his own heritage. Now, Dovian felt a desperate need to somehow cleanse his soul, bring his faith back into the light.

Breathing in deeply, he ran his hands over his face. "It's been far too long," he tiredly spoke. "I wonder how I've managed to fail in everything. I've lived far too long, and it's wearing me thin."

Dovian dropped his hands into his lap, his vivid eyes paling into white orbs as he watched the world outside. Purple clouds stretched in thin streaks over the tangerine sky, the sun beaming rays across the meadows and pastures. Lines of wavering light snaked through the blades of grass as a gentle breeze rolled from the North. The silver lakes shimmered with gold specs; an albatross swooped down to gather a fish. A turtle sank into the waves. A musical song played from a bird's nest in a nearby tree. It was morning, and life was abruptly starting all over again. The idea clicked in Dovian's mind. He had gone so long dwelling on the darkness that he had forgotten the beauty that surrounded him.

Laughter reverberated down the halls. The shrill sound made the gigantic building seem less like a tomb and more like home. Dovian looked over his shoulder, his lips parting as chills shuddered down his spine. Surrounding him was no longer the expected dark and dingy walls, torn curtains, and stained floors. Instead, the space surrounding the man was as beautiful and vibrant as it was thousands of years before. Emerald and plum drapes decorated the bedroom; the teddy bear and various knick knacks appeared as they did in their prime. The stone was polished beneath his feet, and the window next to him was now occupied with a clean pane of glass, opened outward to invite the morning wind. Pink petals blossomed from the bouquet atop the dresser, the scent tickling his nostrils.

Dovian spun, looking out the open door of the room. A blue radiance glimmered down the halls from the ancient text scribed along the surface. He followed the trail, listening to the giggling and chatter of two women. Awed, he slowly approached a room off to the side of the cathedral. It was a large library lit up by massive chandeliers. Crimson banners streamed from pillar to pillar up toward the vaulted ceiling three levels above. Tables filled the center walkway, elaborate chairs occupying the sides. Colorful beads of light highlighted each bookshelf in Legacy. The stone floor was adorned with carpeted paths a shade of red that matched the banners; gold fringe lined the edges.

The tittering sound came again, and Dovian moved his sight toward the end of one aisle. His throat constricted as the sight before him nearly made him fall to his knees. Lavender robes, tight bodice, and brown curls swooped and pulled onto the top of her head with an ornate clip. I'Lanthe stood at the end of the aisle; her slender hand lightly touching her glossy lips as she laughed quietly. She said something, looking to the side as if talking to another person. There was a pause, and then she laughed again, her white teeth shining in the light, her violet eyes creasing behind long black lashes. She stirred and looked toward Dovian.

"She's been doing that for a while, now," a female voice sounded right beside Dovian's ear.

Dovian jolted, tearing his attention to the strange woman who stood beside him—Lilith. Something wasn't right. As he looked at the sultry female, the scene around her was dim and dreary, what Dovian was used to. He curiously looked back toward where I'Lanthe stood. Ivory, dressed in the same garb with golden locks framing her face, replaced I'Lanthe's form. She mumbled quietly, rolled her eyes, and then gave a high-pitched laugh. Dovian returned his gaze back to Lilith. Once again, the room darkened, the walls and furniture returned to their previously deteriorated state.

"What is this?" he asked.

Lilith gave a raspy chuckle, placing her hands on Dovian's shoulders. "I see a crazy woman talking to herself."

Dovian gaped back at Ivory, who was engulfed in bright light and surrounded by colorful banners.

"You don't see as I see…" he murmured.

"Is there anything else to see? The girl's crazy," Lilith moaned. "Why don't we go someplace private and discuss other matters?" She casually ran a hand between Dovian's robes, running her nails across his abdomen.

Ivory momentarily fluctuated to an image of I'Lanthe. The beautiful woman's purple eyes narrowed as she roughly placed her hands on her hips. She said something through gritted teeth, and the image bounced back to Ivory in her place. The blonde-haired woman stared at Dovian and then looked at Lilith.

"Get your smutty hands off of him!" Ivory snarled, pointing a finger in the woman's direction.

Like glass shattering, the light engulfing the room splintered and burst, evaporating into darkness. Dovian grimaced, rubbing his eyes. Once he opened them again, Ivory was already at his side grabbing Lilith's arms. She tugged the dark-haired woman away from the man, and the two began squabbling. They were still in the library though everything had returned to its gloomy, cracked state.

Lilith's face twisted into one of disgust. Immediately, she recoiled and drew back her hand to smack Ivory. Dovian tugged Ivory away from Lilith and pinned her to his side. He gripped Lilith's wrist and fed her a spiteful glare.

"Why don't you find your way back to Sapphire's cave?" he harshly suggested to the intrusive woman.

Lilith scowled. "You don't expect me to live in that dark cave with the monsters, do you?"

"You are a monster just the same as them! You belong there," Ivory snapped.

Dovian warily eyed the blonde. Her tone was like I'Lanthe's. Their personalities were merging more with each passing day.

Lilith scoffed and ran a hand through her midnight hair. "If I'm a monster, then what does that make you?" Slowly turning on her heel, she winked at Dovian. "If you ever get bored with your little doll, you know where to find me."

Ivory moved forward, but Dovian effortlessly held her back. Together they watched Lilith disappear into the shadows, her boot heels clacking against the stone.

"I can't believe you let her touch you," Ivory hissed.

"She snuck up on me. She has a habit of that," Dovian explained.

Ivory lifted her chin, her eyes glowing. "I wouldn't mind as much if she weren't actually a monster."

Dovian gave a little chuckle, resting his chin atop the woman's head. "Proof that even monsters get bored."

"Well, she can make cave paintings or find something else to occupy her time. I'd prefer her to leave us alone," she grumbled.

Dovian was silent, running his hand up and down the woman's back as he held her to his side. After a minute, he couldn't hold his questions back any longer.

"Who were you talking to?" he asked.

Ivory's eyes dimmed, and she looked at the floor. "I wasn't talking to anybody. I was looking at books."

"You were talking. I heard you laughing," he pressed further.

"Must've been the wind," she said, her voice rising in pitch.

"Ivory," Dovian stepped away but kept his hand on her back, "you were talking to I'Lanthe, weren't you?"

Ivory pressed her lips together.

"Why won't you tell me if this is true? It will not anger me," he said.

Ivory gave an unsure smile. "I know it won't anger you. I just…don't want to upset you."

Dovian weighed her answer. Why would he be upset? It would be great news if Ivory were able to contact I'Lanthe willfully. Perhaps I'Lanthe would be able to answer a few of his questions. If he showed any excitement toward this revelation, however, he could hurt Ivory's feelings. He did not want that.

"I do not think it would bother me as much as my knowledge of the fact may upset you," he spoke softly.

Ivory gaped at him, a look of shame crossing her face. "I didn't mean to hide it. I didn't know how you would take it."

"So you were speaking with her?"

Ivory nodded slowly, avoiding eye contact with him. Even though Dovian knew that I'Lanthe's soul was housed within Ivory's body, each bit of information about her contact with the other woman excited him. Dovian's eyebrows lifted as he tried not to express too much enthusiasm.

"Was this the first time?" he asked.

Ivory chewed on her lower lip. She shook her head.

269

"How many times?" he asked in shock.

"Many." The word was quiet as it passed Ivory's lips.

Many. It had been many times Ivory had communicated with I'Lanthe. Why hadn't she told him?

Dovian rubbed the back of his neck. "When was the first?"

Ivory refused to answer. By this time, she was facing away from him. Her silence sent him on edge.

"I promise I will not get angry. I am merely curious," he said slowly. It was a bit of a lie. If Ivory always had easy contact with I'Lanthe, then Dovian would feel a bit betrayed. Still, he knew of Ivory's feelings, and he did not want to disappoint her.

"The Pendant Hotel," she finally whispered. "In Roma."

Dovian sighed. She hadn't always had contact with I'Lanthe, but she had it the entire time she'd been housed with him in the ruins.

"It was only a few words in my head. But since I arrived here, they have been developing into full conversations. This was the longest yet. It felt so real...as if she were actually next to me." Ivory wrapped her arms around herself. "I'm sorry, Dovian. All of this is very complicated to me. I'm not sure what to say or do. I'm not sure who you want me to be."

The Sorcēarian wrapped his arms around her. Ivory was usually calmed by his touch he quickly learned. And by the way Sorcēarians reciprocated care and love casually through hugs or simple touches, Dovian had grown accustomed to comforting her.

"Nothing to be sorry for, Ivory." He felt her relax at the sound of her name. "Be who you are. I'm glad you are speaking with her. I hope she provides some comfort for you as she once did for me."

"She said that's my job now." There was a hint of grief in her voice. "I'm supposed to comfort you." Ivory turned around in his arms, hugging him around his chest. "I'll try my best."

Dovian smirked, holding her in return. "We can comfort each other."

"If you want, I can try to bring her out again. I know she misses you," Ivory said.

"You don't have to. When she's good and ready, she can come to me. For now, I'm with you." Dovian palmed the back of her head, surrounding her with his embrace. He didn't notice the tear that slipped down Ivory's cheek.

The gusting wind cut through Troy's clothing, chilling him. He gave a forceful shiver and shoved his hands deep into his military trench's pockets. Though the sun's rays were beaming onto the earth, the December air was as cold as ever. It was only a matter of time before Fountains would become coated with ice like Cherno. If it weren't for the sweltering summers, the sudden cold of winter wouldn't seem so harsh. This area of land was always on opposite ends of the weather spectrum. There was probably a month or two between the seasons that may resemble what once was known as spring and fall. Anymore, the high temperature mostly blended seamlessly into freezing within a month. Inside the city, however, was a different story.

Contained between the upper and lower cities of Fountains was a plate that housed the nuclear reactor. The reactor had vents that helped heat and cool the city, giving the artificial presence of actual seasons. Simulated rain and storms were brought to the city simply for the sake of aesthetic and psychological reasons. But take one step outside the main interstates and out into the dead land surrounding the megalopolis, and one could see what the real world was like. It was depressing to some, but for Troy, it was nostalgic. The outside world seemed to be a place locked in time. It was nearly always the same, desolate and quiet. Even now, as he stood on the thick grass of the cemetery, he felt isolated, locked in his own bubble.

Rarely a person ventured outside the city to visit the memorials of the dead. Because of this, Troy had made it a habit to come out in times when he needed to gather his thoughts or get away from humanity. It was peaceful and reminded him of the time when life was simple—when he was a young boy, and his father was still alive.

"How you doin', dad?" Troy muttered, running his hand along the tombstone. He didn't pause at his father's stone but passed on by, making a beeline for Gavin's place of rest.

Troy gnawed on his cigarette, letting the stick roll between his teeth. He stared at the marker a while, not sure how to approach it. He hadn't been to the cemetery since the funeral, and he had spoken to Gavin mere hours before his death. It was strange, but his best friend's demise was finally sinking in as Troy stood alone in silence in front of the stone that was etched with the title of his former buddy. The soldier briefly debated on leaving altogether, but something held him firmly in place. It was now or never. Troy would have to come to terms with the situation at some point. Now was the best time to do it as at any minute Sapphire's army could show up and kill him.

Troy cleared his throat. "Hey, man," he spoke. His voice was soft and crackling–not the tone he had intended to use. He stepped forward. Was he ready for this?

As soon as Troy neared the tombstone, a hologram shot upward from behind the rock. It fizzled like static, sent a light over Troy's body, and registered his voice and confirmed facial recognition. With a quick burst, the hologram imprinted lines throughout the area at the back the stone, creating a three-dimensional form. Within seconds, the blue figure was dotted with pigment, the blotches spreading like watercolors to create an exact replica of the person belonging to the grave. Caramel eyes locked onto Troy's green ones. The bright smile twisted cockeyed as expected. A hand whipped through the hologram's shoulder-length brown hair.

"You gonna stand there all day gawking at me or are you gonna offer me one of your cigarettes?" Gavin asked.

Troy gave a sudden laugh, tears welling in his eyes. It was an exact copy. If he didn't know any better, he'd say Gavin was standing before him in the flesh. This was much harder to deal with than his dad's tombstone. No wonder Aria hated cemeteries.

"Yeah," Troy stuttered, trying to clear the lump in his throat. He patted his pockets and pulled out his box of cigs. Fingering one of the thin sticks, he held it out toward the projection.

Gavin chuckled and took the offered cigarette. Much to Troy's surprise, the graphics field actually held onto it. The hologram placed the item in its mouth but didn't pull the tab.

"How long did you stand there before you grew the balls to come talk to me?" Gavin asked.

Troy laughed, scratching his head. "A bit longer than I wanted."

"Wuss," Gavin taunted.

Troy nodded slowly. It seemed that the hologram was the latest model. As strange as it was, Troy was glad Bio-Tech had been able to gather enough DNA and other samples in order to facilitate the use of the hologram. He wondered if Gavin's mother had been back to the cemetery since. Judging by the overflow of flowers surrounding the memorial, it was safe to say someone had been regularly visiting. Hell, he was surprised the woman hadn't just moved in and made camp. Things like the holograms were meant to ease the pain of a passing loved one, but Troy often felt they were a little *too* real. It almost made it worse. And as he looked at the swirling caramel color of Gavin's irises, Troy couldn't decide yet whether or not he liked the thing.

What if it were Aria? Troy's mind darted to the thought of visiting Aria's grave. He quickly dismissed the idea.

"So, how are things?" Gavin asked. "You look like hell."

Troy glanced around at the colorful trees decorating the land. "Aw, you know…still fighting monsters."

"You still haven't defeated those things? What have you been doing this whole time?" Gavin asked with a sarcastic edge.

"Hey! It's tough, man! Those things are…" Troy paused, "bastards. They're goddamn bastards."

"And what of that weird guy? What was his name again? Do-do?" A confused look crossed his face. Casually, he waved a hand through the air. "Ya know…the magician guy."

Troy pursed his lips together, giving a snort. "Do-do? You mean Dovian?"

Gavin snapped his fingers, smiling. "Ha! Yeah! That guy. He still helping you out?"

Troy's smile faltered. "Uh, I'm not really sure."

"Naw! Forget him! How 'bout that blonde chick?" The pilot eagerly leaned forward, his hands resting on the tombstone. "She is somethin' else, isn't she?" He whistled.

"Yeah, she was," the other man nodded.

"What do you mean was? Did you scare her off like you did all the others?!" The hologram gave Troy a playful look. Then Gavin slapped his forehead. "Oh, dude…you didn't wear the bikini chainmail armor in front of her, did you?"

Troy cringed at the memory. "Stop bringing that up! You're never going to let me live that one down!" He laughed, covering his face. "That was the worst day of my life."

Gavin guffawed. "Best bet I ever won and best use of an entire paycheck ever! It was worth the cost to see you train the new recruits in it all day!"

Troy and Gavin's laughter slowly faded into a couple of snickers and sighs. After a while, the two stood silently, the only sound being the wind brushing against the leaves of the surrounding trees. Gavin waited to hear more, but Troy did not continue. Acting a little anxious, the replica folded his arms. "You aren't all that talkative today. What's that all about?"

Troy shook his head. "I'm sorry. This is hard, man. You're just…" he rubbed his bloodshot eyes, "…you're just too much like him."

The pilot looked down at himself. "Well, that's kinda the point, ain't it?"

"I know." Troy glanced to the sky, slowly blowing out the air in his lungs. "I really wish you were here. Things have gotten so crazy. I feel like I'm losing my mind!"

"I am here!" He held out his arms. "Well...kinda."

Troy gaped at the hologram. How much of this image was just an image? Bio-Tech was capable of cloning. Was there any chance that the DNA used to maintain likeness and memories was cloned so much to the point that the hologram was a new and different form of Gavin? The thought was a little unsettling.

"Go ahead and ask all your heebie-jeebie questions. I know you got 'em." The pilot twirled the cigarette between his fingers.

"How much of you is really...you?" Troy asked.

Gavin laughed. "How in the hell should I know?"

"You told me to ask you!"

"I'm not some scientist!"

Troy gave his friend an annoyed look.

"Alright, fine. I've got the typical amount of DNA locked up inside this device." He tapped the back edge of the tombstone. "Anything happens to this baby, and I'm gone. They say the DNA exposes my memories and mannerisms. Other than that, I can't really tell you much. For as splattered as I was, it's amazing they had enough of me scraped up to put into that box."

"Hey! You watch what you say!" Troy growled, pointing at the hologram.

Gavin held up his hands. "Hey, asshat! I can say what I want; that's my body under there. And you know just as well as I do...hologram or not, I woulda said that."

Troy's anger eased. He stared at the image, his nose crinkling. "Fuck, man! Why?" He crouched in front of the stone, finding it hard to look at his friend. Grabbing a fistful of his hair, Troy fought back his tears. "I need you with me. I can't do this shit all alone! What am I supposed to do? How am I supposed to win this war? How am I supposed to keep her safe?"

Gavin was silent.

Troy finally let go, two heavy tears falling to the ground. "I'm so useless! She almost died! You told me to keep her safe, and I died on her...*twice*!" He lifted his head, his eyes widening. "Shit, man! I died twice! Why couldn't you have gotten a second chance?"

Gavin stared forward, his expression unreadable. "Just wasn't my day. You can't dwell on me. You need to worry about keeping yourself safe."

"I'm sorry, Gavin! I didn't even try to save you! I couldn't do anything about it! That bastard!" Troy snarled, fighting to hold back his emotions.

Gavin shrugged. "Wasn't anything you could do. You can't control assholes. The black-haired freak was out for the kill." There was a pause for a second. "At least I got him, right?"

Troy grimaced.

"Aw, please tell me I at least got that bastard!" Gavin groaned, covering his face.

What should he say? Gavin was just a hologram, but Troy still didn't want to hurt his…or its feelings. He didn't want Gavin to feel like his death was utterly meaningless. But then again, Gavin could always tell when Troy was lying, and he at least deserved the truth.

Letting out a harsh sigh, the soldier stood and shoved his hands into his pockets once again. "You would have gotten him if it weren't for his teleporting capabilities. Apparently, he escaped right before…impact."

"Jesus tits!" Gavin shouted. "I fail! I failed at dying! I couldn't even get…GAH!"

Troy couldn't help but smirk.

"Freakin' worthless..." the pilot grumbled.

"You're not worthless. Don't ever think that," Troy quickly said.

"Ah, well. Seeing as you are still alive, that means I at least posed as a distraction." Gavin tugged on the front of his leather jacket, giving a proud grin.

"You definitely ruined Euclid's day, and you did save our asses. Thanks, Gavin." Troy frowned. Would talking to this hologram even mean a thing?

"Eh, don't get all mushy on me." Gavin scratched his head. "So is that Euclid guy still runnin' around?"

Troy gave a small laugh. "Naw. Dovian blasted his head into a million pieces."

"Brutal!" Gavin hooted, clapping his hands. "Wish I coulda seen that!"

"It was pretty gross," Troy chuckled. "Had a nice blast radius."

"Didn't get ketchup on your shirt, did ya?" Gavin raised a brow.

"Heh, maybe even a bit of meat and potatoes." The soldier mockingly wiped his hands down the front of his coat.

Gavin gave a loud, drawn-out laugh. "HA---A! Ghastly."

"Nightmarish, for sure," Troy agreed.

"Well, I'm glad someone was able to take him out. So if he's out of the picture, then why are you still dealing with monsters?" Gavin questioned.

Troy halted, replaying all the events. Gavin had died so soon in their mission. He had no idea about Sapphire or anything that occurred after their first trip to Ives.

"Long story?" the hologram asked.

"Very long. Scan?" Troy raised his wrist.

Gavin eyed Troy's wrist. He gave a guilty smile. "Why the hell not?" For a second, Gavin's demeanor changed, reminding Troy that he was merely a hologram and not the real thing. Blue lines darted from Gavin's eyes to Troy's wrist. With a flash, all of Troy's collected data was copied from his wrist and into the tombstone's memory device. There was a pause after everything had loaded, and Gavin's face lit up with amusement once again. "That was interesting."

"You know the story now?" Troy asked.

"I get the gist. That little girl is creeptastic to the highest." He shuddered.

"You're telling me."

"I see you're using my best pupil." Once again, Gavin stood tall and proud.

"Oh, Aren?" Troy asked. "Yeah. He's a good guy. He's really pulled through and has proven to be quite the skilled pilot. You taught him well."

"Good replacement." Gavin nodded firmly.

Troy's eyes narrowed. "Nothing will ever replace you, man."

The pilot staggered slightly, eyeing himself once again. "Guess an imitation ain't much either, huh?"

"You're fine! You're…great…I…how the hell do I respond to that?" he asked, exasperated.

"Just messin' with your head is all!" Gavin teased.

"Don't make me feel bad. I already feel like shit," Troy muttered.

"So what's your plan?"

Troy cocked his head to the side. "Plan?"

"Yeah! You've got a psycho child out there killing people, and you're in here talking to me? Where's Aria?" At the mentioning of Aria's name, there was a fleeting glitch. Gavin's body wavered, his face becoming emotionless. It happened so fast; Troy had nearly missed it. "Aria," Gavin stated again.

"Home. She's at home. We're meeting up today to plan our final attack against Sapphire and her army. We'll be bringing the battle to us. All we got to do is figure out when."

"You left her alone?" Gavin asked.

Troy was taken aback by Gavin's question. "Uh, she's got Team Phoenix with her."

"You go straight back to her once you're done talking with me. I don't want you doing your mopey shit. Stay away from the bar," Gavin lectured.

"Okay, okay! Sheesh…" Troy grumbled.

"I'm not around anymore to take care of her." Gavin's voice faded out. Troy looked at the projection curiously. "That's rough to deal with, but it's your job now. I know you're the best man for it. Always have been."

Troy rubbed the back of his neck, his expression twisting. "I'll try my best. Believe me; I'd always risk my life for hers."

"Don't be so eager to. Just take care of you both, ya know what I mean?" Gavin looked upward toward the sky.

Troy nodded in understanding. "We're fighting this war together. We're going to survive. We have to. I just wish I had all the answers, you know?"

Gavin grinned, his eyes still plastered to the sky. "Aw, you know me. Anytime I needed answers, I always looked to the sky."

Troy lifted his gaze, the harsh sunlight blistering against his eyes. He held a palm over his brow, peering at the clouds that momentarily blocked out the glowing white orb. "The sky, huh?"

Gavin's form fluctuated once more, a vibration disrupting the feed. Troy caught the disturbance again as the cloud moved away from the sun. The militant's mouth dropped, his eyes widening. There had been a lot of electrical disturbances lately.

In Saray, right after they had barely won the battle, Troy was sitting at the bar watching a football game on the vid screen. Before that, however, the channel had been set at a science conference.

"I do believe that the solar flares are the cause of the recent electric bursts that have plagued our satellites as of late. After years of study, I have concluded that the sun's magnetic reconnection is increasing exponentially. The solar arcades are ever-increasing within the areas of closely contained loops of magnetic lines of force, creating an enormous helix of magnetic field that is unconnected with the others. The quicker the loops, the more the helix grows, sending out multiple coronal mass ejections. But as it grows larger and larger, the loops are growing faster and closer together, but the flares are slowing down. This is causing a massive amount of energy buildup. I predict that a truly enormous ejection is about to occur in the upcoming month. At any time, it could explode, leaving us with the largest flare in nearly 20,000 years and potentially annihilating not only our satellites, but obstructing all energies on Earth."

"When do you predict the massive ejection will occur?"

"Judging by the rate and speed…around the end of December. Possibly the twenty-fifth if my calculations are correct."

Troy pulled back his coat sleeve, pulling up his DNAIS. The date was the twenty-third of December.

"Holy shit," he gasped. He looked back up to the sun and then over to the hologram of his friend. "Gavin, you're a genius."

Giving a swift nod, the pilot replied, "I know."

"No, seriously. You're a freaking genius!" Troy exclaimed. "I've got to get to Aria!"

"Go my valiant white knight!" Gavin saluted.

Troy saluted the image. His face fell into a sad smile. "Thanks, friend…for all the memories, all the good times, all the drinks, and all the arguments. Nobody will ever replace you. I'm glad to call you my best friend and wish you all the luck and happiness," his smile faltered, "wherever you are."

Gavin folded his arms, looking around him at nothing in particular. "It ain't so bad, truthfully. I'll be waiting patiently to meet up with you and Aria again." At this time, the pilot looked at the cigarette; he scoffed and handed the item out for Troy to take.

"We'll visit…often," Troy spouted, apprehensively taking back the cig.

Gavin shook his head. "No, not here." He tapped the tombstone and then looked over his shoulder. "Naw, I'll have a big party waiting for you guys." He brought his attention back to Troy and winked. "But I don't plan on having that party for many more years!"

Troy stared at the projection in silent amazement.

"Go! You have important business to attend to!" Gavin shooed Troy away, his hands limply flopping up and down. Next, he stood at attention and gave a final salute. After giving a charming smile, the hologram faded away line-by-line back into the tombstone.

"Till next time," Troy whispered. He read the name on the tombstone one last time and spun around, running back toward his car.

If the scientist was correct, then he and Aria only had tomorrow to prepare for the final fight against Sapphire. If the mass coronal ejection were to occur on the estimated day, then the militaries would have a pretty good chance at possibly defeating Sapphire's army. It would put their own equipment at risk, but the frequency disruptions caused by the solar flares could disrupt the energy fields that each monster was equipped with and potentially render her robotic armies inoperable. It was a risky bet. The date wasn't set in stone. The massive flare could occur at any minute, but Troy had faith; he felt it deep within his gut. Finally, things were going to be in their favor. And what better way to feed into Sapphire's desire than to have the last battle on Christmas day? It would be an offer she couldn't refuse.

"Visitation"

CHAPTER 18

Gunfire erupted; a tumultuous thundering of warfare crackled and boomed, threatening to burst the eardrums of the surrounding soldiers. Spoofy crouched behind a wrecked vehicle, the flames making it difficult to see her target. Aiming her weapon, the camera at the tip of the barrel produced an image of the shops lining the streets. Chester's Bar and Grille was set aflame. Half the building had been reduced to rubble by a rogue missile. The woman eyed the broken glass from her optical viewer, her sight traveling across the road. Electric bursts sizzled and snapped from the magnetic rails embedded in the street, the energy causing her neck and arm hair to stand on end.

"Come on, you bastard. Where are you?" she murmured in a raspy voice.

A howl sounded, and a massive shadow blurred past one of the side alleys. Spoofy's eyes narrowed. She held her fingers behind her ear.

"Caught sight of one in-between the dress shops," she warned the rest of her team.

"Heading to that area, now," Zombie responded.

From above, Aria watched her teammates on the lower level. She looked to her right at Nerd as he worked some data into one of his comp pads.

"How's the big guy coming? Can you get him in there?" she asked.

Nerd gnashed his teeth; his brow knitted together. "Tryin', but this damn thing is bein' a bitch."

Aria folded her arms, looking out the window. She could see Spoofy moving down the street, pausing at each obstacle that blocked her path. Zombie was running down the alley to the right of her, reloading his weapon.

Monkey was on a rooftop not too far away, sniping at targets further down the road. Kaino waited patiently to be called upon at the rendezvous point.

"Zombie's gaining on its marker. We need to get it up," Aria said, her voice on edge.

"Damn it, I'm tryin'!" Nerd growled.

Aren sidestepped, looking over Nerd's shoulder. He gave a smirk and reached over the other man, pushing against the screen.

"Oi!" Nerd looked up at the younger man. A moment later, a loud snarl sounded, echoing throughout the streets. "How'd you do that?" he asked.

Aren sat in a chair beside Nerd, a smug look on his face. "You didn't designate the location."

"I did!" Nerd disagreed.

"Nope," Aren argued.

"I pushed it, right here…on the map!" Nerd poked the device in his hand.

"Did you confirm it?" Aren swiveled in a slow circle.

"Of course I…." Nerd scrutinized the screen.

"There's a double confirmation process to make sure you are absolutely positive you want to set those commands. Don't want any accidents out on the field now, do we?" Aren explained.

"Accidents," the Scotty scoffed. "Stupid process," he grumbled lowly.

Aria kept her stare fixated on the corner of the alley where Spoofy had initially spotted the target. Spoofy passed an overturned tank, her robotic arm shoving the giant barrel out of her way. The female crouched, walking stealthily over shards of broken glass. She came to a halt behind a second tank, looking down the side alleys.

"Anything?" she asked.

"Not seeing anything. Can you confirm the location?" Zombie replied.

Once again, Spoofy took in her surroundings, guiding the tip of her weapon around the corners. The left side was void of any living targets, civilian bodies strewn about. The woman eyed a street drain. A hydrant's water mixed with the blood of the dead, a swirling pool of red. Unfazed, she moved her sight to the right. On the other side of the tank was one of the Spewers. It rose, standing tall even on stumpy legs. Hot magma rolled between its teeth and thin lower lip, the acidic substance dripping and sizzling through the wheel track of the tank. Moving its eyes downward, it immediately locked onto Spoofy. The revelation startled her.

"Oh shit!" she cursed aloud.

The sound of her voice ignited the monster's rage. Jumping to the side, Spoofy opened fire upon the beast. She was too late, however, as the bursting magmatic flame gushed from the Spewer's mouth, slung through the air, and poured over the top of her.

"SHIT!" she screamed as the boiling liquid doused over her.

Spoofy looked down at herself; the magma digitized and dropped onto the ground in bursting pixels. The woman angrily folded her arms, her armor twitching in and out of focus. Her brown eyes thinned into slits as she glowered at the Spewer. The beast roared, magma flying in long streams. Next, Spoofy felt extremely heavy, her body forcefully dropping onto the ground. She groaned, struggling to breathe against the constricting force.

"Damn it…" she snarled.

"Guys…I'm dead," she mentally spoke.

"NO!" Monkey called out.

"Need a medic?" Kaino asked.

Spoofy rolled her eyes. *"No. I got melted…totally wasted."*

"Don't worry, princess. I got yer back," Zombie sounded.

The cowboy rounded the corner of the alley behind the Spewer. He aimed his revolver at the magma sacs on the creature's back. He shot three times, popping the upper sacs first. The Spewer howled, its thick arms reaching for its wounds. It spun. Fiery eyes looked upon Zombie as the monster's body began to bubble and swell. Zombie popped a few more shots into the creature's torso before he launched a grappling hook over the side of the building. The beast dove, trying to take Zombie out, but missed and crashed into the side of the complex as the man flew into the air and climbed atop the roof. Exploding, the Spewer took out the lower right side of the structure. Zombie stumbled, holding onto his cowboy hat. Using his hook, he zip-lined down the face of the building. After a rather ungraceful landing, he unclipped himself and ran to the opposite side of the street just as the shop crumbled in massive heaps to the ground.

"Ha! Got the bastard!" Zombie drawled, giving Spoofy a thumbs-up.

Spoofy's face twisted into a look of uncertainty. Zombie's enthused expression fell. He knew it was coming, but he couldn't move out of the way fast enough. A Brute from the opposite alley sent a violent shockwave in the man's direction. The impact slammed against Zombie, throwing his body in two different directions. His top landed not far from his previous position; his legs shot across the road, slammed against the crumbled building, and dropped to the ground.

"Son of a bitch…" he angrily twanged.

He eyed his legs across the road and looked down at his split midsection. He felt heavy, his suit locking him onto the ground so he couldn't move; his head slammed back onto the pavement.

"This is bullshit." He stared upwards at the black sky, the smoke swirling in consistent patterns overhead.

"*Damn. I saw that,*" Monkey said.

"*Guess I'm out, too,*" Zombie added.

"*Need a medic?*" Kaino asked.

"*Not unless you can tape my legs back together.*" Zombie glared at the sky.

"*Ouch,*" Kaino dryly stated.

"*Guess it's up to me now,*" Monkey sighed.

From the rooftop, Monkey looked down at Zombie and Spoofy. The two were sprawled on the ground. Each shared matching agitated expressions.

A deafening crash commenced, tearing Monkey's attention away from his comrades. Grabbing his sniper rifle, the soldier ran and slid to his knees, aiming attentively in the direction of the hospital where Kaino was residing. Through the scope, he saw a multitude of figures rushing down the street toward the hospital. Monkey readied to fire but halted, unsure of which action to take.

"*Are those friendlies?*" he curiously asked.

The mob moved in an erratic pattern and speed, darting from one trashed vehicle to another, leaping over barricades, climbing over walls. The sight was unnerving. What Monkey expected to be monsters were regular human beings, but the way they moved wasn't natural.

"*I'd say no,*" Kaino chimed in.

"*What the hell are they? I haven't seen these in the report.*" Monkey gawked through his reticle at one individual. The man had dark hair spiked with neon-green tips. His skin was pale, and he wore basic military fatigues. The way he ran and leaped three meters into the air was spooky. The man's face was undecipherable, not showing fright, rage, or amusement. The man seemed to be on a mission, all the others following close behind.

"*Shoot them, Monkey!*" Kaino called out. "*We can't let them reach the hospital!*"

Monkey gasped, took aim, and quickly fired. Kaino always had good instincts, so Monkey didn't need to be told twice. Firing, the round burst through the mysterious man's head. Monkey continued on, blasting over and over again into the crowd. He got about a dozen shots in before one person made a sudden stop. It was a woman. She was average looking, her long orange hair waving like a fan as she turned her head to look up at the sniper. The woman was a good two hundred meters away, yet her green eyes locked directly onto his. Monkey shivered.

Reloading, he kept his eyes on the mob. The orange-haired woman was making a mad dash in his direction. Monkey knew his weapon inside and out. He was lightning fast at reloading, dismantling, and putting his gun together. By the time he had the fresh clip inserted into the rifle and was aiming, the lady was at the base of his building. He frowned. Through his sights, he watched as the woman slapped her hands together, and a nightmarish scene unfolded.

An electric whir sounded as the woman's arms snapped out of place. The shoulders curved inward toward her chest, her elbows snapping to the side. Her jaw dropped, hitching onto the top of her arms. From her mouth came a telescoping barrel that locked into the palms of her hand. Her arms vibrated, feeding energy into the pipe. The electric whine rose in volume. This all happened within a second, and after another, blue energy fed down the length of her barrel and detonated like a cannon upward toward Monkey's position on the roof.

"Holy shit!" he shouted, diving out of the way.

The energy exploded upon impact with the roof's entry door, its blast radius expanding as the current moved like fire across the surface of the floor. Lying on his back, the sniper scooted away, sliding the best he could from the rushing static. As he spun to his feet to run, the orange-haired woman floated to the roof's level, her feet now bursting thrusters. Monkey heard the windup; the sound sent chills over his body. Before he could even take a step, the woman's cannon fired again, the blue orb of electric light exploding against his back.

Monkey dropped to his hands and knees, blue light enveloping him. His body appeared to char and blow away in the wind, but quickly pulled back together. He felt a heavy weight push against him, and he was locked onto the roof of the building, staring blankly at the cement floor.

"No need for a medic. I died," Monkey whimpered.

"I'll be joining you in just a moment," was Kaino's solemn response.

There was an orchestra of electrical whines revving up from the streets below. Contorting his face, Monkey awaited the inevitable. Within a second, the whole city was erupting into a devastating roar as each booming cannon device sounded one after another from the strange people. He couldn't see the hospital from where he lay, but the corner of his eyesight glowed with a brilliant light. Everything had fallen silent only for a moment before the world was engulfed in a sizzling hiss. The hospital ruptured into pieces; the pavement lifted off the ground in generous loads, crashing and tumbling into the surrounding buildings. Monkey saw it, the debris of rock and metal as it flew high into the air and then came crashing back down toward his body.

He flinched, wanting to shield his face, but everything suddenly shattered into tiny pixels, sprinkling around him like rain. Then all fell into darkness.

"Stop the simulation!" Aria called out, her voice bouncing through the air.

Slowly, everything lit up into brilliant white.

The woman was leaning against the control panel; her mouth pulled tight as she ground her teeth together. The large training room was void of all replicas. There were no flames, no debris, no monsters, and no buildings. Instead, all was laid out like a colorless obstacle course. Spoofy remained on the floor with Zombie only a few meters away. Monkey was high on a white platform, gaping at the floor beneath him. Kaino was at the far end of the room, leaning against the tall white box that was previously his hospital. He folded his arms and gave a huff of frustration. Franklin sat closest to the training room's exit. The spherical droid had only made it two minutes into the simulation before he was brought down by a Brute's blast. The bot shrieked as it lifted into the air and followed up with a flatulent noise.

"That was awful, you guys," Aria called out, her hand pressing against the speaker switch. "I think that was one of the worst simulations I've ever seen."

"What were those things?" Monkey loudly asked.

Aria's forehead wrinkled. "Those would be the biomechanical androids. Sapphire has a whole army of them. As far as I know, each one is very lethal. We need to be prepared for anything. Always use EMPs. An EMP will give you an immense advantage. I'd prefer you to waste an EMP grenade than not use one. Clarke said he's working with the science team to replicate Camery's electrically-charged rail guns. I'd like you each to have an ECRG form of weaponry. Not only that, but you will also be fitted with new armor. But we cannot use that as an excuse! We must be vigilant at all times! Every corner is dangerous; every step is one step closer to a potential death, and every breath you breathe can be your last. Don't forget it, or this simulation can very quickly become a reality."

She dropped the speaker device and plopped into a leather chair. She eyed Nerd and Aren. The two men were avoiding her stare, feeling like children caught in the middle of a fuming mother's lecture. Out of all the simulations that morning, this one was the messiest.

"Erm, want me to go get you a coffee?" Aren spoke up finally.

Aria eyed her teammates out on the training room's floor. She heaved a weary sigh and snatched up the speaker again.

"Hey, guys. Come in for a break. We'll discuss strategy a bit more before moving onto the next simulation." Her tone was a bit softer.

Franklin was the first into the room, chiming and beeping excitably. Bridgette swirled, giving a squeal, and sped toward Aren's bot. The two machines flashed lights and squawked and tweeted to each other. Aren and Nerd eyed each other awkwardly.

"Bridgette," Nerd called out.

Bridgette ignored her owner and ran her faceplate into Franklin's, a repetitive cheap sounding cheerfully as the two spun in a circle while pressed together.

Nerd leaned forward in his chair. "What kind of malarkey is this? Bridgette!"

Franklin brought out one of his clamps, poking and prodding the other bot. Bridgette squealed in what sounded like delight.

Aren leaned against the control panel and folded his arms. "Seems they like each other."

Nerd scoffed, eyeing the younger man. "Like each other...heh. Bridgette!"

Nerd's droid turned around, running her backside against Franklin, the two honking and flashing lights once more.

"Bridgette! Ya blasted prostitute!" Nerd shouted.

Giving another screech, Bridgette's back panel dropped, allowing Franklin to look inside at her computer parts.

Nerd covered his eyes. "Oh, lordy! Showing off yer posterior parts already. I'm disappointed in ya young lady!"

Aren snickered, watching the scene with interest. Aria was also intrigued by this exchange of communication between the two drones. She had never seen it quite like this before. Franklin this time squealed, his clamps opening and closing animatedly. Suddenly, he reached inside Bridgette, gathering data.

"'Ey!" Nerd screamed. "Get yer dirty clamps offa her capacitors!"

"Did we miss something?" Spoofy asked as she entered the room. Her hair was sticky with sweat, pressed against her forehead. The military woman eyed the two robots that were dancing in the corner of the room. "Aw, did Bridgette make a new friend?"

"How can you stand there and laugh? She's clearly being molested!" Nerd protested.

Aren patted Nerd on the shoulder. "I believe she came onto my Franklin, first."

"She's only a year old, for Christ's sake! She's just a baby!" The Scotty whined.

"Franklin!" Aren said. "Cool it."

Franklin immediately released Bridgette, making a sound of discontent.

Simultaneously, Aren and Nerd pointed at the ground beside themselves, telling their bots to "get over here."

"So, how bad was it?" Spoofy asked, dropping into another chair beside Aria.

Aria feigned a smile, and Spoofy cringed.

"That bad, huh?" Spoofy glanced down at her arm, messing with a loose panel.

"It was pretty bad," Aria said with a laughing scoff.

Zombie trudged into the room, his cowboy hat in his hand. He leaned against the wall, already smoking a cigarette.

"I told you to stop that," Kaino said as he passed the smoking man.

"I'll stop after this ridiculous war," Zombie drawled.

"Thanks for saving me, princess," Spoofy sarcastically stated, eyeing the Southern man.

"You coulda warned me about the Brute," he replied sourly.

"That would be cheating," she said. After a pause, she looked toward the doorway. "Where's Monkey?" she asked in a seething tone.

Jumping from her chair, Spoofy marched directly into the hall and slammed her palms against her hips. Zombie's face contorted, and he placed a hand on the side of his face, not wanting to watch the spectacle. Aria looked at him with interest, mouthing the word, "what."

"JEFFREY!" Spoofy yelled. "You went to the vending machine? Are you kiddin' me?!"

"Babe! I'm famished!" Monkey's voice whined from down the hall.

"Snack cakes? You're eating snack cakes!" she shrieked.

"There's nothing healthy in the machines," he pouted, shoving one of the snack cakes in his mouth as he entered the room. "Mmm. I've been workin' hard all morning," he said with a full mouth. He swallowed hard. "Burnin' lots of calories!"

Spoofy threatened to knock him upside the head with her mechanical arm but stopped when Zombie leaned forward, giving her a warning stare.

"You've just lost a night of sex," she hissed, pointing at Monkey's face. Stomping back to the chair, she sat down, refusing to look at her husband's face. "I swear! I didn't get married; I adopted a man-child!"

Aria giggled, watching Monkey as he angrily stuffed the second cake into his mouth.

"Damn. Aria says that about me all the time…and we aren't even married!" Troy's voice sounded from the hall. He rounded the corner, his military trench flapping around his knees as he leaned against the doorframe.

"Where the hell have you been?" Aria irritably asked.

"Had some important things to deal with," Troy said. Rubbing the back of his head, he avoided her stare.

"Important?" she asked. "More important than stopping Sapphire?"

Troy slumped. "If I hadn't done what I did, I wouldn't have come up with my genius idea!"

"Genius?" Aria's eyes widened. "You and the word genius don't go well together."

Moving his head slowly from side to side and pressing his lips tightly together, Troy filtered his brainwaves before continuing. "If you can just shut your sassy mouth for one damn minute, I can explain."

The black-haired woman crossed her legs and folded her arms, giving the man all her attention.

He cleared his throat. "Okay, so this may sound a bit crazy, but I think I know when we should declare the war."

All eyes were on him, waiting eagerly for him to give details.

"December twenty-fifth," he croaked.

"Are you serious?" Kaino asked.

Aria eyed her partner, weighing his words.

"I know, I know. It sounds crazy, but I think that's the best time to do it." Troy unbuttoned his coat, suddenly feeling a bit warm in the crowded room.

"Christmas day may be appealing to Sapphire. It'd be insanely blasphemous," Aria spoke.

"That's what I thought, too! But there's another reason. One that even you haven't thought of yet." Troy fed her a cocky smile.

"And that is?" she asked slowly.

Troy sank to the ground, taking a crouching position. He stared at the tile floor, deep in thought. It was a habit he had when he was in charge of making plans. "Okay, so you remember in Saray? That *one night* that caused all kinds of trouble?" he asked.

All eyes immediately flitted to Aria. The woman could barely contain her blush.

"Uh huh," she huffed.

"Well, I was sittin' at the bar watching the vid screen, right? And, before the football game, there was that commercial with the girl in the fancy underwear...."

"Yeah," Aria roughly affirmed.

"Well, then the boring science convention was on, and I was like, "the hell is this shit" and had the barman change the channel."

Aria pondered a moment, her eyes lighting up. She recalled the event, her memory as clear as when it occurred. "Yeah!" she gasped.

"The coronal mass ejection?" he asked.

Aria stood from her chair. "Yeah!" she cheered.

"I think there's a good chance that sucker will blow on the twenty-fifth. And if it does, it'll give us one hell of an upper hand!" Troy exclaimed.

"It could fry Sapphire's army!" Aria's hands went to her hair; her jaw dropped.

"Fry her Roman robots, her android clones, and render the monsters' Faze Shields completely useless." Troy smirked.

"Wa-wa-wait!" Spoofy held up a hand. "I have no damn clue what the hell you guys are talking about, but if it can fry all of Sapphire's electronics, wouldn't it mess with ours?"

That was when Troy sucked in air between his teeth with a hiss. "Yeeeah…that would be the only problem."

"I don't care. It's our only chance!" Aria said. "Come on, guys. We've been practicing all day. If that solar flare goes off and kills most of Sapphire's army, all we'd have to deal with were monsters without shields."

"That actually does sound pretty easy," Zombie said.

"We'd be virtually defenseless," Spoofy added.

"We'll have our body armor. We'll have our shields until everything goes down. I mean, it sucks, but it'll even things out. It'll be man versus demon. We can take them out!" Aria slammed her fist into her other palm.

"I say we go for it," Monkey said.

"Just remind me to cover Bridgette in static protection. I don't want to lose my girl," Nerd spoke up.

Aren nodded. "I'll look into figuring a way to protect your guys' armor the best I can. It'd be a stretch, but if we can somehow merge the static protection with our own Faze Shields, we can maybe get them to last through the flare's disruptive energy."

Aria pointed at the young pilot. "You and Nerd work on that!"

Nerd shrugged, shaking his head. "Let me just whip up some magic," he replied sarcastically; then his face fell into a look of determination. "I'll see what I can do."

"So…uh…what day is it?" Monkey asked.

Everybody in the room looked at their DNAIS.

"DECEMBER 23," Franklin droned.

"DECEMBER 22," Bridgette said at the same time.

Nerd smacked his forehead. "Damn leap year….Bridgette! Leap year!

Align time and date with the satellites."

Bridgette beeped. "DECEMBER 23…WEATHER
REPORT…CLOUDY...45 DEGREES FAHRENHEIT, 7.2
CELSIUS…ADVANCED WEATHER WARNING: HIGH SOLAR
ACTIVITY. STAY INDOORS."

"Heh, smart girl." Nerd patted his drone.

"If it's the twenty-third…then that means we only have the rest of today
and tomorrow to prepare for the war." Monkey concluded.

Aria looked at Troy; her eyes held a look of uncertainty.

"That's right," Troy stated. "We've waited far too long. It's now or never.
It's time we put an end to Sapphire. Too many innocent people have died
already." He looked at the floor again.

Aria sensed devastation within Troy. Her lower lip curled inward as she
felt Troy's emotion swirling around him. One word stuck out in his mind, a
name–Gavin.

"I'll call a meeting with Clarke. We'll go over all details and plans with
him, alert the other militaries, and finalize all alliances. Tonight we'll
announce our arrangement worldwide. Let's hope Sapphire responds," Aria
said.

"Are we going to train more?" Monkey asked.

"I want you guys to get rested up. Prepare all you've got. I'll find you all
when I'm finished talking with Clarke." Aria stood at attention. Everyone
followed her actions, saluting. "Dismissed."

Casually, everyone filed out of the room. Spoofy immediately harassed
Monkey. Zombie followed behind, making a quiet joke to Kaino. Aren and
Nerd walked closely together, throwing out ideas as their robots chattered
away behind them.

"You thought of that all by yourself?" Aria asked, tearing Troy's attention
back to her.

He stood uneasily in the center of the room, not making eye contact.
"Well, I sorta had a reminder."

"Gavin?" she asked.

Troy's face held a look of shock. "How did you…? Oh…that mindreading
thing you can do now."

Aria walked forward, wrapping her arms around Troy's neck. She hugged
him, resting her cheek against his chest. The man held her in return, resting
his head on hers. She felt him ease beneath her touch.

"For Gavin," Troy quietly said.

Aria gave a quiet sniff. "For Gavin," she whispered.

Ivory wrung her hands nervously as she waited outside the entry of the dark cave. She hadn't returned to the caverns since the day Dovian brought her to the ruins of his city. Though she had everything planned out in her mind, there was still a risk to her current position. The only moments she had spoken to Sapphire had been during stressful situations, and the child's anger had caused either Ivory or Dovian physical harm each time. Still, it was a risk Ivory had to take. If she could gain any amount of Sapphire's favor, it would greatly help her and Dovian's position.

A snarl came from inside the cave. Ivory jumped at the sound and then quickly gathered her strength. A skittering followed, and a Brawler stepped out into the sunlight, its black eyes squinting. It saw Ivory and hissed.

"You just shut that big mouth of yours," Ivory snapped back.

The Brawler's smiling face was unsettling. Despite the menacing look, the creature seemed to lose interest and backed away into the darkness. Ivory let out a harsh sigh, looking up at the glaring sun. Her readings popped up around her vision, telling her that solar radiation had heightened. The levels were rising more and more each day. Not good.

"Okay. Just get this over with," Ivory spoke quietly to herself.

Pushing her shoulders back, Ivory confidently strode into the cave. The tunnels were much longer than she had remembered. Each channel was infested with hissing, growling demons. Even amongst themselves, they fought. One with a red mane snarled, leaping from one aisle into another, its barb lodging into a Brawler's neck. This stirred up a fight, and Ivory ran past a few more passageways to avoid getting drug into the nasty conflict. As she turned one corner, she collided with someone.

"Oh!" She held up her hands, preparing to defend herself.

A man with dark hair and dark eyes peered at her in interest. Ivory held her breath, unsure as to whom or what the man was.

"Um, sorry. Just passing through," she meekly stated, stepping around the man.

He looked over his shoulder at her, his expression blank. Upon hearing the chaos further down the cave, the man turned, running toward the fight. Ivory walked faster, not daring to look back as she heard the sound of chunking gunfire and monster screeches.

"What is that sound?!" the shriek of Sapphire's voice bounced against the walls.

Ivory took a deep breath and stepped into the crystalline chamber. The orange glass-encased flame bounded and reflected light from the shiny surfaces, giving the room a dream-like appearance. Sapphire sat upon her throne with her fingers splayed out. Beside her was Lilith. Just the sight of the dark-haired woman filled Ivory with frustration.

"Your pets won't stop fighting. I sent one of the androids to quiet them down," Lilith said in her husky voice.

Sapphire noticed Ivory immediately; her blue eyes remained passive, almost careless about the blonde's arrival.

"Interesting to see you here," Sapphire said. There was a hint of distrust in her voice. Could she already tell what Ivory was up to?

Lilith turned her head in the woman's direction. Her eyes glinted in the firelight, the corner of her painted lips lifting upward. "Where's your bodyguard?" she asked.

"Dovian is meditating," Ivory said indifferently.

"And why are you here?" Sapphire questioned.

Ivory's blue eyes brightened a bit, her confidence growing as Sapphire did not seem to be in an especially murderous mood. "I've done a lot of thinking," she began. "And the realization has finally sunk in that I will be spending the rest of my life with you."

Sapphire lifted her chin, her blue-grey eyes watching Ivory with interest.

Ivory walked toward the center of the room. Euclid's headless body remained on the floor in a crystalline tomb. What an awful reminder of a terrible man. Sapphire noticed Ivory's sight upon the trophy of death. Ivory raised her head, her eyes locking onto the child.

"Can't say I'll ever miss him, but the corpse still unsettles me." Ivory looked back at the remains. "It angers me. He was powerful; he had so much potential, but he was also a complete idiot."

Sapphire gave a tiny smile. She seemed amused by this statement. "He never was too bright but was a necessary means to carry out my plan. I'd planted a seed long ago within him. He was the type of temptation that was perfect for luring Dovian to me. A pawn, Euclid was never meant to be part of my final plan. But if it weren't for him reminding Dovian of what was at stake, I probably wouldn't have either of you on my side." Her smile faded. "But you are not here to speak about Euclid."

"You are correct. I came here to speak with you, if that would be alright," Ivory stated.

Lilith crossed her arms, glaring at Ivory. She wasn't trusting of the blonde in the slightest.

"And what would we speak about?" Sapphire asked. Her face twisted back to its previous emotionless state.

Ivory shrugged casually. She clasped her hands before her waist and gave a gentle, motherly smile.

"Whatever you like, Sapphire. I am only interested in getting to know you a bit better. As you said, in the future I will become a sort of mother to you. I would like to prepare myself better for that role."

Lilith scoffed. "You want to be Sapphire's mother? Do you not realize who—" She was cut off by Sapphire's raised hand.

The child looked at Lilith. "Leave us." It was a short order.

Lilith gaped at Sapphire in wonder. Her face twitched and wrinkled as she tried to process Sapphire's words. Seeming upset, even hurt a little by this command, Lilith scoffed and marched out of the room, making sure to pass by Ivory close enough to bump shoulders together. Ivory's brow furrowed in irritation.

"You don't like her," Sapphire stated.

Ivory wetted her lips, choosing her words carefully.

"You can give me your honest opinion. I wouldn't care either way," the child said.

"Well, in that case, no. I don't like her much at all." Ivory brushed away a stray curl in front of her eyes.

"Would you like for me to destroy her?" Sapphire asked.

"Is it that easy for you to destroy someone else?" Ivory returned.

"I will destroy anything that doesn't in some way benefit me. I have known Lilith for many, many years. Her usefulness in this form is very limited, but she was curious to live in this realm. And giving such a title as "he" or "she" is often not necessary. For she is neither," Sapphire explained. "Even though I've been in contact with her for far longer than you can imagine, if she does anything at all to hinder my plans, I will destroy her. So, if you ask it of me, I can kill her for you if that would make you happy."

Ivory's eyes widened. "If it would make me happy? I'm sorry to ask this, but since when do you really care about my happiness?"

Sapphire stood from the throne, her face giving a mocked expression of shock. "Why, Ivory, you're still alive, aren't you? I would say that means I care a great deal about you. Sure, I've done some callous things, but that was only to gain what I needed from Dovian. He's the disobedient one, not you."

Ivory nodded slowly. "So, figuratively speaking, if Dovian and I were ever to do anything to upset you, you would kill us without hesitation?"

Sapphire was silent a moment. "Not until you give me children. If, after we have a stable population, you and Dovian continue to dissatisfy me, I will not need you."

Ivory glared.

"Is that too cruel?" the child asked.

"Are you serious when you ask that question?" Ivory almost laughed.

Sapphire gave a shrug. "I must admit; I've not had a conversation like this in a very long time."

"Well, let's change that, shall we?"

Sapphire cocked her head to the side, unsure of Ivory's meaning.

"You and I will need to communicate more often. If I am to be your mother, I would like to have a better understanding of your viewpoint and situation." Ivory looked around at the cave. "What shall we do?"

Sapphire stepped up to the woman, her head only meeting Ivory's waist. "We could go for a walk."

Ivory nodded. "I'd like that." Then, she held out her hand toward the child.

Sapphire stared at Ivory's hand. She looked up at the woman's face and then back toward her hand. Ivory wiggled her fingers, waiting.

"Have you not held hands with someone before?" the woman asked.

"Is that what you want me to do?" The child timidly raised her hand.

"Isn't that what mothers do?" Ivory asked back.

Sapphire finally grasped her appendage. Ivory's readings fizzled with static, an alarm chiming in her head. The temperature of the child's hand was ice cold and then feverishly hot. After a moment, everything settled within Ivory's insides, and she gently squeezed Sapphire's hand. Together they walked out of the chamber.

"I wouldn't know," Sapphire began. "I didn't have a mother."

Ivory frowned, not sure in what context Sapphire was speaking. As if detecting Ivory's question, she continued.

"I only had a Father. We had a bit of a dispute, and He kicked me out." The child spoke about the situation simplistically.

Ivory knew, from I'Lanthe's knowledge, what Sapphire actually was. The idea of holding the girl's hand was absurd, but Ivory was adamant that she try. She had to gain Sapphire's trust. In order to do so, she feigned ignorance.

"Kicked you out? That sounds awful. Why would he do that?" Ivory asked.

Sapphire giggled. "Because He wanted all the glory for Himself. Why create children, if you do not want them to succeed with you? He only wanted to hold me back, keep the praise for Himself. Do you know what that is like?"

Ivory shook her head. "Did it hurt?"

Sapphire's smile quickly dropped. "No! I was glad He did it! I'm glad I'm not there anymore!"

Judging by the severity of her sudden anger, that was a lie.

"It's okay, Sapphire. Nobody is immune to hurt. I hurt. Dovian hurts. It's an ordinary emotion…especially when someone you love hurts you." Ivory tried calming the child.

Sapphire's face softened. "It's a useless human emotion. I wasn't given that."

"I can't imagine. So you feel nothing at all?"

"I feel! I feel…anger and hate and…."

"No sadness?" Ivory quipped.

Sapphire glared at the woman. "Betrayal. I feel betrayed."

"Does your father know this?" Ivory asked.

"Of course He does!"

"Have you spoken to him since?"

"We used to keep contact on a regular basis, but then He officially cut ties right before He allowed the Sorcēarians to inhabit the Earth. He gave them my kingdom. He left me here to rot in my own fiery grave. After everything we'd been through. I had excellent plans. He disagreed. It was only His way. *Always* His way." Slowly, her eyes darkened, her voice dropping an octave. "I will turn this world into my own Heaven. I will have my own creations, and they will love me!"

As they spoke, they passed by the caverns. Each demon calmed themselves at the mere sight of the pale child. At one point, Sapphire even ran her fingertips across one Brawler's head. The beast gave a quiet cooing sound, its clawed hands digging into the rock floor in what seemed like pleasure.

Ivory looked down at the child, noticing her frustration. "I am not trying to make you angry, only get to know you better. I'd like to understand your situation so I can sympathize with you."

"I don't want your sympathy," the girl barked.

Ivory sighed in response. "Empathy then."

Sapphire nodded slowly. "It makes sense, I suppose. Though, I think it's a wasted effort."

"I don't believe it is. You've already told me much."

Sapphire's eyes narrowed. "I have. And I'm still wondering what your motives are."

"Like I said, I only want to care for you. If you're going to be my child, I want to love you." Ivory said it quickly and casually. However, the words seemed to lock Sapphire in her place.

"What?" the girl asked. Ivory was pulled to a halt.

"Love. Are you not capable of that, either?" Ivory asked with a hint of amusement.

The child did not respond. Ivory gently tugged her hand, and the two stepped out into the sunlight.

"You know, you speak of love. You want everyone to love you, yet you seem so angry," the woman said softly as she led Sapphire to a rock.

"I loved once. A long time ago. It was a waste of time and energy," Sapphire whispered as Ivory released her hand.

Ivory climbed atop the boulder and sat down. She patted her hand against the jagged surface. It was interesting; Sapphire complied with Ivory's requests and never once seemed annoyed by it.

"Love is never a waste. That is what I've learned," Ivory stated.

"You were damned by Him, too. For what reason?" Sapphire asked. "If it weren't for you being in Hell, you wouldn't occupy that vessel."

She was talking about I'Lanthe's soul. Ivory kept her façade.

"I'm unsure as to why I…or she was damned. Still, I won't let that ruin who I am now."

Sapphire was silent. She fidgeted awkwardly as Ivory twisted and ran her fingers through her platinum hair, combing it.

"You have an interesting outlook on things. Someday, you'll believe as I do," the child mumbled, staring blankly at the desert landscape ahead of her.

"You've caused many deaths and wars. You had Euclid abduct me. You have held me here captive. You have hurt Dovian repeatedly, and you have killed my friends. Yet, here I am…combing your hair," Ivory said, trying not to give in to her dark emotions.

"And many would call you a fool. I haven't decided yet if you are or not," Sapphire said.

They remained quiet, sitting on the rock as the radioactive sun beat down on them.

"Sometime you will have to come to the ruins. It's much better than this desert. There's a pond where we can swim." Ivory looked over her shoulder back toward the destroyed city.

"I will not feel it." Her tiny voice was meek.

"Why not?" Ivory asked.

"This is not my body. I cannot feel things until I have my body thoroughly repaired. Even then, it is only a robotic body. Everything will be artificial. I will not be able to enjoy life until I have a physical living body to move into." Sapphire leaned back, lying on Ivory's lap. She pointed at the sky and giggled innocently. "Elephant."

Ivory lifted her sight toward a strange cloud. She wasn't positive what an elephant was, but the shape was a bit funny.

"Do you like to play games?" Ivory asked.

"I love games," Sapphire nodded. "When I win."

Ivory smirked and also nodded slowly. Sapphire did have a certain childish demeanor, but Ivory had to remind herself constantly that this was not a child. There was a severe darkness within this entity. For the time being, Ivory decided to keep things simple. Sapphire had already conducted what could be considered bodily contact with Ivory. Things had gone much more smoothly than she had expected. Then, the child spoke again, and her words filled Ivory with disdain.

"Perhaps you can help me sew a new dress later." The girl kept her eyes locked onto the sky. "I'm going to have Lilith retrieve your friends' bodies. We're going to skin them. Doesn't that sound like fun?"

Ivory gnashed her teeth together, profusely trying to hold in her anger. Sapphire looked at her and grinned. She was a monster of a child.

"Love only gets you hurt in the end, Ivory. You've learned that time and time again. Love is a selfish emotion. There is no equality in the universe. You can love me all you want…but don't expect me to love you just the same. I have my goals; I have my reasons; you are merely a fleeting moment of my existence," Sapphire said. Her face turned calm and cold.

"Since we're both being honest here," Ivory started, "I just want to let you know that I will have no part in your skinning of my friends. Nor will I allow you to desecrate their bodies in any way."

Sapphire sat up, her eyes narrowing. "As if you have any control over it."

"You're a spoiled brat. If ever I give birth and you inhabited the body, the first thing I'll teach you are some manners," Ivory spoke in a seething tone.

"Try what you will, Ivory. You're nothing more than a vessel of a damned human being, a person who had no chance at salvation since the Creator left. You're damned, as is the rest of humanity. I will grant you all a Heaven on Earth, a chance to live as one. It's the same for I'Lanthe. She's nothing more than a fallen angel, a damned creature who, despite her holy efforts, ended up as forsaken as the rest of us. He left long ago. This world is mine now, whether you like it or not." The words sounded bland as they passed the child's lips. During this encounter, Ivory found that she was no longer fearful of the child but simply disgusted.

"Then I suppose you and I are going to have to learn to live together," Ivory grumbled.

Sapphire sighed, drawing her knees to her chest. "Yup."

Ivory wasn't sure what to say next. If anything, she wanted to grab the girl by the hair and tear her head off. But Ivory wasn't that stupid. Sapphire's current form was nothing more than a mirage. She had learned that the hard way in the cave after Dovian's battle with Euclid. Still, the temptation was becoming a bit overwhelming as the woman glared at the humming child that sat beside her. Feigning innocence, Sapphire was an abomination disguised as a beautiful little girl. She was deadly; she was monstrous; she was engulfed in darkness.

The sound of footsteps alerted the two blondes to the fast approaching Lilith. The dark-haired woman was running toward them, her eyes nearly popping out of her head. A blood-red line formed her lips, and her manicured hands balled into tight fists. It was clear; something bad had happened.

"What is it? I thought I told you to leave us alone," Sapphire grumbled.

"Have you been paying any attention to the video feeds around the world?" Lilith asked in a startled tone.

Sapphire gaped at the woman a moment and then looked upwards at the sky. With her eyes rolling back into her head, black consuming the orbs, the little girl took a shaking breath. After a few seconds, her head tilted back at an alarming angle, and the child let out a nightmarish scream, folding forward in on herself.

"WHERE IS DOVIAN?!" Sapphire shrieked.

Lilith jumped at the sound, "I-I will retrieve him immediately."

"DO IT, NOW!" The child's voice boomed with an authoritative tone that vibrated in lower tones and garbled moans.

Ivory watched the spectacle in awe. She wasn't sure what Sapphire had seen, but Ivory wondered if it had anything to do with Aria and Troy. Though the woman didn't know their fate, she still maintained hope that they were somehow still alive.

"Simulation"

CHAPTER 19

The entire world was held in silence as humanity watched their vid screens, personal comps, and DNAISs. Black wide eyes that appeared to be holes in Sapphire's face glared menacingly at the public. Aria's bold emerald eyes narrowed. An expression of delight covered her face. It was a temporary staring contest. The military woman waited for Sapphire's reaction at discovering that she and Troy were still alive. Sapphire gaped back with a frightening expression that made every human, except Aria, quake with fear. Angry, shocked, not amused, the blonde child exuded her feelings through even the digital comps. All wrapped into one ball of furious rage, an energy spewed across the world, making it very clear that Sapphire was finished taking things lightly. She was ready for war.

"You look mad," Aria blurted, her arrogant smile only making the energies darker around her. Still, the woman remained unfazed by the child's antics.

Sapphire did not respond. She kept her black stare fixated on the woman.

"I take it I got your attention. How about you sit on your throne and listen a moment to what I have to say, hm?" Aria haughtily said.

The child didn't budge, but her eyes did swell ever so slightly.

"We've gone long enough playing games your way. How about we switch up the rules a bit?" Aria moved to the center of the debriefing room. Waving her hand over a spherical globe, she highlighted the region of Fountains. "I propose you and I just cut to the chase already. What do you say?"

Aria looked up to the child's face on the screen. Sapphire wasn't making any moves, nor was she saying anything. It was beginning to unsettle Aria.

"Let's set a time, date, and location. We can end this war once and for all, but I'd like for it to be on our terms. So far, we've been chasing your armies all over the world. Seeing as you've still not succeeded in your plans, whatever those may be, why not give us a chance to set some rules for once? Who knows, maybe you'd like our terms." Aria moved her hand over the globe, spinning it.

"AND WHAT ARE YOUR TERMS?" a rumbling voice quaked throughout the room, a voice that didn't seem to come from any audio systems but rather sounded upon the air surrounding them. Sapphire's lips did not move. Aria eyed Troy. He and the rest of her team looked like terrified children. Kaino formed a cross over his chest and commenced some form of prayer.

Aria looked back over to Sapphire, a look of determination on her face. "All of our militaries will come against each other for one final battle. We will do it," she zoomed in on her city, "outside of Fountains." The desert land that surrounded the city-state highlighted in red.

"YOUR OWN CITY?" the malevolent voice inquired.

The structure of Fountains rotated, moving between the pillars that held up the metropolis over the expansive hole in the ground. "I'd like to maintain the battle outside the city–military against military."

"IF YOU'RE CONCERNED ABOUT THE LIVES OF CIVILIANS THEN WHY CHOOSE THIS LOCATION?" Sapphire questioned with her foreign voice.

"Why not? Do you disagree with this location? I figured you'd jump at the opportunity to annihilate our forces before moving to our city," Aria casually stated.

"YOU'RE ASKING FOR COMPLETE ANNIHILATION," Sapphire replied.

Aria shrugged. "We want this war to be over. If it gets you to agree to our rules, then it's a risk I'm willing to take."

"THAT'S A MIGHTY WEIGHT UPON YOUR SHOULDERS."

"I'll take it," Aria stated.

"BUT THERE'S A CATCH, ISN'T THERE?" the deep voice asked. Sapphire's eyes narrowed to black slits.

Aria waved her hand from side to side dismissively. "The day of the battle? How about tomorrow?"

Sapphire's eyes held a blank expression for a second. Then, something registered, and they returned to their glaring form. "CHRISTMAS DAY?

YOU WANT TO DECIDE THE FATE OF MANKIND…OUTSIDE
YOUR CITY…ON CHRISTMAS DAY?”

Aria nodded enthusiastically. “That’s right!”

“HUMANITY HAS A SEVERE FORM OF MENTAL ILLNESS….”

Aria smirked a little. “Who do you think gave us that?”

Sapphire’s eyes widened back into large gaping holes in her head. Aria was
proud to receive that response from the evil entity.

“I ACCEPT YOUR CHALLENGE. BE PREPARED, AS TONIGHT
WILL BE THE LAST NIGHT ANY SINGLE PERSON ON THE FACE
OF THIS PLANET SHALL REMAIN BREATHING. I WILL TEAR
YOU APART, SEVER YOUR HEADS, AND WEAR YOUR SKULLS AS
JEWELRY. I WILL SKIN YOU ALIVE. I WILL BURN YOUR CITIES
AND TURN YOUR MILITARIES TO DUST. AFTER TOMORROW,
THERE WILL BE NONE LIVING. EVEN THE SHADOWS OF YOUR
CORPSES BURNED TO STONE WILL BE HELD AS A MEMORIAL
OF MY VICTORY. AS MUCH AS YOU THINK YOU ARE ONE STEP
AHEAD OF ME, THIS DAY HAS BEEN FORESEEN MILLENNIA
BEFORE YOU EVER CRAWLED FROM YOUR MOTHER’S WOMB.
YOU ARE ALL FATHERLESS. YOU ARE ALL MINE. DAMNED
NOW AND FOREVER, NOT ONE HUMAN WILL BE SPARED OF
MY WRATH. THOSE ARE MY TERMS. THERE WILL BE NO
SURVIVORS. IF YOU GIVE UP NOW, PERHAPS I WILL ALLOW
SOME OF YOU TO LIVE.”

Aria scoffed. “We’re not that stupid.”

“YOU MAY NEED TO RETHINK THAT,” the low drone of
Sapphire’s voice quickly uttered. “SO BE IT. I ACCEPT YOUR TERMS.
BATTLE BETWEEN OUR FORCES WILL COMMENCE
TOMORROW AFTER SUNRISE. BRING ALL THAT YOU’VE GOT. I
ENJOY DESTROYING YOUR HOPE.”

Aria glanced at President Clarke, winking. “Haven’t destroyed mine yet!”
she shouted, looking back toward the child. Aria rested her hands on her
waist and gave a mocking laugh.

Sapphire didn’t seem pleased at all, and the screen shut off to black.

“Well…that went well!” Aria spun around, grinning.

Team Phoenix seemed petrified. Feyette and Clarke seemed overly
serious. Troy looked lost in thought. Kovacevic was the only one who
seemed as enthusiastic as she was.

“It was awesome! You got her all kinds of discombobulated,” Kovacevic
muttered as he chewed on his unlit cigar.

"Wow! I'm surprised you know such a fancy word," Aria stated as she walked by the general of Saray.

"Usually I can't get past much more than three syllables. I reserve that fanciful word only for special occasions." Kovacevic shrugged, following after the woman as she exited the room. "So, guess you got yourself a war for Christmas."

Aria gave an unsure nod. "Going to be one hell of a present."

"Hey, Aria," Troy called out after her.

The woman paused, waiting for her partner. She immediately noticed nervousness contained within him. She peered at Kovacevic, and the general nodded at her in understanding.

"I'm goin' to rally my troops," Kovacevic muttered.

"And I'll do the same. I've got some strategies I'd like to go over with them," Feyette joined Kovacevic's side.

"I'll keep you all updated on any news we develop on our end," Aria replied.

Feyette saluted to her. Kovacevic shuffled awkwardly and did the same, twisting his face into one look of confusion. "You all are far too proper," he grumbled, walking away.

Aria brought her attention to Troy. "What is it? You alright?"

Troy rubbed a tense muscle in his shoulder. "I was, uh, thinking this morning. I kinda came up with another idea that may possibly help us out, but I wanted to discuss it with you first."

Aria looked to the side. Team Phoenix was chatting away in the com room. Spoofy caught her stare, and Aria raised one finger, telling her to give Troy and her a moment. Spoofy gave a short nod and contributed to the Team's banter, pulling Clarke and Grayson into the discussion.

Aria placed her hand on Troy's shoulder, and they walked a ways down the hall, resting around the corner where they could have some privacy.

"Your unusual behavior lately is a bit unsettling, Troy," Aria said. She leaned against the wall.

"Tell me about it. I'm suddenly Negative Nancy, and you became the optimistic one. When did that happen?" He scowled.

"I've just been in a good mood lately despite the circumstances. I dunno. I feel like we're finally making some progress. We may actually win this war."

"I hope so. That's why I want to give it our all. We've got to take every chance we can." The man propped himself against the wall, staring at Aria with anxious eyes.

"I plan on taking risks," she paused, "but…what exactly is your idea?"

Troy gave her a severe look. "Okay, just hear me out for a moment. I don't want any interruptions from you until I'm finished, got it?"

Aria glared at him.

He continued, "Sapphire has that robotic fleet from Roma. Those suckers are just as deadly as our biomechanical androids. They have antiaircraft defense systems. They're armed with an arsenal of missiles, lasers, turrets, everything. On top of that, they have high-end defensive shields comparative to Elixis technology. Within seconds, they can do some serious damage to our fleets. If there is some way, *any* way, we can knock a hole in their defenses…we can save thousands of lives, if not more."

The man looked upward at the fluorescent lights above him, searching for the correct words. "I think I know how we can do that. It's very risky. I know you won't like the idea, but I think we can pull it off. If I can get Aren and Nerd to help, I may be able to put myself in the place of one of those robots. Of course, we'd have to get our hands somehow on one of the suckers. I bet Benvenuto has at least one of those robots on hand. He has to! If we can get that transferred here immediately, then I can have Aren and Nerd hack the thing. We can use it for our benefit."

Aria raised her hand, politely asking for a word.

"I…what?" Troy griped.

"If we hack it, then Sapphire's demons can just inhabit it with their souls like we had seen on Ives," she blurted.

Troy ruffled the woman's hair. "This is why I told you not to say anything until I was done speaking," he said in a condescending manner.

Aria scrunched her face.

"That is precisely my point. Let's play this game Sapphire's way. We're not just hacking this thing to fight for us. We're hacking it with my soul," Troy explained.

"Wait…what?!" Aria shouted.

"Camery's done it a few times. It's how he began the android project in the first place. He wanted to see if the human mind was capable of operating drones while off the field. It'd give the drones a more human response but still save lives."

"Except it didn't save lives! Many of the specimens never woke up from the test! In order for it to work properly, he had to place their brains physically inside the robots, which defeated the purpose of the technology completely," Aria argued.

"I'm doing it, Aria! I'm going inside one of those Roman soldiers, and I'm going to be a Trojan horse, got it?" Troy snapped.

Aria stared at him in disbelief. It was an ingenious idea but also incredibly risky.

He took a slow breath, calming himself. "Listen. I can place myself in her lines. I can try to disengage her nuclear warheads. I can try to find a way to close the portals she uses to transport her army, which will keep her from feeding her soldiers into the battlefield. I can cause enough of a distraction that our other militaries can handle the fight themselves. During this time, we can have a team working at disengaging the portal beneath the city. Not sure what it will do, but perhaps if we close the portal from where she originally came from, we can lock her on this plane. I mean, it's worth a shot, right?"

Troy looked determined. He had a fire in his eyes that told Aria he had made up his mind. There was nothing she could do to deter him away from his plan, and despite her feelings for the man, from a militaristic viewpoint, Troy was property of Bio-Tech. He owed his life to the people of Fountains. He was expendable, as was she.

"It's a good plan, Troy," Aria slowly stated. He frowned, noticing her uncertainty. "But what is your plan for when the solar flare hits?"

The man's brow furrowed. "I was hoping you wouldn't think about that."

"We have no absolute time. The flare can occur as soon as you transfer yourself, minutes or hours later…if at all! If you're in the robot when it hits…what happens to you?" she asked.

"Then I'm trapped in an inoperable machine." He shrugged.

"That's practically a dead body at that point," she sighed.

"We'll worry about it *if* it happens."

She shook her head, not liking the idea. "Maybe we can just hack it ourselves and hope Sapphire doesn't notice."

"No! That won't work, and you know it! Come on, Aria! I have the perfect opportunity!" He folded his arms.

"Troy, you do realize that every person who volunteered for Camery's project had been put into a vegetative state when the transfer process occurred. They were all on life support. You're going to ask Aren and Nerd to place you in a coma?"

Troy gave a harsh exhale. "All they got to do is deactivate my pacemaker." He knocked on his chest.

"You're going to die again," she whispered.

"We have to try it," he reassured her. "Aria, I'm not going to die. I'm going to pull this off. It's going to work."

She shook her head in disagreement.

"Now who's being pessimistic?" he chuckled.

305

"Would you let me do it in your place?" she asked.

Troy paused. A look of terror crossed his face. "No. Fuck no, over and over again."

"Then what makes you think I should allow you?" she argued.

"Goddamnit, Aria! Just let me do something for once that will save you. If I die, I die. I come across these situations on a daily basis. Who cares if I'm in my body or not when it happens? If it's my time to go, then it is my time to go." He stared at the floor, chewing on his lip in irritation.

"It just sounds like a suicide mission."

"We've lived through multiple suicide missions."

"We have no time to test it out first. You don't even know if the transfer will work. You don't even know if Aren or Nerd can even do it." She ran her hands over her face.

"They can. I already asked," he bluntly said.

"You already asked them?! And they were okay with it?" She looked appalled.

"Well…I asked in a roundabout way. They don't really know what I plan to do."

Aria still didn't seem pleased by the idea. In fact, she thought it was ludicrous. Troy must've had a death wish of some sort.

"Come on, Aria. I can make it work," he spoke softly.

Her green eyes flitted to his. "I swear to God, Troy…if you die on me…."

"I'm not gonna die," he replied.

"I've heard that before…many times before." She swallowed hard. The thought wasn't going to do her any good. Taking a deep breath, she pushed the whole thing aside. "You know what? Fine. Do it. Go be a robot. If you succeed, I'll beat the shit out of you for making me worry. If you die, I'm still beating the shit out of you."

He gave her a crooked smile as he ran his fingers through his beard. "Babe, after this war, you can beat me all you like. For now, all I'm asking is that you trust me."

She nodded apprehensively.

Troy held his arms out to the side. "Do you need a hug?" he humorously asked.

Aria pursed her lips and wrinkled her nose. Did he have to work his charms on her? Aria had seen Troy's tricks performed on other women, and whereas before she would roll her eyes, now she couldn't help but find him ridiculously adorable when he directed his attention toward her. The more Troy showed her any affection, the harder it was to order him out on the field. If she could have it any other way, she'd lock him in his apartment. Something felt amiss. She couldn't help but worry now that she let her guard down that Troy was on a death sentence. However, now that Aria had healing capabilities, she was going to be sure not to waste them.

Giving a grumpy moan, she wrapped her arms around the man, squeezing him. "You have to come back to me alive," she whispered.

The shrieks and screams were ear-splitting—a nauseating sound that threatened to shatter the crystallized cavern. Dovian grimaced, trying his best not to cover his ears. Ivory stood in the corner, her hands cupping the sides of her head as she watched, not in fear, but in agitation at the fluctuating image of Sapphire. The child soared back and forth from each direction of the room, her ghostly-white image a blur that intermingled with dark shadows. Streaks of black darted across the room, bursting the glass flames, sending the cave into temporary darkness. A searing heat came from her form and reignited the flames surrounding them. A guttural sound growled in trembling echoes, a noise that was inhuman—animal and musically blaring, almost like the sound of scraping metal. Rocks chunked from the ceiling, crashing and disintegrating into dust as the child threw a tantrum. After a few moments, the lingering darkness swirled into a mass around the vibrating girl. With a burst of black light, a giant of a shadow took a humanoid form. Eyes of white light burst from where the head should be, glaring in Dovian's direction.

"YOU SAID THEY WERE DEAD!" a quaking voice thundered.

Dovian's shoulders sagged. His nonchalant demeanor only irritated the mass further. "They were. Plain and simple, they were dead. Troy was left in a vegetative state; Aria was to bleed out in minutes. There was no chance of survival."

"YET THEY ARE ALIVE!" the voice boomed.

"I saw that," Dovian blandly stated.

"HOW?!" The mass grew larger in size, the light from the surrounding flames diminishing in size.

"Honestly, I haven't the faintest idea." And it was true. Dovian had no idea how it was possible Aria and Troy were even alive. He had seen the helicopter enter Ives, but he imagined whoever was piloting the craft was merely retrieving the bodies. Even though Aria and Troy were presumed dead, Dovian was not expecting Sapphire to be so surprised by the fact that they were actually still alive. The helicopter had even gotten away from her army. Had she not known about that? Were the monsters acting of their own freewill? That would mean Sapphire was leaving a lot of responsibility to everyone else. Dovian wondered to what extent her powers could actually reach.

"HOW DID THEY EVEN GET OFF THE ISLAND?!" The mass turned, its glowing eyes locking onto Lilith.

The woman gasped and began stuttering. "I-I had seen a helicopter. I sent the monsters out to investigate and bring it down. Upon further investigation, we found nothing. The storms had taken over that side of the island. We figured it was simply lightning."

"AND YOU DIDN'T THINK TO CHECK FOR THEIR CORPSES AFTER THAT?!"

Lilith cowered in the corner of the room. Dovian eyed her with interest. The android was afraid. She didn't want to relay the news to Sapphire for fear of losing her life. Now that Lilith was contained within a physical body, Dovian pondered if her destruction would become a permanent one.

"Well…I…." Lilith hung her head. "I'm sorry, my Lord."

Dovian cringed at hearing Lilith's words.

"SORRY?" the darkness questioned. "I WON'T BE SORRY WHEN I TEAR YOU LIMB FROM LIMB!"

The mass dashed forward, surrounding Lilith.

"Wait! Stop!" Ivory shouted.

Everything came to a halt. White-lit eyes glared at Ivory.

"I, I know you are angry, but don't tear her apart," Ivory pleaded.

Dovian gaped at the blonde in wonder. Truthfully, he was looking a bit forward to Lilith's demise. In fact, he figured Ivory would feel the same way.

"AND WHY SHOULD I DO AS YOU SAY?" the darkness asked.

"Because…you said you've known Lilith a long time. To tear her apart would be rather cruel. Why not keep her around? She may still prove useful. Give her a chance to prove herself, and perhaps she can make up for the mistake. Besides…after such a long existence, wouldn't killing her now seem a bit wasteful?" Ivory nervously tugged on her hands.

"FORGIVENESS? I'VE FORGIVEN PLENTY, YET YOU ALL SEEM TO REPEATEDLY FAIL ME."

"Then why not do things yourself?" Ivory asked.

The darkness moved from Lilith toward Ivory.

"SUCH BOLD WORDS…."

"I'm merely asking you a question." The blonde woman lifted her chin.

"YOU'RE RIGHT. I PUT TOO MUCH TRUST IN OTHERS. PERHAPS I SHOULD JUST KILL YOU ALL."

"No! Please…I…Let me out of this body. Don't destroy me!" Lilith dropped to her knees.

Dovian walked to the side, eyeing Lilith. He had it figured out. Lilith wasn't meant for this physical plane. If killed, she'd be trapped between the realms in a never-ending purgatory of sorts. Would it be worse off than Hell? He wondered.

"SINCE THE WOMAN HAS SYMPATHY FOR YOU, I WILL NOT DESTROY YOU. HOWEVER, IF YOU MAKE ONE MORE FALSE MOVE, I WILL NOT HESITATE TO TURN YOU INTO DUST."

"Glory to you," Lilith panted, bowing to the mass.

Ivory and Dovian traded uncertain glances.

"IVORY IS CORRECT. I SHOULD NOT PLACE THE BLAME ON YOU, LILITH. ALL BLAME LIES ON DOVIAN."

Dovian closed his eyes, awaiting the terrible impact that the darkness would inflict upon him. Would he lose a limb this time? His head? Perhaps he would be bisected. Maybe filleted to pieces. He had no idea, and the entity had only grown more creative in its ways of punishment. Still, no harm came his way. Curious, Dovian opened his eyes, finding the darkness around him. White glowing orbs of light gazed deep into his soul. It was nearly suffocating.

"BEWARE SON OF THE FATHER. YOU SHALL FAIL ME AS MUCH AS YOU LIKE. NOTHING YOU HAVE PLANNED HAS NOT GONE THROUGH MY MIND IN A MILLION WAYS. THE ENDLESS POSSIBILITIES OF FORESIGHT IS STILL NOT LOST TO ME. I CAN SEE WHERE YOU'VE BEEN, AND I CAN SEE WHERE YOU ARE GOING. DESPITE ALL YOU TRY, YOUR SOUL WILL BELONG TO ME. DARKNESS WILL RULE YOU, AND YOU WILL PRAISE ME SOON AS YOU ONCE DID HIM. YOU ARE NOT FREE. YOU ARE MINE NOW. FAIL, FAIL OVER AND OVER AGAIN. BUT BEWARE. ONCE ALL IS DONE, I WILL DESTROY YOU WITHOUT ONE MOMENT'S THOUGHT. DO NOT THINK YOU ARE INVINCIBLE TO ME."

The mass drifted away from the Sorcēarian. Ivory gasped, holding her hands over her mouth. Dovian's usually vibrant eyes were now an inky shade. He was choking on what appeared to be black smoke. Coughing, he lurched forward as scaly wings jolted from his dorsal side. He vomited.

As Dovian coughed and took in quick short breaths, Ivory eyed the darkness that suddenly burst into a bright light that composed itself back into the form of Sapphire. Her youthful expression lacked delight. Turning toward the stone throne, the child shooed Lilith away.

"Prepare yourselves. We have a war to win tomorrow. Dovian, do not fail me unless you want Ivory to be disintegrated."

Dovian gasped. If Lilith was so frightened of dying, then that meant Ivory's soul—I'Lanthe—was at equal risk of never reaching the heavens as well. He looked at the discontented blonde; his heart rapidly beat against his chest.

"Leave my sight…all of you," Sapphire coldly barked.

Ivory grabbed Dovian's arm, tugging him up. Lilith was already well out of the cave system before the two even exited the room. Once outside and in the harsh sunlight, Dovian gripped Ivory's arms. She looked at him with an inquisitive expression.

"I know that look, Dovian. There's nothing you can say to make me stay. This is my battle, too. I'm fighting tomorrow." She stood resolutely against him.

"If something happens to you…" he started.

"My life isn't nearly as important as all of humanity," she said strictly.

"But…what about you? What about…I'Lanthe?" he asked.

Ivory smiled this time, placing her hand against his pale face. "Oh, Dovian. At what point will you understand we are one and the same?" I'Lanthe's vocals sounded.

Dovian's grip tightened on her shoulders. Ivory laughed with the same delight as I'Lanthe once had.

"Nothing you say or do will make me change my mind. It is set in stone. This is what I've wanted since I inhabited the body. Ivory knows the risk, as do I." Ivory grabbed his hand. "Our friends are alive. That means there is still hope. I will fight for them. I will fight for them like I did our people."

"But…I can't lose you again," Dovian murmured.

"You never lost me," she replied. Looking ahead toward the city ruins, she smiled brightly. "Come. We should prepare for tomorrow." She put his fears aside.

Dovian watched the woman suspiciously, his angelic wings whooshing outward. He prepared to grab Ivory, to carry her in his arms, but she held out a hand, stopping him.

"One moment," Ivory's natural voice came out. "She's taught me a bit more about this."

Looking straight ahead, Ivory's pupils thinned to miniature dots. A burst of noise erupted from the bionic woman. Large metallic beams slid out from her shoulders, spreading out blade after blade into wings. A whirring commenced as the blonde eyed Dovian playfully.

"Race ya," she quickly spouted.

With a spray of her thrusters, Ivory jetted off high into the sky, soaring through the clouds. Dovian shook his head in amazement. Bending his knees, he leaped, his wings taking control as he pushed after her.

Tomorrow could be the end of all days. Tomorrow could be the day that would bring humanity to light. It could be either the best or the worst day of his life. For now, he wouldn't worry about it. Ivory surely had no intention of letting him brood otherwise.

In no time at all, Dovian was by the woman's side, his gleaming eyes flickering behind the fog of the clouds surrounding them. Ivory noticed him and laughed, pushing further ahead. They raced toward the cathedral where Hector and Petey napped peacefully in the garden beside the lake. Dovian's smile faltered. He lowered as a sudden onslaught of imagery invaded his senses.

Fire consumed the land in a shuddering violent blast. Clouds of black and orange shot toward the sky and plumed outward as it hit the stratosphere, giving it a mushroom shape. The dry and cracked earth momentarily dipped lower before exploding upward in splintered shards. The radius spread for many kilometers, destroying everything in its path.

Dovian fell, dropping to his hands and knees in the grass of the meadow. Petey gave a huff, shaking his tired head in alert at the sound of Dovian's sudden intrusion. The lizard groaned, rising to his feet. Another squawk came from Hector, and soon the Sorcēarian was greeted by the nuzzling of his two lizard friends. Ivory spiraled overhead, watching the man below. She dived and landed smoothly onto the grass.

"Are you alright?" she asked.

Dovian ran his hand slowly over Hector's scales. He frowned. "We need to get our friends to safety."

"You think something may happen to them tomorrow?" Ivory wrapped her arms around Petey's neck; her reach couldn't even make it halfway around his bulk.

"I saw something," he said uncertainly.

"You're having visions?"

Dovian nodded slowly. "They are occurring more frequently. The more decisions I make, the tighter the timeline pulls, bringing everything to the forefront of my mind. Bad things are going to happen, Ivory, and our chances are dwindling. Time is running out."

"Was the vision of Sapphire?" The woman ran her fingers up and down

Petey's snout. The creature wheezed a purr, his gold eyes rolling back slightly.

"I'm unsure. The war holds much weight for both sides. Anything is possible. I will not hold any doubt that the battle will be brought to Ives if needed. If that is the case, I would like for Petey and Hector to retreat further south away from the caves."

"Poor babies," Ivory whispered.

"Petey," Dovian began. The lizard became alert, licking his chops in anticipation. "You are to take Hector to the south."

Petey snorted in response.

"There is a beautiful place near the mountainside. It's full of freshwater, fish as far as the eye can see, and trees full of albatross. I know of a location that has a cave by a waterfall where you can sleep. Retrieve as many of your kind as you can. Leave now, and you can, hopefully, make it there by morning. You are not to come back here until things are over. In fact, you may just want to stay there," Dovian sternly stated.

"Stay?" Ivory asked, shocked.

Dovian's eyes fell. "In case anything happens, Ivory. I do not want them coming back for us and getting hurt."

Petey's golden eyes shifted between the two humans.

"Listen to me, Petey. You are a magnificent creature. I need you to take care of the island while I am gone. After the war, I will come back for you. But, if for some reason I never return to you, know that I love you and Hector both." He kneeled next to Hector, rubbing his fringe. "You've kept me company for many lifetimes. I leave Ives to you. Make the best of it."

Hector hissed, his tongue moving across Dovian's hand. The creature crawled on his lap, and Dovian's eyes closed. He refused to get teary-eyed over this.

"You are my children. This is for your own safety. Go to the south. Be fruitful and multiply."

Ivory patted both lizards with tears in her eyes. "Dovian, what happens to Petey?"

Dovian narrowed his eyes. "If ever anything were to happen to me that would prevent me from living another day, I assume Petey's tie with me will become severed. He will be mortal. He will live and die like all the others."

"But you said you can't die," Ivory said.

Dovian smirked. "I haven't yet. Still, there isn't a day that I don't doubt it a little."

"But I've seen it," she said.

"I'm merely laying out ground rules. I will not tell them that I will come back for them. It will only break their hearts more if something were to happen which would prevent me to do so. They're grown lizards. They need to understand." Dovian lifted Hector in his arms, carrying him like he had done when he was a baby monitor.

Ivory frowned. "It makes sense. It just makes me feel horribly sad."

Dovian put the palm of his hand against Petey's forehead. Immediately, the lizard's eyes turned milky-white as Dovian placed the information and visions in the creature's mind. The giant reptile barked and hopped back, shaking his head in aggravation. Ivory watched with her hands clasped tightly before her chest.

Dovian scowled. "We're wasting time, Petey. Don't get so upset. You knew this day would come."

Petey snorted, ramming his forehead against Dovian's shoulder. Slowly, Dovian pressed his forehead against Petey's and lifted Hector higher into his arms, hugging the animal. These creatures were all Dovian had known for thousands of years. These were his children, family, and friends.

"Go you blasted scaly fiends...before you make me cry," Dovian muttered lowly.

He pulled away from Petey and gently set Hector onto the ground. Clearing his throat, he straightened his robes.

"Go! You must leave now. Gather as many of the others as you can and take a little vacation in paradise. Really, Petey, the desert? There are much better places for your kind on this island. Why not go exploring! Have some fun! Play your...lizard games and swim for a while." Dovian grinned, waving his hands. This gesture and the tone of his voice got Petey excited, the lizard flinging his tail back and forth. Hector eyed Dovian; he wasn't as easy to fool. "Go my sweet boy. You worked hard at helping our friends. You deserve some time out and about with your own kind. Go have fun. We shall see each other another day." Petey was running in circles now, honking in excitement. "Well, what are you waiting for?! Onward!" Dovian lifted his fist into the air.

Petey gave a war cry of sorts—a shrill, oscillating noise that echoed over the lands. Around them, the grass moved. Lizards from all places waddled from their hiding spots. Ives was alive with the reptiles. Soon, Petey was rushing through the pasture, all the others following behind. Hector made it a few meters before he stopped and looked back. His tongue poked the air.

Dovian raised his hand and spoke to Hector, his dialect falling to Legacy.

"Tӧӧðæ'ē, μ' фrℓєнъδ."

"Goodbye, my friend."

WWW.ARCREBS.DEVIANTART.COM

"Saying Goodbye"

314

CHAPTER 20

Morning came entirely too fast. A hint of sunlight crested over the barrier of the lower floor of the city, spewing an incandescent pinkish-orange hue that bounced from the glass of each building, beaming upwards into Aria's apartment. Staring out into the city, the woman gave a shiver. There was no movement, no cars, no sound. All was in a still silence as the civilians stayed inside their homes. Everyone knew what was about to happen. Fountains was a city of sitting ducks. There was no refuge. At any minute, the metropolis could become nothing more than a giant tomb.

Aria lowered her head, her armored hands running over the faux stone countertop. The sunlight glinted across the silver crucifix that lay between her hands. Her eyes locked firmly onto the item. She tensed. Finally, her nerves were getting to her though she wasn't worried about herself as much as she was worried about everyone else. For a while now she had come to terms that she could die, would die, in battle. Even so, she never dealt well with people she knew meeting their demise in such cold and abrupt ways. Most of all, she feared for Troy. Nothing she could say would change his mind. He was as bull-headed as she was, and he was going through with his plan. She could only pray it would work in his favor.

Turning her head to the side, Aria eyed the two pink boxes sitting on the counter beside her—the containers that held the chocolates from Saray. A sudden flash of memories played through the woman's mind as vividly as they had occurred. One box was shared between her, Troy, Dovian, and Ivory. Dovian had teased Aria about tossing it into the trash, but it turned out he had actually transported it to her apartment as she had asked. The second was the container at her hospital bedside after Dovian and Ivory had become stranded on Ives. No doubt about it, the Sorcēarian had given her those chocolates. But why? Why would he bother with something like that when he was so eager to kill her and Troy? It remained a mystery to her, and it plagued her for some reason.

Aria sighed, her fingers trailing over the note atop her "get-well" present. The tiny smiley face drawn in the corner of the parchment sent a tinge of sadness through her chest. In the end, Dovian had failed at destroying her and Troy. Was it deliberate or just some unforeseen accident–a miracle? She wasn't sure. Dovian's motives had always been somewhat unclear to her. As far as Aria could tell, Dovian was always a conflicted man. It was foolish, but she hoped he would somehow stay away from the conflict. Not for his sake but humanity's. She had seen more than enough of what Dovian was capable of. He could've destroyed the world countless times with nothing more than a flap of his wings. And that's what confused her the most. If he was as monstrous as he liked to perceive himself, why wouldn't he just finish things quickly? Unless he was as sick and twisted as Sapphire, then that would mean he enjoyed playing with her emotions. Was he any better than Euclid at this point?

Something else left a sinking in Aria's stomach. During the last world transmission, she had not seen any evidence of Dovian. Were he and Ivory even alive? Were they safe? Aria wasn't positive of the child's abilities, but she imagined Sapphire could have easily destroyed Dovian and Ivory for their transgressions and failures at complying with her requests. In fact, Dovian was no better off than Euclid. That fact alone made Aria fill a bit more optimistic. Perhaps he had a plan. She just hoped it was a plan beneficial to humanity.

The ideas flip-flopped in her brain–Dovian good, Dovian bad. Just as she was about to go crazy over the thoughts, there was a gentle knock at the door before it slid open. Aria spun, leaning back against the bar. Troy slipped in, shutting the door behind him. Tall, masculine, and covered in shining body armor, he looked ominous and powerful. He stood before the entry, staring at her from behind his helmet. Aria fed him a twisted smirk, her helmet not yet in place.

"How's it feel?" she quietly asked. Even though she had been awake for nearly an hour, the sound of her voice seemed terribly loud, and she was afraid she would wake up the entire city.

He nodded, looking down at himself. "New modifications seem pretty grand. Can't wait to try it out. You ready?"

She twisted and snatched up the silver crucifix. "Almost," she mumbled. Diligently, she fiddled with a thin cord, pushing one end through a tiny hole at the top of the cross. Next, she tied the two ends around her neck, fashioning the item into a necklace. The silver clanked against her armor.

Troy stared at her chest, silent. It made her slightly uncomfortable, reminding her of the argument she had with him in the Underbelly.

"The man who told me to take this...he said that they were afraid of it. If so, then I'm going to wear it. I'll be their symbol of fear," she spoke slowly, running her fingers over the decorative grooves.

Troy stepped past the woman, casually opening and closing the drawers in her kitchen. Aria peered at him curiously. After the fourth drawer, he pulled out a large roll of colored tape. Giving a small grunt of victory, he pulled off a long strip and stuck it to the front of his armor over the company and city-state insignia.

"What in the hell are you doing?" Aria asked, giving a small laugh.

Pulling a second strip, he said, "This isn't a battle for Bio-Tech, isn't a battle for Fountains. It's a battle for humanity, a battle for us, for Dovian and Ivory."

Aria hesitated. "I dunno. Maybe you were right about Dovian. What if he does plan on destroying us?"

Troy shook his head. "I don't think so. I mean, think about all he's lost. After all this time, why change now? I get why he is doing what he is doing. He's doing it for some chick, right?"

"I'Lanthe," Aria corrected.

"Right. If it were me," he slapped the second strip across his chest, making a cross, "and it meant that I could have you back after losing you...then yeah...I'd do it, too. I don't know what his final plan is, but this war is about him just as much as it is about us. Dovian may be a bit messed up in the head, but he isn't evil. He's not like that. If he were, we wouldn't be here. I believe there's something else going on."

"You think there's still a chance we can end this war and have Dovian and Ivory back?" She eagerly awaited Troy's answer.

"...I think so. I guess it all starts with having...." He looked back down at his chest.

"Hope?" Aria asked.

Troy rapped his knuckles against his makeshift cross. "Faith. We just got to have a little faith...in all of us."

Aria gave a weak smile before nodding. Timidly she grabbed her helmet.

"This is going to be one hell of a war." She slipped the armor over her head.

"Damn right it is. And no matter what happens, Aria, I'm glad I'm fighting alongside you." He walked up to her, placing his hand on her shoulder.

She grabbed his shoulder, giving him a rough shake. "Let's kick some ass!" she snarled.

"Fuck yeah!" Troy cheered, shaking her in return.

They gathered their gear and left Aria's apartment, the woman giving one last long look at her home before closing the door, and rushed to the elevator. The ride seemed to last an eternity as it silently crawled down the floors of Bio-Tech. As the elevator chimed and the doors slid open, she and Troy hurried and hopped aboard a hovering humvee. Once on the ground level, a few kilometers away from the city, Aria became pumped on adrenaline. As far as she could see, her military stretched along the horizon.

Aria had all of Bio-Tech adorned in full armor and state of the art EMP weaponry, the best pilots in the world operating the Hawks and fighter jets, robotic tanks, and missile-loaded mechs. She had gained the support of the other corporate militaries of Fountains. Saray took to the fringes of the Bio-Tech line, equipped with a multitude of mini-drones and a variety of mechs and armored vehicles. In the back of the line was an assortment of rogue soldiers from the surrounding city-states of the United Americas. Their fleet was small, but they were a much-welcomed addition to the family. Mingled among the rest was an unexpected sight. Britainia had even joined in on the fight. Though the entire military seemed vast and powerful–more than she had ever seen gathered in one place–Aria feared it wasn't enough. She looked toward the center of it all where a large convoy surrounded Feyette, Kovacevic, Team Phoenix, and President Clarke with Grayson.

"James?!" Aria shouted, running toward the older man. "What are you doing?" she panted, looking at Grayson. "You let him come out here?"

Grayson cleared his throat, staring at the dusty ground.

"This is my fight, too. I'm not going to sit in the city while you and my entire military take on Sapphire's army," James protested, rolling his shoulders inside his armor.

"He wouldn't have it any other way," Grayson said.

Aria folded her arms, glaring at James as she wondered where his blasted helmet was. "Just…just keep an eye on him, alright?" She pointed accusingly at Grayson. "If the enemy draws too close, get him the hell out of here."

"Let the man have some fun," Kovacevic barked. He sat atop a nearby tank, chewing on his unlit cigar.

"This isn't fun," Aria growled.

"Eh. To each his own, I s'ppose," the rough man grumbled.

"And what about Lebedev?" she questioned.

"His soldiers will be a bit late. They had to make a pit stop in Roma to retrieve that prototype android you were needin'," he ground out.

"ETA?" she asked.

"Beats the hell out of me. I reckon any minute now. That is if they haven't run into any trouble. Communication with the team went out nearly thirty minutes ago." He looked at the sky. "'Round the time of sunrise, actually."

Aria peered over at Troy. Perhaps the solar flares were already kicking up. He matched her stare.

"Everybody got their static protection activated?" she asked. An outbreak of nodding commenced amongst the warriors.

Feyette stood on the ground, eyeing the empty desert before them. "I've not seen anything out there. Not even a gust of wind."

Aria approached the man's side; her sight dropped to Feyette's mechanical leg. She had nearly forgotten that Ivory almost killed Feyette during the scuffle below the city. If he had been killed, how differently would events have played out? Aria didn't know, but for the time being, she was glad that the man was finally on her side once again.

She brought her attention to the same location Feyette's was directed. With her jaw clenched tight, she grinded her teeth and looked toward the sun. Though it was still morning, it wouldn't take long for the sun to begin to bake them all inside their suits despite their cooling systems. She was starting to think her plan was asinine. All Sapphire would have to do was keep them waiting all day as the radiation slowly beat against their shields.

"Interesting choice of jewelry," Feyette coolly stated. He glimpsed the woman out of the corner of his eye.

"I've heard the demons fear it," Aria replied.

This brought the attention of the neighboring soldiers. In a flurry, each man slowly moved to whisper to their comrades. The sea of soldiers momentarily waved, and one by one each man down the line began creating crosses of their own over their chests, helmets, and forearms. They used paint, their own blood, tape, and whatever else they could get their hands on. The sight was nothing short of amazing, if not humorous. Feyette grinned and reached inside his armor to pull out his own cross that he had been wearing around his neck.

"Only thing I have left of my former life," he quietly said. "Was my mother's. Only thing she left me."

Aria smirked behind her helmet. There was an assortment of snickers and giggles behind her. Looking over her shoulder, Aria resisted the urge to slap her palm against her forehead. Kovacevic had fastened together two cigars in the shape of a cross and pinned it to his shirt with the assistance of a small staple gun that he found in the toolbox at the back of his transporter.

"Glad everyone's marking themselves. Would be nice to have a symbol to distinguish who's a friendly and who isn't," Michelle spoke up. "With these numbers, things are bound to get messy out there."

She and Team Phoenix rested against one of the tanks. Nerd and Aren were busy working with various electronics, their spherical drones dancing around them in a failed attempt to provide some help in their project. Kaino, Zombie, and Monkey were busy calibrating their shields and discussing battle tactics. Waiting was the worst part of missions. The longer things were quiet, the more anxious the men grew.

Without warning, a loud thumping came from behind them. Aria spun on her heel, fearing the worst, but was captivated by the sight of a line of soldiers heading their way. Ornamented with crosses and massive battle rifles, a faction of nearly 4,000 Soldiers of God stomped toward the line in a serious fashion.

"We saw the news feed and decided that it was time we lend a helpin' hand," a large man spoke—most likely the leader of the group. His voice was intimidating and deep and contained a southern drawl.

"We'll take all the help we can get! I'd be more than grateful to have you and your men fighting by our side, sir." Aria shook the soldier's hand.

"After what happened in the Underbelly, we realized our purpose was more than protectin' the churches. There's a greater battle being fought today, and our sole purpose in life is servin' our Lord," the man said. "What better way to serve Him than to fight against mankind's worst enemy?" Looking back toward his men, he gave a bellowing shout. The other militants twisted and marched in timely beats to their places along the line. "We've got the best riflemen. All are class A-5 sharpshooters. Our weapons are fully auto and also have sniping capabilities. We will have one eye in the foreground and the second in the back."

Aria nodded. "I appreciate you coming out here. You're a valuable asset to our line."

Giving a quick nod, he turned about-face and walked a couple steps into his place before turning back around and taking a readied position. The sight of the enormous men made the woman feel a bit more at ease. Humanity was pulling together on this.

A slight quake shook beneath Aria's feet. It lasted only a millisecond. Giving an unsure look toward Feyette, she pressed a couple buttons on the side of her helmet, trying to gain some readings. The man stared down at his own two feet. He lifted his robotic leg and stamped it back down in response to the tremor. A loud beep alerted Aria toward Team Phoenix's position.

"Picking up some readings, ma'am," Aren spoke up. Poking at the armband of his armor, he looked into his DNAIS, his brow wrinkling. "Tremors are from the west headin' our way."

"What the hell is it?" Aria impatiently asked.

"Erm…hold on, gathering data." Aren fingered his DNAIS as another quake shook the desert floor. "Seems mechanical, ma'am!"

"Mechanical?" Aria turned toward Troy.

"The Roma fleet?" he suggested.

"Multiple bogies." Aren shook his head in disbelief. "One is enormous!"

"Everybody on the ready!!" Aria shouted.

Was Sapphire's army simply going to burst out of the ground from beneath their feet?

"Hold it," Clarke mumbled. "At ease."

"At ease?!" Aria looked at the older man. His face was hard, revealing nothing. "Did you forget to tell me something, sir?"

"I wasn't sure if they would make it," Clarke replied.

"They? Who in the hell are they?" Aria asked.

The ground shuddered; an earsplitting roar followed, growing louder and louder each second. Aria felt the worst of the vibration travel from behind her to the front of her, a deep crack bursting and shooting at a high speed away toward the empty desert. In an explosion of noise, the earth split open, rock and dust spreading across the land. Aria gaped in awe as an enormous mechanical drill spiraled up and out of the hole in the ground. The machine churned into the air, twisting and giving an ominous alarm of warning. Jolting from the sides of the mechanism was a pair of legs that crunched into the floor. Cranking, the middle cylinder spun up and out, another pair of arms breaking away as a large piece lifted further, topping the machine with what looked like a head. As the giant mech morphed–rising higher and higher–the eyes lit up with a ring. A loud roar followed. It stood well over thirty meters, towering over the military like a menacing statue. A siren blared, and the mech growled again, stomping forward with large animalistic feet, its tail whipping to the side.

"What the hell is that?" Troy stammered.

A few more quakes arrived and from the same hole popped a series of armored vehicles, all with skids and drills. The convoy sped around the desert, circling the massive android. Clarke gave a quiet chuckle and moved forward toward the swarm.

"James!" Aria trotted after him; Troy followed not far behind.

"Don't worry, Aria. These are friendlies." Clarke moved his arms out to the side, giving a hearty laugh as one of the lead vehicles' doors shot open.

Troy kept his eyes locked on the mechanical giant. "Why couldn't we have one of those?"

"I hope we are not too late to the party," a foreign voice called out.

From the vehicle stepped a man covered in armor that revealed the mysterious military's origins. He wore split-toed boots, an armored chest piece that attached to what looked like a waist skirt, and massive shoulder armor. A frightening mask covered the man's face, topped with an ornate helmet that horned out at the sides. He was a samurai.

"General Yoshitaka! I am so pleased you received my message!" Clarke announced, eagerly shaking the man's hand.

"Holy shit! I thought Dai-Ni-Tokyo was wiped out!" Troy garbled.

As the samurai removed his mask, the pieces separated and disappeared into his helmet. Yoshitaka gave Troy a firm look. He appeared to be Clarke's age and purely of Japanese heritage with dark hair, brown eyes, and neatly trimmed facial hair. "We nearly were. The rest of our people are taking refuge in our underground tunnels. The city below has held up the past few weeks, but I do not know how much longer we can last. Many districts have been completely annihilated. Believe me, it was a hard decision to leave my people, but I do owe Mr. James Clarke a favor." Giving a crooked smirk, he moved his attention to the President. "Being a man of honor, I am reporting for duty."

"Understand that you have my utmost gratitude right now. Your fleet is a priceless asset. I know your people are currently defenseless with you here, but if we can end this battle today, humanity will be safe," James said.

"I certainly hope you are correct," Yoshitaka spoke with uncertainty.

Another figure eagerly approached the group, his garb designed quite differently with thin, sleek armor painted a midnight-black. A filtering mask covered the lower half of his face, and a hood covered his head. Aria eyed the newcomers. There seemed to be two different militaries among them. Judging by the robotic enhancements the second army had on their bodies, Aria guessed they were from one of the more rebellious factions.

Pointing at one particular soldier with bladed hands and optical goggles, Troy leaned toward Aria and giddily whispered, "Freakin' ninjas! How cool is that?"

Yoshitaka twisted, holding an arm out to the approaching man. "Let me introduce you to Hattori, head of the Iga clan."

"Iga?" Clarke asked, perplexed. "This is certainly a surprise."

Yoshitaka gave a wry smile, looking toward Hattori. "It took much persuading, but Hattori eventually agreed to lend a helping hand. In this time, it is better to make enemies your ally as greater threats are at hand. During this war, it is humanity against…monsters. To fight amongst ourselves would leave us weak and open to attack. Now is the time to pull together. If we cannot help each other, then we are all doomed."

"Couldn't agree with you more," Clarke said. Holding his hand out, he introduced Aria and Troy to the Japanese men. The two militants raised the faceplates of their helmets and gave a respectful nod to each of the foreign men.

"Owarimashita ka?" Hattori belted out in a harsh voice. One of his eyes was nearly all black, the other a silvery color which had a pupil that dilated and constricted as he looked toward the others of the group. It was an optical reader of some sort.

Yoshitaka frowned as Clarke gave the ninja a strange look.

"You must forgive Hattori. His clan insists on sticking to old customs. They prefer to speak in ancient ways." Yoshitaka glared at the other leader. "And he is being rude."

"Only as rude as necessary…" Hattori spoke in English this time; his accent was thick. "We waste daylight speaking in grandiose ways. Should we not be looking for the enemy?" His voice was gruff and had a rumbling to it as he snarled.

"Perhaps you are correct, Hattori. Why don't you get our men lined up with the others? And if you have any *grandiose* speeches to make, maybe you should spend those words trying to unify them," Yoshitaka spat out, matching Hattori's callous tone.

Hattori gave a loud scoff and rushed away, yelling in Japanese at his troops.

"Having trouble with the kids?" Aria asked.

"Hattori and I may have come to an understanding. However, our men are not as enthusiastic about the idea and have been fighting amongst themselves since we've come into contact."

Yoshitaka eyed his men, twisting his face into a look of dissatisfaction as one of his soldiers was lined up beside a member of the Iga clan. There was an exchange of Japanese mixed with broken English, and the two began fighting. Hattori barked an order, and the men straightened up right away. Once Hattori turned away, the Iga soldier slammed his clawed fist into the other soldier's back. Hattori spun at the sound of the samurai's cry of pain. Growling an order, Hattori grabbed his own soldier's head and shoved him facedown into the dirt. He then looked toward Yoshitaka and gave a rumbling chuckle while he muttered in Japanese.

Yoshitaka slowly ran a hand over his face. "Let's get this war over with," he sighed.

They all agreed and made their way to the front line except for Troy, who remained in his place gawking at the giant mech. "Question," he blurted.

Yoshitaka paused, looked to Troy, and then up at the robot. "I forgot this may be the first time you had seen something like this."

"What is it?" Troy asked. "Besides every teenage boy's wet dream?"

General Yoshitaka gestured to the machine. "That is a Feline Intelligence Firmware Integration. We call her FIFI."

"FIFI!" Troy exclaimed, slapping his hands joyously together. "Wait...feline? You mean that is a robotic cat?"

Yoshitaka smiled. "That is a tiger."

FIFI twisted, giving a hearty roar at the soldiers beside her feet. Troy kept his head crooked to look upward at the machine's open jaws and bent back ears. It even had whiskers. "Bitchin'," he whispered.

Aria stared in awe. "You mean to tell me that you integrated a tiger's brainwaves into a giant mech?"

"We did. FIFI has the brain of a tiger." The samurai nodded.

"But tigers are extinct." Aria watched FIFI as it swiped its tail back and forth, creating a dust cloud around a small grouping of soldiers.

"Not when you clone one," he explained.

"You cloned a tiger's brain and placed it inside a giant mech. Isn't that against the terms of war?" she asked.

Yoshitaka quietly chuckled. "The reason why you've never seen her before."

"Illegal or not, that thing is badass!" Troy exclaimed, gesturing toward the mech.

"I figured she would come in handy," Yoshitaka nodded.

"As long as she doesn't eat our soldiers," Aria groaned.

"FIFI is very friendly," Yoshitaka stated, feigning a hurt expression.

FIFI snarled. Crawling on all fours, her massive hand swiped at a group of ninja soldiers.

"Now, I can't say that she will be peaceful among the Iga clan," he added.

"Hmm," she hummed, watching the mechanical beast. "I'm interested to see how she does in combat. I know there will be a use for her. Sapphire's got a monster roughly that size."

"We have not seen one that big," Yoshitaka gasped.

"You're lucky. We only caught a glimpse. In a matter of seconds, it destroyed the entire hydro complex at the Amazonian Desert and nearly annihilated our forces in one strike." Her relaxed attitude slightly unnerved the Japanese man.

Aria climbed atop the hood of a transport vehicle beside Team Phoenix. Yoshitaka's expression suddenly turned into a look of dread. He glanced over at his men and then took in the sight of Aria's militia. It was the largest he had ever seen. In fact, there were so many men; he couldn't see the end of the line on either side. With all the leftovers of the United Americas, Britainia, Saray, and what was to come from Cherno, the number was a staggering two hundred and eighty-seven million soldiers. It was unheard of, yet she and the generals were left with mixed feelings.

Feeling a bit anxious, Aria brought her attention to her team. "Why aren't you guys in position yet?" she muttered, flipping through data on her DNAIS.

"I tried to get him to move, but he won't listen to me!" Nerd whined.

"Hey! If you guys want this done right, then I need to have an accurate reading," Aren retorted.

"What's the problem, Aren?" Aria asked.

"We can't go beneath the plate until I know for sure the entry point of Sapphire's army. Beneath the plate, with all this electrical interference we're getting from the sun, my readings can be inaccurate…and you don't want my readings to be off." Aren continued calibrating Franklin.

"And what happens if they enter from beneath the plate?" Aria asked.

Aren gave a drawn-out exasperated sigh. "Just hope that they don't."

"Team Phoenix, get your asses to the mining district. I need your eyes on the portal that was drilled out four months ago. Make sure those pillars remain stabilized at all times. Aren, you remain here. Troy will wait by your side until you have your readings and Cherno arrives with the Roman soldier. You'll take one of the buggies down to the lower level and continue on with the rest of your mission. Understood?" Aria ordered.

"Understood!" The Team gave a quick salute and hopped atop their vehicles. With revving engines, the bikes pushed upward and hovered above the ground, blue lights twirling in circles beneath. Spoofy took the lead, making a hand signal, and they all sped off, the bikes jumping over the cliff edge into the mining district beneath Fountains.

"Troy, stay by Aren's side. Once the battle starts, you guys need to get your asses down there ASAP. Every minute counts in this fight," Aria advised.

"I'm ready. All I've got to do is gather the coordinates, and I can move on," Aren replied.

Aria nodded slowly, beginning to feel concerned. They had already been out on the line for an hour at least, and there still was no sign of Sapphire. She wiped a bead of sweat from her brow. What if she didn't show? What if Sapphire wasn't going to play by the rules? Aria always hated waiting, and with her recently enhanced senses, time seemed only to creep slower. The woman stared eagerly out onto the horizon, mentally calling out to Sapphire and her army. Her military was becoming restless, the men and women chatting amongst themselves.

"Look at these numbers! I can't even see the end to our army!" one man exclaimed.

"Don't you think it's a bit overkill?" another asked.

"Heh, your city-state wasn't hit that hard. You haven't seen what these monsters are capable of."

"Well, I've seen it, and with a military this size, I don't see how they can defeat us! Together we have every piece of weaponry and technology at our fingertips! How can we lose?" a third spoke up.

"Hell, I'm excited. I don't know about you guys, but I think this is going to be fun!" a female voice cheered.

Aria closed her eyes, taking a slow breath. It felt as if the air was becoming denser. Something ate away at her nerves. Yesterday she had felt hopeful and ready for anything, but as the seconds ticked by, her whole being was sinking with dread.

"God! Let's just get this over with!" Aria hissed through gritted teeth.

A distortion buzzed along the horizon. The land filled with silence. Aria narrowed her eyes, watching carefully to make sure it wasn't just her vision straining to focus. Another electric sizzle snapped along her line of sight, followed by a second. Then there was a third, and the area erupted into a mass of darkness, a thunderous sound crackling as the landscape shattered like glass. It swelled, growing larger and larger, eating away at the desert scene. The blackness was immense, something unlike Aria had ever seen. With one more groaning boom, the shade expanded into the sky and zipped back down into nothing, disappearing altogether. In its place was a hair-raising sight. Sapphire's army stretched for kilometers along the desert. There were monsters of all shapes and sizes, androids among the group with bored expressions, the entire Roman fleet on guard, and a tall structure in the center of it all.

Made of what appeared to be human bones, a tri-legged throne towered high above the enemy fleet. Sitting atop it was none other than Sapphire, her black eyes staring directly at Aria. The female militant jumped from her seat atop the vehicle and took a few strides out before her forces. Aria's optical camera focused in on a flicker of yellow and purple. There was a secondary throne in the center of the structure halfway down. Sitting upon it was Ivory. The blonde sat stiffly upright, one hand tugging on the other. Aria's breath caught in her throat. Ivory was still alive, and she was stuck in the middle of the fight. Moving her sight along the enemy line, Aria found no sign of Dovian.

"Holy shit. I knew her army was going to be big, but…goddamn that's insane," Troy cursed. He pressed a button on his helmet, gathering a reading. He twisted his head all the way to the left and then the right. Aria awaited his answer. "Eight hundred million," he choked on the words, devastation saturating his voice.

Four times the size. Sapphire's army was four times the size of Aria's entire fleet. Whispers and groans rippled throughout the military as the soldiers beheld the sight of their enemy. Morale just took a sudden plummet.

Aria eyed the generals behind her. "Shall we make the first move?" she asked.

Yoshitaka stepped forward. "No. Let her make the first move."

"Are you sure that's a good idea?"

He nodded, his mask shifting in pieces back over his face. "Trust me. I have another card up my sleeve."

Hesitantly, Aria made a noise of understanding.

"Phoenix. Status?" she mentally called out.

"In position. Nerd is almost finished calibrating the Electrostatic Cannon onto the drill," Spoofy replied.

"Great. I will send Troy and Aren down as soon as the package arrives."

"Roger."

"Well, Yoshitaka. I hope the card up your sleeve is an ace," Aria moaned.

"Just keep your eyes low." Yoshitaka pointed toward Sapphire's army.

Aria's sight traveled across the desert floor, over the expanse between the two armies, up to Sapphire's glaring face.

"ARE YOU READY TO MEET YOUR END?" Sapphire's oscillating voice echoed throughout the land.

Feeling a bit more determined, Aria flipped down the faceplate of her helmet. "Come at us with all you got."

"Feline Intelligence Firmware Integration"

CHAPTER 21

With nothing more than a flick of Sapphire's wrist, her front line of monsters rushed forward at erratic speeds. Some beings jittered across the landscape; others moved so fast that they were merely a blur. The sound became a garbled mix of rumbling rock and monstrous shrieks and groans. The weighted footsteps vibrated across the desert, threatening to shatter the Earth in half. Aria raised her hand as she spoke through her mental chip, telling her soldiers to remain on guard and to have all projectiles ready to fire. Yoshitaka waited beside her with his sight fixed on the desert floor. As the evil army neared their position, Aria's eyes flitted from the dangerous force to the Japanese man beside her.

"There," he spoke suddenly.

Aria kept her gaze straight.

A flicker on the dusty floor sizzled only for a split-second. With her fist still raised, Aria leaned forward, her optical viewer gathering data.

"Did I just see that?" Troy asked.

"I saw it," Aria responded.

Another crackle of static streaked across the land, bursting upwards. With a sudden jolt, the ground heaved upward, knocking out a large portion of Sapphire's line. Aria made a strange noise, not quite understanding what she was seeing. It appeared that enormous rocks were darting back and forth, smacking the violent beasts. As one creature would break through the line of stones, another line would shoot upwards, blocking its path. It took a few moments to register what was going on. After Aria's eyes had focused, she realized that what she thought were rocks were actually people.

"That is some kickass camo." Troy gawked at the scene.

"Yoshitaka, who are they?" Aria asked.

"They are of the Dilong monastery." He turned his head to look at her. "All that's left of Beijing."

"We lost communications with them weeks ago. We were left to believe there were no survivors," Aria said quietly. "I'm glad that someone survived."

"We intercepted them while digging through the tunnels. They had multi-purpose vessels that allowed them to move both underwater and drill through the earth. They had nearly crashed into our fleet as they broke through the crust. It didn't take much to convince them to come with us. Despite their beliefs, they are on a mission for revenge," Yoshitaka said. "They have nothing left."

Aria solemnly watched as the monks fought effortlessly against the beastly creatures. They moved with a dance-like grace that was unseen in typical combat, using their weapons in traditional ways mixed with martial arts. It was impressive. Equipped with little armor, the monks stuck as close to tradition as possible. Outside of their optical camo, they wore yellow and orange outfits topped with slender pieces of metal to provide some form of protection. Their weapons were either a type of spear or sword, the blades buzzing with electrical currents. Piece-by-piece, the smaller monsters were torn down. As the Brutes and Spewers arrived, the monks finally appeared to have met their match.

One particular fighter stood out from the rest. It was a woman. She was handling the monsters two and sometimes three at a time. She was tiny in every sense of the word. With rapid movements, the woman darted right and left and flew through the air in ways that seemed unnatural. Her lithe body arched and twirled, her weapon guiding her among the mass. Leaping, she brought her double-sided spear through one of the Brutes, pulled out, and stabbed a second that was located behind her. Looking over her shoulder, she assessed her men with glaring brown and gold-specked eyes. Blowing her black hair out of her face, she shouted an order. The entire assembly simultaneously stepped away from their targets, regrouping as they slowly trudged backward toward the military line to join the others.

"Who is that woman?" Aria asked.

Yoshitaka smirked. "That is General Jiao."

"General?" Aria asked, her voice rising in pitch. "I like her already."

Jiao folded her spear in half, snapped it into a different shape, and then held the weapon over her head. The blades rotated like a fan, lifting the woman off the ground. She traversed above the battle to where Aria and Yoshitaka stood.

"Do it now!" she cried out.

Yoshitaka gave a quick nod. Holding his arm out toward the fight, he shouted an attack command. The warcry was ear-piercing as the Japanese troops took off to join in the chaos, Hattori leading the way. Yoshitaka then placed his hand on Aria's shoulder, to which she finally threw down her fist, shouting her own orders. An earth-shattering rumble and boom followed as every tank and missile weaponry detonated one after the other down the line. It started as a couple of bursts that quickly fell into a crash so undecipherable that it became nothing but a hissing white noise. To Aria, it sounded like glory.

Enormous craters developed in the landscape. Rock, fire, sizzling blood, and messy particles of demonic flesh scattered among each impact. There was one aspect of Sapphire's monsters that seemed to benefit the human army. As projectiles hit the Spewers, their bodies exploded outward, annihilating mass amounts of other demons. Within seconds, nearly all of Sapphire's first wave was demolished. Aria held her fist in the air, screaming as the soldiers prepared for their second attack. A loud laugh brought her attention toward Kovacevic. He was shouting into his radio; every other word was a colorful obscenity as he spoke to the fringes of the army. From a distance, she saw a grouping of his drones and mobile tank mechs heading out to battle. Aria then looked to Feyette. He busied himself with orders to the rest of the Fountain militaries, sending out their various robots and unmanned war machines. Yoshitaka did not letup, calling out orders to a man named Saito.

"Saito! Unlock FIFI!" The Japanese man waved his hand in the air.

"Oh, this is gonna be SO good!" Troy rubbed his hands together.

With a cranking whine, FIFI's eyes pulsated with light. The enormous tiger-mech stamped forward, roaring with ferocity. Each pounding step had a banging echo effect. The sound was like a warning, causing many to pause and watch. With one giant swipe of its clawed hands, FIFI took out nearly two hundred enemies. The oversized feline must've been enjoying itself as it gave another howl and pawed at the monsters. FIFI stomped the demons into the dust, sawed them in half with razor-sharp claws, and sent them soaring toward Sapphire's tower with a slap of its tail. This boosted the human's morale as the men began cheering and chanting their own war songs.

Aria locked gazes with the satanic child once again as half of one of her pets slapped against the side of her throne, hot blood splattering over her white dress.

"Having fun yet?" Aria arrogantly asked.

Sapphire slowly stood from her seat, her black eyes narrowing. Pressing a white shoe against the messy carcass, she kicked it over the side of her throne, the body tumbling past a flinching Ivory onto the sandy ground with a disgusting splat.

"THE FUN IS ONLY BEGINNING," the eerie voice piped over the battle.

The little girl lifted a palm, releasing her second wave which contained the biomechanical androids. As she raised the other hand, a large crackling black hole burst open behind her once again. Aria frowned. She knew there was something Sapphire had been holding back, and she had a pretty good inclination as to what her next move was.

"Feyette!" Aria spun around. The man abruptly halted his communications. "Get the Hawks and whatever else we have on hand ready for the sky!"

He didn't question her, but merely nodded, switching up his orders for half of the army. Within seconds, the thumping drone of the revving Hawks pounded in Aria's ears, followed by the growing hum of the neighboring jets. Kovacevic followed with orders of his own, the second half of the line responding in the same manner.

In only a couple of seconds, the biomechanical androids were even with the remaining demons, filling the line. Aria and Feyette knew exactly how they would operate. As the droids communicated their calculations to one another, their various weapons dropped, slid out, and warped out of their bodies. They were an army of nightmares. Dislodged jaws revealed cannons; arms morphed into rifles; some folded in on themselves to create electrically-charged rail devices, and others had legs that morphed into treaded wheels that tore away at the rocky ground. Aria could barely get a word out before the androids released their arsenal upon the humans.

"Take cover!" she simultaneously mentally and verbally shouted.

Her words fell upon deaf ears as the excruciating, pulverizing, blare of the assorted weaponry drowned her out. Aria covered her head, twisting away from the blast into a crouching position, Troy doing the same by her side. The noise grinded into an electric hiss; the sound of crunching flooded from all directions. The horrendous noise had lasted a good thirty seconds before all androids halted either to cool their systems, reload, or recalibrate. The closest thing to silence on the battlefield followed next, but it could have been possible that the sound had blown Aria's eardrums. Trying to regain her equilibrium, Aria craned her neck to check out the damage.

Of course, it was as devastating as she had imagined. Many of their war machines had been obliterated, split in half, crushed, overturned onto soldiers, and melted into a sizzling pile. As far as she could see to the left, a mound of bodies in all sorts of disfigurement littered the desert floor. It was horrifying, but a large portion still had survived thanks to their shields and for taking cover behind vehicles. The sudden calm wouldn't last long, however. The androids only needed a few moments to ready a second attack.

"Give all you have! Fire when ready!" Aria commanded.

A horrid bellowing interrupted her; the call warped as it moved toward the humans. Aria slowly stood, her wide eyes locked upon the black swelling portal behind Sapphire's tower. It was just as she had feared.

Out of the dark mass came a fluctuating silhouette. Massive, lumbering from side to side amongst a murky dark mist, it was the Colossus, the beast from the Amazonian Desert. As quickly as it stepped out of the black ring, the portal suctioned closed. Aria immediately noticed a pair of electric-blue eyes. Standing upon the monster's shoulder was none other than Dovian; the sultry woman with long dark hair stood on the opposite side. Dovian was already watching Aria from the expanse of the battlefield. His face was pulled tight, revealing no emotion as the humans were dropping dead by the handfuls each second. As the Colossus worked its way around Sapphire's tower, its feet crushing a few of its own kind, Dovian cocked his head to the side, finally giving some sort of response to Aria's presence. That was when Aria realized Troy had been calling her name.

"Aria! Move!" Troy yelled, shoving the woman out of the way just as a Brute's blast spiraled past them. The sickening plop of the poor soul behind them being torn to pieces sent chills down Aria's spine.

"You alright?" she called out, helping Troy to his feet.

He pointed a finger toward the battle as he stood. Aria turned her attention to the monsters that were in the process of surrounding them. She waited no longer, lifting her rifle to join in on the violence. Grimacing, Aria sidestepped, moving further and further away as the demons forced the two apart. As she relentlessly fired into the creatures, her bullets ripping through their shields and flesh, she caught the sight of a Spewer heading directly for Troy.

"Watch out, Troy," Aria spoke into his mind.

Troy rolled to the side just as a pile of magma sludge gushed toward him.

He somersaulted backward over to his feet, firing at the Brawlers and Brutes that annoyed him more like bugs than anything. With one giant stride, the Spewer pulled back and swiped at Troy, knocking the man onto his back. Air rushed out of his lungs upon impact. Troy shook his head, trying to steady his spinning vision just as a large hand clamped around his rifle and pulled. Troy flew up and over and slammed onto the ground on the opposite side of the beast. He recoiled instantly and released the weapon. Holding his hip, Troy glared at the Spewer. Its golden eyes watched him. As the monster roared, it pulled on both sides of Troy's gun, tearing it in half. Troy quickly pushed to his feet, taking a couple of staggering steps back.

Pointing an accusatory finger at the creature, he spoke, "You, sir, are a dick!"

The Spewer eyed him carefully, circling slowly to the side. Troy swallowed thickly. Looking over his shoulder, he took in the sights of the war around him. Humans were being torn apart by demons and androids alike. Bullets whizzed by; some would've impacted his body if it weren't for his own Faze Shield. The ninja and samurai were doing alright with the monks at their side. Their weapons were excellent for both long distance and close range. Troy watched General Jiao as she easily fought hand-to-hand against a Brawler, her small hands snapping the creature's neck as if it were no effort at all.

"Okay," Troy sniffed, shaking out his hands and rolling his shoulders. "Let's do things the hard way. You and me. Mano a mano….Whatever the hell that means."

The Spewer lurched forward, snarling. Troy quickly moved to the right with his fists held up before his face.

"Alright!" he cheered. *'Just like the virtual simulators at the club…'* he thought.

Ducking, he avoided a collision with an oversized fist. Troy rotated to the side of the Spewer, punching one of the magma sacs on its back. He had to be quick, shaking off his fist before the liquid fire could melt through his armor.

"Whoo-hoo-hoo! Hot!" Troy hissed.

The Spewer twirled with its arms held out to the sides as it made a whirlwind attack, fire bursting from its mouth. Troy turned, continuing in a circle around the beast as it chased after him. He stood, leapt to the ground, and rolled between its legs. Hopping to his feet, Troy popped two more sacs along the creature's back. He squinted, trying to formulate a way to burst the sac at the base of its skull. Eyeing his broken weapon, he dove for the scraps but was intercepted by the monster's fist. Troy cried out as he slammed into the rock once again. He made an awful sound upon contact, his helmet cracking. The Spewer continued, throwing Troy onto the opposite side. The man groaned, reaching out for his shattered gun as the Spewer stood over him and readied to vomit liquid fire atop his body. Grabbing a fistful of ammunition, Troy mustered all his strength and threw the bullets directly into the monster's mouth. The heat of its fire ignited the ammunition, causing the Spewer to draw back. As it turned away, Troy pushed to his feet and threw the remaining shells at the magma sac behind its head. The ammunition pierced through the bubbling welt, causing it to explode. The Spewer went wild, howling and clutching at its wounds. Troy backed up, trying to avoid the careening monster that was already beginning to expand.

"Incoming!" he shouted, running toward Aria, who was surrounded by monsters.

"Wha–?" Aria gasped, her eyes widening at the sight of Troy running toward her, a bloated Spewer ready to blow.

Tory grabbed her by the elbow and tugged her around to his side. She used her momentum, spinning, and pulled him in return to avoid the tumbling creature. Aria, however, was obscenely stronger than she used to be. The two soldiers crashed violently into an overturned tank.

"Holy shit!" Troy groaned. "What? You have superhuman strength now?"

As they gathered their footing, Aria and Troy dropped and crawled under the vehicle just as the Spewer exploded, taking out a massive ring of enemies.

"Hot damn!" Troy laughed.

"Are you finished with the one-liners?" Aria shouted. "You about killed us both."

"Hey!" he whined, his visor sinking into the sides of his helmet. Blood dripped from his head, beading over his brow onto his cheekbone. "I helped you! Took out that group that was pinning you down."

"I wasn't getting pinned. I had it under control," Aria replied, her hands instinctively reaching for his face.

"Uh huh," he mumbled, letting her touch his skin. Continuing, he used a sad impression of Aria's voice. "No, thank *you*, Troy. I don't know where I would be if I didn't have you around to save me all the time."

Aria glared at him. "IVES!"

It was one word, and she said it loud and slow. It stung.

Troy moaned. "Okay! Let's not bring that up *ever* again."

"Are you two alive under there?" Kovacevic asked through their mental chips.

"We're here," Aria replied. She worked at healing Troy's wounds. The man's dilated pupils returned to normal. "You had a concussion," she quickly muttered to her partner.

"Damn. You're better than a pain pill. *You're* still a pain, though." He gave her a stupid grin.

Aria ignored him.

"Looks like your Roman soldier is here!" Kovacevic added.

Aria and Troy locked nervous gazes. There was an explosion, the shockwave of dust suctioning beneath the tank, covering them.

"Cherno has arrived," Kovacevic laughed. His celebrations abruptly halted. *"Wait a minute. We have a new report. Apparently the war has broken out across the world. City-states from all over are being attacked by those monsters. That little bitch is attacking everyone else while we're busy with her army here."* The man no longer sounded amused.

"Troy," Aria coughed, trying not to inhale the dirt. It was as she feared. Sapphire was taking the opportunity to destroy the other city-states while all the militaries were outside Fountains.

"I'd better hurry," Troy blurted. "If I can get those portals closed, maybe we can keep her monsters from traveling to the other cities. If anything, they'll lose contact with her." He reached forward, beginning to pull himself out from beneath their shelter. Aria's hand on his shoulder stopped him.

"Please," she hesitated, "...be careful."

He fed her one of his boyish grins. "Don't worry about me. This will be fun. I've always wanted to be a kickass robot!"

Aria gave him a severe look.

Watching the Colossus, Troy's face became stern. "I can imagine what your next action is," he murmured.

Aria drifted her green-eyed stare toward Dovian, who was still riding upon the giant's shoulder. The monstrous being was swiping at the aircraft. In one swoop, it took out three Hawks. Dovian waited patiently atop the creature, keeping his balance without much effort, his shields protecting him from projectiles. "I'll figure out a way to deal with him," Aria whispered.

Lowering his face shield, Troy looked back toward the woman. *"You* be careful. When I'm done, I'm heading directly back to you. In the meantime, you've got to survive. Dovian's dangerous."

Aria lowered her eyes to the dirt. "I'll be on my toes, trust me."

Troy patted her on the back, shaking her. "I always have."

Aria waited, staring at the man. His face was unreadable behind the mask, but the tension overflowed from his being. He was struggling for words, but as he pulled himself out from beneath the tank, his mind swirled with a desperate need.

'Not sure why I can't just say it, but you know that I care about ya. A lot. Always

have, always will,' his mind whispered.

He stood outside the tank, Aria pulling herself out beside him. As she rose, she gave him an embarrassed smile. Troy lowered his head, rubbing the back of his neck nervously. He figured Aria had just read his thoughts.

"You're so good with words," she mumbled, walking forward as she signaled to the Cherno troops hovering above them in their craft.

"Erm…I try my best," he said, barely audible.

"Survive. Help me end this war, and then you can say them out loud to me. Besides, you owe me a drink from Chester's." Aria waved her hands, guiding the soldiers who were lowering the robotic Roman soldier.

"Can we go now?!" Aren's shrill voice called out from behind.

Aria and Troy looked back at the pilot. He had nearly been crushed by a large piece of metal that appeared to have been a war machine of some sort at one time. He had his arms covering his head; Franklin was busy encasing their bodies with a large domed shield.

Seeing Aren's desperation, Troy ran ahead and snagged the Roman soldier. Not far away, a biomechanical android had its sights locked upon the hovercraft.

"Go! Go!" Troy waved, severing the cord the Roman bot was strapped to.

Aria took careful aim and fired upon the biomechanical enemy, distracting it just enough for the Cherno soldiers to back away into the air. With a pulsing hum, the craft twisted, fired a missile that obliterated the android to nothing more than scrap metal, and then sped directly toward the Colossus.

"Get your ass to the mines! This war is getting out of control! We need those portals closed!" Aria shouted. Reaching into her belt, she pulled out a beacon and slapped it upon the Roman soldier. "I've got my eyes on you. All soldiers will see you marked as a friendly. They've already been briefed."

Troy nodded, carrying the robot in his arms as he trotted toward Aren. A mechanical roar sounded, bringing Troy's attention momentarily back to FIFI. The robotic tiger circled the Colossus.

"My only regret is missing the epic fight between that cat and that ugly crud-monster!" Running faster, he approached the panicked Aren. "Hoverbike?" he asked the younger man.

Aren lifted his head, gaping at the bike a few meters away. He pointed with a shaking hand. The vehicle had been knocked over and covered in debris.

"Damnit!" Tory cursed.

Aren immediately stood, regaining composure. "It's not inoperable! It should be able to get us down there. Franklin! Run diagnostics!"

"RUNNING DIAGNOSTICS…CLEAR," Franklin chimed, his scanner flowing over the shape of the hoverbike.

"Good enough for me," Troy said, strapping the Roman soldier to the back of the vehicle. "Get on, Aren!"

Aren didn't need to be told twice. As soon as the pilot hopped onboard, Troy sped off without much warning. The young man urgently wrapped his arms around Troy's chest. Franklin gave a shriek, reaching with outstretched clamps to grip the Roman bot. With a jolt, the bike soared over the edge of the cliff, sinking down several hundred meters toward the mining center. The sight was unbelievable. From above, Troy and Aren watched in awe. A battle had broken out in the mines as well. A large hole had been drilled at an angle into the floor, a yellowish light shimmering from it—the opening to Sapphire's origins. More and more monsters climbed out of the portal, the beasts taking to the walls and floor toward Team Phoenix.

"We need extra soldiers down here!" Troy mentally called out over various channels.

Feyette responded first. *"I've got the church mercenaries heading your way."*
"Perfect."

"I've got to help them!" Troy looked over his shoulder at Aren.

The pilot gaped at him as if he were crazy. "I'm sorry, Troy, but there's no time. We've got to get you into this robot."

Troy glared at the monsters, watching Spoofy, Monkey, Zombie, and Kaino as they struggled to fight the small onslaught. Nerd was cursing, Bridgette zapping a series of electric currents onto the massive driller. As Troy pulled up, Aren hopped off the bike.

"What's the problem?" Aren asked. Franklin zoomed to his side.

"Damn battery is dead on the blasted drill! We need it to run the electrostatic cannon!" Nerd growled, running his hands through his hair.

"Franklin! Grab the other side. You and Bridgette fix this damn thing!" Aren shouted.

Franklin complied without issue, clamping on one side of the battery while Bridgette took the opposite. Together the bots fed currents back and forth, the drill humming and quaking. Within a few seconds, the heavy machinery sputtered to life.

"Back away from the drill!" Nerd cried out.

"About damn time you got that thing running! We need to get that portal closed, or we're all going to be slaughtered!" Spoofy shouted.

"Come on!" Aren yelled, grabbing Troy's arm. "The clinic is just over here!"

THE ESOTERIC DESIGN

"You need me to come with ya?" Nerd asked.

Aren gave an uneasy look toward the spinning drill. "What about the cannon?"

"It's gonna take a few minutes to build up enough power to fire," the Scotty explained.

"Nerd, if you're going, hurry! We can hold them off for a few more minutes but get your ass here ASAP! We need to fire immediately!" Spoofy called out.

Monkey, Zombie, and Kaino shot from behind cover of the mining vehicles. For now, only monsters were filtering through the portal.

"You're going to have to spare me. I need to be in there to make sure all of Troy's vitals are stabilized," Kaino suddenly spouted.

"Damn it!" Spoofy grit her teeth. "Go! Just…hurry!"

"Got my alarm set!" Nerd waved a hand, running after Aren and Troy.

Kaino groaned a confirmation and rolled around the corner, following the others.

"We're goin' to die," Zombie drawled.

"Think that way, and we already are," Spoofy sighed.

As she took down a few enemies, giving a fleeting stare in the direction of the half of her team entering the clinic, an invisible force sliced the truck Spoofy was hiding behind in half. The woman screamed as she was tossed backward, a massive tire slamming only centimeters away from her head. Moving toward her was a large group of Brutes. Their arms were raised; their claws noisily clanged together as they prepared for their next attack. Spoofy tried to move but found her leg pinned beneath the bumper of the lopsided vehicle. She gasped, looking up at her enemy.

'I'm dead….' It was her only thought.

Unexpectedly, two of the monsters' heads burst into a splatter of red, the loud *BA-DOOM* of a sniper rifle following. The other beasts met a similar fate, their heads exploding outwards into pieces, the thunderous sounds coming immediately after.

"Check it out!" Monkey cheered.

In a flash, the mine was full of Soldiers of God. They fought relentlessly against the demons. They were an impressive team, each one singlehandedly taking out handfuls within seconds. Soon, the infestation of monsters had become a manageable game of picking-off.

One soldier came to Spoofy's rescue, quickly lifting the backend of the truck from off her ankle. "Is your leg okay?" he asked with a deep voice.

Every member of the Soldiers of God was a massive creation. Not only were they tall, but they were beastly with muscle hidden behind equally large body armor. They could give Feyette's Goliaths a run for their money.

Spoofy moved her ankle slowly, testing it out. It ached a little, but nothing felt broken thanks to her armor. "Feels fine. Thank you."

The man nodded, pounding his hand against his chest as he bowed. "Anything for a lady." Spoofy couldn't help the blush that crossed her face.

Monkey's expression twisted into a pout as he was momentarily distracted by the other elite soldier. A Brawler leaped from the top of the vehicle near him, latching onto his head.

"WAH!" Monkey screamed, batting at the beast with his hands.

Spoofy sighed, shooting the monster in its skull. The creature dropped to the ground, sputtering into an uneasy death. Monkey looked at her and then lowered his head dismally.

"You are a good shot as well. There are few females in our group. Perhaps you should look into joining our ranks," the Soldier of God suggested.

Spoofy smirked. "Heh…never really thought about it."

"She can't join your ranks!" Monkey stomped toward the man. "She's already in…my…my ranks!"

Despite Monkey being a large man himself, the Soldier of God still towered over him. The two men participated in a staring match.

"Quit it!" Spoofy spat. "We've got more important things to worry about!"

The soldier immediately broke free from Monkey's dagger-like glare. "I am at your command."

Spoofy liked the sound of that. With a little sway of her hips, she smiled. "Well, then…." She pointed toward the clinic. "I need you and your men to keep that clinic safe at all times. No matter what."

The soldier pounded his fist against his chest, gave another nod, and stomped toward the clinic with a fervor unseen in most men.

"He's ambitious." Spoofy placed her hands on her hips, watching the Soldier of God as he rounded up a group of his troops.

"I…I'm ambitious, too," Monkey whined, moving to the front of her.

"Yes, you are!" Spoofy spoke to the grown man like he was a dog, rubbing her hand over his helmet. Monkey did not seem pleased by her teasing. "Come on. We've got work to do. Let's secure the drill." She looked at her DNAIS. "Nerd only has a few minutes left."

She peered at the clinic window. From her position, she could see Troy strapped to a table. Kaino, Aren, and Nerd were scurrying about like madmen.

340

"We've got ya all hooked up!" Nerd exclaimed.

Troy looked down at himself and then at the Roman robot he was hooked up to, his heart pounding as his nerves took a nosedive. Puffing out his cheeks, he let out a whoosh of air. A large hand rested on his shoulder.

"You ready for this?" Kaino's rugged features wrinkled more as he gave Troy an unsure look.

"Yeah!" Troy sputtered. There was a multitude of wires connected to his chest, arms, neck, and temples. He felt like a science project. "Totally ready. Why wouldn't I be? I mean, I'm just going to…um…go through cardiac arrest, die, transfer my mental being into this robot over here, and sabotage Sapphire's portals. No problem. Easy-peasy. Why wouldn't I be ready?" His eyes bugged out as if the realization of his insane idea finally hit him.

'Oh, damn…where's Aria?'

"You don't have to do this, Troy." Aren worriedly gazed upon the man strapped to the med table. Troy's vitals blipped in front of the pilot's face from his DNAIS.

An explosion sounded outside, alerting the men to the war.

"No…I'm doing this. I'm ready. Let's just get it over with," Troy firmly stated.

"You're sure?" Aren hesitantly asked.

"Just do it, Aren!" Troy shouted.

The pilot cringed at Troy's outburst.

"Okay, okay…" Aren whispered. He looked to Kaino and bobbed his head.

"Administering the sedative now," Kaino grumbled, injecting a liquid into Troy's IV.

"Yer goin' to get a little bit sleepy. When you wake up, you should be inside the Roman robot," Nerd spoke softly to Troy.

"I *will* be. I'm going to make this…work…." The male soldier's breaths slowed, his eyes fluttering closed.

Kaino looked to Aren.

"Vitals are stable." The pilot looked to Nerd and Kaino. After a long pause, he continued, "Shutting off the pacemaker now."

As Aren clicked a few buttons, Troy's vitals spiked. After a couple of erratic heart beats, the pulsating line jolted up and down, racing only for a couple seconds before dropping and stopping altogether. The pulse line turned red, an abrasive alarm chiming from the medical equipment around them. Troy remained still, his body unmoving. Nerd winced, quickly turning off the alarms. Truthfully, the silence made it worse. All three men waited impatiently, staring at Troy with uneasy expressions.

Aren eyed a clock on the wall, the seconds flitting by until a minute had passed. "Damnit," he hissed.

"I knew Aria should have come down here. What are we goin' to do?" Nerd whispered.

"Did we kill him?" Kaino muttered.

Beep!

A small ding sounded from the second set of equipment connected to the Roman soldier. Aren and Nerd dashed to the control panel, gaping with their mouths open.

"Did I hear…?" Nerd asked.

Beep!

"That!" Aren pointed at the screen. "Holy shit!"

"Did it work?" Kaino asked. "It's not moving."

Both Troy and the Roman soldier remained as still as ever.

Nerd pushed a series of codes on the panel while Aren ran a diagnostic scan on the bot.

"Initiate?" Nerd asked, looking to Aren.

"Ummmm…." Aren dropped his arm, looking at the panel. "Yeah! Yeah…try it."

As soon as Nerd confirmed initiation, the Roman robot flew upward in its bed, a garbled electric sound blaring from it. The three men ecstatically watched the robot as it flailed its arms in the air in panic. It hopped from the bed and continued making loud noises—a series of beeps, twits, and honks. Its movements were neurotic, looking over its shoulders at the men and down at itself, then over at Troy's body.

"HONK BLEEP CUUUURNNCHHHH!" The Roman soldier blared while holding its hands on its head. It ran to Troy's bedside, peering closely at the man's face. It pointed, looked to Aren and Nerd and garbled another expression in tech speak.

"I think he's tryin' to talk to us," Nerd said in a hushed voice.

"Um…Troy?" Kaino asked.

The robot spun, pointing at Kaino. "KRaaaaaNnnn!" It pointed at itself. "REEEE ERRR AAA ERRRAA!"

"Uh…yeah…you are Troy…and you are in a robot body," Kaino spoke to the machine as if it were stupid.

Aren scanned the Roman soldier, finding a strange electrical field contained within it. "This is insane." Taking this as proof that Troy's consciousness was safely contained within the robot, Aren returned to Troy's panel. He quickly restored the pacemaker. They needed to keep the body alive in at least a vegetative state. The first part of the plan was complete, now he hoped they would be able to figure out a way to get Troy's consciousness to return to his body later.

The robot made another squeal and ran to the mirror on one of the opposite walls.

"That thing is Troy, right?" Nerd nervously asked.

Humorously peering at its reflection, the bot slammed its metal hands against its waist, rotating them. It looked at its face and then looked at its backside, shaking its rear back and forth while it made an eerie noise similar to the sound of mechanical laughing. Franklin and Bridgette gave high-pitched shrieks, floating toward the mechanized Troy. Together they danced, the Roman soldier moving its hips and arms in a fashion that Kaino and Nerd had seen many times over at the nightclubs.

"Yup...that's Troy." Nerd covered his face and shook his head.

"Troy!" Aren screamed.

The bot abruptly stopped, Bridgette and Franklin clanging against each other.

"I know you're having fun being a robot and all, but we seriously need to get a move on. People are dying," Aren dryly stated.

"Yeah! We've got to activate the cannon; it should be ready by now. We got to close that portal!" Nerd added.

The bot nodded quickly as he looked to each of the men; his palms lifted as he made a series of crunching computerized sounds. No one understood what Troy was doing. The Roman robot stomped to the control panel, plugging his finger into a port in the back.

Aren leaned forward, catching some words that scrambled onto the screen.

"I am a badass robot..." Aren read aloud, not impressed. Looking to the bot, he glared. "Yes, yes you are. I'm glad we didn't kill you."

More words covered the screen.

"You have an idea?" Nerd asked. He read some more. "What do you mean? Don't close the portal? But we got to!"

Troy shook his mechanized head, a red brush atop his helmet bobbing back and forth. More words came.

"You want to go through the portal first? Before we close it?" Nerd asked.

Troy nodded.

"You want to go through and you want us to close it at your signal?" Nerd questioned.

Troy nodded again.

"Ohhh…that makes sense. He can just go through the portal and find his way to Sapphire's side. He won't have to travel across the battlefield." Aren smiled.

Troy held his hands out toward Aren, clapping. It was like a game of charades.

"Whatever! We just got to do it quickly!" Nerd growled, heading for the door as he adjusted his tweed cap. "As in NOW!"

Troy ran with high knees toward the door. His posture was a bit wobbly as he had difficulty controlling his body.

"Ya know? I kinda like this version of Troy," Kaino chuckled. "It's quiet."

A flatulent sound came from Troy.

"Aw, you learned that from Bridgette and Franklin!" Nerd scoffed.

On cue, Bridgette and Franklin added their own noises to match.

They neared Spoofy, the woman reloading her incredible weapon. "About time you guys showed up! I was…worried…." Spoofy turned around and gawked at Troy. "Holy shit! Did it work?"

Troy marched to the woman, his arms in the air going willy-nilly. Spoofy pointed at the awkward robot as it anxiously moved from side to side.

"This…is this Troy? Did the transfer process make him stupid?" Spoofy asked.

"I thought he was before," Zombie laughed.

"KURRNCH CHHHUUUU." Troy held up a middle finger to Zombie.

Spoofy cackled, holding onto her stomach. "That's definitely Troy!"

"Yes, yes…we have to get him through the portal. Let's go!" Nerd shoved the robot toward the eerily glowing hole.

"I'll get the cannon!" Aren announced as he snatched up the control codes for the electrostatic cannon calibrated with the drill. He climbed into the vehicle.

Spoofy and Zombie moved with Nerd and the Roman soldier, providing cover fire. As they passed Monkey, Spoofy tapped his shoulder, bringing him to their side.

"Woah! Robo-soldier!" Monkey rooted. "Robot Troy! Yeeahh!" He curiously poked the robot.

Seeing the strange Roman soldier, a Soldier of God spun and aimed directly at Troy. Team Phoenix hastily protested aloud and pointed back. Troy held his hands in the air. He was at the mercy of the soldiers.

"Why does this robot say friendly on my reader? Is it not one that is possessed?" the large man asked.

"This is the one that's on our side. You should have been briefed," Spoofy said.

"We were a bit late to the line. Rumors had reached our ears, however. I was merely alarmed by its presence. I will relay the information to the others that the friendly Roman soldier is active." The man fisted his chest and bowed, returning to his position in the battle.

"Those guys are a little odd," Zombie drawled.

Eagerly, Troy and the others continued forward. By the time they arrived, the monsters were coming in droves. As everyone provided cover fire, Troy tiptoed closer and closer to the portal, looking anxiously about at the monsters scurrying in all directions. The static from the hole tickled his senses. Rubbing his metal hands together, he stepped through, the light engulfing him.

The world around Troy instantly changed, but this was not what he was expecting to see. It was incredibly hot, the heat becoming unbearable by his readings. He stood upon a shiny black rock ledge that overlooked a world scorched by fire and magma. There was a deep rumbling that quickly turned to white noise. Screaming. He could hear horrible, terrified screaming all around. It sounded like the entire planet was shrieking. As he gaped over the ledge, hundreds of meters below, he inwardly shuddered. The churning lake of molten lava and black rock coiled and twisted around what appeared to be millions, no…billions of humans. Some were odd to look at, appearing to not be exactly human. Hovering above them all was a plate of rock held up by pillars.

'Where the hell am I?' Troy thought. Then he noticed the enormous throne in the center of the rocky plate. Chains of diamond were severed and scattered across the ground.

Far below, at the edge of the rock wall Troy was standing upon, fiery beings rose from the magmatic ooze. The goop dripped from their flesh, the creatures hissing and shrieking. In a mad flurry, they dug their claws deep into the rock wall he was standing on and climbed upwards to where Troy was. They were Brawlers, and they weren't too happy to see Troy there as they hissed, shrieked, snapped, and swiped at the robot.

'Definitely the wrong place!'

Troy twirled and stepped back inside the portal, coming back out into the mines. Making an assortment of noise, he waved his hands back and forth.

"What are you doing? Get back in there!" Spoofy hollered, shooting the enemy.

Troy refused again pointing at the portal and shaking his head.

"Wrong location?" Aren asked.

Troy nodded.

"Figures…" the pilot sighed. "Let me recalibrate this sucker. Perhaps if I use a low wave frequency, I can alter the destination of the portal."

It took a few moments of Aren tweaking his tech before the cannon kicked on. Nerd joined his side, helping with the project. With a quiet whir, the cannon shot a thin blue beam at the portal. Slowly, the gap shifted, turning in a circle. The beasts that were exiting the portal were severed in half as it reconnected with a different location. After a full revolution, the gateway twisted into a black hole.

"Okay! Try it now!" Aren hollered as he shut off the beam.

This had better not send me spiraling through the great dark abyss of the universe….' Troy gaped at the ominous opening. Giving a shrug, he passed on through.

He was surrounded by darkness this time. Troy inwardly sighed. He wasn't on the battlefield; still, once his optics gathered enough data, he realized he was inside the cave system on Ives. Before him was a gathering of Brutes and Stilt-Men. The beasts all turned their attention to the robot, drool seeping between their jagged teeth.

'Um…hello.' Troy waved a hand.

Looking to his right, he noticed another portal. There was a second to his left.

'Door number one? Door number two?' He weighed his options between each hand.

Number one—to his right. He may as well check that one first. Casually stepping into the portal, Troy nearly slipped over a black rocky ledge. It was hot, fire and magma gurgling far below in the valley. He heard the screams, saw the throne, and threw his arms into the air.

'For the love of….' He immediately returned to the cave on Ives.

Taking a couple of steps toward the beasts, he held his arms out toward them.

'How in the hell do you idiots even know where you are going? Do you just stand there and wait and play rock, paper, scissors?!' The robot expressed itself in loud noises. The creatures merely stared at the bot, their expressions never changing. *'Ya know what? Screw you guys! Stay right here. Don't move! When I come back, I'm blowing all your asses to pieces. Stay!'*

Troy eased his way toward the other portal choice. Light emitted from this one as well, but there seemed to be a thumping noise coming from the other side.

'This has to be it.'

As he stepped through, the world exploded into a circus of noise. Troy looked up. He was directly beneath Sapphire's tower. Looking to the seat in the middle, he noticed Ivory was not on her perch. A vicious skirmish had unfolded between FIFI and the Colossus. Even Dovian wasn't in his place. Troy narrowed his eyes, noticing that the City of Fountains looked a little off. Then he realized that one of the pillars had been completely obliterated, and the city was slowly teetering on the edge, threatening to cave-in on itself and smash Team Phoenix and the other soldiers in the mines. He had to work fast.

'Shit! Shit! Shit, shit, shit!' Troy mentally cursed.

In front of him was the entire Roman fleet. And directly beside the portal was a container with a pulsating orb of blue—a nuclear reactor that Sapphire undoubtedly was waiting to use on the humans. And next to that was the Elixis Electro-Static Frequency Tuner Euclid had stolen. It couldn't be any more perfect.

Sneaking toward the other Roman soldiers, Troy carefully opened the general robot's back panel and tugged on the wires. There was a slight interruption, causing Troy to halt. His computer was linking with the enemy soldier. This was the key to the entire robotic military. Hacking the system, Troy changed the code. Things that wouldn't normally make sense seemed natural to the man as his computerization took the lead. The Roman fleet was a legion of demons at this point, the general being the host. All he had to do was override the orders, and he had each vessel in his control. He had very little time, however, as the demons that possessed the Roman soldiers would eventually figure out Troy's scheme. Whereas he wanted to use the entire fleet to attack Sapphire, the best option was to destroy them all.

'Set to…self-destruct…no!' Troy stopped. Would the self-destruct function destroy Troy's body as well? Was he tied to this particular general? If his robotic form did self-destruct, would he make it back to his human body? What would happen to his consciousness?

An alarming cry echoed over the land. Troy looked up just as a massive explosion took out the center of Sapphire's tower. He only had a split-second to choose.

SELF-DESTRUCT?

YES.

Light, noise, heat, and shrapnel surrounded Troy's world.

Aria only looked back once to see Troy and Aren fly over the edge of the cliff on their hoverbike. With Troy no longer at her side, she didn't have time to worry about him. Out of sight, out of mind. Her focus could now be centered on the task at hand—getting to Dovian.

Looking back to the Colossus and FIFI, Aria was shocked to find that Dovian was no longer located on the giant's shoulder. He was nowhere to be seen.

"Typical," Aria hissed.

She had waited only a breath before she spun around with a cocky grin on her face. Dovian was directly behind her.

"You're getting slow in your old age," she said, taking only a second's attention away from the Sorcēarian to shoot a nearing beast.

"And you are getting more perceptive," he replied, his cold eyes staring down at her. He, too, took a moment to disarm one of her soldiers, pushing an invisible shockwave at the man that sent him flying back several meters. Dovian injured the man, but he did not kill him.

"Going a little soft?" she asked.

"Why not have a little fun while fighting?" he asked, finally tearing his gaze away from hers. He smirked, walking to the side, his hand launching separate waves of energy at any human that came too close to him, bullets disintegrating against his force field.

"Ah, yes. Sorcēarians do enjoy slaughter-fests, don't they?" Aria snidely remarked.

Dovian gave her a sideways glance, looking irritated. Lifting one eyebrow, he took in the sight of the battlefield. "This was not at your own request? I'd say humanity indeed enjoys the slaughter. You all are practically sacrificing yourselves for Sapphire's cause."

Aria noticed how many men had fallen in merely minutes. Her lines were looking rather pathetic since the biomechanical androids took over in the fight.

"Better to fight than to lie down and die," Aria scoffed. "I'd rather fight for my survival than rot away behind closed doors waiting for my death." She looked him up and down, and Dovian gaped at the sky and released a harsh sigh in annoyance. "Or waiting for the opportunity to turn my back on everything I've ever known for my own selfish benefit."

Now that statement grated on Dovian's nerves.

"Listen here you little ungrateful twit." He grabbed her.

Aria pressed the barrel of her rifle under his chin. Dovian didn't seem at all impressed by her nerve.

"There's nothing you can say that will offend me any more than what you did back there on Ives," her icy tone crackled. Dovian's eyes flickered if only for a second.

He finally lowered his hands, knocking back a Brute's invisible force that was plummeting their way.

Aria was livid, remembering all that they had been through and how easy it was for Dovian to shoot Troy right before her eyes before he turned around and did the same to her. But it wasn't the act of doing it that hurt her; it was the way he had done it, acting as if he was an insane murderer. He even seemed to enjoy it. It was a sickening display.

Overwhelmed by her anger, she shoved the man, sending him flat on his back. He looked at her in awe, his eyes wide and his mouth hanging open. How had she mustered the strength to do that to him, he didn't know. He immediately boiled it down to an armor attribute.

"You are awful! The most terrible, horrible thing I've ever known!" she shouted.

Now her emotions were a spiraling whirlwind. Ever since she had received her strange powers, her mind had been all over the place. Not just because of her heightened senses, but because of her mood swings. No wonder Dovian was an emotional rollercoaster. Were all Sorcēarians like this?

"When we first discovered you, I thought you were the key to humanity's survival! I thought you would be some savior of some kind! Instead, you're no better than we are! You just have magic powers!" she shouted, emptying her grenade clip into a group of Brawlers. "You're manic, you're reckless, you're thoughtless, and you...you're mean! You are just a mean old man!"

Dovian was standing now, watching the woman with interest.

"Goddamnit, and I slept with you! You stupid bastard!" She gestured toward him with an arm, her voice dripping with dread.

"Well...now that I know how you feel...." Dovian gave her a lazy stare.

"Don't give me your lax attitude! Look around us! Look at this war! You blame this on us? How about the fact that this was a war that began millennia ago?! Long before you and I even existed! You were meant to save us! Instead, you're allowing our destruction. And you don't even have the guts to do it yourself! You couldn't even off Troy and I, which says something." Aria placed one hand on her hip. "Either you suck at killing humans or you have a reason behind all this." She waved her hand out toward the chaos surrounding them.

Dovian sucked air in-between his teeth. "Ah. You see...that's where we have a bit of an issue." Dovian continued his pacing, his fidgeting making

Aria all the more anxious. Stopping, twirling to face her with his palms together, he gave her a guilty look. "You weren't supposed to live. I mean, I actually tried to kill you. I didn't think there was any way around it, but apparently I do suck at killing humans, so you are alive! And you gathered up a big, strong army to fight the enemy! That's good!"

Aria glared at him. "Is that supposed to make me feel better? That you really did try to kill us but failed?"

Dovian scratched his head, not making eye contact with her. "I suppose not, but you're alive and that's all that matters, right?"

Aria stomped toward the man, clutching his robes. "You tried to *kill* us!!"

"I didn't want to," he muttered.

"But you did!" she growled.

"But I failed!"

"Doesn't matter! You still *tried*!"

Dovian grabbed Aria, holding her against his chest. She struggled against him, and he chuckled deeply, rocking her back and forth. "And how glad I am to see that I failed. I've never been so happy to fail at something in my entire life!"

Aria harshly pushed him again, and he stumbled back a few steps, laughing joyously.

"You're crazy! You are bat-shit insane!"

"And I have no idea how in the heavens you survived, but I am so glad you did!" Lifting his staff, he formed a bubble around the woman, enclosing her in a sphere of energy.

"What is this, Dovian?" she asked in irritation.

"Now that I see you are alive, I'm not letting anything happen to you, understand?" Dovian gleefully stated. Swinging his staff suddenly, Aria quickly guarded herself, waiting for him to knock her senseless with it. Instead, she was clipped around the ankle by one of the wings, the staff locking her firmly to the desert floor.

"Hey! What do you think you're doing?" she yelled, tugging on the staff.

Dovian poked a finger against her helmet. "That staff will provide you with endless energy to keep you safely contained inside this orb." Snapping off the second wing of his staff, he morphed it into a large knife.

"I don't want to be safely contained inside an orb! I need to be killing monsters and defeating you and Sapphire!" she screamed.

Dovian walked away from her, using the makeshift knife when necessary to combat the human soldiers that dared attack him. He never once killed a man; he only disarmed or injured them.

"DOVIAN!" Aria shrieked.

It didn't take long before she was surrounded by Sapphire's demons. The creatures were snarling as they pounded against the force field around her. Aria was beginning to panic. Each fierce impact vibrated the dome. Giant mouths nipped and barked at her, the beings' hunger rising by the second. As if things couldn't get any worse, a massive detonation took place behind her. Looking back, Aria caught the sight of an android revving up its blasters to make a second attempt at taking down Aria's shield. Dovian's staff or not, Aria did not trust the hold of the sphere around her. Giving a cry, she tugged on the weapon once more.

"Release, damn it!"

And the staff released. Aria swung the weapon around, blue light swirling around her. Slamming the pole into the ground with all her might, she activated a violent blue shockwave that detonated outward, sending all of the surrounding beasts in a ten-meter radius into ash. The wave etched toward the android behind her, shattering it to a thousand pieces.

The thunderous boom that echoed behind Dovian made him freeze. A look of horror crossed his face, and the Sorcēarian spun, eyeing the crater that was now surrounding Aria. She was kneeling, his staff in her hand. The blue light danced around her like a whirlwind. Dovian staggered forward, starting slow before he took off in a mad dash in her direction.

"No…not possible. Not even remotely possible!" he sputtered.

He saw it, her hand on the staff. She had used his weapon, and it was impossible. No one else could use his weapon. He forged it only for himself. Not even another Sorcēarian could use it to its full extent. It was bound to him by his DNA. The power was his. It only released its magic at his touch. This was entirely impossible.

"Aria!" he shouted.

"You left me there to die you miserable asshole!" she growled.

"How did you do that?" he quickly asked.

Aria was taken aback by his question.

"I grabbed it and pulled really hard! How else?" she quipped.

"That, that's impossible!" he stuttered. He looked shocked, amazed, mortified.

Aria lifted her face shield. "Obviously, it's not impossible." Her glaring eyes were glowing like bright-green embers.

Dovian's hands slapped against the sides of his face as he came to an abrupt stop. "A-Aria…have you noticed any changes lately with your body?"

Aria dislodged the weapon from the rocky ground. "Yeah, quite a bit actually...ever since you failed at killing me. In fact, if it weren't for you somehow passing your powers to me, I wouldn't have been able to save Troy. He was practically dead."

Dovian groaned, spinning in a circle. "No, no...not possible. It doesn't make sense."

"You did it!" she cried, not understanding his trepidation on the matter.

Was it possible? Had he somehow transferred his powers to Aria when he had shot her? There was no way. At least, he wasn't conscious of it. He had only heard of Sorcēarians passing their life-force into other Sorcēarians. It was how his mother had rescued him and allowed him a healthy life. In order to do something like that, one would need to focus their soul energy on it. If that was what happened, it occurred completely without his knowledge or will, which also meant that his plans had considerably changed.

Dovian gasped, another explanation coming to mind. Unless it wasn't by his will that it occurred.

"Oh, God!" Dovian gasped again. "By the will of the Father."

Aria eyed him warily. "What is your deal? Is this a bad thing?" she asked.

"No...no," he whispered, trudging toward her. Dovian looked paler than ever, as if it were possible. He clutched the woman, firmly placing his palm against her stomach.

"What the hell are you doing?" she irritably asked.

"No, no, no-no-no-no!" He shook his head.

Now Aria was beginning to feel panicked. "For the love of God, what?!"

Dovian spun away from her, his hands on his head. Tugging at his hair, he twirled back to face her. With his hair messed in all directions, the man looked like a crazed lunatic–his eyes wide and his expression twisting into a look that was a mix of fear and astonishment. Taking a deep breath, Dovian finally forced out the words he wanted to say.

"You're pregnant?!" he shouted.

Aria shook her head, dumbfounded. "WHAT?!"

"New Allies"

CHAPTER 22

"What are you talking about?! I'm not pregnant!" Aria's voice was shrill to Dovian's ears, yet his face didn't falter as he looked at the woman with a matching expression of astonishment. She leaned forward and whispered with a hiss, "Am I pregnant?!"

"How have you not noticed?" Dovian's voice rose over the booming of the battlefield.

"I've been a bit busy! You know…surviving!" she shouted.

"I thought you said…you were on…" Dovian hesitated, pursing his lips as he grasped for the appropriate words, "a birth control of some kind!"

"I am! Wait…don't tell me. You have magic…*junk*?!" She gestured to his pelvis to which he promptly looked down at himself.

Speechless, Dovian ran his fingers across his forehead. "I…my…I have…what? Magic what? What does that even mean?"

The chaos was getting out of control. Bullets and Brute blasts were colliding around the couple, fire flying past their heads. The explosive noises were becoming unbearable. Dovian ran his hands through his hair and over his face, groaning in irritation. Reaching for Aria, he snatched her wrist.

"No. Nope." He shook his head defiantly. "Timeout. We're taking a timeout. Enough of this."

Twisting the pendant on his scarlet coat, the two instantly disappeared from the battlefield. Aria barely had time to respond to Dovian's touch before he tore her away from reality. With a sizzle, the world melted from the center of her vision outward, the browns of the dusty earth dissipating into blackness with specks of navy and white, pinks and yellows blurring around her. Aria turned to the side, her breath catching in her lungs as she felt her whole body cover in goosebumps. Far off in the distance was a burning mass of orange, different orbs of various shapes and sizes and colors churning slowly around it. As far as her enhanced vision could carry, she saw a multitude of glittering sparks. Nebulas of foggy hues intermingled with specks of white and pale blue. A flickering tail would shoot by as a rumbling rock or two would quake around them. The woman's eyes sparkled in the light as it was the most beautiful sight she had ever seen.

"Oh my God," she whispered, breathless. "This is…" she paused, choking on her words. Lifting her head to Dovian, she awaited an explanation.

Looking past her at the spinning orbs, he gave her a sad smile if ever so slight. "This is the edge of time." His voice was barely audible. Looking at the woman, he placed his thumb on her chin, guiding her to look downward.

"Holy crap!" Aria gasped, her hand covering her mouth.

Beneath them was a familiar sight. She had seen it before, but nothing quite like this. Below, with spiraling clouds of white and massive blotches of brown and blue, was the Earth. From where she stood, she could not see the battlefield.

"Sometimes I would come here…only to sit and meditate. It was a quiet place. I could be here for days, and no one would know any different as to them, I was gone mere seconds," he whispered.

"I thought you said humans were incapable of traveling through the use of your frequency tuners," she said.

"Yes. And right now, you are not human."

Aria looked down at herself, her hands covering her stomach. How could she have missed it? How could the hospital have not noticed? Aria grimaced, pulling up her DNAIS. Sure enough, she had a multitude of missed calls from the clinic. She didn't have time to mess with them. Perhaps that was what the strange anomaly was on her lab results, not her nanomites. She felt like bashing her forehead against a wall for being so careless.

"This is…insane." She lowered her head, suddenly not feeling well.

"Imagine how I feel," Dovian chuckled. Aria tore her gaze to the Sorcēarian. "I nearly killed the mother of my own child."

Aria moaned, slowly sitting upon the invisible floor. "Don't say that. That's so weird to hear," she grumbled. "I'm pregnant?" Aria stared at Dovian's boots, her mouth wide open as the revelation finally set.

"I can't let you go back out there," Dovian firmly stated. "If Sapphire finds out...."

"What does she want, Dovian?" Aria asked. "What is the purpose of all this chaos?"

Heaving a tired sigh, Dovian waved his hand through the empty air. From his fingertips, an image appeared, replaying the events of the war that they were supposed to be fighting. Everything seemed to freeze in place, nobody moving, no creature snarling, no bullets piercing. Time had stopped. The image spun, zipping upwards to Sapphire's tower, revealing the little girl with black eyes.

"Sapphire wants to wipe the world a clean slate. She desires to re-inhabit it with human-Sorcēarian hybrids. Her plan is to use Ivory to house and birth the children." He looked at Aria, knowing her question. "Yes, she has a Sorcēarian gene and apparently can have children despite her bionic state."

"And...I'm assuming that means you are expected to help in the repopulation process," Aria spoke slowly, an edge of bitterness coating her words.

He nodded slowly, not matching her stare.

"Really? Is that why you stayed in Ives?" she scoffed. "You're somethin' else."

"I did not remain on Ives merely to...impregnate Ivory!" he roared. Immediately, he looked away, staring at the faraway sun. Actually, that kind of was why he was there. He was tempted by the idea of living a life with I'Lanthe once again. Though, he never truly wanted it. He knew better than that. His purpose was of greater meaning. "It's come to the time I should probably tell you everything."

Aria pushed to her feet, glaring daggers at the man. "You probably should have told me the truth from the very beginning!"

He held up his hands dismissively. "Even I didn't know the whole truth. Not until recently."

"How can I even trust a single word you've said? Betrayal. That's all you've shown me." Her expression was both angry and hurt.

"It's not how I wanted things to be, believe me." Dovian's frown curved further.

She scoffed. "Just tell me what the hell is going on."

He cleared his throat, waving his hand over the image he had projected. "Since the beginning of my life, God had preordained a plan for me. No one knew of this plan, except for Gaius. Even today, I have no means of telling exactly what will happen, exactly what my end will be. But as I near the final point, the point I was tasked to do, the timelines, though always a never-ending spiral of possibilities, condense further and further, telling me the way to go. At first, when I had met you, I had only known what was about to happen, not how it would end."

As Dovian spoke, flickers of his life flashed across the projection. Aria intently watched, finally grasping the beauty of Ives and its people. As time sped by, it came to the point where Dovian first met Aria and Troy. Dovian halted the replay by holding up his palm.

"If you can stop time, control it like you do, why can't you go around and kill all of Sapphire's army?" Aria asked, amazed.

"There are specific rules a Sorcēarian must follow. Time disallows certain things. There are paradoxes, the possibility of creating wormholes. It's a delicate process. Euclid was a master of these things. It's how he was capable of doing all that he had done. He had found loopholes in the system, ways to create chaos without much repercussion involved. But, perhaps his repercussion was me. He got away with much, but in the end, his chaos always came to an abrupt end. At too great a cost, I realize."

Dovian grasped outward, pulling invisible strings that expanded a particular series of scenes. From the frames, Aria could see Gavin's death, replayed a many times over, slight differences each time. Sometimes he and Troy died. Sometimes she died along his side. Others, the whole team burned inside the helicopter. The scenes unfolded across their entire journey together. No matter what, Gavin always died.

"There are times where my mind reveals things to me, like a form of premonition. I have a fleeting moment to react, to choose the right path. So far, I had done all that I could to keep as many alive. Everything I've done was to ensure the best possible outcome—agreeing to come with you in the first place, sending Hector out to find King Petey, buying chocolates in Saray, to giving the sermon in the Underbelly. It goes as far as a swing of my staff, to one wrong step or word uttered from my mouth. I've told you; the things that work inside a Sorcēarian's mind are beyond what humans can comprehend. There's always a miniature universe of knowledge at work." He frowned at one scene in which he had narrowly missed saving Aria, the woman dying in his arms. "And it is indeed very tiresome."

"You see all this?" she asked, appalled.

"Every second of every day," he grumbled.

"How…do you filter through it all? How do you even know what's real?"

"There are plenty of ways of telling. Believe me when I say that it is as natural as breathing to us."

"Why am I not experiencing this?" she questioned.

Dovian hummed a laugh. "Because you are still a human. You may experience heightened senses and quicker reactions, but your mind isn't capable of something like this. If may just blow that pretty, little head of yours to bits."

Aria rolled her eyes.

His amused look faded as quickly as it came, however, as he saw the entire world break into pieces.

"So many possibilities, so many chances, so little time." His eyes rapidly darted back and forth as the images flooded at an impossible speed, the man tracking each one. "Here, so close, but everyone dies at the last second. Here, Euclid lives, but everything ends fifty years from now. Here, you all die before you even get to Ives. Here, I refuse to come with you. Here…it must have been a very bad day. I kill all of you and send the world to ashes, living amongst the burnt debris for a lonely eternity." He shuddered.

"But you said it narrows," Aria spoke again.

"It does. We're getting closer to where I need to be, closer to my purpose. I see everything now in nearly a straight line. The gates are closing in around me, and there are few choices left, few possibilities." The projection slowed down, reflecting on the night Aria had shared with Dovian. She awkwardly looked away, feeling the heat rise to her face. "Of all the possibilities…." He waited a moment. "When Sapphire ordered me to destroy you, I was at a loss. Every path led to me doing what I had done. There was no way around it, no way without destroying the entire world in the process. Yet, here you are. Of course, I had to shoot you. I had to kill you and Troy. There was no other way. But never once had it ever occurred to me that you were pregnant."

The scene unfolded of the time when Dovian firmly held Aria in her place, pressing the gun beneath her ribcage. He solemnly closed his eyes, inwardly cringing at the display. Watching the replay, Aria noticed this time a hint of sadness in Dovian's eyes; she saw the quiver in his lip as he tried to appear merciless. It soothed her somewhat. And Dovian had noticed once again the pain and traumatic mental distress he had placed upon her.

"That child being inside you was essential in not only your survival, but it was necessary for the whole of the earth. You would not be here; these militaries would not be here," he said, pointing to the vast abyss.

"But I still don't understand why you can't simply do it all yourself," Aria added.

"Because…for what purpose does humanity deserve to survive if they do not fight for themselves? The free path had already been given in the past, yet you all still forsake what was given. For what reason would I desire to save you all if you had not offered to die trying? It's much more complicated than it seems. And without you and Troy…there would be no survival. In any revelation where you two were not alive, I had failed. The darkness would come quickly without you two." Slowly turning to her, he further explained. "It is because of you, Aria, that humanity has lasted this long. You maintain hope when others do not."

"Hope?" Aria's brow wrinkled. "I understand the cliché of maintaining hope, but what does hope have to do with anything?" She looked at the projection, the images flickering once again to the war outside their time. It appeared futile. "Look at us, Dovian. We're dying out there. Despite all my hope, it's done nothing but lead us to failure. Me having hope has not helped us. In fact, it has led Sapphire to our doorstep and has allowed her to attack the other unprotected city-states. I have failed everyone. We are doomed."

"Aria…." Dovian's lips parted as he looked at the woman in wonder. "Hope is a thing that, despite all that moves against us, defies the physics of pain. It may hurt now. Yes, things may seem utterly doomed to failure. Life may seem like a dark hole caving in around us, but hope digs us out. Hope floods a light upon the darkness that is failure. Hope is the bandage to our pain. It holds us together, inspires us to keep moving when our feet feel stuck, motivates us in a way that doesn't make us dreadfully ask 'why me' but leads us to passionately question 'what can I do.' Failing is not what dooms us. Losing hope is."

He approached her and gently placed his hands on her shoulders. "And you've maintained hope this entire time. You've united the world with that stubbornness of yours. You've done more in the past few weeks than any leader I've ever known. You are the key to all of this because there is something inside of you that won't stop. You simply won't quit. You not only maintain hope, but you instill it in others. You've joined the nations, moved armies, and ignited a passion within the innocent that makes them cheer for you. So, despite feeling like you've failed, you've got to realize how much the hope of one person can spread across the world. There's a power within you Aria that you've always had. Don't ever forget that." There was something in his eyes that told Aria there was more to it. He forced a smile that was obviously not natural.

"What else aren't you telling me?"

"I need to keep you safe, Aria," he said, avoiding her question.

"Why am I so important? Just because I have hope? I don't believe that," she said, folding her arms. "I'm just some military grunt."

"You are with child; I must keep you out of harm's way."

"I'll be fine!" she argued.

"No. Sapphire cannot find out. If she does…." He looked to the timeline, pulling out a foggy vision. It revealed a multitude of horrors. Aria could be kept alive to birth a child, the process killing her. If by some incredibly rare chance she could handle birthing a Sorcēarian half-breed, the rest of Aria's days would be spent in a terrible and painful existence. Then, there was also the possibility that Sapphire would simply kill her outright, Aria's child being the only creation that could stand up against her future army of demon-inhabited hybrids. In a fleeting moment, Aria saw all of the possibilities. She saw herself dying. She saw herself birth a beautiful little boy with white hair and watched him grow to become a formidable opponent against Sapphire's future species. Alternately, she saw him used as a tool to benefit Sapphire. He sat upon a throne of bones, a matching crown atop his head made of human teeth. He could possibly be humanity's savior, or he could be their ultimate demise. Nowhere did she see Dovian. Would he be needed at that point?

Aria watched in horror, tears stinging her eyes. Dovian quickly closed the visions altogether.

"I know that look in your eyes, and believe me when I tell you that you do not want to take the chance," Dovian turned to her. "That child will most likely kill you. In fact, you are in danger every second it is in your womb."

"But there is a possibility," she whispered.

"There is a possibility, in the event that we fail today, that he could someday rise against her, but that all relies on your safety. That is why I cannot let you back out on that battlefield. You need to hide. If anything happens, you can try all that you can to give birth to him. I would only pray you live through it to raise him right. If Sapphire ever got her hands on him, she would have the perfect tool to destroy."

"She will have it either way…because of Ivory," she argued.

Dovian covered his face, swaying as he thought.

"Why don't I just sit here for nine months? I can just hang out here…and have a baby. I'll have you to heal me. We can wait until he grows up and then unleash him on the war out there," Aria offered if not a bit sarcastically.

He removed his hands from his face, giving her a curious look. "We would have no food."

"You can gather it for me. I'll just wait here," she looked at the planets.

"This will not solve anything. By the time that all happened, the war could be over. Time doesn't completely stop while we are outside the timeline," he explained.

"Why not go back in time?" she asked.

"Aria! Things do not work that way! Are you trying to drive me mad? You would create the worst kind of paradox, and your entire world would fold in on itself. Your soul would bend in two, and your very being would create the demise of the whole universe. Is that reason enough?" He looked flabbergasted by her questions.

"Good reason not to go back…" she quickly sputtered.

"You think I wouldn't try it? To save my people?" he questioned.

Growling in frustration, she threw her arms into the air. "So what do we do?!"

Turning, Dovian grabbed her hands. "I am going back out there to fight before Sapphire detects that the both of us are missing and she comes here and finds out everything. You are going someplace safe to hide. As much as I hate the idea, if something does happen, and we fail today, we need to have the chance that you will healthily have that boy and give humanity one last chance."

"I'm not hiding! I can't do that! Troy's out there! My team is out there!" she quarreled.

Dovian rolled his eyes. "Curse the genes that make you as stubborn as you are!"

"If it weren't for my genes, I wouldn't be here!" she sassed.

"We haven't the time for this, Aria." Dovian wrapped his arms around her suddenly. "You listen to me, woman. Listen to me well. All the things I am about to do are for you, our child, and for the human race. Any move you make can jeopardize the entire thing. Do as I say, and all will go as I plan." His mouth was near her ear. "Just remember that when you wake up."

"Wake up?" Aria's face wrinkled with confusion.

She was answered by a sharp pain as Dovian whipped the side edge of his palm against her neck. A quick yelp sounded, and the woman collapsed into the Sorcēarian's arms. He held her tightly, staring at the brilliant sun. Deciding not to waste anymore time, he spun the dial on his tuner, abruptly reappearing inside Aria's bedroom in her apartment. Carefully, he placed the woman on her bed. He watched her for a moment and then softly put his palm on her stomach, feeling the gentle tingle of life energy contained inside her. With sad eyes, he smiled and then swallowed hard.

"Forgive me, Aria. I may have failed in all aspects of my life, but I will not fail at this. No matter the cost," he whispered.

An obnoxious boom interrupted the silence. Dovian set his crystalline eyes upon the horizon, feeling the floor beneath him shudder and quake. A riotous groan echoed throughout the city, sending a wave of fear over the Sorcēarian. One of the pillars holding the city had been hit. Grabbing his tuner, he disappeared again, finding his way to the mines beneath the city.

Ah, how smart the humans were. He could see a team of soldiers diligently working at annihilating the beasts that were funneling in through the portal. One person in particular caught his eye—Aren, the pilot. The young man was focusing his attention on the cannon at the face of the drill he was seated upon. He shivered, looking back toward where the Sorcēarian stood. As the city continued to groan, all eyes fell upon the structure overhead.

"Dovian!" Aren cried out. He leaped from the vehicle and made a mad dash toward the silver-haired man. "The clinic! Troy's in the clinic! Help! Cover it!"

Aren surprisingly seemed trusting of the Sorcēarian despite all that had happened. Dovian tore his attention to the building the pilot was waving his finger toward. From the window, Dovian saw Troy's setup. He was barely clinging to life, which seemed odd, but then Dovian was fully aware of the situation as he noticed Troy's consciousness was missing.

"What trouble have you gotten yourselves into this time?" Dovian muttered, waving his arms in the air. A bulbous barrier of electric-blue ignited around the clinic.

"He's inside a Roman soldier. We've traded frequencies on that portal. He's supposed to be in Sapphire's lines at the moment," Aren roughly explained.

Dovian nodded, gathering all he needed from Aren's words and discombobulated thoughts. The corner of his lip turned upward.

"So…he's the Trojan horse, eh?" The Sorcēarian smirked. It seemed Troy had taken Dovian's story about the Trojan horse a bit too seriously.

Aren gaped upwards at the blue light that engulfed the clinic. Another groan sounded, and a second pillar shattered beneath the added weight.

"We've got to get out of here!" Aren shouted.

Dovian wasted no time, raising his staff in the air. With eyes snapping with electricity, Dovian sent another rush of power up toward the support beams, sputtering a few incantations. The light firmly locked into the cracks and gaps of the pillars, holding them in place.

"I can give some power, but you will need to find a better way to hold this structure. My energy will not last forever," Dovian coolly stated.

Aren was already on his way to one of the maintenance vehicles, shouting orders to Soldiers of God, the brutish men responding with valor and enthusiasm. In a matter of seconds, Aren had a team working to strengthen the structure.

"Seems he's a natural leader," Dovian mumbled.

A sudden chill washed over him as he felt a portal momentarily open behind him. With his hands still raised, power flowing from his staff, Dovian looked over his shoulder and grimaced. He had no time to respond as a palm ruthlessly slapped him against his face.

"You asshole!" Aria screeched, slapping him repeatedly.

"Ow! Stop! I'm trying to save your people!" Dovian groaned, flinching under Aria's tiny fists.

Another projectile hit beneath the city, narrowly missing another pillar. Aria abruptly halted her physical assault, gaping at the damage that had been inflicted.

"We need to get up top!" she shouted.

"How did you even get here?" He looked at her in amazement.

Aria shoved a frequency tuner in the man's face. "Lucky for me, Camery had a few prototypes lying around in his lab!"

Dovian eyed the piece of tech in her hand, and then stared at the woman with tired eyes. "You could've been shredded to pieces using that."

Aria shrugged. "Better than staying locked up in my room awaiting the destruction of my city!" she growled. Her eyes were blazing with anger, making her all the more curious to watch.

"Come, we mustn't waste anymore time," Dovian sighed, giving up all effort to argue with the woman. *"Aren..."* he mentally called to the pilot.

"Go! Do what you can to stop those missiles!" Aren replied.

Dovian gave one more burst of energy, directing it toward the pillars and the clinic housing Troy's body.

"Where's Troy?" Aria finally asked.

"Don't worry about him right now. We've got more important matters to deal with," Dovian quickly stated, grabbing Aria's hand. A portal swallowed the two whole, leaving Aren and the Soldiers of God to handle the support beams.

"Everything alright?!" Spoofy mentally shouted, her voice bouncing in Aren's brain amongst the sound of gunshots.

"YEAH! Just dandy!" Aren waved at her, operating some heavy machinery that had two massive arms. As he pulled the stick on the control panel, the arms swooped up, clamping against one of the broken pillars. Two other vehicles joined in, their arms lifting for support. *"Where's Troy?"*

"Not back yet." She seemed irritated.

From one of the drilled caves off to the right of the pilot, there came a rambunctious noise. Aren's eyes fell upon a flurrying group of biomechanical androids. He gasped, signaling to one of the Soldiers of God.

"We're going to need him soon. Sapphire's sending reinforcements! We have to get those portals closed!" Aren reported to Spoofy.

Spoofy spun on her heel, feeding Aren a panicked expression. The pilot hopped out of the vehicle and paused, every hair on his body standing on end as he came face-to-face with a very familiar, yet horrifying, sight. He gave a sharp intake of air, his eyes bulging. Blocking his path to the drill was a tall, slender woman. Blonde curls framed her face. Blue eyes watched the pilot, void of any emotion. Aren shuddered, slamming his back into the big machine behind him as he recoiled.

"Fi...Fiona?" his voice cracked.

Aren tore his eyes away from the woman's face for only a millisecond, gathering sight of a handful of familiar faces from the other androids surrounding them. They were the citizens of the Underbelly. Not only had Walten killed them all, but he had used their bodies to be converted into hosts for Sapphire's demons.

The young woman clamped a cold hand around Aren's neck, squeezing.

"No!" he choked. "Fi-on-a!"

Aren palmed at the woman's hand, trying to pry her fingers away from his throat. Tears stung his eyes as he helplessly watched his beloved girlfriend slowly strangle him. All around, war broke out. The androids were killing the soldiers with far too much ease. Death was everywhere. Still, Aren couldn't pull his gaze away from the beautiful eyes of Fiona. If ever he were to die, he never thought it would be by her hands–her beautiful, soft, tiny hands. The same hands that were once used to attack him with tickles had become a lethal weapon. Whipping back her other hand, Fiona's arm extended outward into a fan of sharp blades. She pointed the strange weapon at Aren's head and readied to push it deep into his skull.

"What have they done to you?" Aren whimpered.

The young pilot closed his eyes in anticipation of his death, when a loud pop sounded. A miniature missile collided against Fiona's body, sending her soaring backward. Aren dropped to the floor. Franklin floated by, one of his arm clamps smoking hot.

"Not Fiona," Franklin chimed.

"Yes, I know. Good Franklin," Aren coughed.

Noticing a rifle on the ground that belonged to one of the elite soldiers, Aren snatched it up. He aimed at Fiona's expressionless face as she fidgeted to sit up. A large hole was burrowed deep inside her chest, making Aren's heart ache. He fired once directly at her head as he tightly closed his eyes. A single tear fell down his cheek, and Aren lowered his head. Franklin gave a reading of the corpse.

"Terminated," Franklin said with a proud tone.

Aren kept his eyes fixated on the ground. Blood and hydraulic fluid swirled around the tiny pebbles, mixing into a dark mud.

"Thanks…Franklin," he whispered dully.

The young pilot felt a bit sick, his mind spinning with a type of numbness that he hadn't known in many years. Somehow, this was worse than finding out Fiona had been killed, worse than seeing her death on the security feed. Despite being a fleeting moment of his entire life, pulling the trigger was the single hardest thing he had ever done. Yet…it was still easy to do. Rational senses told him he had to. But the sinking feeling in his belly, the shaking of his hands, the sour taste in the back of his throat, and the weakness in his knees made Aren want to collapse and cry like he was a small child once again. Only for a second could he reflect on his current feelings.

Multiple thunderous crashes sounded one after another in a series. It started outside the city but seemed far away. Another quickly followed that came from the portal Troy had passed through earlier, and a third echoed above as the city began to sink slowly toward the mines.

"Evacuate!" Aren shouted.

A thick cloud of murky dust flooded downwards, coating and threatening to snuff them all before the quaking metropolis became the lid to their coffin.

"Damn it, Feyette! What the hell do you think you're doing?" Kovacevic swore up and down that the other man had officially lost his mind.

General Feyette crouched low to the ground, his hand clutching his opposite arm. The joint in his armor had cracked, blood generously seeping from the shoulder area. Feyette steadied his breaths, eyeing the medic symbol on his forearm. He moved quickly, tapping the button. A low moan sounded from him, and he grabbed his injured arm once again.

"Saving you from being torn to bits." Feyette struggled with his words.

Kovacevic and he had been surrounded by Brutes and forced into the battle. They seemed to be holding off pretty well until a rogue shockwave was sent their way. Feyette instinctively reacted, and he shoved Kovacevic out of the way, his left shoulder taking the brunt of the force. Even his shield couldn't withstand a direct hit, and his arm was nearly severed.

Kovacevic stood over the man, cursing as he shot the enemies slowly surrounding them. "Don't lose an arm on the account of me. I ain't worth an arm."

Feyette groaned, his hand reaching for his chest. The damage seemed to be worse than he initially thought. Pulling up his DNAIS, Feyette found that his ribs on the left side had shattered along with his entire arm. His heartbeat was erratic; a shard of his sternum had cracked, and his lungs were trying to sink against his heart. The armor was holding him together. He gently pressed against the med symbol again, gratefully accepting a double-dose of morphine.

"Nothing to worry about. I'll simply get it replaced with an artificial…just like my leg." He gave a deep chuckle.

Kovacevic suspiciously eyed the other man. He barely caught sight of Feyette's DNAIS before he stubbornly stashed it away. It was enough to realize the severity of the situation. Feyette wasn't going to last long if he didn't seek immediate medical attention.

"Where's the President?" Feyette groaned, trying not to make pained noises as he rose to his feet.

Kovacevic spared a look behind him. "Shit. They're back by the barricades. Looks like it won't be long before they're overrun as well."

Just as he spoke, the barrier President James Clarke was hiding behind was shattered by a Brute wave.

"Son-of-a-bitch," Kovacevic spat angrily.

Stepping to the side and activating a temporary flare screen that blinded the enemy, Kovacevic provided cover fire, allowing Grayson to regroup with Clarke. The silent bodyguard eagerly guided James to safety. Despite Kovacevic's efforts, the monsters kept crawling toward James and Grayson.

"Save your ammo," Feyette said.

Kovacevic letup, but he kept firing when absolutely necessary. He couldn't see Feyette's face behind his helmet, and that fact made him nervous. The general of Bio-Tech marched forward, his good hand resting on his utility pack around his waist. His fingers dipped into the top of the pouch that housed an assortment of grenades.

"Now, don't do anything foolish…" Kovacevic warned.

Feyette didn't look back at the man. "I devoted my life to the protection of the Walten family. This war is just as much my fault as it was his. I owe the world better."

Kovacevic noticed Feyette's staggering steps and the dark blood trail he left in his wake. The man wasn't going to last much longer.

"Once Walten was gone, my duties transferred to the protection of the President. At this rate, he won't be lasting much longer, either." Feyette pushed aimlessly toward the gang of monsters that were slowly overpowering Grayson. One leaped atop the bodyguard, snarling, biting, and scratching. This sent Feyette into a mad state.

"HEY!" Feyette shouted in his baritone voice. With one fluid tug, he removed his helmet and threw it to the group. All the attention immediately moved to the crazed man. "You want some? You want a taste?!" Cupping his hand, he gathered a stream of blood and threw it at the beasts.

Kovacevic watched in amazement; his unlit stogie clung to his lip. "Holy Hell…" he grumbled, trying his best to provide cover fire. "You damned idiot!"

A flicker of red and electric-blue caught Kovacevic's interest. It was Dovian and Aria, exactly who he needed.

Waving a hand, he mentally shouted, *"Aria! Get your asses over here real quick! Feyette's about to do something stupid! He needs some of that magic voodoo!"*

Aria twirled, her eyes gathering in the tragic scene. Though she was gone only minutes, everything had gotten out of control. There was no order; it was nothing but chaos. Monsters were bleeding into their lines. They were tearing men apart, blasting them with shockwaves, melting them with fire. One poor man was stabbed by the barb of a Stilt-Man. It didn't take long before the soldier's flesh began burning, and he was melting to the ground. Aria cringed at the overwhelming sight.

"AHHHH!" Feyette screamed. All attention was on him.

He pulled at something on his belt and then jerked his arm away from his midsection and dropped to his knees, allowing the beasts to swarm him. Grayson caught on quick, covering James Clarke with his body. After a second, a massive explosion took place, blowing Feyette and all the creatures around him into nothing put particles.

Kovacevic gaped at the scene, his mouth wide open. His stogie dangled from his lower lip and then dropped. Aria ran past him, sliding toward the blast scene. She instantly tore her gaze away, slowing to an uneasy trot.

"Damned…idiot," Kovacevic murmured. He rubbed his brow, slowly letting out his breath.

As Aria neared James and Grayson, a projectile sped directly over her head. She shouted and dropped to the ground just as it ignited around her, shrapnel blasting in all directions. Lifting her head, she found Dovian's familiar force field around her. Looking at him, she noticed his frown. Sapphire had undoubtedly caught sight of this. Aria pushed to her feet, and Dovian expelled the bubble around her.

"This is why I wanted you to stay in a safe place!" he barked.

She opened her mouth to speak but paused once she heard Clarke call out.

"Grayson?" The President's voice was muffled.

Covering James Clarke was Grayson's body. Aria couldn't help but gasp. Grayson's form was full of sharp spikes of metal. Pieces of all kinds of shapes and sizes lined his spine, one shard being nearly half a meter long.

"James?!" Aria called out, running toward the two.

"Are you alright, sir?" Grayson's dull voice rumbled.

Aria knelt and placed a gentle hand on the bodyguard's shoulder. "Grayson?" she asked in amazement. "You...how are you alive?"

As Grayson pushed away from Clarke with ease, Aria cringed yet again. A portion of the bodyguard's face on the right side had been sliced off, his sunglasses cut in half. Grayson noticed, and his mouth set in a tight line. Gingerly gripping the shades, he dropped them carelessly to the ground before moving his gaze to James. Grayson's eyes were not normal. His pupils dilated and constricted at random intervals. They were a dark brown with a spiral of silver near the center.

"Sir? Are you alright?" he asked again, reaching out to James. As he spoke, metal moved from where his skin had been.

"Grayson...you...you are...." Aria couldn't help but stare.

James took Grayson's offered hand, groaning as he moved to his feet. "He's a biomechanical android."

Aria was stunned. Never would she have believed Grayson was an android. Troy and Gavin, on the other hand, had predicted it more than once before. Nevertheless, she still bet those two men would have been just as surprised as she was.

"Incoming." Grayson pointed to the sky, shoving James behind a destroyed vehicle.

Aria turned, watching as another missile passed directly over their heads, smashing into another pillar beneath the city.

"Who keeps shooting those things?!" Aria shouted.

Her vision pushed forward, detecting the trajectory and wind speed, her brain calculating where the missile had been fired. Her optical camera zoomed in, highlighting the dark-haired woman who had previously been riding the Colossus when Dovian first appeared on the battlefield.

"Lilith," Dovian growled through his teeth.

"Another one of your girlfriends?" Aria snidely asked.

"She'd be so lucky," he grunted.

The woman started at a saunter, her hips swaying back and forth in a ridiculous way. She spread out her arms as another missile prepared to fire from her chest. Aria readied herself but was halted by Grayson's hand on her shoulder.

"Protect Mr. Clarke," Grayson said in a lethal tone.

Before Aria could protest, the man tore off, running at a speed most unnatural.

"Shit!" Aria peered all around. The battle was unmanageable.

Her senses began to overload–detecting the other military leaders caught in the midst of violent battle, highlighting over the frightened thoughts and screams from the surrounding soldiers, counting the losses to the human army and the gain to Sapphire's. The child's army was only growing larger and larger, the thought causing Aria's chest to ache as each soldier they lost was replenished as a number in Sapphire's demonic fleet. The woman's balance failed her only for a second, and she nearly dropped to her knees. Feyette was dead; Kovacevic was barely handling himself, blood seeping over one of his eyes. General Yoshitaka had lost half of his men, and he was currently avoiding a Spewer. Her eyes scanned over the pandemonium, her despair growing by the second as she physically felt the turmoil of the battlefield.

Hattori of the Iga clan was going head-to-head against an android. His right arm whipped, a chain spiraling from his elbow joint. His fingers dislodged into large blades, and he continued swinging, swiping for the android's head while taking out monsters at the same time. The enemy android raised its arm, catching Hattori's chain-whip. With one vicious tug, the machine ripped off the ninja's arm. Hattori growled in response behind his mask and continued his fight, using his left arm to wield an electric blade.

A flash of yellow caught Aria's eye. General Jiao of the Dilong monastery was having difficulty against a particularly feisty Brawler. They tussled about for a while before the creature dislodged its jaw and ferociously latched onto the woman's shoulder, crunching her armor and embedding its teeth deep into her body. She gave a cry and continued with her fight, trying to pry off the wriggling beast that was gnawing at her flesh.

A horrendous rumble alerted Aria of the city that was falling in slow motion to her senses, threatening to cave-in on the mines. Her team and Troy were down there. They would be dead any second. James Clarke was injured, blood covering his chest. The poor man finally appeared his age–worn and weary. Despite his prestige accomplishments and experience in war, the man was past his prime.

There was a noise, alerting Aria back toward the battle of the woman named Lilith and Grayson. They were fighting one-on-one, tugging and pulling, throwing and punching. Grayson had appeared to have the upper hand when Lilith suddenly impaled his midsection with one of her arms and fired a cannon-like shot directly through him, his insides blasting in a thousand metallic pieces over the battlefield. With one careless swoop, she lifted him and threw his body over the distance to Aria's feet. Aria jumped to the side, narrowly avoiding being smashed beneath Grayson's weight.

"Grayson!" she screamed.

James scooted across the desert floor toward the bodyguard, reaching out to him. "Grayson…" he whispered sadly.

"Forgive me, sir. I was not…not good enough," Grayson muttered, his voice crackling. His body was not moving, his fingers twitching and giving a strange buzz.

James shook his head. "You've done far more than enough."

Grayson's body quaked, black fluid leaking from him. His eyes twitched, trying to register James' face. "I cannot see you, sir."

James struggled, and his expression twisted. He tightly grabbed a hold of Grayson's shoulder. "That's quite alright, Grayson. You just need some sleep. It's been far too long. You deserve your peace."

Grayson's mouth, for the first time Aria had seen, tilted upwards into a gentle smile. "Oh, sir. I *can* see…it's…just…too bright." The man's voice cutoff, his last word dipping an octave as a mechanical sputter jolted his body one final time.

James was silent, his fingers digging tightly into Grayson's arm. "I damn myself for allowing you to die twice, Grayson," his broken voice quivered.

Aria reached out to touch James, to console him in whatever way she could, but Lilith did not wait. The female android fired once more in Aria's direction. Dovian held up a palm, protecting the humans around him. The missiles missed their intended target, blasting against the shield instead. Dovian's glare locked with Lilith's.

"Seems we have a traitor in our midst. I'm not surprised," Lilith's silky voice rang out.

"Just leave them be, Lilith. You have plenty of other humans to pick-off," Dovian snarled.

Lilith ran her hand through her hair. "I have specific orders to annihilate these pests. I won't let anyone stand in my way, especially a failure such as you."

Dovian stepped forward but was halted as something landed directly in front of him, blocking his path to Lilith. Mechanized wings were spread wide, spanning a few meters across. The burning of thrusters crunched loudly. Giving a sudden flap, the wings folded downward. It was Ivory. She held out a hand to halt the advancing Lilith. Simultaneously, she looked back toward Dovian with shimmering cerulean eyes.

"You let me handle this one. I'm tired of sitting back and watching," the tone of I'Lanthe's voice sounded from Ivory's vocals.

Dovian meant to protest, but his words were interrupted by a sudden siren of noise that shrieked across the land.

On the opposite side of the battlefield, the Colossus and FIFI were coming to an end of their battle. FIFI sidestepped, avoiding the Colossus' fist, and countered with a harsh punch to the monster's face. Grabbing the demon's jaw, FIFI pulled down, dislocating it. The Colossus shrieked, and the giant mech reached inside its mouth. Grabbing the back of the beast's neck, FIFI crammed its entire forearm down the creature's throat. Giving a sharp tug, the mech removed a pulsating yellowish-orange sack. Was it a stomach? A heart? Aria wasn't sure, but she gaped at the nightmarish scene in awe. After giving the sack an intense onceover, FIFI twisted to the side and threw the fiery organ directly at Sapphire's tower. The bag burst, annihilating the center of the child's perch, magma rain falling down toward the Roman forces. Aria's vision zoomed in; her heart raced for the possibility that Troy was down there. After a moment, a blue blip temporarily highlighted near the base of Sapphire's throne, but it only lasted a millisecond. The woman sighed, hoping her partner had accomplished what he had planned and was nowhere near the series of explosions that were beginning to take place down there.

An angry scream sounded from Lilith, gathering Aria's attention once again.

"What's wrong Lilith? Things not going as planned?" Ivory smugly asked.

"Maybe not according to Sapphire's plans, but once I'm through with you, I will be satisfied!" Lilith sneered.

Another deep rumble erupted from Sapphire's direction. Lilith and Ivory paid no mind to the disastrous noise. Instead, they took off, each flying into the air.

So much. There was so much going on. Aria had no idea what to do, and she momentarily wished she was in bed sleeping. She felt utterly useless on this battlefield. That is until Dovian slammed his staff into her palm.

"Get James away from this battle. Use the staff to hold up the city. It will drain your energy fast so I will make quick work of everything," he forced the words out quickly. Looking back to where Sapphire was located, Dovian shuddered. "Aria. Sapphire has seen my transgressions. It will not be long before she joins in the fight. I must put an end to all this madness before she kills everyone."

Fire surrounded the child, the flames tickling the edges of her white dress, scorching the lace. The child watched Dovian with large dark eyes. Slowly, the tower folded in on itself, the legs snapping and breaking, the massive throne falling to pieces and smashing the robotic fleet that seemed to be blowing apart one after another down the line. The swirling portal behind the girl expanded outward, and Dovian's mind revealed the same vision he had seen the previous day of Ives being hit by a weapon of nuclear proportions.

Fire consumed the land in a shuddering violent blast. Clouds of black and orange shot toward the sky and plumed outward as it hit the stratosphere, giving it a mushroom shape. The dry and cracked earth momentarily dipped lower before exploding upward in splintered shards. The radius spread for many kilometers, destroying everything in its path.

Dovian held his head, praying that Hector and Petey were safe and far away from the destruction. He only allowed his thoughts to travel to Ives for a second before he was pulled back to reality, watching the inferno eat the entire horizon. The portal extended, letting out haunting sounds that hummed and vibrated the air. With a loud whoosh, the anomaly zipped backward and imploded in on itself. What followed next was a series of portals closing all over the world. Dovian could feel the relief of the planet as the fight was severed and Sapphire was no longer able to feed monsters to any location. He caught Aria's hopeful stare. Now was not the time to celebrate. In fact, Dovian felt the worst was yet to come as he looked upward at the child that remained levitating in the air, the gaping holes in her face watching him in return. It sent a horrible chill throughout his body.

"Dovian!" Aria's voice tugged his awareness back to her.

The woman was standing several meters back, James staggering beside her. She pointed abruptly to the sky to where Ivory and Lilith had taken their battle. The two biomechanical androids were nearly a kilometer away. Dovian's optical camera flickered to life, pulling in the sight in better detail. What he saw made his face flush.

Ivory and Lilith spiraled around each other. Ivory's wings flapped, allowing her to move throughout the air with grace. Lilith's thrusters burst from her feet, giving her force and speed, but not allowing her much control.

Lilith continued an assault of gunfire and missiles, trying to knock Ivory back. After several volleys, Ivory latched onto the woman.

"Stop your efforts now, Lilith. You will not win," Ivory calmly stated.

Lilith gave Ivory a wild look, her dark hair twisting around her face and neck. "Oh, I will win! There's nothing you can do to stop me!"

Lilith opened her mouth, spitting a spray of bullets in Ivory's face. The blonde woman withdrew, shielding herself. Lilith cackled as her chest opened up, revealing a massive bomb hidden inside. Ivory's calm resolve was now broken. It was a reactor core, rigged up to be used as a weapon.

"Lilith!" Ivory cried out.

"You can't stop me! Even if I have to crash my body into the city!" The terrible woman sped off, her thrusters pushing her further and further away from Ivory.

Without hesitation, Ivory aimed her hand toward Lilith as it cracked and broke apart. The appendage snapped and reformed together into an Amasser Particle Beam, giving a mechanical whine.

"Locked on," an automatic reply sounded from inside Ivory, and she released her power into one straight line.

Lilith looked over her shoulder and gave a sly grin, spinning to the side as she released all of her remaining weaponry. Ivory aimed at the other woman's body, pulling the beam with her. The sound was atrocious, the blast crystallizing the surrounding earth and whatever else it hit in the process. After roughly ten seconds, Ivory's weapon sputtered off. She frowned, furiously shaking it.

"Is that all you got?" Lilith taunted. Her feet planted firmly against the crystalline bridge that formed from the rocks and debris that had shot upward in response to Ivory's weaponry.

Ivory smiled in return, causing Lilith to stir uncomfortably. Finally, the dark-haired android noticed the glass encasing the pillars supporting Fountains. Ivory had soundly secured the structure. Lilith's eyes narrowed to slits, and her hands balled into tight fists. The evil woman wanted to scream, wanted to throw a fit. She wanted singlehandedly to annihilate each and every human being on the face of the planet. But first and foremost, she wanted to murder Ivory.

The blonde's smile faded, however, as she gathered her reading. She had never fired her weapon twice before, and her system was already alerting her to an overload. It was mandatory that she waited for the beam to cool. Lilith must've known as her smile widened once again.

Ivory shot a quick beam toward Lilith, causing the woman to flinch and

A.R.CREBS

move upward. Despite it being a momentary blast, the heat created fractures along Ivory's right side. She didn't care, however, and sped forward, colliding with Lilith's body.

"You are nothing more than a fool!" Lilith shouted in Ivory's face.

"No. You are the fool!" Ivory retorted, latching onto the nuclear core in Lilith's middle.

Giving a shrill scream, Lilith tried to free herself from Ivory's hold. Pointing her fingers together, Ivory pushed with an immense force, impaling Lilith through her stomach. Ivory then locked her legs around the other woman's, forcing her to lean back.

"If I go out…you're going out with me!" Lilith screeched.

"That's the plan!"

Spreading her wings, Ivory forced her thrusters to move at maximum velocity. The two spiraled backward away from the city. Slowly, Ivory's Amasser Beam gained energy and cooled, but it wasn't enough to fire. She frowned.

"Let go!" Lilith screamed. She pushed against Ivory's face, squirmed, and shrieked.

Gradually, Lilith unlocked her upper body from Ivory's. Growling, the temptress twisted her hand backward, a broad blade pulling out from deep within her forearm. Ivory scowled. Just as Lilith hacked through Ivory's left arm that had impaled her, the blonde stopped all of her power to her wings. Lilith continued pushing away from Ivory at an incredible speed. Aiming, Ivory fired her beam once again.

The Amasser Particle Beam gave its shrill wind-up. However, this time it burst outwards into a thick band rather than a concentrated beam, most of the force exploding out the front tip of the weapon. Ivory continued firing until the blast finally made contact with Lilith's body, the dark-haired woman's screams hidden behind the monstrous roar of the lethal weapon. Ivory grit her teeth. Her entire right arm exploded, and she immediately cut the power. Falling, the blonde kept her eyes fixated on the sparkling glass-encased Lilith. The enemy android flipped a few times in the air, the sun glinting against her shiny surfaces, before bursting into an impressive blast that rushed against Ivory. The violent wave added to the force of Ivory's fall, her body crashing into the earth violently in a heavy heap. Dust and rock ruptured outward from the impact.

At the point of the detonation, Lilith was several kilometers away from the city. The shockwave traveled fast, though, shoving every combatant onto the ground. Once the terrible grind of the wave fell into silence, Dovian pushed to his feet, his wings unfolding from his back.

"Dovian! Wait!" Aria called out, but her words were upon deaf ears.

Leaping, Dovian's body burst forth, his form breaking the sound barrier. In a flash, he was at the crash site, dropping to his hands and knees beside the broken and battered Ivory.

"Ivory!" he hollered.

"Do...Dovian?" the sweet, melodious tone of Ivory's voice replied.

The Sorcēarian looked over her, wanting to hold her hand but found none. Both arms were completely destroyed. Instead, he placed his palm gently against her cheek.

"Oh, Ivory...look what you've done," he whispered softly. His eyes peered down at her with a sadness she had seen many times over in the past few weeks they had known each other.

"Did...did we get her?" she asked, her voice weak.

Dovian nodded slowly as his gaze scanned over her again. Black fluid pooled around her, the liquid seeping into the cracks in the earth.

"I can...I can heal you. Let me..." he hesitated, "let me...." His eyes were beginning to burn.

Ivory slowly shook her head. "It's okay, Dovian. I don't feel a thing. *We* don't feel anything."

"You saved the city," he mumbled. "You saved the humans."

"Hm..." she hummed. "Not yet. You still have to get Sapphire."

Dovian nodded apprehensively; his lips pulled tightly against his teeth.

"WARNING. SYSTEM OVERLOAD." A robotic voice echoed from deep inside Ivory.

"Ivory!" Dovian shouted, his hands glowing blue.

Nothing was working. He couldn't sense any living organs, no brainwaves, and no light. To him, she was already dead biologically. Only the machinery was keeping her alive.

"I'm sorry, Dovian. I wish...I could have been a better woman for you," Ivory sadly stated. "Like she was."

"You're lovely, Ivory. Lovely in every way," he quickly uttered, placing a palm on her cheek.

"Don't lie." The words were like the sound of the wind.

"I'm not lying!" He fervently shook his head. "You're lovely. Always have been."

"I wish I could touch you," she quietly stated.

Dovian leaned in closer, running his hand through her tangled curls.

"And I..." Ivory whispered, tears lining her eyes. "I wish I could have gone...."

Dovian sucked in air, blowing out slowly. The black fluid was soaking through his robes; he could feel it against his skin. "Gone?" he asked.

She fed him one of her lovely grins, her blue eyes shimmering in the sunlight. "Ice-skating...."

"WARNING. SYSTEM OVERLOAD. SYSTEM SHUT DOWN."

The inner voice droned, the gentle hum sinking lower and lower into an odd silence. Dovian cupped Ivory's face, his thumbs smearing the dark fluid splatters that dotted her cheeks. The glow of her eyes was gone. The brilliance that was once her smile was now only parted lips. Slowly, a tear dropped from the corner of one of her eyes, and Dovian's resolve finally broke.

"I...Ivory?" he harshly whispered, his expression twisting into a horrid look of pain.

The beautiful woman did not stir. She made no noise. There was no giggle, no confused questions, and no cheerful solutions to his suffering. All that was left was a shell, an empty shell that no longer housed the woman named Ivory nor the soul of I'Lanthe. What happened to her? Where was she? Where was either of the two?

"Ivory," he barely managed her name again.

Giving a low, drawn-out moan, Dovian curled around the woman, lifting her into his arms. He hugged her, swaying gently. Ice-skating. She just wanted to go ice-skating. That was all. Why couldn't he simply give her that? It was what the world was supposed to be–simplicities and joy. Not this. Not endless war and death. Dovian clenched his arms tightly around the woman; his cheek pressed against hers. An occasional groan popped past the man's lips until his body was trembling. Slowly lifting his head, Dovian let out a thunderous, guttural scream.

A portal opened beside him, and he did not stir. Aria emerged from it but remained still, her eyes locked on the corpse in Dovian's arms.

"You should not see this," he harshly hissed.

Aria didn't say a word but fell to her knees next to him. She removed her helmet and dropped it in the dust. Just like that? In a matter of minutes, Ivory's life was taken away. She covered her mouth, devastation slowly taking over. Dovian and she remained silent for a while. Neither moved nor spoke. Dovian held onto Ivory, his hand holding her head as he rocked her. Soon, his face fell into an empty expression. His eyes kept their light, but still seemed dead. Aria watched him carefully.

"Now what?" she asked with a scratchy voice. Her own eyes were bloodshot from the tears she was struggling to hold back.

Dovian slowly lowered Ivory to the ground. For a moment, his muscles twitched. His jaw jutted from side to side as he grinded his teeth together. His countenance chilled Aria to the bone. The Sorcēarian had had enough.

"I end this," he said. Dovian pushed to his feet.

"How?" she asked, rising with him. She eagerly held out his staff for him to take.

Dovian shoved the weapon back toward her. "For once, do as I say." Aria listened intently. "You will activate a shield that will protect you and everyone else on the battlefield. You will hold that shield for as long as you can."

"Won't you need your staff to fight Sapphire?" she asked.

"No," he numbly stated. Looking to the sun, he closed his eyes. "I can see the path narrowing. Everything is falling into place. There are few options left, and I know what I must do. I do not plan on fighting from a distance. If I need to, I will use my hands."

Dovian's wings fluttered open, the white color glittering with gold and silver light.

"Dovian," Aria took a couple steps toward him. Finally, he looked at her face. "Thank you. You know…for helping us." The woman looked at Ivory. Her gaze moved across the battlefield, her optic camera scanning for Troy's beacon. Looking to the city, realizing the amount of debris that had fallen into the mines, she still found no sign of her partner. She gave a quiet sob, fighting desperately to remain calm. The outcome was looking bleak.

Dovian merely gave her a quick nod. With a sinking feeling in his gut, he pulled the woman toward him, giving her a lazy hug.

"Do you think you can succeed?" she nervously asked, leaning against his chest.

Dovian's brow furrowed. "Of course."

"How can you be sure?"

He glared, not at her, but at the vision in his mind as the gates closed, locking his fate into place. Dovian gave a harsh sigh and lowered his head. Guiding Aria's chin upward, he pressed his lips firmly against hers. She gave a quiet squeak, surprised by his sudden actions. It was a simple kiss, quick and soft.

Looking at her with brilliant eyes set aflame, Dovian uttered the words in Legacy, "Æēçאüßē Є אµ tпē אræℓtгאför. Ŧпē çпöℓçē ℓß µℓhəē."

Aria replied with a weak smile, understanding him completely.

"Because I am the Arbitrator. The choice is mine."

Not saying anything else, Dovian turned away from her, his body bursting with light. As if made of fire, Dovian's robes took to a hue of gold and silver, his wings becoming four—a pair of white and a pair of obsidian. His unruly hair magnified in a halo, matching the pale lightning sizzling from his irises. He barely moved his body, and he shot away to where Sapphire was levitating and waiting.

WWW.ARCREBS.DEVIANTART.COM

"The Gates Are Closing"

CHAPTER 23

The child had been watching Dovian since the very beginning. She saw him disappear for only a short moment and saw him save Aria's life with his power. Sapphire was not surprised by any of this. In fact, she almost expected it. Still, the anger that burned within was becoming overwhelming. No matter about her throne being blown to bits, but Sapphire did notice the rogue Roman soldier that slipped through her portal and destroyed her entire Roman fleet. That robot had life contained inside, and it was not life that she had granted it. It had also gotten away, taking with it the Elixis Electro-Static Frequency Tuner and her nuclear weapon that was then used to destroy both her cave and the demonic forces based there. After that, the large gateway closed in on itself. On the opposite end of the battlefield–deep within the mines–she felt the doors close there as well. One by one Sapphire's routes were blocked. Not only that, but Lilith had failed. Her terrible ego caused Ivory's death, which had nearly ruined all of Sapphire's plans. At the moment, she wanted nothing more than to finish the game and blow the city to pieces. That was precisely what she was going to do.

As Dovian neared her at an impossible speed, Sapphire finally activated her system. With a hum, her thrusters guided her upward, metal wings sprouting from her back in long flapping blades. Her sight remained locked on the Sorcēarian. His hands were held out, whips of fire licking across her demonic forces, burning them to the ground. He spiraled, bursting forth with a deafening rumble. His flame turned blistering white, crawling up his arms, around his torso, covering his entire body. Sapphire, though tiny, held out her arms to embrace Dovian as he crashed into her. Her palms remained steadfastly against him, halting him.

"You think you've won, Dovian, but what will you do when I kill your precious humans? What will become of you once all the humans are gone?" Sapphire questioned in her child-like voice.

"You won't be killing anyone. You're too late. The pride inside of you has allowed you to waste all of your time," Dovian rumbled through his teeth. "Your portals are closed. There is no escape for you. You're locked on this plane."

Sapphire's face fell, her anger exuding from her, filling Dovian's lungs. He struggled with her, pushing her shoulders as she pressed against his.

"We can fight an eternal battle, Dovian. You will never defeat me."

"And you will never defeat me," he returned.

From far below, Sapphire saw a bulbous dome-shaped light emerge over the battlefield. Aria had Dovian's staff, blue light growing around every figure on the cracked dry land. Sapphire's eyes enlarged.

"My plans are not all ruined!" she ecstatically exclaimed. "The woman is with child!" Sapphire gave a shrill laugh, thrilled by this revelation. "Your child I presume?"

Dovian grimaced, his grip tightening. He gave no word.

"I will destroy the city and take the human woman as my slave! Her child will be mine!" Sapphire shouted, flying higher and higher, her chest opening to reveal her nuclear warhead.

"You won't be doing any of that," Dovian lethally stated.

"You can't stop me. No one can stop me! This world is mine!" Her tone dipped down into a menacing growl.

Dovian looked upward at the sun, sweat beading on his brow. "No. *I* can't."

Sapphire's face fell into a look of confusion.

A vibrant pulse of light spiraled from the white orb in the sky. It followed up with a few more flickers, the sun spraying waving beams. A moment later, a horrendous gasp sounded from the child.

"What is this?!" she screamed.

Suddenly, the whole world fell into silence as an invisible force smashed against the planet, creating an EMP disturbance so grand it wiped out every electronic device around the world. Each and every single one of Sapphire's androids fell to the ground and remained motionless. The demonic creatures were abruptly dropping with ease as their shields no longer protected them. Sapphire's numbers were dwindling fast. The child's body sputtered and gave a dull hum. She suddenly fell heavily against Dovian, no part of her moving.

"THIS ISN'T POSSIBLE!" the voice inside her screamed.

"All things are possible," Dovian reminded the girl. "And I am no longer hesitating."

Reaching for the bomb, Dovian activated it. It was better for her to detonate in the sky rather than on the ground, and her previous velocity was sending them faster toward the earth.

"YOU MAY HAVE ENDED THIS BODY, DOVIAN, BUT YOU WILL NOT SAVE THE HUMANS. EVEN WITH HER SHIELD, SHE IS NOT POWERFUL ENOUGH TO SAVE THE CITY. THE FORCE WILL ANNIHILATE HER AND EVERYONE. YOU WILL FAIL," Sapphire grimly stated.

Dovian gave the child a sorrowful look. "Then today...we both fail."

Closing his eyes, Dovian focused on all of his energy and pulled it to the surface. White light engulfed both him and Sapphire in spidery tendrils. As the radiance tightly stretched around them like a taut web, a black shadow moved out of Sapphire's body.

"WE MAY HAVE FAILED, BUT NOT TOGETHER. FAREWELL, SORCĒARIAN. I ADMIRE YOUR RESOLVE, NO MATTER HOW FOOLISH IT MAY SEEM," the shadow spoke, the words like clanging metal and music.

Dovian didn't care to chase after the dark mass, allowing it to extract from Sapphire's body. Dovian clenched his fist, power exploding outwards as he detonated the warhead. A brilliant flare expanded outward, stretching Dovian's protective orb to its limits. As soon as it warped as far as the expanse of the visible sky, the sphere sank inward and burst back out into a large ring of fire. Dovian's body launched from the light. His form along with the power of the blast shattered Aria's shield to pieces.

Dovian's wings were blazing, charring, and flickering to tiny black bits. He kept his eyes locked onto the gleaming sun overhead, feeling completely drained. Limply, he fell, his arms flowing in front of him. All he could hear was the wind in his ears, and he relished in the strange peacefulness only for a second before his body collided harshly with a pile of broken metal from a destroyed mech. He made only a quiet groan, his blood splattering from his torso as a giant spike cut through him. Dovian was pinned to the earth, his blood coating his robes. He felt entirely too heavy. The act of moving was impossible, and his breaths were quick and shallow. The white of the sun kept his attention.

"Dovian!" Aria's voice echoed from far away.

A black silhouette blocked the sunlight, and his heart ached with each loud cry that came from the woman peering down at him.

"Dovian!" she cried again.

She was on her knees, moving scraps of metal out of the way. From behind, the war raged on, monsters and humans fighting one another. Dovian did not respond to her. Instead, he continued to stare blankly into the blue sky.

Aria's hands lit up. She urgently touched the man's body and gave a ragged gasp as she detected that nearly every bone was shattered. It was a miracle he was even alive, or conscious by Dovian's standards.

"Dovian. Can you hear me?" she weakly asked, gently pressing her fingers against his chest.

Finally, his white eyes looked to her, his fire extinguished.

"Ar...ia," he croaked.

"Let me heal you," she whispered.

"N-no." He reached up with a shaking hand and dropped it atop hers. "You are too weak."

"I can at least help a little until you can fully heal yourself," she replied quickly, setting the staff next to him. Aria gave a troubled intake of breath, noticing the light in the orb of his weapon was also missing. She worriedly looked to the man. "Dovian...are you going to be okay?"

He was straining to breathe, trying to lift the corner of his mouth into a smile for her. "I'm...going to be just fine."

Aria reached for him, placing her hand on his forehead. "I don't believe you."

"Ah," he tried to laugh but groaned in pain instead. "Stubborn."

"Dovian!" she screamed, her hands flickering as she tried to mend his lungs.

He snatched her hand with a weak grasp, his eyes watching her. He looked distressed.

"No. You mustn't. This...it...has to be...this way. Please. I...I want it this way." His voice quivered as he talked. "I...I am *so* tired."

Aria's lower lip trembled. "What do you mean? You said you can't die! Are you dying?"

Taking in a slow, shaky breath, Dovian spoke, "I learned a thing or two...from my mother. The life-force...can do many things."

"You gave up your life-force? To stop Sapphire's attack?" Aria questioned.

Dovian gave a weak laugh. "It worked...didn't it?"

His face was colorless, and his body was turning cold. Aria's shoulders quaked as she barked a sob.

"Yeah, but was it worth it?" She palmed away her tears. Staring at her hand, she noticed the coat of blood on the side of her palm. "You're dying!"

Dovian gave a smile, his thumb running over the back of her hand. "Yes. You are alive, are you not?"

"You can't do this to me, Dovian! You can't…" she paused, noticing that he had a faraway look in his eyes. "What's next on the timeline? What do you see?" she frantically asked.

Dovian's attention was brought back to her. Like in a drunken state, he struggled to look at her face. "Hm…no. All…all I can see is…you." He tiredly placed his hand on her cheek.

Large tears fell from Aria's eyes.

"Aria…" he whispered. "You can't…you can't have the child. It will kill you."

"Don't tell me that. You know I won't give up." Her hands were shaking. The man was not moving. "Dovian!"

He stirred; his expression was empty, sight aimed at the skies. "My…only regret…is not being there," he took one last scratchy breath, "…for…you."

Immediately his hand dropped from her face, smacking against the metal beneath him. Aria gaped at him, wide-eyed. Eagerly, she placed her hands on his chest, feeling him. No life signs. No energy. No blood was pumping. No brainwaves.

"No," she meekly whimpered, shaking her head back and forth.

She had not noticed the crowd that had gathered around her–Kovacevic, James, a mixture of battered soldiers of varying nations, the other generals. Aren, saturated with a powdery dust and blood, pushed through the crowd. His mouth opened to speak, but upon seeing Aria, he stopped mid-step and made no sound. The rest of Team Phoenix emerged, covered in grime.

Aria gripped Dovian's robes, shaking him. "No!" she screamed. "NO! NO! NO! Don't you do this! Don't you do this to me!" Her eyes stung, her face bright red as she lost her composure. "Damnit! You planned this, didn't you?! You knew this would happen! You knew all this would happen! You're not dead! You can't die! You told me that! You said that over and over again! Why? Why would you lie to me?! DOVIAN!"

The Sorcēarian's body remained motionless with his pale eyes open. Aria abruptly halted. A drawn-out wail sounded from the woman as she looked the man up and down. It was a miserable sound.

"Ooooohhhh." She shakily drew breath. "Oh…no."

She curled over him, covering his torso as she sobbed quietly. Slowly, she ran her hand through his hair. Even the strange hint of light that once haloed around his head was missing. She couldn't believe it. She refused to believe it. It simply was not possible.

Aria's memories rushed into her all at once, as crisp and clear as the moment they occurred. She saw Dovian absorbing the light in his cathedral, the way he swung his blade in battle, his awkward posture while in her apartment, his youthful smile as they chatted alone, his brooding stories, his charming laugh as he held her in bed, and relived the feeling of his lips upon hers. It didn't help. It only made it all the harder to deal with as the man was no longer living. Aria's chest heaved as she choked on her sobs.

"Aria?" Spoofy finally called out. Her voice held a hint of urgency but was still apprehensive.

Aria flinched when she felt the other woman's hand on her back. Lifting her head, Aria looked at her friend.

"We need you," Spoofy whispered, pointing toward Team Phoenix.

Aria's eyes darted to the group, not caring that everyone had seen her momentary breakdown. Letting out another whimper, Aria stumbled to her feet. As if it were even feasible, things had just gotten worse. Held in Monkey's large arms was Troy's body. To her horror, Troy was unconscious. Kaino was holding the Roman soldier. It also was unmoving.

"Can you bring him back?" Aren asked. "He was fine, but then the EMP disturbance wiped out the bot. We were in the process of trying to transfer him back to his body when everything went offline."

Aria ran to Troy, her hands shakily covering his face. Monkey lowered him to the ground, and Aria went to work. She tried to pull up his DNAIS but realized it was offline as was her own.

'Troy?" she attempted to call mentally. She was met with a kind of silence inside her mind that she had not known since she was a child. Even the mental chips were incapable of functioning. Aria's body chilled. That meant Troy's artificial heart was most likely not working either.

"How long?!" she asked.

"Only a couple minutes," Aren said. "Somehow his heart's capacitors didn't fry. Most likely thanks to the static protection in his suit along with the barrier Dovian placed over the clinic. But his heart isn't self-sustaining yet. That damn blast from the sun knocked out all of our equipment, and then we lost all readings on his vitals. Can you keep his body alive? Can you help him?"

The rest of the team nervously watched.

Aria let out a growl of frustration, tears gathering at the corners of her eyes as she realized that Troy was probably dead as well. She fed electric currents into his chest, trying to kick on the device. She looked upward at the sun, hoping that it would keep its solar flares at bay.

"Come on!" she screamed. After a second shock, she felt a small bit of relief when she detected a pulse. Aria sent another jolt into his system, and the pacemaker kicked on. "I have a stable pulse…" she stammered. Placing her hand on his forehead, she concentrated. "But…but he's not waking up. He's…he's not in there." Any amount of hope she had quickly expired.

There were groans from her teammates.

"TROY!" Aria screamed in his face. "Wake up! Wake up!" She shook him violently. "Wake up! Goddamnit! Just wake up!" She hugged the man, burying her face into his neck.

Spoofy averted her eyes to the ground. She knew that Aria was never going to recover from this. She and Troy had been lifelong partners. They were basically one entity. Just as much as Troy couldn't ever function without Aria, she could never function without him.

Aria sat on her knees, embracing Troy. This was not happening. She refused to believe any of this was real. She could only wish that she were merely dreaming and was still unconscious in her bedroom where Dovian had tried to leave her. But the sounds of warfare were too real. She could hear the thunders and cracks of mortar and guns alike, could hear the screams of the injured. The memories she felt spiraling within her mind was suffocating as she relived her life from her parent's death up to this point in time. What was the point? What would she do now? So many people that were so close to her were now dead. How could she go on without them?

WAAAAAAAAAAAAAAMMMMMM!

An alarm sounded from up high. It was unlike anything Aria had ever heard. It was a foreboding, chilling noise—the sound of a thousand horns and creaking metal. It intermingled with chimes and dings. It silenced everything.

Aria raised her head, looking at the sky. A cold breeze rolled by, whipping her hair across her face. Had she finally lost her mind?

Pushing through the white puffy clouds was an unimaginable object. It was enormous, triangular in form, peaking at the top like a pyramid. As it shoved through the atmosphere, clouds and fire and smoke plumed around it while a portal of stars and nebulas swirled.

Another alarm blared followed by a second, and more ships pushed into the visual realm. The entire sky south of the City of Fountains was covered in nothing but silver and gold metals. Gems and jewels glittered in the sunlight.

From the center vessel, a sudden beam of light emanated. Shooting from it was a stream that streaked downward in the blink of an eye, crashing a few meters away near Dovian. From the glowing crater spiraled a golden flame. It churned into a vague humanoid form. Sparkling wings sprayed from behind the strange anomaly. Aria felt its eyes upon her.

Standing, the military woman slowly walked toward the energy of light.

"Aria?" it questioned in a deep voice, the sound oscillating.

"Y-Yes." She tried to appear stern, but her nerve was gone.

The being gave a short bow to her, its hand pressing against its chest. "A pleasure to meet you, my dear."

Aria cocked her head to the side, watching the flames of light curiously. "Who are you?" she asked, finding his term of endearment toward her oddly familiar.

Straightening its posture, the being lifted its chin in a regal manner. "You can call me Gaius."

"Gaius?" Aria exclaimed. "You...you mean you are the original Sorcēarian."

"That I am and Dovian's great-grandfather." After saying this, Gaius turned to look upon Dovian's body. "A tragedy in every way, yet the only way for things to end as they did."

A shriek sounded from the battlefield causing Gaius to huff in annoyance. Waving a hand through the air, a series of booms commenced, and golden specks flew from the airships, crashing like meteors into the earth. The lights streaked across the landscape, burning all the remaining demons to ash in an astoundingly effortless manner.

"You're saying that this all was meant to happen?" Aria asked.

Gaius held a hand out toward Dovian. "As complicated as it all seems, there was a reason behind all of this. Dovian followed each step precisely as was pre-ordained to him. Once he fulfilled his duties, Dovian was granted the gift he had wanted since the day he was born—death."

"Why give him such a terrible fate?" She glared at Gaius with vibrant green eyes.

Gaius was not insulted by her tone. "Oh, no. Don't misunderstand. Dovian volunteered for this."

Aria's mouth dropped. She remained silent for a moment. "He volunteered?"

"Unfortunately, the earthly plane diminishes the heavenly memories that a soul once had. Dovian was a high member of the warrior class of angels. At the time of the Second Fall, which I was responsible for, Dovian agreed to become the Arbitrator. His sacrifice was in losing his memories. Only the first generation of those who fell with me, the Elders, had kept our memories intact. My role was to guide him and ensure that he followed the path best suited for him and humanity. I kept many secrets from him, and it pained me to do so." Gaius explained.

"But he killed all of you," Aria whispered.

"As was the only solution to ensure the survival of humanity. Can you see the destruction and devastation created by the humans alone? It takes only one man to turn the world upside-down. Once birthed on this planet, the angels' genetic code became tainted by sin. Imagine a world with matching evils but in the form of Sorcēarians. Do you think humanity would have lasted long?" he questioned.

Aria had not wondered about that. She only knew of Euclid becoming evil. She did not think of the possibility of many more to follow in his footsteps.

"Dovian saw something that I had not. I was confident the angels would remain pure. Yet, I had underestimated the faults of the original Fallen. I had too much faith in giving my kind freewill. Even with our angelic powers, we were no better." Gaius turned suddenly, eyeing Troy's body. "And as I speak, *he* still continues to stir trouble."

Aria turned to look back at Troy. A commotion had started. Seeping from the cracks in the ground emerged a tall, thin shadow. The mass quivered and vibrated, darting back and forth before leaping into Troy's body. The gathered crowd quickly backed away.

"Troy!" Aria shouted.

"Don't get too close," Gaius calmly advised.

Aria didn't listen and ran directly toward Troy. The man's body jolted, his eyes popping open, overshadowing in an inky black. He glared at Aria, his mouth twisting into the worst scowl she had seen him make.

"I WILL DESTROY YOU, EVEN IF IT'S THE LAST THING I DO!" the dark voice that had once inhabited Sapphire erupted from Troy.

Aria slid to a halt just as the man's hand clasped around her throat. His menacing stare locked her in place, filling her with dread. Something gathered his attention, and his eyes fled to Gaius. He gave a cry of terror.

Gaius simply held up a hand. "Michael, if you will do me a favor...."

Another rambunctious noise came, and an immense figure of light materialized beside Aria and Troy. It was twice as tall as Gaius with flames made of silver. Whipping its arm outward, a lasso of light snapped around Troy's form.

"NO!" Troy screamed in the lethal tone.

Giving a tug, the entity named Michael ripped the darkness out of Troy. The soldier's body immediately went limp, and Aria caught him, kneeling. A horrible screech sounded from the shadow, and Michael held it firmly in place, containing it inside what seemed like an invisible cage.

"My, my...Lucifer, I thought you would have learned your lesson by now," Gaius mumbled. He looked carefully at the irate shadow. "Let me tell you that He's been watching your every move. Did you really think He would not have noticed? You certainly tried hard to get His attention. Did you mean for that?"

"THIS WORLD IS MINE!" the darkness shouted.

"Not any longer. You see, He has decided to bring you back home," Gaius explained.

The shadow halted its writhing and howling. Glaring at Gaius with piercing eyes, it arrogantly rumbled, "I'M GLAD HE FINALLY SEES THINGS MY WAY."

Gaius gave a hearty laugh, slapping his palm against the barrier around the evil being.

"Ah, yes. So does that mean you forgive Him?" Gaius asked.

"ME? BOW TO HIM AFTER ALL HE'S DONE TO ME?" the shadow snarled. "HE SHOULD BE BOWING TO ME!"

Gaius lowered his head, sighing impatiently. "There really is no hope for you." Clasping his hands together, Gaius looked confidently upon the captured blackness. "I'll tell you what. We're going to try something a bit different. Since you won't accept your prison here on Earth, where you've been tormenting and causing suffering to the human race...the kind you hate so much, you get a special prison in the heavens. You'll be locked up for the rest of eternity under severe guard. You'll hear nothing but that praises for Him from those that are granted in his house–the praises from those you loathe. You will have no sight but for the bright light that shines for Him. You'll have no speech either. How does that sound?"

This sent the blackness into another fit of rage.

"NO! I WANT SALVATION!"

Gaius chuckled, walking toward Aria and Troy. "You should have thought about that before you decided to fall."

As it pounded against the barrier, the entity screamed in pain. "NO! I'LL STAY HERE! LEAVE ME BE!"

"Michael, if you will be so kind. Please, take him away," Gaius called out, not bothering to look back.

Michael didn't need to be told twice. In an instant, he and the horrible darkness disappeared from sight, traversing back into the ships. The painful roar of anger quickly vanished with it.

Crouching beside Aria, Gaius stared intently at the man in her arms. "Let's get you patched up," Gaius gently stated, holding a hand against Troy's forehead.

Being so close, Aria could make out vague details of Gaius' face. His light eased the pain in her heart, and she nearly smiled. He looked like an older version of Dovian. His jaw had more of a square shape, but his eyes held a kindness that Aria had seen a time or two from the Sorcēarian she knew.

"Come on, now," Gaius mumbled, watching Troy attentively. He didn't speak to Aria and the others, but kept his concentration on the lifeless man. "Well…that's your decision. Yes. They are all waiting." Gaius eyed Team Phoenix. "Aria is waiting. You've got her very worried."

Aria eagerly gazed at Troy's face. Slowly, his olive eyes fluttered open. It took a moment to gather his bearings, and he locked onto her, recognizing her instantly. Aria's breaths quickened as she watched him in amazement. Troy gave his usual cockeyed grin.

"I was a robot…" he whispered.

A laugh slipped past Aria's lips, tears falling from her eyes. She pulled Troy into a tight hug, crying into his shoulder. Troy held her, looking sheepishly at the people around him. He froze when he saw Gaius. Then his eyes fled to the airships in the sky.

"Holy shit!" he tiredly garbled. Aria pulled away. "Freakin' aliens!"

Gaius laughed and rose to his feet. This brought the male soldier's attention back to the flaming form.

"Who is that? Dovian?" Troy questioned with a confused expression.

Gaius' faint smile faltered as he peered over at Dovian's dead body. He slowly moved toward it.

Aria grabbed Troy's hand. "No," she said in a hushed tone.

That's when Troy noticed Dovian's still form a few meters away. Giving a panicked groan, he struggled to get to his feet, but his body wouldn't move.

"What happened? What did I miss?" Troy asked a bit more seriously.

"I'll explain later," Aria whispered. Scanning his body with her enhanced senses, she gently patted his knee. "Sit here and rest a bit. Your body will be functional soon."

Troy dejectedly remained seated. Aren and the others gathered around him, all bursting with questions and retellings of the events he had missed. Aria folded her arms and made her way to where Gaius stood. He was silently staring at Dovian's corpse, the wind licking his form.

"I can see why he took a liking to you," Gaius murmured, his glowing eyes looking at the black-haired woman. "You are a bit like I'Lanthe in certain aspects. Very strong, yet full of emotion."

"What happened to her?" Aria asked.

"Currently she awaits in the heavens for him." Gaius chuckled. "That girl is always waiting! After her initial death, I'Lanthe's memories returned. She chose to wait in Hell until the moment came where she could be of use to Dovian once again. She knew of the plan, and she gave up salvation…all for Dovian."

"That's amazing," Aria whispered.

"Sadly, the vessel she occupied…Ivory, was it?" he pondered. Aria nodded. "Ivory's brain had been damaged. This created a type of split personalities. But know this. She was never once Ivory. All that you had known was I'Lanthe though a bit more of an innocent character when her memories were sealed away. During times of her remembrance, she could not speak of her reasons for being in Hell, for fear of ruining the grand design. Dovian had to decide. She could not interfere but merely guide."

"Would Dovian ever have chosen to join Sapphire's side?" Aria asked.

Gaius turned to her. "Depends. Sapphire had tempted him in the best way. It is only a mixed blessing that she…*he* did not realize that Ivory could not bear children."

"But…I was told that Ivory still had her reproductive system," Aria stated.

"Oh, yes. She did. Unfortunately, the woman was sterile. Funny…how things work like that. Sapphire's plan would never have come to fruition even if she had slain you all." He spoke plainly of the matter, much in the way Dovian had spoken.

Aria's head was spinning. "So many coincidences."

"But are they?" Gaius suddenly placed his hand on the woman's stomach, causing her to flinch.

Aria lowered her gaze.

"Ah, he is a strong one." A faint smile appeared once again on Gaius' face.

"I imagine he will be as stubborn as his father," Aria whispered sadly.

"And the one before his, and so on," Gaius chuckled. His laughter quickly faded, and an uncertain emotion flooded through him. "But I must take him."

Aria gasped, taking a step away. Did she hear him right?

"Do not fret. It is meant to be." Gaius held out his hand. "The portals have all been closed. Earth will be locked from the other realms and will no longer be able to merge. In order to make this happen, I must take anything and everything with me from the other realm. I must remove all evidence of the Sorcēarians and Ives. That includes your child."

Aria placed her hands on her stomach, looking down apprehensively.

"All things divine must be taken out of this world. Only then can you as humans make the correct choices to follow your paths. We cannot interfere. Evil cannot interfere. It will be up to you and your freewill. It is His will for it to be so. Don't worry; you will see your child some day. He will be safe with me." Gaius reassured her.

"I…no. I can't," she fearfully refused. She replayed the visions Dovian revealed to her. She could have a beautiful and powerful son. He would have his father's smile.

"It must be this way, or everything you and Dovian have fought for and lost will all be in vain. It will mean nothing," Gaius softly stated.

Aria timidly withdrew her hands, watching as Gaius moved forward. In a flash, he removed a swirling orb of light from her abdomen. Reaching out, Aria made an unsure squeak. She didn't expect it to be so quick and painless.

Gaius held up the illuminated ball. "See? All is well."

Aria lowered her hand and stared at the sphere in wonder. Contained within the small white orb was a sparkle of light. It flickered with brilliance, giving off a surreal sense of peace and joy. It nearly broke Aria's heart as she realized the tiny speck was what saved her and Troy's lives. And now that it was gone, she felt empty inside. She no longer felt the high of the Sorcēarian powers, and that was an incredibly lonely feeling.

"We all start out as a little flicker of light and *poof;* we become amazing things," Gaius cheerfully spoke. She noticed his eyes dart in Troy's direction. "I know it saddens you, but you will have your own family some day." Aria felt a blush spread over her face. "For now, let me borrow your son. I've got my own plans for him."

Bending over, Gaius snatched up Dovian's staff. It lit up radiantly as he placed the tiny orb inside, and then he tapped Dovian's foot with it. "Come now, lazy bones. You have plenty time to sleep."

As Gaius turned away, Dovian's body set aglow. Growing into a blinding flash, he shattered into golden dust, spiraling into the sphere on the staff. From the dust, an illusion formed. Aria could have sworn she saw Dovian's face.

"Wait!" she called out.

Gaius paused.

"Is…is he alright?" she asked.

Gaius looked to his left at what appeared to be nothing, giving a broad grin. Looking back at the woman, he scoffed. "Who? Dovian? Oh, yes. He is perfectly fine. Much better now." Gaius pointed the staff to the left. "Standing right beside me, in fact. Oh…you cannot see him." Gaius gestured with his hands. "He is currently outside time. I will have to guide him back to where he belongs."

Aria felt her tense body relax. In a way, Dovian was still alive. He was merely going back home where he belonged. It pained her, but it also eased her. He would be much happier from now on. After all this time, he deserved some peace.

"So long, Aria! I do look forward to our next visit! It will be here before you know it!" Gaius waved a hand as he walked away. He quickly looked to his left again, whispering, "What? Oh, I guess that did sound a bit ominous, didn't it?"

Aria gave a small laugh, watching as Gaius burst into a beam of light and returned to his ship. All was quiet in the sky for only a few more seconds, and then the alarming sounds came again. Each ship slowly sank backward into their colorful portals. Once completely vanished, and each portal had sealed shut, a beam of light–like a rainbow–spread over the entire sky, washing over the atmosphere multiple times before dissipating.

Aria stayed in her place, silently staring at the clouds. There was a stillness that made her believe that this was the last time she would ever see any signs of angels or demons. Breathing out her nose, she finally relaxed her tense muscles. The day's events had been overwhelming, and now she wasn't sure what to do with herself. All was calm. The desert was lacking any evidence of Sapphire's creatures but remained littered with shards of metal and destroyed androids. A soothing breeze flew from the south, and it felt cold against the sweat on her skin.

"Hey!" Troy called out.

Aria turned about-face, smiling at the weak man who remained seated upon the ground. As the beaten and battered military generals spoke to one another about the next step in revitalizing civilization, Team Phoenix directed their attention to Troy.

"You know what sounds good?" he asked, scratching his goatee. "A big, nasty, greasy cheeseburger from Chester's sounds good. You think he's open today?"

Aria laughed as she approached him. "He'd better be!" she replied. "You owe me a drink!"

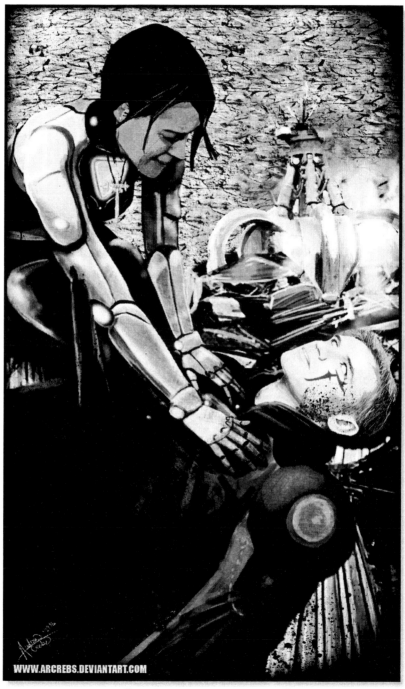

"I Want It This Way"

CHAPTER 24

All was quiet in the room that was lit aglow from a string of tiny white lights that dangled from the apartment windows. Outside in the night, the flicker of construction lights blinked in alternating beats with the traffic signals. The colors complimented the holiday decorations that caked the tiers and balconies of the surrounding corporations and apartment buildings, a sight that Troy had only now noticed. He set his olive gaze on the window, his chin resting in his hand as he lazily yawned. For once, the silent peace was welcomed by the man. The past week was spent doing interviews and going to global meetings pertaining to the restoration process of the city-states. He barely had a moment's peace and was enjoying the dull calm of Aria's home. As he stretched, his spine cracked and popped, and he gave a loud groan as he eyed the digital clock on the upper corner of the kitchen window.

"Hey! You ready yet?" he called over his shoulder, looking down the hall. "Everyone's waiting at the bar, ya know?"

Aria's voice sounded from down the hall. "I don't know why we have to go out tonight. I'd much rather stay here." She gave a quiet exhale as she entered the living room, putting on an earring.

Troy gave a smile upon her entrance. The woman paid him no mind and snatched up her coat. Her hair was treated, having a sleeker look than usual. Surrounding her eyes was dark liner and even some eye shadow, the kind that made her emerald irises pop. There was even a hint of blush on her cheeks and a touch of lip gloss. A tight dress wrapped around her body. It was black around her top and faded into a silver sequined bottom that stopped mid-thigh. Her feet dipped into tall heels. After slipping on her coat, she fussed with her hair, her long silver earrings tinkling together. Once settled, she finally noticed Troy's stare.

"What?" she asked, her voice coated with annoyance.

Troy chuckled. "Nothing. You look nice is all."

Aria gave an awkward smile, her fingers fiddling with the buttons of her open jacket.

Troy finally stood from the stool beside the kitchen bar. "And I have to take you out for New Year's Eve, especially when you look like that." He gave a snort for a laugh.

Aria fidgeted some more, pulling her hair behind her ear. "Ivory made me buy some makeup the last time we were at the market."

Troy was silent a moment, his hand resting against the side of her arm. "Well...she has good taste in makeup. I'm surprised you knew how to apply it."

Aria slapped his shoulder. "I'm not completely hopeless when it comes to womanly things." She smirked, swaying a bit. "Okay...I looked up a tutorial on my DNAIS."

Troy laughed, his eyes looking her up and down.

"Shouldn't we be going?" she asked.

"I'm just looking at you. Give me a minute," he said in a husky voice.

Aria's face warmed under his scrutiny. "You've got all night to look at me."

"And I plan on staring all night as well," he replied. "And so will Kovacevic."

Aria rolled her eyes, giving a shiver. "You enjoy making me feel uncomfortable, don't you?" she grumbled, turning to face him as he placed his second hand on her other arm.

"I plan on taking as long as I like from now on to do the things I enjoy." He leaned down and firmly pressed his lips against her forehead.

Aria grinned. "And what kind of things are those?" she whispered.

"Oh, you know...taking you out on dates. To places like the museum and the theater and whatever fancy cultured thing you want to do. Spoil you with things like fine dining and wine. Drag you with me to the club so we can work on your horrible dance moves." He held her, and the two gently swayed back and forth in a slow dance. Pressing his cheek against hers, he clasped her hand. "Make love to you for hours on end. Things like that."

Aria gave a mocking laugh. "And where would you find all the time to do that?"

Troy looked upward at the glowing white lights surrounding them. "In retirement."

Aria pulled away, looking at the man with a worried expression. "Retirement? You're leaving?"

Troy nodded slowly. "Yeah. And you're retiring with me. We've done more than enough. We saved the damn planet and lost our lives a few times while doing it. I think we've earned our retirement. Been doing things like this for nearly our entire lives."

"Yeah…but," Aria stammered.

"No buts. You know Clarke would grant it," Troy said. "Besides, there's no more war! We're out of a job anyway unless you want to be a part of the cleanup and restoration crew."

"And what would we do? Just laze around my apartment all day?" she asked.

"I may still help out with things around here. Maybe I'll pick up a job at Chester's if I get too bored. Perhaps I'll take up dancing. Who knows?" He grabbed her again, forcing her into an awkward two-step. "And you're going to paint and make pretty pictures, and they'll hang them up in the museums. Who wouldn't want a painting from the world's hero?"

Aria had to admit; the idea did sound appealing. Still, she couldn't imagine just quitting the violent career she had spent her life doing.

Resting her head on his shoulder, she mumbled, "Could we handle that lifestyle?"

"I thought that's the lifestyle you were wanting. You know, living like normal people. We can go shopping, get groceries, fight over what color of drapes we should hang, and you can wake up next to me every morning." He twirled her slowly. "Have kinky sex every night."

"That's really all you want, isn't it?" she scoffed.

"Every night, with you? Hell yeah, I want that. I may even buy you some handcuffs…my sassy lil weasel."

Aria wrinkled her nose. "Since when were weasels sexy?"

"Erm, I couldn't think of any other animal off the top of my head."

Something white flashed by the kitchen window, catching Aria's attention. "Cat?" she asked, perplexed.

Troy gasped. "Cat! Why the hell didn't I think of a cat? That should have been the obvious choice."

Aria slipped from the man's grasp. "No! Cat!" She pointed to the kitchen window and then darted down the hall, her legs stiff in her tall heels.

"Cat?" Troy looked over his shoulder at the window, then back toward the woman. Confused, he quickly followed after her. "Are you on hallucinogens?" he asked, strutting into her room.

Aria was moving at an alarming speed as she tugged open the blinds to her window and then moved to slide back the pane of glass. The bedroom instantly blared with the loud sounds of the city traffic. A frigid gust of wind overtook the warmth of the room. Troy took a few more eager steps forward and then shook his head in disbelief. There was a cat sitting on Aria's windowsill. The sill was barely as wide as the palm of her hand and stretched the whole expanse of the building. It was unbelievable the feline hadn't fallen off the side due to the winds that swiped across the skyscrapers.

"Here, kitty," Aria anxiously whispered. She carefully reached out to the cat. "What are you doing out here?"

The animal had long hair that was a strange mix of white, silver, and gold. It must've been a genetically enhanced breed. At Aria's touch, the furry thing didn't stir or fuss, but gratefully accepted her grasp and sank toward her, resting against her chest. Aria quickly shut the window and then twirled toward Troy. The expression on the woman's face was a rare sight.

"Look at this beautiful baby!" she exclaimed, running her fingers through the cat's fur.

Troy eyed the creature suspiciously. It had vibrant blue eyes that seemed to glimmer in the dimly lit bedroom. The fur was extraordinary in a way that what little light there was reflected against it, giving it a surreal appearance. Troy quickly folded his arms, his lips twisting into an unsure expression. The cat smiled, closing its eyes as it loudly purred.

"Really, cat?" Troy asked.

"What?" Aria replied, confused. The long-haired feline moved in a way so that its paws stepped on Aria's chest, and it gained enough leverage to press its head against her lips. Aria laughed, giving the animal a series of kisses. "I wonder who he belongs to." Aria scratched the cat's chin. "He doesn't have a collar."

Troy glared at the cat, locking eyes with its abnormal glowing blue ones. "Guess he belongs to you now."

Aria lifted her head. "You think?" she asked. "No, I can't. I bet he was someone's Christmas present, and he somehow got out."

"So, we'll hang fliers. If no one responds in a couple of weeks, then he's yours." Troy shrugged, finally moving to pet the animal. The cat accepted Troy's touch and continued its purring.

"Really? You think I should keep him?" Aria nuzzled the animal. It was the happiest Troy had seen her in ages. "Can I?" she hopefully asked.

Troy shrugged. "Why couldn't you? You're an adult. Have a damn cat, Aria! You need one!"

Aria giggled, hugging the animal. It gave a tiny meow in response. "Oh! What should I name him?"

Troy cocked his head to the side, inspecting the animal's strange characteristics. Dovian, Sorcēarian, angel, Ives, lizard. The words and correlations swirled through his brain and then he smirked.

"Hector?" he asked with amusement.

"Hector?" she repeated, bouncing the cat gently in a motherly way. The cat's eyes enlarged, and then he bumped her again. "I think he likes the name Hector." Then, the connection hit her.

Aria stared down at the feline. With its silvery-gold hair, brilliant blue eyes, and aloofness, there was no wonder why this cat made her feel at ease. Aria held the animal tightly against her, scratching its neck.

"Hector is a lovely name," she sadly whispered.

Troy moved toward her, placing his hands on her hips. "Does that mean I'm going to take the backseat to a cat?"

Aria shook her lonely thoughts away, meeting Troy's stare. "No."

"Good, because…as I was saying…before we were interrupted by the flea-bag…" Troy stated sarcastically.

Hector meowed in a defensive way.

"Oh, yes, you were mentioning handcuffs," Aria snickered.

"Hmm, yes. Get you a fun outfit or two…." Troy was silent a minute. "And then we can have chubby babies."

Aria's amused expression quickly fell. "Have a baby?"

"Yup!" Troy chimed.

Aria lowered her head. Truthfully, she had been pondering about it lately, especially right before the battle with Sapphire. After she had found out she was pregnant, her heart had grown heavy with a strange feeling of love and fear mixed. The idea of being a mother was actually exciting to her, but would she be any good at it? The thought both thrilled and terrified her.

"Aren't you moving a little fast?" she asked.

Troy laughed. "Is it too fast to think about the future? We don't have to have babies now, but I expect my wife to give me children at some point."

"Wait! W-Wife?" She nearly dropped the cat.

Troy's trademark cockeyed grin spread across his face. "Yeah. Cuz we're going to get married. I figured that was a given; ya know? We practically already are! We argue like a married couple. I eat all your food and drink your beer. I leave half of my shit in your apartment all the time. Hey! I've just been missing out on the best perks to being married–seeing you naked whenever I want!"

Aria turned and gently set the cat on her bed. Giving a sly smile, she wrapped her arms around the man's neck. "Marriage and babies, eh?" Hector meowed in protest and then commenced giving himself a bath.

"Sounds much better than fighting until the day I get blown to bits," Troy grimly muttered.

"With me?" she asked.

"Um…yeah." He nodded quickly, his eyes wide. "Who else?"

Aria giggled. Pausing to think only for a second, she finally gave one stern nod. "Okay!"

Troy leaned back, eyeing her carefully. "Okay?" he asked. "That's it?"

"Yes! I would like that very much!" she said with a laugh.

"Okay, then!" He laughed with her.

They remained in the bedroom holding each other for just a while longer until another blur of white caught their attention. Tiny flakes were dropping from the sky, something that had never happened before in the City of Fountains.

"Is that snow?" she asked.

"I hope so. That would suck if that were nuclear fallout…" Troy mumbled.

Aria laughed and grabbed the man's face, kissing him tenderly.

If the way she felt at that moment was any indication as to how she would feel in the future, Aria wasn't going to question it. She knew life wasn't going to be perfect; it never was. But not dwelling on the next mission, not wondering when she or Troy were going to die tragically in battle, relieved a sort of tension she had been holding onto for longer than she realized. No, she wasn't going to question it at all. She wasn't going to ask 'what if' but was going to live by Troy's words—why not.

And Aria did pretty well for the remainder of her life living by those words. No, things were not always perfect. She and Troy fought, and they fought a lot. When times like that occurred, she found solace in the company of her cat—a cat that Troy was desperately jealous of at times but secretly had his own moments with. The feline stayed with them for all their years, living far longer than any animal of his kind should have lived. Hector got to see Troy and Aria's wedding and the births of both their children–a boy and a girl. The cat was around to ease Aria's pain during the difficult time of President Clarke's passing–a peaceful death due to old age. The animal lingered, becoming the playmate of the couple's grandchildren and eventually their great-grandchildren and even their great-great-grandchildren. He was around to watch Aria and Troy grow old together. He remained by her side during the devastating time of Troy's passing due to heart failure and stayed in bed with her for the entire week following until she finally passed at the old age of one hundred and fifty-four. She lived a long life. A life that she was able to claim was somewhat quiet and comforting and full of joy—a life that left her with very few regrets.

Once all was done, and Aria and Troy's bodies were laid to rest in the same beautiful cemetery that housed their previously passed friends, Hector finally took his leave. He was simply gone, with no evidence left as to his whereabouts. And he was never seen again.

"Aftermath"

EPILOGUE

20,000 years earlier: O S.F....

Watching Saturday cartoons was becoming a dull and painful process for nine-year-old Brody. Every station had some form of boring newscast. Where was his typical superhero cartoon? He had waited all week to find out whether or not Captain Brawn had actually died by the hands of the evil Lord Vice and his creepy monkey minions. The boy was slouching on the couch, a can of soda in one hand and the remote in the other. He heaved a tired sigh, his eyes only darting to the open window a fleeting moment as a harsh wind rushed through the trees, tossing the cream curtains about. Impatiently pressing the channel button again, he found the next station was, of course, another news broadcast. Something about this report, however, caught his attention.

The video on the television was taken from a large naval carrier. Ocean waves splashed against the sides of the ship. Men in their uniforms scurried to all edges, pointing and shouting while some gave orders. The camera jolted over the rushing crowd upwards to the sky. Zooming in, the camera fuzzed and blurred as it tried to gain sight of the strange dot in the clouds. Once focused, the video revealed a massive structure in the air. It was triangular in shape and seemed to be made of shiny metals. Brody sat forward in his seat, his mouth hanging open. The video condensed in size and replayed in the tiny corner of the screen as a female news anchor gave her report.

"As recent events have tossed the world into disorder, and confusion plagues the nations, yet another bizarre event has occurred, this time taking place over the Indian Ocean. What was first thought to be a hoax recording of a strange unidentified aircraft hovering over the ocean waters southeast of the southern tip of Africa, has been verified as truth. Dozens of videos, all from different sources, have surfaced along the coastlines of that continent, providing more unexplainable evidence. Officials are reminding citizens to remain calm and to stay inside their homes until further notice. I repeat: stay calm and remain inside your homes. Previously covering a story on a recent oil spill, NCB News was close enough to get in on the action. Our team is currently onsite where we will be receiving live video coverage from our reporter, Scott."

The television switched to a live newsfeed, revealing a man wearing goulashes and a funny yellow hat. A rogue wave washed up against the side of the boat, crashing against him. He sputtered, holding tightly onto his microphone. Pointing to the sky, he led the camera to the sight of his angle on the strange airship.

"We can verify that the bizarre phenomenon is indeed very real! For the past hour, that aircraft has reportedly been sitting in the air, not moving, not doing much of anything. As the entire world waits, we can only hope that whatever this is, wherever it came from, that it has peaceful intentions." The man came back into camera view, his eye taking up nearly the entire screen as the cameraman struggled to zoom back out on his face. "It seems to be hovering. It hasn't moved an inch. It has been quiet. We're not sure how it appeared, as once we were on location it was already in place. We're currently probing other sources to see if any militaries can confirm whether or not this is their aircraft."

A loud horn blared in alarm. Scott turned, staring upward at the craft as the camera zoomed back in on the foreign vehicle. A vortex twisted around the ship, burst open violently, and immediately closed. Two other similar ships had suddenly appeared directly beside the first one. It took a few seconds before a massive shockwave of noise hit the man who was recording, the sound rumbling through the television speakers.

"Brody! Turn it down!" Brody's mom shouted from the kitchen.

"Unbelievable! This is unbelievable! Out of thin air! Those two ships just appeared out of nowhere!" the news reporter hollered in amazement.

"Brody! What did I say?!" his mother shouted again.

"Mom!" Brody cried out. "Mom! Come here! Quick!"

On screen, the camera kept zooming further and further. A white light flickered from the main ship. Something seemed to be happening on the front of the craft.

"We've got activity! We're detecting movement!" Scott shouted.

"For the love of God, what?" Brody's mom grumped, stomping into the room with her glass of wine. Could she simply have ten minutes alone to finish off her mid-day drink? That's all she ever wanted.

She gaped at the television, not impressed. "What? You brought me in here for one of your cartoons?" she asked. Looking out the window, feeling the fresh breeze from the gusting wind, she rolled her eyes. "Why don't you go outside and play? It's nice out. Take the dog with you."

"What do you see? What's happening? I can't see!" the reporter on TV asked the cameraman.

"Uh, it looks…it looks like someone's coming out. There's a front deck on the ship. It appears to be a man of some sort," the cameraman stuttered.

"Aliens, Mom! There are aliens! They just appeared out of nowhere!" Brody exclaimed, looking back at his mother.

A horrendous blaring noise echoed in vibrating beats. It seemed to start out low and then burst through the family's window. Brody's mom looked at the trees outside, watching as the branches danced against the harsh wind that flowed with the sound. It was the same sound that had come from the television speaker only moments before. The mother's eyes locked onto the television screen, watching the camera jitter from side to side as it gained sight of a giant man adorned in golden robes, a halo of light shimmering around his head. Her glass of wine slipped from her hand, spilling all over her brand-new white carpet.

It appeared to be a man. He looked no different than any human, perhaps a bit intimidating in his ethereal way. He had hair that shimmered in silver and gold, almost as if made of light. The sun beamed against him, encasing him in a glow. Gold markings lined his middle-aged face; his jaw was tight and square. Narrowing his eyes that seemed to burn with white fire, he stepped forward, moving with purpose across the deck of the airship. Firmly gripping the metal bar fencing him in, he stared deeply into the blue waters far below. He searched carefully, tilting his head a little as he remained silent. After a minute, he nodded. Holding a hand out before him, the giant of a man concentrated, and the planet began to rumble.

From the deep oceans, an immense chunk of earth heaved upward, the crust moving and adjusting beneath it. Soon, an island formed. Beautiful colors of nature sprang to life from the dirt mound that lifted from the lower depths. Trees pushed up in all directions as if they had been there many years. Grass and mountains formed; rock churned and twisted into caves on one part of the island; plains of green speckled with colorful flowers sprouted elsewhere, and rolling hills jolted and formed around massive silver lakes. As the ocean waters gushed off the land, falling back to where they belonged, the foundation of a beautiful new world was set.

The strange man in the golden robes looked down upon the earth, his eyes watching the trees as birds of all sizes and colors took to the skies, chirping and shrieking. Fish jumped from the clear lakes. Deer and other furry creatures pranced through the plains while rams joyfully hopped along the mountaintops. Lizards darted from the rocks, their tongues poking in every direction. Butterflies danced from flower to flower. It was stunning. It was perfect.

"So…what do you plan to call it?" A second man had joined him. He was even taller, sharp-cut with bulky muscle, dark-skinned, and had eyes the color of the sun. Armor of gold and silver covered his body; a cape of scarlet was chained to his back. His voice was deep and rich, but very gentle.

The golden-robed man smirked. "Ives," was his simple reply.

"A grand name, Gaius. I'm sure the others will approve," the other man said.

Gaius turned to face the man. "Go ahead, Azera, and tell the others that I am ready. We still have much to do."

Azera bowed slightly, pressing his fist against his chest. Then he turned, his cape swooping out behind him as he reentered the ship.

Gaius turned his gaze down toward Ives, giving an amused expression as he muttered, "We have a lot of building to do."

WWW.ARCREBS.DEVIANTART.COM

"Gaius"

Aria's DNAIS

SEARCHING...

Caution!

The following content contains
- Character Bios
- Bestiary
- Weapons & Armor Listings
- And More

Spoilers may lurk within the DNAIS.
Please read with caution.

BIOGRAPHIES

Aria Ivanov

- Age: 52
- Height: 198cm, 6'6"
- Weight: 81.6kg, 180lbs
- Eye Color: Green
- Hair Color: Black
- Blood Type: 0-
- Old Nationality: Italian-American, Russian

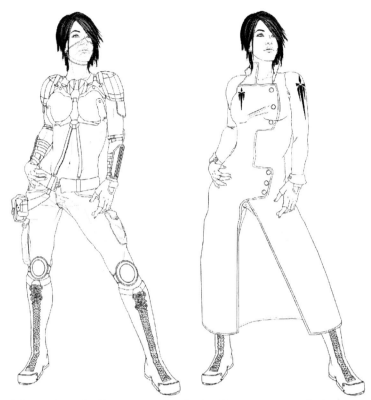

Aria was born in Cherno, Russite. Both of her parents worked at a university—her father a professor of literature and mythology and her mother a teacher of art and music. At the age of nine, Aria's upscale life was turned upside-down when her parents were killed right before her eyes in a tragic accident that left her an orphan. Not long after the incident had taken place, Aria was rescued by a soldier named James Clarke. He comforted her during her loss and took her into his home at Bio-Tech Military Corporation in Fountains where he taught her all there was to know about hand-to-hand combat and weaponry.

By the time she was a teenager, Aria was at the top of her class. Seeing her potential as an elite soldier, James paired Aria with Troy. After years of successful missions, both were upgraded to high-status in their twenties and put in charge of their own Delta Squad—later dubbed Team Phoenix after the False Syndicate War. Now, Aria and Troy are deployed on Bio-Tech's most top-secret missions. When not being used as a backup for the two soldiers, the rest of Team Phoenix is sent out for special ops and espionage around the world.

Despite surviving countless battles and the suicidal False Syndicate War, Aria has seemed to have met her match in the latest enemies threatening not only hers, but the entire world's militaries. Fighting in a war against humans had become an easy task for Aria. The question is whether or not she can master the art of war against monsters.

Troy Moreau

- Age: 55
- Height: 218.5cm, 7'2"
- Weight: 140.6kg, 310lbs
- Eye Color: Green
- Hair Color: Brown
- Blood Type: 0+
- Old Nationality: French, American

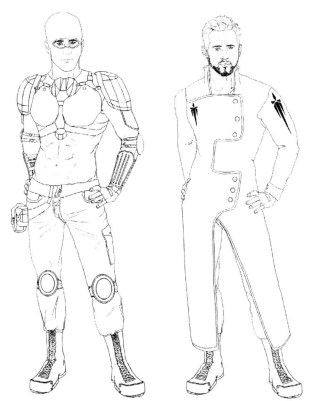

Losing his mother while he was still an infant, Troy was raised by his father within the military. Like many soldiers, Troy's father did not live a long life. He was killed in action when Troy was only eleven. With his father having been owned by Bio-Tech Military Corporation, Troy's transition into the military was simple. Bio-Tech adopted him, allowed him to keep his father's apartment, and began training Troy the next day. Having been raised by a military man, Troy was already adept with weaponry and was named a prodigy in marksmanship. Not one to be good at giving orders, Troy was always good at taking orders and following them to a tee or adapting when necessary. He was the perfect soldier.

By his teens, he was second in the class behind Aria. The two were paired together where they were seen as polar opposites but equal in talent. Needless to say, the two often competed for dominance over the other. While in their twenties, Troy and Aria were given the opportunity to train their own squadron, but there could only be one leader. During the final exams to determine who would be the leader of the Delta Squad, Troy missed the opportunity by a few points when he was late to his final exercise due to a laxative placed in his morning coffee. Having questioned Aria about it, she never confessed but did proclaim that whoever had done it was a genius and that all was fair when it came to war.

Despite having their differences and sometimes butting heads, Aria and Troy have always proven to be the perfect team. In the current war, where Troy's understandings and beliefs about the world are repeatedly questioned, he must choose what to believe in and the adverse effects it could have on his relationship with Aria.

Dovian

- Age: 17,000+
- Height: 249cm, 8'2"
- Weight: 174.6kg, 385lbs
- Eye Color: Blue
- Hair Color: Silver/Gold
- Blood Type: Unknown
- Old Nationality: Sorcēarian

Dovian is the sole survivor of the Sorcēarian race. His great-grandfather, Gaius, was one of the original angelic beings to come to Earth, forming Ives out of the Indian Ocean and beginning the Sorcēarian settlement. Sorcēarians were given the task of preaching the word of God to the human populace. After a few thousand years, the Sorcēarian race became tainted with sin, and an immense war eventually broke out between the human and angelic race. Details of the war remain unknown, and from that day forth, the race was extinguished. Only Dovian knows of the tale, and all he wishes to share are hints of the once great existence of his people, giving only few facts pertaining to their demise and his supposed fault in it all.

Being small in stature compared to other male Sorcēarians, Dovian was somewhat of an outcast growing up. He felt immense amounts of pressure being from the Gaius lineage–a grand and powerful leading lineage that was dubbed the most fearsome of family lines. Thought of as weak, Dovian proved the doubtful Sorcēarians wrong when his temper had gotten the better of him as a child, and he nearly destroyed one of the cathedrals in his home. It was a turning point in his life as people no longer doubted as much as they feared his strength, only making Dovian all the more estranged.

Gaius was a prominent figure in Dovian's life, acting more on the fatherly role than Dovian's own father, Gaius III. He had placed a lot of faith on Dovian and developed preventive measures to help control the young Sorcēarian's energies. In the end, Dovian's controlled actions seemed to cause more bad than good, and he feels he is to blame for the race's annihilation, leaving him depressed and full of regret. Upon meeting Aria and Troy, he agreed to help them in their battle though his true motives remain unclear.

Ivory

- Age: Unknown
- Height: 213cm, 7'0"
- Weight: 88.5kg, 195lbs
- Eye Color: Blue
- Hair Color: Blonde
- Blood Type: Unknown
- Old Nationality: Unknown

Very little is known about Ivory. Having been discovered unconscious on Ives by Aria and her team, Ivory has no recollection of her past or how she had gotten onto the supposedly impassable island. Not knowing of her purpose or past life, Ivory joined the team in hopes of discovering her true identity and eventually finding her way home. However, due to Walten's interest in the strange woman, Ivory was placed in Aria's company and protection. As battles arose, Ivory began to develop lost time and seizures which caused shifts in her personality. Originally thought to be a symptom of post-traumatic stress disorder, Ivory's alternate personality revealed a much more unnatural connection to a past that did not belong to her, a past that belonged to Dovian.

Living in both confusion and fear, Ivory keeps her thoughts mostly to herself, creating a wedge between her and her teammates. Now stranded on Ives with Dovian, Ivory finds that her inner struggle is only worsening. With the pressure of wanting to save her friends weighing her down, her desire to be closer to Dovian growing, and Sapphire's violence surrounding her, Ivory must come to a solution. Should she remain as she is, or should she allow I'Lanthe to take complete control?

Gavin Sigo

- Age: 54
- Height: 208cm, 6'10"
- Weight: 127kg, 280lbs
- Eye Color: Brown
- Hair Color: Brown
- Blood Type: A+
- Old Nationality: Native American, American

Gavin was a spunky, light-hearted pilot for Bio-Tech Military Cooperation. He was one of the few in the military who was born and raised as a civilian and still had living parents. Expected to go to college and follow through with a pilot's license for commercial airlines, it was his parent's horror when the young man decided he was going to enter the military to pilot the Hawk 90. Many think it was due to Troy's constant persuasion that Gavin finally gave in and signed his rights away to Bio-Tech, but it was actually because of his sense of justice and desire to do more for the people of Fountains—and possibly a secondary motive involving the safety of a certain green-eyed beauty he had met through Troy—that he decided to become a pilot.

Knowing Troy throughout his entire military career, Gavin was eventually introduced to Aria. Having passed all tests with flying colors and mastering the Hawk 90 in half the time most recruits do, Gavin was quickly given a Class C-5 status in the Air Force and immediately assigned to Troy and Aria's unit. For nearly 30 years, Gavin had been the eye in the sky for Aria and Troy. Doing what he always did best, Gavin made sure his comrades were safe before he ever bailed from the Hawk 90. Fighting for his friends until his untimely death at the hands of Euclid, Gavin was awarded high honors and buried in the beautiful cemetery outside Fountains.

When questioned about his reasons for becoming a pilot, Gavin always replied, "Everyone thinks a hero needs to have a gun. Nobody thinks of the heroes that take to the sky. Though the ones on the ground always have all the fun, I always preferred to fly."

Sapphire

- **Age: 8**
- **Height: 129.5cm, 4'3"**
- **Weight: 23.5kg, 52lbs**
- **Eye Color: Blue**
- **Hair Color: Blonde**
- **Blood Type: Unknown**
- **Old Nationality: Unknown**

Despite appearing beautiful and innocent, there's a darkness within Sapphire that seems to make the bravest of men cower. Leading the demonic attacks, Sapphire plots to cleanse the world of all of humanity. Through the use of Dovian and Ivory, the child wants to create a race of Sorcēarian-human hybrids. Having no souls, the hybrid vessels will house the souls of the damned, and a new kingdom will rise on Earth with Sapphire as the ruler.

Aren Hagar

- Age: 28
- Height: 200cm, 6'7"
- Weight: 90.7kg, 200lbs
- Eye Color: Hazel
- Hair Color: Brown, Orange
- Blood Type: AB
- Old Nationality: Spain, American

Born in Fountains, Aren was brought up within a wealthy family. Having a type of philanthropic side, Aren often ventured to the Underbelly for charity purposes. During one of his travels to the lower city, Aren met the young, beautiful, upbeat Fiona. Together they held fundraisers for the churches, orphanages, and the preservation of old family businesses. It wasn't long before the two developed a relationship. After a while, Aren strived to do more for not just the people of the Underbelly, but for the entire City of Fountains. After having read a book about the survival of Team Phoenix, Aren dreamed of becoming a hero someday and quickly signed his life away to Bio-Tech, much to Fiona's displeasure. It was because of her paranoia of him getting killed in battle, that Aren transferred to the Air Force where he was trained to be a top Hawk pilot under the supervision of Gavin Sigo.

James Clarke

- Age: 78
- Height: 206cm, 6'9"
- Weight: 120.2kg, 265lbs
- Eye Color: Brown
- Hair Color: Grey
- Blood Type: O-
- Old Nationality: English, American

James Clarke is the President of Bio-Tech Military Corporation. He organizes and overlooks all of the corporation's military operations. Given almost complete control, Clarke works beneath Walten, who is the CEO and financial owner of the company. Anything Walten says, however, overwrites Clarke. This sometimes creates an awkward tension between the financial and military side of Bio-Tech.

Born and raised in Fountains, James Clarke's father was a military genius who spent the majority of his life fighting. He trained James to be one of the best, and by the time James was in his early twenties, he was leading his own squadron. James was a rare individual. Despite seeing the horrors of war, he had a strong devotion to civilian and family lifestyle. Wanting to maintain some sort of normalcy, he met a woman named Courtney and quickly settled into a domestic relationship with her. It wasn't long before he became engaged to the woman and she was pregnant with his child. James' small amount of peace was destroyed, however, when a commercial airliner was taken down by Cherno forces, killing Courtney and her unborn child only days before the scheduled wedding. This ignited a war with Cherno.

With his squadron, James was sent to Russite where he was able to track down General Lebedev and end the war, but not without casualties. James had accidentally given the wrong coordinates to a mortar team, and a civilian district was hit. Upon investigating the site, James found a child pinned beneath her father; her mother was dead a few meters away. This was his bargaining chip with Lebedev as the child was in the center of the gunfight. James decided to spare Lebedev's life and take full responsibility for the child if the man agreed to call off his war and assent to peaceful solutions between the two city-states. With no options, Lebedev approved, and James adopted the little girl named Aria and raised her as his own.

Grayson

- Age: 75
- Height: 208cm, 6'10"
- Weight: Unknown
- Eye Color: Unknown
- Hair Color: N/A
- Blood Type: Unknown
- Old Nationality: American

Having served by James Clarke's side for many years, once Clarke was promoted to President of Bio-Tech Military Corporation, Grayson gratefully accepted the offer to serve as his personal bodyguard. His unwavering loyalty to Clarke and his enigmatic nature makes Grayson appear menacing to those who don't know his history. Still, Grayson does hold a few secrets of his own, which often spiral with rumors about who he actually is and his shadowy past.

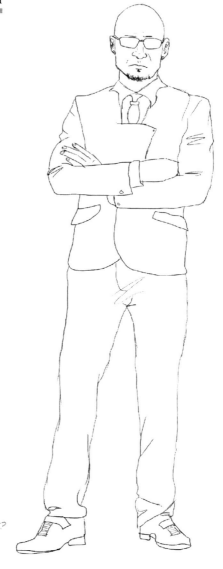

Dr. Camery

- Age: 61
- Height: 206cm, 6'9"
- Weight: 108.8kg, 240lbs
- Eye Color: Grey
- Hair Color: Brown, Grey
- Blood Type: A-
- Old Nationality: English, American

Dr. Camery has been a scientist for Bio-Tech Military Corporation for most of his life. Having multiple Doctorate and Master Degrees, Camery is one of the highest renowned scientists in the world. He jump-started the Biomechanical Research and Development program and created the first clone army. Using cloned DNA and blending with robotic technology, Camery created biomechanical androids. Having been awarded for his genius development, it was a shock to Camery when Bio-Tech pulled the plug on his program, destroying all he had developed and taking away his life's work. Having no real purpose, Camery was crushed and desperate for his life to return to him.

Due to the recent attacks around the world and the strange evidence that points in Camery's direction, it's no surprise that the doctor is a key suspect. How far would he go to achieve his goals within his program? For what purpose would he be helping the enemy? Is he the one equipping these creatures; did he make the creatures himself, or are all these events simply a coincidence? These are the factors that pull Camery into the design. Whether he wants or not, he is involved.

Mr. Walten

- **Age:** 38
- **Height:** 208cm, 6'10"
- **Weight:** 99.8kg, 220lbs
- **Eye Color:** Brown
- **Hair Color:** Brown
- **Blood Type:** A
- **Old Nationality:** German, American

Walten is the CEO of Bio-Tech Military Corporation. After the sudden death of his father, Walten inherited the family business at the age of thirteen. While the boy was considered too young to manage the company, Walten's father had stated in his will to give full control to President James Clarke until Walten was of a mature age. Walten was insulted, claiming that he was better off ruling on his own without the help of a military-based President. He still had his way within the company, however, thanks to General Jeron Feyette. Making sure James Clarke played by Walten's rules, Jeron managed certain military groups and actions behind Clarke's back due to the young CEO's demands. This eventually created a tense relationship between not only the financial side of Bio-Tech but on the military side as well.

Now a grown adult, Walten runs the whole of Bio-Tech along with fifty other industries. As the days pass, his wealth and control over businesses and city-states increases. Walten, watching his father waste his own potential, yearns to have mass control over all major industries around the world. Whether it is for the betterment or worsening of mankind is unknown, though Walten is not notorious for being compassionate. With the current events around the world disrupting the predictable flow of the consumer and military finances, many begin to wonder if Walten's strategic blows to the stocks have all been a coincidence or are part of a more elaborate plot. The question remains if it is Walten who is in control or if it is someone else entirely pulling the strings in this esoteric design.

Jeron Feyette

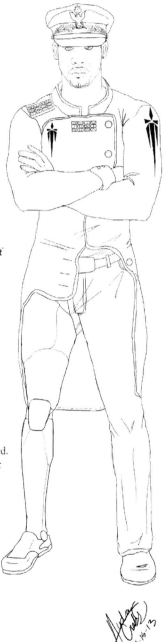

- Age: 65
- Height: 223.5cm, 7'4"
- Weight: 183.7kg, 405lbs
- Eye Color: Brown
- Hair Color: Black
- Blood Type: B+
- Old Nationality: African-American, French

General Jeron Feyette is a native to Fountains. Born with genetics deemed abnormal, Jeron was abandoned by his mother at an orphanage in the Underbelly. Growing up in the lower level of the city, Jeron often got into trouble due to theft and violence. Being different, even while in the Underbelly, Feyette had to train himself to be strong and capable of not only protecting himself but the other children in the orphanage as well. Jeron grew to be enormous in height and had incredible strength. He was in his teens when the Bio-Tech recruiting squad showed up on his side of town. Feyette was in the middle of a brawl, sending away thugs who were trying to steal money from the children of the orphanage. Impressed, the recruiting squad offered Feyette a job. With much hesitation, Feyette agreed to join the ranks of the military, the figures of his income an overpowering temptation as it was more than enough to care for himself and much of the orphanage.

It wasn't long before Feyette became a general and the late President Walten's personal bodyguard. Feyette owed his life to the company. If it weren't for Bio Tech, his orphanage would have been closed, and the children would have wound up on the streets or given to the front lines to serve in the wars. The President had guaranteed protection over Feyette's home, to which the general was eternally grateful. So when the late President had died and left a final request for Jeron to watch over his thirteen-year-old son and protect him with his life, General Feyette gratefully accepted and became the young boy's shadow, taking him in as he had done for the children of the Underbelly.

Team Phoenix

Spoofy

- Age: 53
- Height: 200.5 cm, 6'7"
- Weight: 87.5kg, 193 lbs
- Eye Color: Brown
- Hair Color: Brown
- Blood Type: B-
- Old Nationality: American, English

Nerd

- Age: 54
- Height: 206cm, 6'9"
- Weight: 118kg, 260 lbs
- Eye Color: Green
- Hair Color: Light Brown
- Blood Type: A+
- Old Nationality: Scottish, American

Originally Delta Squad 5, Team Phoenix received their mythological title after their miraculous survival of their suicidal mission during the False Syndicate War. Thought to be dead, there was no chance of search and rescue. With Aria and Troy as the team leaders, the elite fighters fought to the edge of their lives and despite the odds, pulled through their mission. Losses were not void, however, as life threatening injuries were sustained and a team member was lost. Rising from their presumed death, Delta Squad 5 was dubbed Team Phoenix. Current members include Aria, Troy, Spoofy, Monkey, Zombie, Nerd, and Kaino.

Monkey

- Age: 57
- Height: 211 cm, 6'11"
- Weight: 145kg, 320 lbs
- Eye Color: Green
- Hair Color: N/A
- Blood Type: AB
- Old Nationality: American, German

Kaino

- Age: 46
- Height: 216cm, 7'1"
- Weight: 143kg, 315 lbs
- Eye Color: Brown
- Hair Color: Brown, Red
- Blood Type: A-
- Old Nationality: Native American, Samoan

Zombie

- Age: 50
- Height: 208cm, 6'10"
- Weight: 131.5kg, 290 lbs
- Eye Color: Grey
- Hair Color: Brown
- Blood Type: A
- Old Nationality: American

Kovacevic

- Age: 70
- Height: 211cm, 6'11"
- Weight: 131.5kg, 290lbs
- Eye Color: Brown, Grey
- Hair Color: Bald
- Blood Type: A+
- Old Nationality: American, Bosnian

Kovacevic was born in America and raised by his single mother in the Columbia city-state. His father, a soldier from Saray, had been fighting in a war within Columbia over natural resources. Having been severely injured, the soldier was discovered by Kovacevic's mother. She was a nurse who pitied the injured man and snuck him into her home for fear of the military finding him and making him a prisoner of war. Nursing the man back to health, Kovacevic's mother had developed feelings for the soldier, and the two had a short-lived relationship. Once the soldier had healed from his wounds, he disappeared, leaving Kovacevic's mother alone and pregnant in the war-torn city. After years of war, Kovacevic's mother had died in some crossfire on the streets while trying to gather rations, leaving Kovacevic to fend for himself at a very young age. Living on the streets, the boy joined the military as soon as the option arose with one goal in mind: find and kill the man who caused his mother so much pain. His only clue was his own last name—his father's name.

As an adult, Kovacevic became a well-renowned soldier. He had fought for many years before he was given the chance to infiltrate Saray for a reconnaissance mission. Kovacevic went against orders and abandoned his team in search of his father who was then the general of the army of Saray. Having successfully chased down and killed the man without any effort, Kovacevic found himself captured, beaten, and taken as a prisoner of war. His own city-state didn't dare rescue him due to his abandonment and going against orders, and so Kovacevic stayed in Saray. Eventually, the man was given the option to fight for the enemy military, to which he gratefully accepted the offer. Within a few short years, Kovacevic had risen through the ranks, bettering the best of all of Saray's soldiers where he eventually became general of the military he was once a prisoner for. Having killed his father didn't relieve any pain or anger he held inside, for the man hadn't even remembered Kovacevic's mother in the sea of women he had past relations with. Now, Kovacevic fills his days with the one thing he knows best—fighting.

Yoshitaka

- Age: 74
- Height: 211cm, 6'11"
- Weight: 136kg, 300lbs
- Eye Color: Brown
- Hair Color: Black
- Blood Type: A+
- Old Nationality: Japan

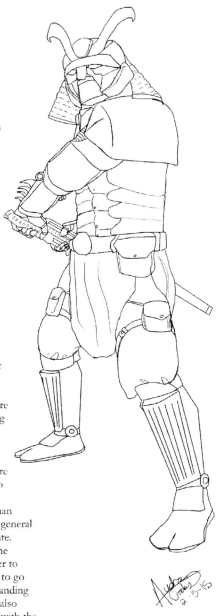

General of Dai-Ni-Tokyo, Yoshitaka was born and bred in the high-society based samurai clan of warriors. In his early years, he worked as a military weaponry scientist and engineered a way to integrate projectiles with basic weaponry. Mastering his own creation, Yoshitaka joined the lines and quickly flew through the ranks. Training his own men, his military became a force to be reckoned with between their use of modern and ancient warfare. Though he was a mastermind behind the revolutionary weaponry, Yoshitaka quickly became a target of the Iga clan—a rebellious faction of military dropouts who fled the city to live in a more traditional style. They believed Yoshitaka's creations were a slap in the face of ancient heritage. Holding onto old ideology, the Iga clan believed that Yoshitaka and the elitists he served were the downfalls of the city-state, claiming freedom didn't exist due to the severe division between classes of rich and poor. Because of this, Iga claims that those who follow the samurai code were natural born enemies, only feeding into the hate of the already feuding society.

At the request of James Clarke—a man whom Yoshitaka owes his life to—the general gathered his troops and left his city-state. Though the sacrifice would be great, the samurai knew it was a necessity in order to protect his own people. Yoshitaka had to go straight to the source of the attacks. Banding together with James Clarke, Yoshitaka also formed a tolerable alliance of his own with the Iga clan. What better weapon to use against a greater evil, than your own enemy?

Hattori

- **Age:** 65
- **Height:** 206cm, 6'9"
- **Weight:** 127kg, 280lbs
- **Eye Color:** Black, Silver
- **Hair Color:** Black
- **Blood Type:** A-
- **Old Nationality:** Japan

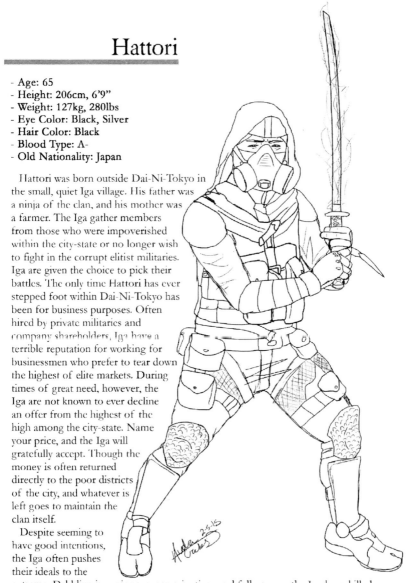

Hattori was born outside Dai-Ni-Tokyo in the small, quiet Iga village. His father was a ninja of the clan, and his mother was a farmer. The Iga gather members from those who were impoverished within the city-state or no longer wish to fight in the corrupt elitist militaries. Iga are given the choice to pick their battles. The only time Hattori has ever stepped foot within Dai-Ni-Tokyo has been for business purposes. Often hired by private militaries and company shareholders, Iga have a terrible reputation for working for businessmen who prefer to tear down the highest of elite markets. During times of great need, however, the Iga are not known to ever decline an offer from the highest of the high among the city-state. Name your price, and the Iga will gratefully accept. Though the money is often returned directly to the poor districts of the city, and whatever is left goes to maintain the clan itself.

Despite seeming to have good intentions, the Iga often pushes their ideals to the extreme. Dabbling in espionage, assassination, and full-on war, the Iga have killed more than a few leaders who were fit to provide positive change to the Japanese society. Thus, the Iga clan sometimes drives a wedge further between those caught in poverty and those who are wealthy.

With the recent monstrous attacks around the world, the Iga too were affected, their number declining fast as their village was nearly wiped out overnight. With much reluctance, when Yoshitaka's unit offered a momentary truce, Hattori agreed knowing that not only his people but the impoverished of the city needed saving as well.

Jiao

- **Age:** 45
- **Height:** 190.5cm, 6'3"
- **Weight:** 75kg, 165 lbs
- **Eye Color:** Brown, Gold
- **Hair Color:** Black
- **Blood Type:** B+
- **Old Nationality:** Chinese, Mongolia

Born in the Beijing province, Jiao became an orphan of war at a young age. Found wounded on the steps of the Dilong monastery, Jiao was brought in and cured by the monks. Despite the tradition of no females allowed to live within the monastery, the men quickly became attached to the beautiful child. What was expected to be a temporary refuge became Jiao's permanent home. The woman was raised among the men and trained just the same. With her small frame and agility, Jiao became an interesting project for the leaders of Dilong. Soon, she was allowed an official soldier title among their temple.

In her young adulthood, a nighttime raid was brought upon the monastery, killing many. The leaders were taken as hostages, and few monks were left alive. Thought to be nothing more than a servant, Jiao was captured as well and locked within the enemy encampment to be used as a form of entertainment for the male soldiers. During her first encounter with a man in her cell, Jiao quickly killed him, stole his uniform and weapons, and took over the encampment on her own. She freed the Dilong leaders and safely returned them to the Monastery. It was after this that Jiao became general and head of the temple.

With all of Beijing wiped out, Jiao moved her troops toward the main battle outside Fountains. Ignoring all traditions, she and her men are looking for revenge. In order to maintain peace, they must defeat the evil that is suffocating the world.

Lilith

- **Age: Unknown**
- **Height: 203cm, 6'8"**
- **Weight: Unknown**
- **Eye Color: Brown**
- **Hair Color: Brown**
- **Blood Type: Unknown**
- **Old Nationality: Unknown**

Lilith, a decommissioned biomechanical android from Bio-Tech Military Corporation, became inhabited by a demonic spirit during Sapphire's opening of the portals. With a seductive attitude, it isn't known what type of creature Lilith was before merging with the vessel, but speculation is she was either a succubus or incubus. Given the role of governing the rambunctious demons and other androids, Lilith has other plans for herself. Using her seduction as a form of manipulation, Lilith wants to be able to rid the world of Ivory's presence—despite Sapphire's need for the other woman—and keep Dovian for herself.

BESTIARY

Brawler

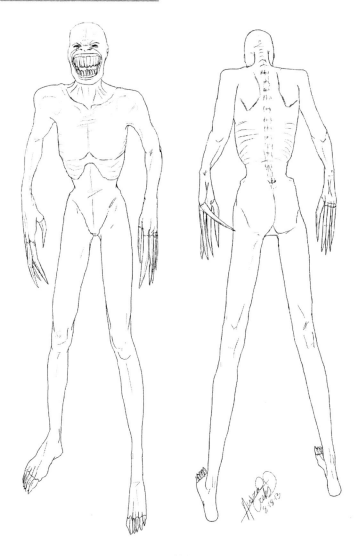

Brute

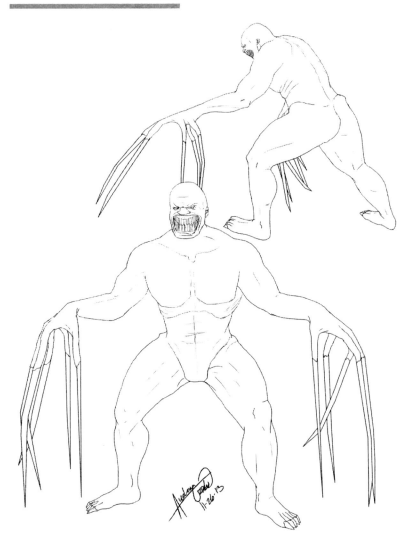

Spewer

Stilt-Man

Colossus

Hector

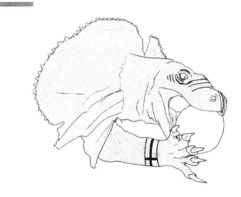

King Petey

ARMOR

Cherno Armor

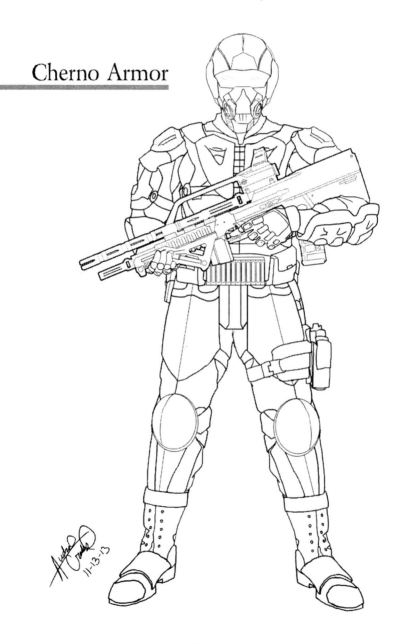

Fountain Armor

Soldier of God

Goliath

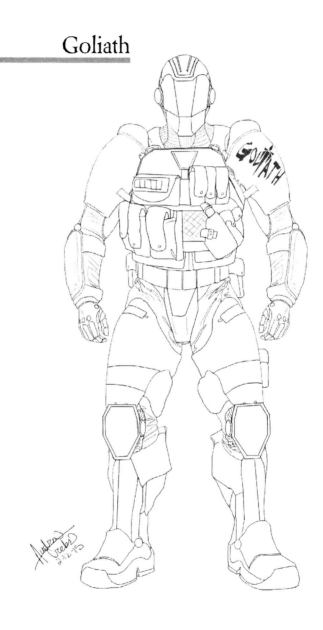

Roman Soldier

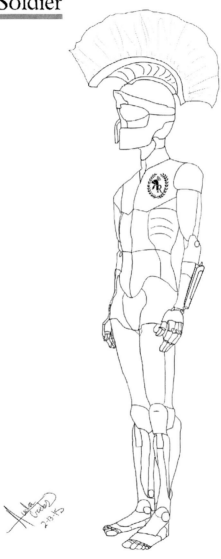

WEAPONS

20mm EMFD Sniper Rifle

Auto-Aim Standard

ECRG-15

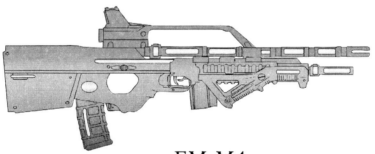

EM-M4

EM-36C

Ignition Rifle

Fernstal 300

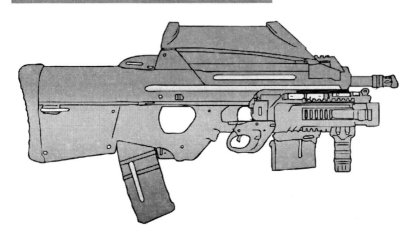

Sub-Fernstal P20

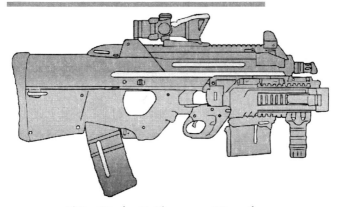

.50 Cal. Liberty Eagle

Mini Liberty Eagle

Amasser Particle Beam

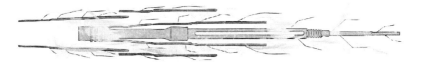

M28 Shredder

Banana Sniper Rifle

.68 Magnum Tex

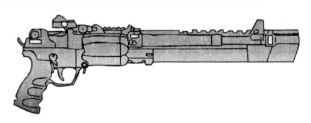

MP Katana

Iga Thunderstorm

Dilong Lotus Staff

Dovian's Arm Band & Back Apparatus

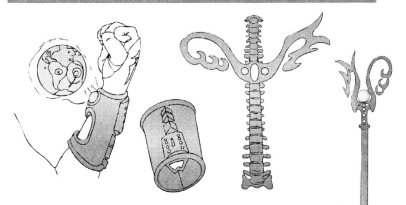

Dovian's Optical Camera & Staff

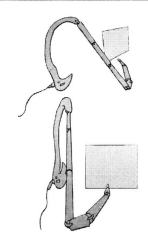

WORLD INFO

City of Fountains

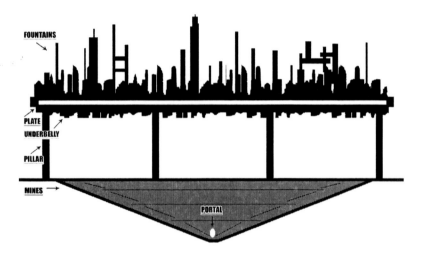

The Underbelly, a separate city beneath Fountains, is dirty, poor, and full of the strange and outdated of society. Anything that doesn't meet the middle ground of the majority in civilization is often frowned at, thus flourishes in the Underbelly. Designer genes are often used during pregnancy to prevent genetic differences such as pale or dark skin, too light or dark hair, or diseases of all kinds. Sometimes, however, the designer genes clash with the embryo's genetic code and create deformities or other undesirable effects. Because of this, a child is either aborted for their differences or moved to the lower level of the city to take their chances at survival there in the orphanages or the streets until the military snatches them up for their armies.

The Underbelly thrives on genetic differences and old technology so much that the people of the lower level often hold resentment for those above. This creates animosity and rivalry between the two districts despite being part of the same city-state. Though the Underbelly welcomes differences with open arms, violence is not a rarity. The streets of the Underbelly are dangerous due to criminals who dwell in the poor district and from civilians of the upper plate who receive pleasure from abusing and murdering those who reside in the lower half.

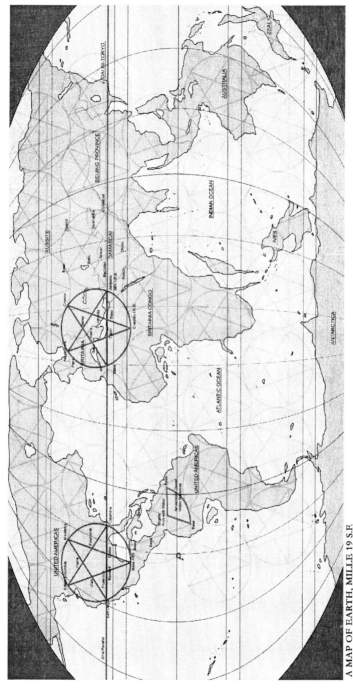

A MAP OF EARTH, MILLE 19 S.F.

After thousands of years of nuclear war, Earth's plates have shifted. Ground penetrating nukes, which were used to hit fault lines and underground bases, have created geological upheavals, causing some islands and coastlines to be submerged. Nuclear winter has caused permanent icecaps to form along the northern continents. The rest of Earth is a desert, void of organic life. Constant warfare has also damaged the ozone. The planet's water resources have dwindled massively as a result of pumping large quantities of water into the upper atmosphere to reflect and absorb the sun's solar radiation. A high percentage of the remaining water is contaminated due to nuclear radiation. Fresh aquifers deep underground provide the last amounts of natural fresh water. Corporatism has formed a monopoly on the reserve, only causing more warfare over the final remains of Earth's resources.

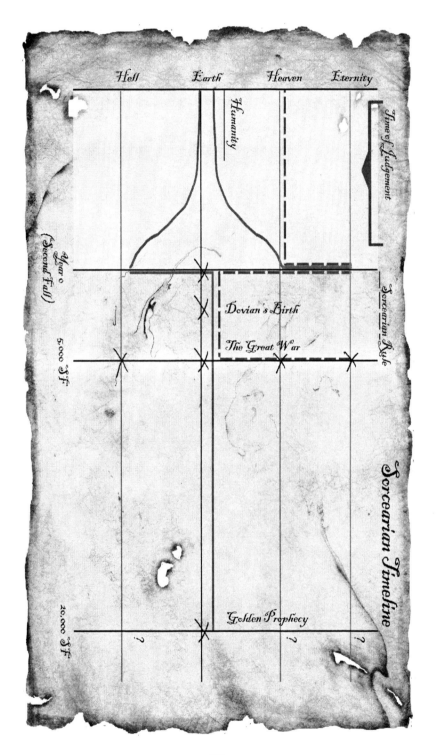

Legacy Alphabet

Capital A: א	Lower g: r	Capital N: Hb	Lower t: ŧ
Lower a: א	Capital H: ה	Lower n: Hb	Capital U: Ÿ
Capital B: Æ	Lower h: ה	Capital O: Ö	Lower u: ü
Lower b: æ	Capital I: €	Lower o: ö	Capital V: B
Capital C: Ç	Lower i: ℓ	Capital P: P	Lower v: в
Lower c: ç	Capital J: J	Lower p: p	Capital W: ι
Capital D: Δ	Lower j: j	Capital Q: ﻕ	Lower w: ι
Lower d: δ	Capital K: K	Lower q: ﻗ	Capital X: Ξ
Capital E: Ē	Lower k: k	Capital R: R	Lower x: ξ
Lower e: ē	Capital L: Λ	Lower r: r	Capital Y: '
Capital F: Φ	Lower l: λ	Capital S: Ŝ	Lower y: '
Lower f: φ	Capital M: M	Lower s: ß	Capital Z: 3
Capital G: Γ	Lower m: μ	Capital T: ϝ	Lower z: ɜ

Legacy, the native language of the Sorcēarian race, is comprised of letters from multiple languages around the world. Thought to be a unique language used only by the Holy, some speculate that Legacy was once the dialect used by the entire world before the time of Babel.

ABOUT THE AUTHOR

A. R. Crebs spent her youth playing video games, watching action and horror films of the 80s and 90s, and used her imagination as a form of entertainment for her family and friends. It wasn't until she was in her early teens that a friend introduced her to the fantasy genre of gaming. Crebs was hooked. What started as fan art of her favorite characters turned into a passion for designing a world of her own. Thus, Dovian was born. The creation of Dovian's world grew throughout the years where new characters and creatures were made. While in college, Crebs sparked the idea to write her story of Dovian and his adventures in The Esoteric Design series. After graduating from the Rocky Mountain College of Art + Design with a BFA in illustration, Crebs began to piece together the artwork and ideas from her youth. Together she formed a novel with chapter illustrations, bios, and a glossary. Dabbling in multiple art styles, A. R. Crebs felt that changing the look of the illustrations would coincide with the imaginations of others. While everyone has a different mind, hopefully, one of the images depicted in The Esoteric Design matches the reader's imagination whether it is through style, mood, or subject matter.

You can check out A. R. Crebs' websites for updates, full color artwork, and to participate in future contests.

www.ARCrebs.com

www.ARCrebs.deviantart.com

www.facebook.com/ARCrebs